Threads

Small Things Vol. 2

by

Joe
DeRouen

Small Things Press

Visit Joe's website at www.JoeDeRouen.com

First Printing: October 2013

Second Printing: October 2021

ISBN 978-0-615-84301-8

Cover by Mallory Rock, rocksolidbookdesigns.com

Author photo by Jasmine Teramura

FIRST EDITION

Printed in the USA

* * *

Small Things Press | www.SmallThingsPress.com

For Bruce Diamond, a great writer and an even greater friend; and for Jenny Kuzbury, Annie Sturdivant, and Robin Raven, three women who continue to inspire me.

Novels by Joe DeRouen

The Small Things Trilogy:
Small Things
Threads
A Pattern of Shadows

Memories of a Ghost
Splinter the Ghost*

Leap Year

Short Story Collections by Joe DeRouen

Odds and Endings: Fiction Short and Otherwise
Untitled Patreon Stories*

Anthology Appearances

Klarissa Dreams Redux: An Illuminated Anthology
May the Fourth: A Collection of Stories Across Time and Space
The Cat, the Crow, and the Cauldron: A Halloween Anthology
Mistletoe Magic: A Christmas Anthology

* Not yet published

Acknowledgements

I'd like to thank everyone who contributed to helping make this novel happen, including Andee and Fletcher DeRouen, Bruce Diamond, Paulette Wallis, Burgundy Wisrock-Eckert, Robin Raven, Tony Vazquez, all the folks associated with NaNoWriMo, Jonathan Carroll, and Richard Matheson.

Special thanks also go to Irene Knouff, Rebecca Fitch Gibson, Pan Sticksell, Angela Herring, Paul and Ruth SoRelle, Lacey Henegar, Megan Earley, Zoom Beezie, Jennifer Battering, Angie Henderson, Paul Leone, Cheryl Smith, Jim Reader, Dee Dee Dean Kahs, Madeline Francisco, Shelley and Dave Darling, Heidi Simmons, Steve Lynch, and Jim Fishback.

Threads

Small Things Vol. 2

Prologue

Halloween, 11:47 PM

Elminster the Large knew that he would bite the big one someday, but never in a million years had he imagined that it would end quite like this.

Skittering around the corner of a deserted convenience store, his robe flowing behind him, he ran down the length of the dark alley and straight into a metal trashcan. He spun as the hem of his robe caught the edge of the can, pulling it over with a thunderous clang that echoed through the street. He stumbled, feet going out from under him, landing with another loud crash against the corrugated tin container. He watched helplessly as his glasses tumbled from his face to disappear somewhere in the darkness.

It was all supposed to be a joke, just something to impress the goth girl from their D&D group and get Jason laid. Now they were both dead, their blood spattered all through Jason's apartment, and he was going to be next.

Elminster wasn't his real name, of course, just the name of the half-troll wizard he'd been playing for nearly three years in his weekly gaming group. If he were really Elminster the Large, he would call lightning down from the heavens and burn the demon alive. And then he'd raise Jason and the girl from the dead, and everything would be normal again.

He rose on shaking legs, heart hammering, squinting, looking for a way out. But there was nowhere to go. He was trapped. He'd run through the streets of Chicago like a madman, screaming for help—but tonight was Halloween, and no one took him seriously. Nothing was chasing him, they said. He must be drunk, stoned, or worse.

He ran until his sides were in stitches and he thought his lungs would burst, but still the thing pursued him, its fetid breath hot on his neck. It was toying with him. The thing was seven feet tall and covered in yellow, oozing lesions, its face an open maw of needle-sharp teeth that dripped green venom and blood.

"For the love of God, somebody fucking help me!" he rasped, his throat raw from screaming.

But still, no one came. Every muscle in his body ached, and his hands and feet were freezing. He was sure he'd been running for hours, though some rational part of his brain told him it had only been fifteen minutes at best.

He heard the demon's footsteps, echoing against the building. If he could just—there! He wedged himself behind the rusty dumpster at the back of the store. If he held his breath, held on for a few more minutes, maybe the thing would think he'd escaped.

The street lights around him suddenly went out with a loud pop, and that was when he knew it was over. The night turned pitch black, but he could make out an unearthly red glow coming from the other side of the dumpster. The light grew closer, throwing dancing shadows against the side of the building. And then the dumpster was gone, thrown aside like a toy, and he stood face-to-face with the demon he had inadvertently called up from hell.

"You know what they say," a voice bubbled from somewhere within the oozing monstrosity. "Play with fire…"

"Oh fuck, oh fuck, oh fuck," he screamed, biting down hard on his tongue.

Blood was everywhere. He turned to the wall, frantically clawing and scratching, trying to scale the smooth tin siding. Something touched his shoulder…

Ethereal met earthly and the demon fell apart, collapsing in on itself in a rain of green and yellow ichor. The oozing liquid flooded the little alleyway for the briefest of moments before drying to a near-transparent dust and then vanishing into the night, blown this way and that by the fierce Chicago winds.

The tall, blond man in the black robes turned around, licking the tangy red blood from his lips. He smiled. He was alone in the alley. He looked up into the night and could just make out the outline of the full moon behind the clouds, reflecting light down upon him.

"...and you get burned," he said, marveling at the way his breath turned to frost as it hit the cold night air.

He stripped off the robes, finding a faded pair of blue jeans and a University of Chicago sweatshirt beneath. He crumpled the costume into a ball and casually tossed it aside.

He took a deep breath, filling his nostrils, enjoying the feel of the frigid night air pouring into his lungs. It'd been decades since he had tasted the wind. He stared up into the sky, watching as the moon finally found its way out from behind the clouds. Truly, it was going to be a beautiful night.

Reaching a hand under his sweatshirt, he pulled a silver pentagram up and over his head, the chain wrapping around his wrist as he freed it from his long blond hair. He held the star tight in his fist, moved his hand to his mouth, and whispered something into the silver. Brilliant blue sparks shot out from between his fingers, brightening the alley for an instant in a blinding display of fireworks, and then all was dark again.

He dropped to his knees, placing the object on the dirty cement pavement. Touching a finger to his bleeding mouth, he used the red fluid to draw a small pentagram around the necklace, enclosing it within a perfect circle. He rose to his feet and waved a hand over the drawing, moving his fingers in an intricate pattern as he whispered indecipherable words of power into the night. The necklace began to glow, blinked once, faded, and then was gone.

"And so it begins," he said to himself, breaking the circle with his foot. He walked through the alley and out into the night without so much as a glance behind him.

Chapter 1

Three Days Later

Katy Ruskin awoke tangled in covers, bathed in sweat, breathing hard and on the verge of screaming. She'd had another one of the dreams, this one worse than the last. She was in the house again, the house that Henry Spencer had turned into apartments before she was even born, and was running, running, running for her life. Running from some unseen menace, constantly looking over her shoulder, hiding in the shadows, scurrying away from God only knew what.

She'd been having the dreams since she was twelve and, though they varied from time to time, the theme was always the same. Something she couldn't see, had never managed to see, despite her abilities, was chasing her, mocking her, calling to her, wanting her dead. They usually happened at least once a week, sometimes more but rarely less, and she wanted them to stop. She needed them to stop. But instead they seemed to be getting worse.

Rarely had she had the dreams two nights in a row, but last night was the third time in as many days she'd found herself trapped in the house. She'd been terrified out of her mind, unable to escape, with whatever chased her hot on her heels and closing in fast. And it was getting closer.

At first, she'd just had the sense that something dangerous was following her. Later, she heard fragments of a voice, and lately she'd almost been able to see the thing. The dreams were progressing, and she feared what might happen when her pursuer finally caught her.

The house in her nightmares was different than the real house, but apparently that hadn't always been the case. She'd asked questions about the building and had long ago confirmed that, without the partitions and remodeling that had turned it into an apartment building in the late seventies, it had once looked exactly like the house that she so feared.

Sighing, shaking her head, Katy rose from her bed and padded to the bathroom. Running a brush through the tangles in her straight brown hair, she blanched as she caught her reflection in the mirror. The night had not been kind to her. Puffy bags hung from under her deep brown eyes and she looked as if she hadn't slept in days. In fact, if she didn't know better, she'd almost think she had aged a good ten years overnight. Katy was only 24, but, this morning at least, she looked and felt much older. This definitely did not bode well for her date tonight.

"Are you okay?" asked a tentative voice from outside the bathroom. "The way you ran in there…"

"I'm fine, Mel. Just a bad dream, that's all. Give me a sec and I'll be right out."

"No rush. Go ahead and take a shower, my first class today isn't until ten."

"Cool," Katy said, picking up her toothbrush with one hand and a half-used tube of Crest with the other. "fifteen minutes and the bathroom's all yours."

Melissa Fleming was Katy's best friend and roommate. They'd been paired up in their first year of college at Western Illinois University in Macomb, and, discovering to their amazement that they had a lot more in common than their incredibly good fashion sense, had quickly become friends. After earning their bachelor degrees—Mel's in journalism, Katy's in art history—they'd decided to move to Chicago, where

Mel was from, to pursue their Master's and find their fortunes. That was nearly two years ago, and they'd remained roommates ever since.

They'd been close since that first year of college, but Mel had really become her touchstone when Katy's father died shortly after graduation. Sure, she was close to her mother, but her Mom had been too torn up by the loss of her husband to even breathe. And she and Sam, who was eighteen years her senior and the product of her mother's first marriage, had never really been as close as she would have liked. But Mel had really come through for her, even going so far as to drive with her to Carthage for the funeral. That, more than anything, had cemented their friendship.

Katy stripped off her faded WIU nightshirt, finally ready to shower before schlepping off for another day of work at the gallery. She chanced a second look in the mirror and frowned at her disheveled appearance. She'd never been what anyone would call beautiful, but at she wasn't exactly ugly either. She was 5'7" tall and 135 pounds, her B-cup size breasts had yet to start their inevitable journey southward, and she had reasonably firm, muscular legs with an ass to match, honed to perfection (or at least as close to perfection as she was going to get) by years of track in high school and college. She had pale, porcelain-like skin, and her straight brown hair was cut in a classic page boy bob.

She was intelligent, had a good sense of humor, and knew a lot about a wide variety of subjects. And while she wasn't a knockout, she knew that she was definitely cute, maybe even approaching pretty in an abstract sort of way. Her brown eyes matched her hair, both inherited from her father, while her delicate features and bone structure she had managed to acquire from her mother. All in all, not a bad package: so why weren't more guys interested in her?

Mel had told her on more than one occasion that she was simply unapproachable. Guys were interested, Mel insisted, but they couldn't get past the emotional barriers she had built. She had to be more open, more willing to give people a chance.

"You'd have barriers, too, if you spent your nights running from monsters," Katy mumbled to herself, stepping through the steam and into the shower.

Chapter 2

Emily Spencer was in a bad mood. She lay on her little bed in the tiny room that barely had space for all her stuff, fuming. It was bad enough that her brother had the big bedroom, had a driver's license, got all the attention, and was practically richer than Bill Gates. She could deal with that. What she couldn't stand was him breaking promises.

Ben had promised to drive her to the library after school and here she was, ready to go, but he still wasn't home yet. And it's not even like he had school as an excuse anymore. Lazy bum that he was, he'd decided to take off a year between high school and college. Big brothers sucked. Worse yet, being thirteen sucked. She flopped herself down on the bed, long red hair fanning out behind her.

She was supposed to meet Brandon behind the library at four-thirty, so it's not like she was only going there to study. But Ben didn't know that, and he was going to ruin everything. Maybe he was happy to live his life pining away for someone who didn't even know he existed, but she wasn't. Brandon liked her, and she wasn't about to let Ben screw things up.

She wanted him out of the house, out of the big bedroom, and out of her life. Ever since she could remember, life had given him everything on a silver platter while she had to work her ass off for whatever scraps were left over. He got good grades without even trying, while she actually had to work at it. And he thought he was so *special* with his *abilities*, so unique. Sure, he could always win at Monopoly, and he defi-

nitely kicked ass at video games, but so what? Being lucky wasn't everything.

Wait until he saw what *she* could do. Then he'd be sorry. They'd all
be sorry, from her freakishly forever-young parents to her self-
absorbed brother, and even Katy. Everyone would know just how special she really was.

She'd finally come into her own powers six months ago but hadn't
told anyone, while she learned how to control them. Once she was
ready, she'd show up her brother and laugh as he fell flat on his face.
And then she'd be the special one, while he—

The room began to spin, and she felt like she was going to throw
up. She tried to sit up but tumbled off the bed instead, her red wool
skirt flipping up around her hips as she landed. She rocketed up off the
floor and into the bathroom that connected her room to Ben's, stumbling the last few feet to the sink. What was happening?

She caught her reflection in the mirror. Her green eyes were wide
in alarm, her pixie-like face white as a sheet. She looked like someone
she didn't know. She vaguely recalled that she'd been waiting for
someone, and then...

She stared at her face in the mirror, feeling everything around her
slipping away. The face stared back, and she wondered who was looking at her.

"Help me," she whispered, but then she was gone.

* * *

Ben pulled his candy-apple red Mustang into the driveway. Glancing down at his Rolex, he felt a sense of dread. He'd promised Emily
he'd be home at four to give her a ride to the library, and he was nearly
an hour late. He wished he could blame it on the weather, but though it
was cold and windy, Chicago had yet to produce the season's promised
first snow.

He stared at his parent's white four-bedroom, ranch-style house. Something seemed different, but he couldn't quite put his finger on it. And then he realized Emily had finally got around to putting her 10-speed bicycle in the garage. Maybe she intended to run him over with it.

Steeling himself to face his sister's wrath, the blond-haired, green-eyed teenager rolled out of the driver's seat, pulling his leather bomber jacket tight around his chest as he readied to brace the Chicago cold. The library didn't close until six. There was plenty of time.

"Hey, Sis, sorry I'm late," Ben called out as he pushed through the front door, "Come on, we need to get going."

He watched as a peach-colored postal slip fluttered to the ground. He stooped to pick it up, wondering why Emily hadn't answered the door. The postman rarely arrived before 3:30, and she was almost always home by then.

He looked at the slip; something for his father, from an address in North Carolina. Probably that toy he'd won off eBay. He slipped the paper into his back pocket and shrugged off his jacket as the heat from the house finally hit him.

"Emily?" he called a second time, stepping inside. He'd half-expected to see her standing at the front door when he drove up, impatiently tapping her watch. But she hadn't been there, nor was she in the living room.

"Look, I'm sorry I was late, okay? I just got tied up at the bookstore."

It wasn't a total lie. He did have a part-time job at Barnes and Noble, something his dad had insisted upon when he decided to put college off for a year, but his shift had been over at three. He'd been shooting hoops at Will's house and lost track of the time.

He moved toward Emily's room. "Em, we still have time..." The words stuck in his throat as he pushed open the door to his sister's room.

The room, painted blue three years ago, was white again, and filled with filing cabinets and storage boxes. Not only was Emily not there, but her bed and dresser, her stereo, all of it—everything was gone.

Chapter 3

It was nearly five o'clock before Katy found another chance to reflect on her love life. The first part of her day had quickly gone by in a whirlwind of activity. For whatever reason, the gallery always did its best business Thursday and Friday mornings. She'd managed to sell nearly $3,000 worth of paintings and sculptures this morning, which meant a $150 commission on her paycheck at the end of the week. Not too shabby for a part-time working-your-way-through-grad-school type of job.

Katy sat by herself at a table in the corner of Starbuck's, nursing a tall caramel frappuccino. The coffee house was just across the street from the gallery where she worked, on Miracle Mile, so she came here often. In fact, this is where she and Mel had run into Tom Logan.

She thought about Tom and the date they'd made for tomorrow night. She regretted saying yes almost from the moment that he asked her out, but matchmaker Mel had practically pushed her into it.

They knew each other from school, had been in a lot of the same classes, but didn't seem to have much in common beyond that. Still, he was cute, and seemed intelligent, so she may as well give it a shot. It'd been so long since she'd been with a guy that she was tempted to just jump him in the car and get it over with.

She sighed, for a moment forgetting her troubles and just letting herself enjoy the sweet smells of cinnamon and chocolate. Katy enjoyed the smell of the café just as much as she did the drinks. She allowed herself to relax, pushing back her hectic day for just a few more seconds.

And then the world caught up to her. Katy glanced at her watch. Ten more minutes until the end of her break, and another three hours before she could go home. Between school and work she was exhausted. She was this close to finishing her degree, and the sooner she got her papers the sooner she could get a real job and begin to carve a niche for herself in the real world.

"Excuse me, are you using that?" asked an older woman at the next table, gesturing at the old-fashioned sugar bowl.

Katy smiled, wordlessly passing the bowl across the aisle, noticing that the woman's dress looked a lot like the dress her sister had been wearing when she'd visited Carthage last Christmas.

She suddenly felt herself gasping for air, as if she'd momentarily forgotten how to breathe. She rocked back in her chair and nearly fell over, then slumped against the green-covered table. The bowl fell from her fingers, shattering at her feet, broken glass scattering everywhere.

"...are you okay? Miss, are you okay?" It was the woman who'd asked for the sugar.

"I think so," Katy replied, feeling confused.

What happened? She was thinking about her sister Samantha, who had died the same year Katy was born, and then...nothing. It was like her mind had gone completely blank. She blinked, staring at the woman in the pretty floral dress.

"Are you sure you're okay? Do you need me to call someone?"

"No, I think I just swallowed funny," said Katy, gesturing toward her half-finished drink. "Caffeine rush, you know. I'm okay now."

"Ma'am, is there a problem?" asked a voice from behind her. It was the girl from the counter, a pretty blonde around her age. "Is there something wrong with your drink? Do you need me to get you another one?"

"No, no, I'm fine." Her cheeks reddened. "Just went down the wrong pipe, I think. I'm okay."

The woman in the floral dress sat back down, concern still evident on her face. She smiled at the counter girl, who looked back at Katy.

"Are you sure?" the girl asked, kneeling to clean up what remained of the sugar bowl.

"I'm fine, I promise," she said, rising to her feet on shaky legs. "I'm sorry about the sugar. I should have been more careful."

The words sounded lame even to her. She needed to get out of here, get back to work. She pulled her green Bernardo nylon jacket from the back of the chair and slung it over her shoulder.

"Well, if you're sure…" the woman said, trailing off, her eyes darting toward the counter and the ever-increasing line of customers.

"I'm sure. Thanks, though," Katy mumbled, her face a crimson red. The whole café was looking at her. She dropped a twenty dollar bill on the table, said it was for the sugar bowl, and started toward the door.

"Ma'am, that's really not necessary," said the girl, but Katy was already gone.

Chapter 4

Ben tried but failed to quiet a growing sense of panic deep in his gut. It had been almost five hours since Emily disappeared, and no one else in the house seemed to notice. At first he thought it was an elaborate joke, but now he wasn't so sure. He'd considered the fact that he might be going insane, but, damn it, for all he'd cursed Emily, he'd never wanted her to disappear. If he was crazy, why would his psychosis take the form of wishing away his sister?

Other things had changed as well. His best friend Matt had pretended not to know him when he'd texted him this afternoon, and his high school diploma now listed him as "Benjamin Paul Spencer" when his real middle name was Tanner. If this was a scam, someone had gone to an incredible amount of trouble to pull it off.

He flipped through one of the family photo albums he'd grabbed from the den. Not only was Emily missing, there were some other discrepancies as well; Grandpa Paul was nowhere to be found, the family vacation to the Grand Canyon in '96 had apparently never happened, and, in all the shots featuring the Ruskins, it was usually just a very young Katy and her dad, occasionally Katy and her mother, but never the three together, and he couldn't find Katy's sister Sam anywhere.

He shuddered, closing the album. What in the hell was going on? He sat cross-legged on his bed and booted up his laptop, waiting for it to connect to the wireless network in the den before tapping in a series of addresses he knew by heart. His Dad's website was gone, and none of his books were listed on Amazon. Apparently, he'd never written *Small Things* or any of the other novels that had made him famous. As

Katy would say, this was definitely descending into "weirdness," and he knew that it wasn't him who had gone crazy.

He casually mentioned something about Emily to his father, who looked at Ben like he was nuts. That blew any chance of confiding in his parents. After all, if his father had never written any novels, and his mother had never given birth to a daughter, what else might have changed? He felt bad keeping this from them, but, until he knew more about what was going on, he didn't want to talk to anyone other than Katy. He hoped she'd return his call soon.

His family had long been touched by magic—real, live magic, the kind you read about in books—and he knew full well about his parents' involvement with a magical talisman years before he was born, and the resulting deaths that had followed. His father had chronicled all of it in his first novel, the one that didn't seem to exist anymore. Could this somehow be related?

On a whim, he Googled the terms "Paul McGee" and "Carthage," followed the results to the Carthage *Journal-Pilot*, and nearly fell over when he read the article the link provided:

From the Carthage Journal Pilot, Wednesday October 31, 2007

The Halloween Murders: A Retrospective

By Ashley Allen, Managing Editor

It was 30 years ago today that the first of what would come to be known as the Halloween Murders took place in Carthage. Many theories as to motive have been developed during the last ten years, but none have shed any real light on the spree or the culprit behind it. The crimes remain unsolved.

The following is a timeline of the events in the Halloween Murders case:

October 31, 1977—Paul McGee, a security guard at the Marine Trust bank in Carthage, was found murdered in his garage at approximately 8:15 p.m. He was bludgeoned repeatedly with a crowbar before his throat was slit. McGee was found by his 18-year-old daughter Jennifer.

McGee was survived by his wife Abigail West McGee and their daughter Jennifer, both of Carthage. This was the third time that tragedy had struck the McGee family; McGee lost a sister, Margaret McGee Ruskin, to a 1963 murder in Chicago; and McGee's son, Benjamin Tanner, drowned in 1975.

Jeremiah Watson was arrested on suspicion of murder three days later but was never formally charged with a crime and was released the next day. Watson, a drifter, had sought work on the crew remodeling the Spencer Heights apartments (later renamed Huffman Heights in honor of decorated Korean War veteran Bruce "Brody" Huffman, who had worked on the crew and was killed in a construction accident on September 3, 1981) of which McGee was the foreman. Watson had applied for work and allegedly argued with McGee over not getting the job.

"He was the only suspect we had," said Sheriff Jesse Floyd of Carthage. "Once we eliminated him, we were never able to develop a solid lead. There just wasn't any evidence."

October 31, 1978—Ellen Jones Spencer, a schoolteacher at Ferris Elementary, was found by a patrolman at 4:38 a.m. hanging by her feet from a tree in the county courthouse courtyard, on the north side of the square. Her mouth was covered with duct tape and her throat had been cut. She bled to death.

Spencer was survived by husband Henry Benjamin Spencer and their son Shawn, both of Carthage.

"It was the cleanest crime scene I've ever witnessed," said Floyd. "We never did find the murder weapon. There was absolutely nothing to go on."

Special agent John Aiken was brought in to consult on the case. Aiken, a fifteen-year FBI veteran, put together a task force and worked on the case for three months but was never able to put together a strategy for finding the killer. Aiken, convinced that the two murders were related, referred to the culprit as "The Halloween Killer" in an interview with *Journal-Pilot* reporter Michelle Owings and the name stuck.

October 31, 1979—Aiken was once again brought in. Together with Floyd, they set up a 24-hour patrol of the city from October 30 through November 1. Halloween was cancelled that year, as it was every year until 1985. 25 uniformed police and ten undercover FBI agents were assigned to cover the city, and Floyd claimed, "This time, we'll be ready."

Despite the patrols, Candace "Candy" Martin Ruskin was attacked at 2:45 p.m. behind Ruskin's Pizzeria, the restaurant she owned with her husband. This was the first attack to happen during daylight hours. Ruskin had been emptying the trash in a dumpster behind the restaurant when an unknown assailant slipped a burlap sack over her head and began punching her repeatedly in the ribs.

Her husband, Frederick James Ruskin of Carthage, had left the restaurant to make a supply run and was in his vehicle when he "felt something was wrong." Ruskin, a former Chicago detective and Sheriff of Hancock County from 1965 to 1975, later said he had learned to trust his instincts. (His first wife, Margaret, mentioned earlier in this article, was murdered in 1963.)

Ruskin ran into the restaurant, asking his wait staff the whereabouts of his wife. An employee indicated that he had seen her take out the trash. Ruskin immediately ran through the kitchen and out the back door, coming face-to-face with his wife's attacker. The assailant, wearing a Frankenstein mask and dressed entirely in black, had Candy Ruskin on his shoulder and was carrying her away from the restaurant.

Ruskin ran at the assailant, tackling him, pulling the mask from his face. The unconscious woman fell from the assailant's arms as he and Ruskin stumbled to the ground in the struggle. Afraid for his wife's life, Ruskin rolled away from the attacker to verify her condition. After checking her pulse and breathing, he pursued the assailant on foot but was unable to catch him.

Candy Ruskin suffered multiple broken ribs and a concussion but was otherwise unhurt.

Ruskin stated that, "I must have hurt him, because he was limping after he got up, but I still couldn't catch him." According to Ruskin, the killer wore a black ski-mask beneath the

Frankenstein mask. The mask was the first tangible piece of evidence that the police had, but ultimately didn't serve to help bring the killer to justice.

October 31, 1980—Aiken and Floyd doubled the patrols and renewed the Halloween ban. Everyone was to stay in their homes after dark. Samantha Ruskin, 17, and Arthur Cook, 19, were found murdered at the Jaycee Park on Halloween morning at approximately 8:30 a.m. Time of death was estimated to be between 12:00 a.m. and 1:00 a.m. that morning. Both teenagers were beaten and strangled. Ruskin was survived by her mother Candy Ruskin and step-father Fred Ruskin. Cook was survived by his mother Janice Cook of Carthage.

"They weren't supposed to be there," said Floyd. "If they hadn't ignored the curfew, they might still be alive." Floyd was terminated from his position on January 13, 1981, and Fred Ruskin was re-appointed Sheriff two weeks later.

October 31, 1981 — Sheriff Ruskin, working with FBI investigator Aiken, canvassed Carthage with nearly eight dozen FBI agents, local police, and state troopers. Curfew was maintained, and Halloween passed into November 1 without incident.

"The killer took my step-daughter," Ruskin said in a town hall meeting the next day. "He took four innocent lives, and we will not rest until he is brought to justice."

It was only recently revealed, 30 years after the fact, that in each of the murders a hole was sawed into the victim's chest and the heart was removed from the body. This information was held back by the police in an attempt to draw out the murderer. The hearts were never recovered.

As of Halloween 2007, Carthage has remained free of the "Halloween Murderer." Ruskin, however, was never able to fulfill his pledge; he died from cirrhosis of the liver in 1997. Ruskin was survived by his daughter Katherine Grace and ex-wife Candace Martin.

None of this had ever happened! Both sets of his grandparents were still alive, and he'd seen Sam just last year, during Christmas. Everything was changing around him, but he was the only one who knew it.

But *why* did he know it? Was it because of his powers? His parents were convinced that he and Katy's abilities were a result of what had happened years ago. When his dad had used the nickel to heal himself, Mom, and Fred Ruskin after they had nearly died doing battle with an ancient wizard named Aupuch. That using the magic had somehow altered their DNA, which in turn they passed on to their children. If so, maybe Katy had also noticed the changes. He'd already left her a message at home, so he picked up the phone to try her at work.

Chapter 5

Katy lay on the couch, exhausted. Between her graduate classes and the job at the gallery, she didn't have a lot of free time. She hadn't gotten home until after nine and by the time she'd finished dinner and managed to catch a couple hours of TV she'd recorded on the DVR, it was half past midnight. Thank God tomorrow was Friday.

Of course, tomorrow was also her date with Tom Logan. Nervousness replaced relief in an instant. The longer she thought about it, the more she considered calling him and canceling. She'd almost choked to death on coffee. A night at home by herself would probably do her a world of good.

"Hey, I almost forgot. There was a message from Ben on the voicemail when I got home," Mel said, wandering into the living room in her nightshirt.

Like her, Mel was a night owl, and they'd just finished watching a marathon session of *The Bold and the Beautiful*, the soap they were both hooked on. When would Ridge ever figure out that Brooke was cheating on him, anyway?

"Shit," she said, forgetting about Tom and flashing to earlier in the day. Ben had called her at the gallery, and she'd been too busy to talk. She'd promised to call him back but, with her work and catching up with Mel afterward, she forgot. "What did he say?"

"I dunno, something about things changing and how it was, and I quote, 'really, really important' that you call him back as soon as you got the message. He has it bad for you," Mel said, with a grin.

She felt awful for ignoring Ben. She knew he had it bad for her, too—had for years, in fact—and she did like him, but only as a friend. Maybe even as the little brother she never had. Still, she'd ignored him, and that wasn't cool.

"Yeah, I guess so," she said, wishing it weren't so late. He still lived at home, and she didn't want to wake his parents. "He called at work today, too. I'd call now, but it's after midnight."

"So dreamwalk, girl," Mel said. The two shared everything, and Mel had known about her abilities for years. "Find out what he wanted. You know it'll give him a thrill."

At first Mel had found it hard to accept, but since then she'd had more than her own share of the supernatural. It was amazing what someone could accept once it happened to them.

"Shut up, you," Katy said, secretly knowing her friend was right about giving Ben a thrill.

The two times she'd dreamwalked with Ben, the boy hadn't been able to stop talking about it for weeks. She didn't want to lead him on, pretend there was an intimacy there that wasn't, but at least they'd get to talk.

"I'm about to hit the hay," Mel said, laying a hand on Katy's shoulder. "Don't do anything I wouldn't do."

Katy stuck her tongue out at her friend before rolling off the couch, turning off the lights, and heading to bed.

* * *

Katy lay in the bathtub, surrounded by warm water and bubbles. The lights were off, and candles glowed all around her. Soft jazz music courtesy of Fourplay drifted from her CD player, and still she couldn't fall sleep. It was almost one thirty, which meant only six and a half hours until morning. While she could control her own dreams and enter others' at will, the one thing she couldn't do any better than anyone else was fall asleep.

She'd tossed and turned in bed for nearly an hour before deciding to try a bath. Insomnia was no stranger to Katy; she'd suffered from it almost as long as she'd been having the dreams. She supposed her psyche was trying to protect her from the nightmares—the only dreams she couldn't control—by not letting her sleep. But it wasn't exactly working. She still had the dreams, she was just sleepier than usual the morning after.

Katy closed her eyes, lying back in the bathtub, concentrating on the rhythm of the music. She imagined warm, white waves of energy rolling over her body, relaxing her, protecting her, draining away the tensions of the day and the fear of her dreams. She could feel herself floating, drifting away, bubbles enveloping her body to carry her up to the ceiling...

Finally! Katy found herself in a small cabin in the woods, the safe place in her dreams. She'd created the little house when she was just a girl, before she'd even learned to control her dreams. It was where she'd always go when she was upset, feeling depressed, or just sad. It had always kept her safe, even if it was all just in her head.

She was floating in a tub of warm water scented with rose petals, candles lit all around her. She pulled herself out of the antique claw-footed tub, (unlike the run-of-the-mill bathtub in her apartment) quickly toweling herself dry with a fluffy pink towel. She plucked a terrycloth robe from the hook beside the tub and wrapped it around her body.

She looked at herself in the mirror above the sink of her cabin, and the girl looking back at her looked refreshed and awake, and the bags beneath her eyes had disappeared. Her normally shoulder-length straight brown hair had turned a long, curly blonde and hung down the middle of her back, while her deep brown eyes had changed to a beautiful shade of blue. She was also a generous C-cup now instead of her usual B. If only she could look like this in real life. She sighed, turning away from the mirror to pad through the door and into the living room of her dreams.

The little imaginary cabin in the middle of a forest that didn't exist was decorated with some of the most exquisite artwork from some of the most exclusive museums around the world; among them a beautiful bronze sculpture by Giacometti, Van Gogh's *Sunflowers*, a self-portrait of Leonardo da Vinci, and Paul Klee's *Rooftops*. Katy changed the artwork periodically, depending upon what she was studying and her mood on any given day.

Katy's attention was drawn to the window; it was snowing, just like it always was. Thankfully, the little fireplace in the corner of the room was already blazing. Wood popped and crackled as she dropped herself to the overstuffed leather couch in front of the 60 inch widescreen television, picked up the remote, and turned it on.

Mel's face appeared on the screen. She was dreaming about high school again, walking naked through the hallways, looking for the class that she could never seem to find. Katy laughed, then pressed a pre-programmed button on the remote; Mel looked shocked as a pretty little Dianne Von Fursternberg wrap knit dress appeared around her naked form, and a pair of Jimmy Choo black satin mules formed around her feet. And, lo and behold, the very next door she tried was her home economics class.

Katy knew this dream like the back of her hand and had long ago programmed her dream-remote to automatically fix it. She didn't even have to enter the dream to work her magic, not if she knew the subject well enough.

She pressed another button and watched as her mother came into view. Candy Ruskin, in her early sixties, still looked beautiful despite the hardships she'd endured throughout her life. Her first husband had left her with a one-year-old daughter to raise and then, sixteen years later, happily married to Katy's father, that same daughter had been taken from her when...

Katy's thoughts stopped cold. She looked down at the remote. One of the buttons was labeled "Sam," which was her sister's name. But she didn't remember programming a button for anyone else named Samantha, and her sister had died nearly a year before she was born.

The world around her began to waver, which usually meant she was about to wake up. Closing her eyes, she concentrated on staying asleep, on holding the cabin together. There. She slowly opened her eyes, her gaze falling down to the remote; there was no button marked "Sam."

And why would there be? She must have zoned out for a minute, thought she saw something that wasn't there. Of course her sister was dead. She'd grown up an only child, but had always been aware of an incredible sadness that shadowed everything her parents did. Even though she never said the words, Katy knew that her mother—long divorced from her dad—blamed him for Samantha's death up until the day he died. She probably still did.

She stood up from the couch, letting the remote fall to the cushion. It was time to visit Ben. Only after she'd crossed the room to the frosted glass door on the north wall of the cabin did she realize that she'd forgotten to look in on him. Shrugging, she reached out to close her fingers around the handle.

"Ben," she whispered, pulling the door open. And then she stepped through, finding herself somewhere that was all too familiar.

She was back in her own apartment, standing in the living room. Weirdness. What was Ben doing dreaming about her apartment? For that matter, where was Ben?

And then she heard a low moan coming from her bedroom. Her spine tingled as she glided across the floor and opened the door. Ben was lying in her bed, covered in sweat, as a woman with short brown hair slowly rode his hips. She had her back to the door, and neither she nor Ben noticed her. Maybe she should just leave. But why was he having wet dreams in her bedroom?

"Katy, I want you so much," Ben whispered, pushing up into the woman as his hands wrapped around her hips.

It was only then that Katy realized that *she* was Ben's dream woman. She felt stupid, and a heated anger flashed through her chest. She found herself striding toward the bed, fist clenched.

"Hey, asshole!" she yelled, placing a hand on the other woman's shoulder.

The dream-Katy turned around, her brown eyes huge with surprise and her face white as ash. Katy ignored her doppelgänger, and instead reached out to slap Ben across the thigh.

"Wake up!" she ordered, and then everything went dark.

She was back in the real world again, still floating in the bathtub. She quickly pushed herself out of the tub, water splashing over the side to soak the rug. How dare Ben use her like that?

She glanced at herself in the mirror. She was definitely back in the real world. Her blonde hair and blue eyes had both turned brown, and she looked like she hadn't slept in days. It was only then that she realized that Ben hadn't seen her how she wished she was, but had actually dreamt of her real self. And, somehow, that made her even angrier.

Wrapping one towel around her wet hair and another around her body, she stomped out of the bathroom and down the hall to her bedroom. Screw waking Ben's parents up—he had some explaining to do.

Chapter 6

Ben knew he'd screwed up. Sure, it had been a dream, and, unlike Katy, he couldn't exactly control his dreams, but he'd still screwed up. He wasn't really sure how, though. He just knew he'd done it.

He'd had a crush on Katy since at least his twelfth birthday, possibly longer. She'd given him a copy of Charles de Lint's *Trader* that year, a book he'd come to love. The problem was, she still saw him as the same boy he'd been seven years ago. Try as he might, he couldn't seem to get her to give him a chance.

He looked at the clock: it was just after two in the morning. Ben sighed, stretched, and forced himself out of bed. Where was his vaunted luck now? He could always roll sevens, got straight A's in school, and never failed to buy a winning lottery ticket. So why couldn't he get 24-year-old Katy Ruskin to realize that, in the grand scheme of things, a five year age difference just wasn't that important?

Sitting at the foot of his bed, he thought about his life. He had offers from all the best colleges across the country, (some that he'd never even applied for!) and a bank account that most people his age would die for. Sure, it had all come easy—too easy, perhaps—but that wasn't exactly his fault.

If he actually studied for a quiz and tried to give the right answers, he'd usually top out at a B; but if he randomly picked answers, especially on a multiple choice test, he'd get them all right every time. *Every single time*. He'd had the talent since he was thirteen, and he'd have been a damned fool not to use it.

Of course, Katy knew about his talent; maybe that was why she wouldn't give him a chance. She knew everything had come easy for him and didn't want to include herself on the list. But it's not like she didn't have talents of her own. They were both special, gifted with the magic his father had briefly possessed years before either one of them was even born. Weren't they supposed to be kindred spirits?

He looked at the cell phone charging on his nightstand; he didn't want to make the call, but he knew that he should. This didn't have to be a big deal, and he needed to make her see that. Emily having been erased from reality was a much bigger deal than who he had wet dreams about.

He reached for the phone and rolled over on his stomach. Sighing, he selected Katy's number from his phone book.

Before he could dial, however, the little silver Nokia began to play his favorite Avril Lavigne tune. *Shit.* He glanced at the caller ID: it was Katy. He tentatively pressed the answer button.

"Umm, hello?" he said, bracing himself for what he knew was coming next.

"What the *hell* was that about?" yelled Katy Ruskin into his ear. She had a temper just like her old man, and he'd always hoped to stay on the other side of it.

"Katy, listen, I can explain…"

"What's to explain? Jesus, Ben…you were fucking me!"

"Katy, if you'll listen…"

"I actually felt bad that I couldn't talk when you called this afternoon. Little did I know."

"I can't help what I dream!" He said, all thoughts of Emily forgotten. "You're the only one who can do that, remember? And who asked you to come into my dreams tonight anyway?"

"That's not the point. We're supposed to be friends, Ben. If I can't trust you…"

"Trust me?" he interrupted, his voice trembling with emotion. "When have you *not* been able to trust me?"

"Tonight, that's when," she snapped. "I really didn't need to see that, Ben."

"Of course not, because then you might have to face the fact that I'm not a kid anymore."

"Ben, I know you're not a kid," she said, her voice growing softer, "it's just that, well, I'm even less of a kid than you are."

"Five years, Katy. Five years! Your dad was, what, twenty years older than your mother?"

"That's not the point. Look, you know I love you like a brother. A little brother. I'm just not interested in anything else, okay? I just don't need the weirdness."

"...Yeah, okay," he finally said, giving up. "I'm sorry about the dream."

"Well, like you said, not your fault. I'm sorry I was so angry. So," she said, stretching the word out, "what did you want to talk to me about?"

"Katy," he took a breath, "what can you tell me about your sister?"

"My sister? What a weird question."

"Just tell me everything you know," he insisted. "It's important."

"Not much. As you know, she died almost a year before I was born. I sometimes forget I even had a sister. I barely even remember my father, and he died when I was six."

Shit. Whatever had happened to his life was affecting her too, only she didn't remember it. "Well," he whispered into the phone, almost afraid to speak, "what if I were to tell you that she's alive and living in Carthage, and that we both had Christmas dinner with her last year?"

Chapter 7

Ben stared wordlessly at the cell phone in his hand. She hung up on him. He couldn't believe it. She'd actually hung up on him. He was screwed. He was royally and completely screwed.

He opened Facebook on his phone and went to Katy's page. Good, she hadn't blocked him. He sent her a message, and a few seconds later she answered:

Katy: What???

Ben: Katy, I'm sorry. I'm not trying to make you angry, but it's real. I swear to God, it's real.

Katy: Come off it. I don't know what kind of game you're playing, but if you think saying my sister is alive is somehow going to get you into my pants...

Ben: No! Please, just listen. Let me call you, okay?

Katy: Say whatever you have to say here. I don't want to talk to you right now, and I don't want to wake up Mel.

Ben: Things have been changing, Katy. Your sister is alive, your father didn't die until just a few years ago, and I have a little sister. Her name is Emily Margaret. The middle name comes from my great aunt, your father's first wife.

Katy: Are you insane??

Ben: I don't know. Maybe!

Katy: So what do you want me to do about it? You should talk to your parents, or maybe your psychiatrist.

Ben: I tried talking to my dad and he looked at me like I was nuts.

Katy: And this surprised you why…?

Ben: Because it's all true. The Halloween murders… I read about them on the Web, but they never happened. My grandparents, your sister, they're all still alive. At least they were until this morning, when everything started to change.

Katy: So if things are changing, how do you know about it?

Ben: I don't know. Maybe the magic? I was hoping you'd noticed the changes, too.

Katy: No changes here other than my honorary kid brother going nuts and wanting to bed me.

Ben: Ha Ha. And I'm not your kid brother, will never be your kid brother. Katy, do you have any idea how I feel about you?

Katy: No, and I don't want to.

Ben: Fine, then. So what do we do?

Katy: About your past changing, you mean? What else has supposedly changed?

Ben: Most of my friends don't remember me, and those who do remember a drastically different version of me.

Katy: How about that girl you were dating? Cerulean or Chartreuse or something?

Ben: Sigh. Her name is Burgundy. Burgundy Wisrock-Eckert. But we broke up months ago. I hadn't even thought to call her.

Katy: I'm sure that's for the best. Burgundy was probably just a pigment of your imagination anyway.

Ben: Ha. I'm not sure now is the best time to be making jokes. It's your past, too! And my parents, and your mom's, and for all I know everyone else's. It's all changed, and I'm the only one who can remember. Hell, even my middle name changed!

Katy: So it's not Paul anymore?

Ben: It was never Paul! It's Tanner. Benjamin Tanner Spencer.

Katy: Always been Paul to me. Named after your grandfather, right?

Ben: But that's just it, it's not right. My grandfather is still alive. At least he's supposed to be.

Katy: Stuff like this only happens in books and movies, Ben.

Ben: Much like the stuff that happened to our parents, hmm?

Katy: Okay, good point. So let's pretend for a moment that I believe you. What can I do?

Ben: I don't know. I just need your help, okay? Can you come over tomorrow?

Katy: Can't, dude. I have a date. A dreamy grad student by the name of Tom Logan. ;)

Ben: Are you trying to make me jealous? Just cancel it. This is way more important.

Katy: lol. No can do, sport. But how about Saturday? Mel and I are going to see the new Marvel movie, but I can stop by after.

Ben: It might be too late by then.

Katy: What do you mean?

Ben: One or both of us might disappear by then.

Katy: Gee, I hope I stick around long enough for my date.

Chapter 8

What was he going to do? Everything had changed, and he had absolutely no idea what to do about it. It was ten in the morning but he felt like he had hardly slept. After his Facebook discussion with Katy, he had stayed up the rest of the night researching his new "past" on the Internet. He had many questions, but precious few answers.

He and his parents had long ago decided that his abilities helped him to affect causality. When he rolled a pair of dice, his father hypothesized, some part of him reached into an infinite number of alternate universes and plucked out the pair that came up a four and a three. It made sense, once you wrapped your mind around it.

Maybe that would explain why he was the only one who noticed the past changing all around them. If he could affect causality—always getting the desired results, never failing to buy a winning lottery ticket—then maybe he himself was the desired result, the one person whose memories of the real past couldn't be changed because a little part of him existed in all the different infinite universes.

That would help explain why the altered past deleted his sister but left him intact. He still existed because he'd found a universe—perhaps the only universe—where, despite the alteration of the past, his parents had still managed to procreate at the exact necessary moment in time to produce him.

His past had changed around him, but he, Ben Spencer, the Ben Spencer he was before any of this happened, the memories he had created over nineteen years of life, had not.

That was a lot of maybes, and he had the feeling he was missing something. Was he making himself too important in all of this? After all, who would want to alter his timeline? What purpose would it serve?

He thought back to the stories his father had told him about the summer of 1975. He knew that his parents and Fred Ruskin had gone to battle with the wizard Aupuch over an ancient magical charm given the form of a Buffalo-head nickel, and that the charm currently resided in a safe in his father's bedroom. He knew that Aupuch had turned his great-great-uncle Colin Wainwright into a demonic creature called a fetch, and that the fetch had murdered his uncle Tanner and almost killed Ruskin and his parents.

His father had briefly wielded god-like power when he held the combined magic of the nickel and the four other corresponding charms in the palm of his hand. He'd given it all up and pledged to Michael the archangel (a freaking angel!) to safeguard the nickel for the rest of his life, but not before using the magic to heal his party of their injuries. That was, according to his dad, when the magic permanently altered their DNA and made it possible to pass the magic on to their progeny. The supernatural power had given him and Katy the ability to tap into the wild magic that existed all around them, allowing her to dream walk and him to circumvent the randomness of chance.

If someone else was after the nickel—and that was certainly a possibility, because it had happened before—how would altering the past help them obtain the charm? According to his father, copper contained an inherent ability to mask the energies of the nickel. He kept it hidden in an old mason jar surrounded by hundreds of Indian-head pennies, so how would anyone even know where it was?

Even with the proof of his and Katy's abilities staring him in the face, he'd always had a hard time believing his parents' stories. But if all of that had really happened, if his family had been indelibly marked by magic, then anything was possible.

There was no putting it off. He had to talk to his parents. He'd been dreading it, because he was afraid of what else might have changed. If they couldn't help, he could only imagine what might happen next.

Chapter 9

"We've been over this time and again," said Shawn, staring across the dining table at Ben. His father looked like a slightly-older version of himself, sandy-blond hair and all. "No one changed your past. How could they, and why would they want to? You're off your meds again, aren't you?"

"What meds?" Ben asked, his eyes darting from his father to his mother. His heart thrummed wildly in his chest, and he felt punchy from lack of sleep. "Mom, what's he talking about?"

"Maybe we should see the therapist again," his mother offered, brushing her short red hair back from her face. "We seem to go through this every few months, honey." She reached out to stroke Ben's cheek. "You know we take everything you say seriously, but the past is set in stone, as far as anyone knows. Nothing has been changed because nothing *can* be changed. God knows I wish things were different, that your grandparents and Samantha had never been murdered. There isn't a day that goes by when I don't miss them, Ben, and when I don't miss my brother Tanner. Not a day."

"But we just saw Grandpa McGee last month! And we spent last Christmas with everyone in Carthage."

"Son, you need to take your medicine. Everything will become much clearer if you just take your meds."

"I'll be right back," his mother said, rising from the table and disappearing through the hallway.

"I've never taken medicine," Ben insisted, his eyes wild with panic. Everything had gone horribly wrong. "I'm telling you the truth."

"Okay," said Jenny, reentering the room. She held three pills in the palm of one hand and a cup of water in the other. "Ben, you really need to take these."

"No!" he yelled, standing up from the table. He felt like running, but he had nowhere else to go. "You have to believe me."

"Please," his mother pleaded with him, tears trickling down her freckled cheeks. "We can't go through this again. Just take the pills. It'll all be better in a few days, I promise."

Ben felt defeated. He reached out to take the pills from his mother's hand, throwing them into his mouth.

"Gone," he said, opening his mouth and sticking out his tongue. "I'm going to go back to bed now, okay?"

"Ben, I love you," said Shawn, standing from the table to take his son into his arms. "I love you so much. You know that, don't you? We both do."

"Sure, Dad, I know," he said, returning his father's embrace. "I just need to go to bed. I'll be better tomorrow, I promise."

"I know you will, Ben," Jenny said, squeezing his shoulder. "I know you will."

Chapter 10

Katy sat at home, half-heartedly watching a movie on Netflix. Tom was late. It was nearly 7:30, and he was supposed to have picked her up thirty minutes ago. She'd tried calling his cell phone, but to no avail. She had to face facts. She'd been stood up.

Instead of anger or disappointment, she felt strangely relieved. She hadn't really wanted to go out with him anyway, and could use a night at home. Maybe she should scrub off her make-up and red nail polish, ditch the diamond stud earrings and get out of these uncomfortable date clothes—a Donna Karan "little black dress" with a pair of Manolo Blahnik black leather pumps, not to mention her way-too-expensive Prada purse—and into her pajamas and just hunker down on the couch with a cup of hot cocoa and a book.

Mel was out with her new boyfriend, a mixed martial arts fighter, of all things, by the name of "Gentleman" James Duncan. She'd met the guy a few times and he seemed nice enough and even intelligent, so who was she to throw stones? At least Mel actually *had* a boyfriend. The closest thing she had to a beau was a nineteen-year-old kid with a crush.

Why had she been so mean to Ben? She needed to be more understanding of his condition. She'd practically rubbed it in his face that she had a hot-and-heavy date tonight, and more or less treated him like dirt. She'd just been so angry when she'd walked into his dream. Seeing him making love to her doppelgänger somehow left her feeling betrayed, but for the life of her she couldn't really figure out why. Worse yet, why had it bothered her so much that he saw her as she really was and not as the hot fantasy chick she liked to portray in her dreams? She shrugged to herself, willing the thoughts from her head.

She stared at the phone, feeling guilty. She finally slid across the overstuffed Pleather couch and away from watching Wreck-it-Ralph on her television. She was free tonight, apparently, so she might as well pay Ben a visit. She picked up the phone and dialed his cell.

Chapter 11

Ben awoke with a start. He heard music. Had someone turned on the TV? No, it was his cell phone. He'd gone online to do more research after the confrontation with his parents but had apparently fallen asleep. He checked the time of the last article he'd bookmarked—2:15 p.m. That was—he glanced at his clock, trying in vain to focus his eyes—only five hours ago.

He could still taste the bitter tang of the pills he'd thrown up earlier. Things were so screwed up, he found himself almost wanting to believe that he really was schizophrenic. But he knew it wasn't true. The world had changed around him, and he felt powerless to set things right again.

The phone rang again, and Avril Lavigne sang at him, asking him why he felt the need to be so complicated. He wished he knew.

Suppressing a yawn, he reached across the bed to snatch the phone from his night stand. "Hello?" he mumbled into the phone. "This had better be good."

"Ben, are you okay? You sound awful." It was Katy!

He thought back to last night. He hadn't been able to convince her, and the more he thought about it the more he could understand why. How do you convince someone of something that they have no memories of and of which you have absolutely no proof?

"As okay as I'm going to be with my life changing around me and my parents thinking I'm nuts," he finally replied, "but I'm surprised to hear from you."

"I'm sure. And I'm sorry I was so rough on you last night."

"I probably deserved it."

"So, anyway, if you still want to see me tonight..."

"Well, yeah, sure. I mean, don't you have a date or something?"

"Truth be told, he stood me up. Story of my life. Bad for me, dude, but good for you," she said.

"The guy's an idiot."

"I won't argue with that. So, I'm still coming over?"

"Most definitely," he said over the phone.

"Cool. Be there in fifteen."

"Do me a favor?"

"Almost anything, Ben," she said hesitantly. "Shoot."

"Meet me in the backyard. I'll leave the gate open."

* * *

"You look like shit," Katy said, as she stepped through the open wooden gate leading into Ben's backyard.

She was wearing her old leather jacket, an incongruous contrast to the more stylish clothes she had on underneath. She probably should have changed, but didn't feel like going through the whole rigmarole again.

Why Ben had wanted to meet this way was beyond her, but, after the way she'd treated him, she figured she owed him at least that much. Still, today's forecast had called for rain, and she definitely didn't want to ruin her shoes. She'd give him five minutes, tops, and then it was either go inside or she was out of here.

"Yeah, well, that's what two days without sleep will do to you," Ben replied, his eyes jumping from Katy's dress to the sliding glass doors that led back into the house. He looked like he was about to say something and then thought better of it. "My parents think I'm schizophrenic."

"Well, aren't you?" She asked, shivering against the cold. She glanced up at the sky. She was pretty sure she'd felt a drop or two of rain while walking around the side of the house. "Oh God, Ben, don't tell me you went off your meds again?"

"What meds? I never took any fucking meds!"

"You need help, dude. Let's go inside and talk to your parents." She reached out for his arm, but he pulled away.

"Katy, everything has changed, and I'm not crazy. Look," he pulled his wallet out of his back jeans pocket, flipping it open. "Even my license..." his eyes grew large, and he fell silent.

"What?" she demanded, feeling frigid drops of rain pelting her hair and shoulders.

"My license—it has my real name on it. Everything else has changed, but my license is still real."

Katy moved closer. The ID read 'Benjamin Tanner Spencer'. "Okay, big deal. You could have easily changed it. Is that supposed to prove something?"

"Everything else changed, everything else is wrong, even my high school diploma." He removed the license from his wallet, pressing it into her hand.

"Again, so?" she turned the license over in her palm, and her breath caught in her throat. It clearly said 'Benjamin Tanner Spencer,' and then—it simply didn't. She blinked, reading the words 'Benjamin Paul Spencer' on the laminated card.

"How did you do this?" she asked, her concern with the weather all but forgotten. Screw the shoes. Something was definitely happening, and she had a feeling it wasn't good.

"Do what?"

"It just changed, Ben. I was staring at it, and it changed. Your name was wrong, and then it was right."

"Let me see," he said, taking the card back. His middle name had changed to 'Paul.' "But that's wrong! A second ago... hold on a minute." He flipped through his wallet, looking through the photos until he found a family portrait of himself, his parents, and his sister.

"She's still here," he whispered, finding Katy's eyes in the darkness. "Emily's still in the picture. Look."

Ignoring the rain, Katy moved her face close to Ben's, peering over his shoulder. A red-haired teenager, maybe thirteen or fourteen, stood with Ben and his family, smiling for the camera. "Let me see," she asked, reaching out to slip the photo from its jacket.

The girl was still there. She backed up from Ben and watched in amazement as the teenager faded from view. The other figures in the photo adjusted themselves to make up for the empty space. Katy thought she was going to be sick.

"What?" Ben asked, noticing the look of horror on her face. He snatched the photo back from Katy, blanching when he saw that his sister was missing.

"It's like," Katy said, trying to formulate her thoughts, "if it's in contact with you, or close to you, it stays the same. When it leaves your sight, it changes. For good."

"Do you believe me now?" he asked her, eyes wide with fear. "We are truly and royally fucked."

"Not necessarily," said a voice from behind them, "though I do have to admit that it's looking pretty grim."

Katy whirled to see a tall man in a tan trench coat standing at the open gate. His hair was long and blond, and he looked to be about 25 or 30. The man looked oddly familiar, yet she couldn't place his face. "Who are you?"

"I've looked in on you many times, Katy," the man said, seemingly reading her thoughts. "My name is Michael, and I've come to help."

Rain dripped off his coat and fell to the grass as he stepped forward, closing the gate behind him.

"Michael," Ben said reverently. "The Archangel Michael?"

"One and the same," he said, "Ben, you are the only one who can see that things are wrong, and the only one that can put them back together again, the way that they were meant to be. But we must work quickly."

"Wait a minute," Katy said, looking back and forth between the two men. "This is getting way too weird. The past really has changed, and you're supposed to be an angel?"

"The past really has changed," said Michael, lifting his shoulders. "That much I can tell you. But the past is now a darkened glass to me. The date on which the path diverged was October 31, 1977, and whatever changed it came from the old house on Randolph street, but beyond that I cannot see."

"And you're an angel? An honest-to-goodness, real live angel? I don't think I ever really believed it…"

"The Halloween murders," Ben whispered, pulling a folded print-out from another pocket. "All of those people should still be alive."

"Exactly," Michael agreed, "and you must go into the past and set things right again."

"Me?" Ben asked, his eyes falling to the paper in his hands. "But what can I do?"

"You must go into the past and stop the murders. This I can help you with," he said, reaching out a hand to touch Ben's shoulder, "but once you're there, you will be on your own."

"You're not coming with me?"

"I can't," Michael explained. "I am…anchored to this place and time. Humans are not. You are not."

"So, I'll be alone."

"No, you won't," Katy said, making a decision. She was scared to death of entering that house, but she couldn't let him go alone. Her hand found Ben's, their fingers automatically intertwining. "You won't be alone because I'm going with you."

Ben looked at her in surprise.

"But don't get any ideas, Spencer," she said, squeezing his hand.

"This path is very dangerous, Katherine. Ben can walk it because he can see it, because he is a part of it. He exists in all realities because he can affect all of those realities; you cannot, and thus do not."

"You said dangerous, but not impossible. And this affects me too. I'm going."

"Katy," said Ben, finding her eyes. "I couldn't live with myself if anything happened to you…"

"My mind's made up," she said. "I'm coming. I *can* go, right?"

"You can go," Michael said, though he didn't look very happy about it. "But, because of his abilities, only Ben can read the spell. If you try, it will likely kill you. And when you're ready…"

His words were interrupted by the antiquated ring of an old telephone. Katy blanked for a second before realizing that the sound was coming from her purse. She'd just gotten a new iPhone and had quickly set the ringer to the "old tyme" option but forgotten to change it to vibrate.

"Katy!" Ben yelped, reaching toward her purse.

"I got it," she said, fumbling through the bag until she came up with her cell.

The caller ID said it was Mel, probably calling to check up on her date. It rang again. Damn it, why hadn't she bothered to read the instructions? She tapped a series of buttons in random order on the virtual screen until the phone finally stopped making noise. Her heart beat fast, and she breathed a sigh of relief as she slipped the phone back into her purse. "Sorry about that."

"Do you have access to the nickel?" Michael asked Ben, as though the interruption had never happened.

"The nickel?" he asked. "Why?"

"Because you'll need it."

"It's in my parents' bedroom, in a wall safe. If we talk to my dad…"

"We cannot," said Michael. "This path is not his. He's part of this new reality, as is your mother. They won't believe you, and they may not even believe me. We must do this now, tonight, before any other changes are made and it becomes impossible to intercede."

"So how do we do this?" Katy asked, letting go of Ben's hand. "Is there, like, a time machine or something?"

"Nothing that extravagant," Michael said. "I've prepared a spell for you, but the nickel must power it. And you will need a focus, something from the past, an object that means something to the people you wish to save."

"Do you think this'll do?" asked Katy. She reached under the neckline of her dress and pulled out a twisted hunk of metal that hung from a silver chain around her throat. "It belonged to my father."

"It will do," Michael said before turning to Ben. "And you can get the nickel?"

"Okay," Ben said, glancing at his watch. "It's a quarter 'til nine, so my parents are still up and awake. This is something I probably need to do alone. Give me fifteen minutes and I'll meet you in the garage. You can get in through the side entrance, just outside the gate and around the corner. The key's above the door."

"Now you tell us," said Katy, glancing up at the rain.

Her shoes were definitely ruined. She wondered what the chances were of finding a cute pair of pumps in 1977, finally deciding they were somewhere between slim and none. All time travel jokes aside, this was definitely going to be one long trip.

Chapter 12

Ben pried open his bedroom window, slipping back into the house the same way he'd left. He was careful not to make any noise; all he needed now was his parents coming in to check on him.

So what did one take on a trip to the past? He scanned the room, looking for anything that might help them. His eyes fell on his laptop. He didn't want to risk altering the past any more than it had already been altered, but the information he'd uncovered about the Halloween murders could prove invaluable.

Information, he knew, was the most valuable commodity that existed in the 21st century. Perhaps it would serve them equally well in 1977. He quickly located the laptop bag and set it on the floor beneath the window sill. Moving to the laptop, he loaded Website Extractor, a research tool capable of autonomously downloading huge amounts of data from the Web and programmed it to find everything it could relating to Carthage, circa 1975 to 1981.

Leaving the computer to its task, he kicked off his Nikes before quietly opening the door and slipping into the hallway on stocking feet. He could hear his parents talking in the living room, so it was now or never. He carefully padded down the tile hallway, past the room that used to be Emily's, and into his parent's bedroom.

Willing his luck to hold true, he slipped past the huge oak dresser to a painting of a sunset and carefully removed the canvas from the wall. Yes, the safe was still there. He laid a hand against the small Fire-King and slowly turned the dial left to 12, then right to 7, and finally left again to 2. He pulled the handle, but nothing happened. And then he realized—the combination had been Emily's birthday. Without Emily, the numbers made no sense.

Ben tried to clear his mind. He reached out and set the dial to zero, then spun the dial randomly to the left. He watched as it settled on the number one. Then he spun the dial to the right and smiled as it came to rest on 12. He didn't need to rely on his luck for the last number. The combination was his birthday. He turned the dial to the correct number, and then pulled the handle. The safe swung open with a satisfying click.

And there it was—the old Mason jar filled with pennies. The nickel, he knew, would be inside. Brushing aside a sheaf of papers, he carefully removed the jar. The pentagram necklace his father had used to open a secret doorway into a hidden room in the old Spencer house was also there, along with a small handgun his mother had purchased after a rash of burglaries hit their neighborhood. On impulse, he grabbed the necklace and the handgun. He figured they could use all the help they could get.

He rifled through an envelope of cash his parents always kept for emergencies. Most of the bills were post-1977 fifties and hundreds, but hidden behind the larger bills were twelve crisp 1976 two-dollar notes. He had 24 dollars, plus whatever bills he might be able to use in his wallet. Not a lot of money, but at least it was something.

Breathing a sigh of relief, he carefully closed the safe before hanging the painting back on the wall. He traced his steps down the hallway and back into his bedroom.

He looked at his watch. It was just a few minutes before nine. He hurriedly rummaged through his closet before bringing out an old blue duffel bag he'd gotten as a freebie at a computer show a few years ago. It would do. He dropped the jar and the gun into the bag and slipped the necklace around his throat, carefully concealing the pentagram inside his shirt.

"What's going on, Ben?"

Ben's heart went staccato in his chest as he turned to see his father staring at him from the hallway. Ben's bed separated him from the doorway, so his father hadn't yet seen the duffel bag. He let the bag fall to the carpet, pushing it under the bed with his foot.

"Not much. I just woke up and need to take a shower."

"Are you feeling okay?" his father asked, moving into the room. Ben quickly crossed the floor to meet him.

"Definitely better," he said, doing his best to be convincing. "I'm sorry about earlier."

"So your medicine helped?"

"I guess so."

"Good." He reached out to embrace Ben, pulling him tight. "I love you, son. We'll get through this, I promise."

Ben felt tears well up in his eyes. "I love you too, Dad," he said, returning the hug.

"Well, I'd better let you get to your shower," his father said, pulling back from the embrace. "Everything really will be okay, Ben."

"I know it will," he said, smiling.

If things went well, he'd be returning to parents who didn't think he was nuts and he'd regain two grandparents and a sister in the process. He could think of no better trade-off than that.

He was moving again the moment his father shut the door. Quickly slipping his shoes on, he powered down the laptop and shoved it into its carrying case, and then shoveled everything into the duffel bag. It was now or never, and there wasn't any time like the present—or at least there wouldn't be once he'd set everything right again. With that thought in mind, Ben let himself out the window and into the rainy night beyond.

Chapter 13

Summer, 1975

Reverend David Allan Dowd (or "Dad", as many in his flock liked to call him) sat in a tent on the outskirts of Rector, Arkansas, getting ready to give his sermon, when he felt the Evil. It was as if a hundred—no, a thousand, maybe more—tortured souls suddenly called out, and only he could hear their cries. Only he could witness their screams. He began to tremble, and tears ran freely down his cheeks. Satan had just stepped foot on Earth, and God's chosen children must rise up against them or forever be doomed to the fiery depths of hell.

It had happened somewhere to the north, he knew that much, and soon he would know more. He'd seen a flash, just the hint of a vision, but it was enough. An old priest stood helpless against an evil trinity, ready to die for the Lord. A young, red-haired whore and a blond teenager—the Anti-Christ, Dowd was sure of it—stood against him. With the help of a Roman soldier, they struck down the priest and consumed his soul. The priest was gone, and his betrayer held the power of Satan in his fist. But the priest would find glory in heaven, and he, Dad, would track down the evil and avenge the man's murder. He'd destroyed Satan's minions before, scores of times, in fact, and he'd do it again. It was his mission. He was a soldier of the Lord, and he would not fail.

This was the second time in a week that he'd been blessed with a vision, and he knew that they both came from the same place. The first vision was confusing—a young man and woman lying motionless in an alley behind a church—but he knew they must have been sinners, for God hadn't the need to show him saints.

He'd first felt the calling years ago, after waking up from the accident that had left him in a coma for more than a month. He was only twelve, but he felt God calling to him, handing him the mantle, choosing him to preach His word. And, more than that, to be His sword, to smite those who sought to undo His good works. To grind those damned souls under his righteous heel, to bury them and then pray for their immortal souls.

His first victim had been a common whore. He'd seen a vision of her using black arts to gain the affections of a married man. He followed the path God laid out for him, from his hometown of Grainfield, Kansas, to Acton, Maine, but he'd been too late. By the time he'd hitched rides across the country and found the hotel room, the deed had been done—the whore had corrupted her would-be lover, dirtied him with her filthy loins—and he'd been forced to put them both down. He buried them outside the city, five miles into the forest that surrounded the north side of the town. He could still remember the rain on his skin, the sweet smell of pine, as he dug their graves.

He'd never gone home after that. At the age of thirteen, he left his family and joined a traveling ministry, helping to bring the word of the Lord to thousands of unsaved souls. A year later, after he discovered the minister stealing money from the flocks, he'd struck the man down and taken control of the ministry. That had been fourteen years ago, and he'd traveled across the globe ever since, spreading the word of God and smiting those who refused to listen. He'd never once looked back.

Dowd looked down at his notes; his sermon tonight was on coveting thy neighbor's wife, but he let the cards tumble from his fingers. He'd been inspired to a higher cause, and that's what he would preach on tonight. He picked up his worn, leather-bound Bible and clutched it tightly to his chest.

Rising from the old lawn chair he carried from town to town, the Reverend pushed aside the tent flaps to the cheer of his followers. He quickly walked past his helpers, through the throng of true believers, and onto the little stage they'd erected the night before.

He was met by silence, but he expected that. His face was marred by the devil as surely as his heart was clenched in the fist of the Lord. David Dowd stood a huge six foot seven inches tall, weighed a muscular 270 pounds, and wore his hair in a military burr with a ponytail in back. An angry red scar ran diagonally from the left side of his forehead, through where his eye used to be, and ended at the corner of his mouth. But when he started to speak, he knew that they would listen. Oh, how they would listen.

He looked out into the crowd of nearly a hundred and felt their pain, felt their fear. And they should be afraid. They *have* to be afraid!

"My friends," he said, the soft Kansas accent evident in his voice, "we don't have much time. Hell on Earth is coming, and the demons prepare to wage their war against all that is good and holy. The wrath of God burns against them, and yet their damnation does not slumber; the pit is prepared, the fire is made ready, the furnace is now hot, ready to receive them, and still they come; the flames do now rage and glow, and they are doomed to fail, but they will come, and they will take you with them if you allow it." He looked on from his makeshift pulpit, Bible in hand, and let his words reverberate through the little crowd.

"Revelation 20:10 says, 'And the devil that deceived them was cast into the lake of fire and brimstone, where the beast and the false prophet *are*, and shall be tormented day and night forever and ever.' And so he shall. But he has been set free, my friends, and I feel him even now ravaging the lands asunder. Armageddon is coming, and the rapture will surely follow. Are you ready? Are you ready?"

The crowd was already starting to respond. He could see the fire in their eyes as they chanted "Hallelujah!" and he could feel the spirit enter their souls as he fed upon their energy. He only took a little, not enough to hurt them—just enough to help him do his good work. The Lord helps those who help themselves, after all. And the Lord always provides.

Chapter 14

"About time," Katy said, as Ben walked through the garage door. "We were worried."

"Sorry, I had an impromptu visit with my dad."

"You didn't tell him anything?" asked Michael, running his hand through his wet blond hair.

"I didn't tell him a thing," Ben said.

The rain was coming down harder now and the temperature had dropped to around 40 degrees. He wished he'd thought to bring his jacket. The green sweatshirt he'd been wearing since Thursday morning was doing precious little to protect him from the cold.

He dropped the duffel to the dusty garage floor, reached in, and pulled out the jar of pennies. He quickly unscrewed the lid and dumped the copper into the bottom of the bag. And there it was—the Buffalo-head nickel, silver gleaming in the dim overhead light.

"So what do we do now?" Ben asked, snatching the nickel from the sea of copper. He scooped the pennies back into the jar, then zippered his duffel bag closed.

"Take this," Michael said, producing a folded piece of paper from one of the many pockets of his trench coat. "I've prepared the spell for you. Concentrate on your time and destination—the morning of October 31, 1977, in Carthage, Illinois—and hold the nickel in your hand. Katy, hold Ben's shoulder and concentrate on your necklace. Think about where it was during that time, and then hold it in your mind."

"So that's it?" Ben asked, unfolding the paper to reveal five lines of Latin on college-ruled notebook paper.

The spell was written in a spidery hand, and the words seemed to dance before his eyes. By the penmanship, he guessed it'd been a few years since Michael had actually been forced to write anything.

"That's it," the angel said. "You will have to find the murderer on your own. Keep your eyes open, and trust your instincts. And be careful who you interact with. You're going into the past to set things right again, try not to change things any more than necessary."

Katy reached out to touch one shoulder as he shrugged the duffle bag over the other. He clutched the nickel tight in his fist, then said, "My Latin's more than a little rusty—as in non-existent—but here goes:

"Abbas vicis matris terra verto vicis sands, preteritus exsisto tendo quod tendo exsisto preteritus, meus sententia destinatus intertractus aeris, meus immortalis animus reus ut angelus Eblis, fortuna absum, dissolutus" he stumbled through the words, hoping the spell would work. He felt suddenly dizzy, as though someone had pulled the floor out from under him.

"Be careful, my friends," whispered the angel, laying a hand on Ben's fist, "and Godspeed."

Ben felt electricity course through his body at Michael's touch, and then the angel was gone. No, that wasn't quite right. It was them who had disappeared, not the angel. He watched in fascination as the world around them began to unravel.

"Jesus," said Katy, her eyes wide in wonder as her fingers dug into Ben's shoulder. "Did you see that?"

The garage had all but disappeared. They watched in awe as a group of construction workers quickly dismantled it, leaving nothing but cement in its wake. The cement quickly turned to dirt, and then to grass, which turned brown and died only to bloom again, bright, green, and beautiful.

And then everything fell away, and there was only light. Red, blue, yellow, green, gold and silver—streaks of bright luminescence wrapped around the pair, moving this way and that, and Ben thought for sure he was going to vomit. The pressure behind his eyes grew so strong that it was all he could do to keep from passing out.

"Hold on tight!" he yelled, wrapping his arms around Katy. "I think this is about to get interesting."

Chapter 15

"God, my head hurts," mumbled Katy, pressing the palm of her hand hard against her eyes. She was lying on the ground and could smell something sweet in the air. Doughnuts? She rolled over on her stomach and forced her eyes open.

She was in an alley behind an old building, surrounded by tall oak trees and a huge tin storage shed on the other side of the walkway. A bright silver trashcan stood a few feet to her left, beside the back door. Ben lay passed out to her right, the duffel bag draped over his leg. She crawled toward him, mindless of the rough cement ripping into the knees of her stockings.

She shrugged out of her leather jacket. She was burning up. At first she thought she had a fever, but then noticed the bright sun directly overhead. It had to be 90 degrees. She'd grown up in Carthage and couldn't remember even a single hot October. The air, however, was exactly how she remembered it; unpolluted, clean, with just a hint of pig manure from the surrounding farms—a far cry from Chicago. They'd truly done it. They'd traveled through time and space into the past.

"Ben," she whispered, shaking his shoulder. "Wake up. I think we're here."

Ben's eyes flew open as he lurched to a sitting position. "Jesus, I've got a killer headache," he said, forcing himself to his knees. "That was... incredible!"

Katy pressed down on his shoulder, trying to use Ben to stand up, but tumbled into his lap instead. "Tell me about it," she said, her cheeks reddening as she looked up into his eyes. She rolled off of him and scrambled to her feet.

"You could have stayed for a while," he said, climbing to his feet as well.

She rolled her eyes and then punched him hard in the shoulder.

"Ouch," said Ben, the smile never leaving his face.

"You know, I need to say something," said Katy, still feeling embarrassed. "I'm so sorry I didn't believe you. I mean, when Sam vanished, I should have..." She trailed off, her face turning ashen white.

"What's wrong?"

"I remember everything. It's like...I have two sets of memories, Ben. The one where my sister was murdered and you're schizophrenic, and another where she's alive and well and you're just goofy." She said. "Wow. This is way weird."

"Tell me about it," he said, for the first time seeming to notice his surroundings. "Where in the hell are we anyway?"

"I don't know, but I smelled doughnuts when I woke up. That can't be bad, can it?"

"One can only hope," he said, throwing his duffel over his shoulder. "Say, did you notice how hot it is?"

"I did," Katy said, "and I don't ever remember hearing about a heat wave in Carthage in October."

"So let's go find out where we are," Ben said, already moving through the alley toward the front of the building.

Chapter 16

She couldn't believe it. Standing right there in front of the Immaculate Conception Roman Catholic Church was her father, an unlit cigarette in one hand and a book of matches in the other. He was a good 50 or 60 pounds heavier than she remembered him and considerably more haggard, but it was him. He was wearing his Sheriff's uniform complete with a badge and gun and had a box of doughnuts cradled under one arm. She started toward him, and then felt Ben's hand on her wrist.

"Don't," he whispered, yanking her back around the corner of the building.

"But that's my dad!" she said, pulling against his grip. "I need to see him. I need to warn him."

"Excuse me," said a voice from behind them. It was her father! "I'm out of matches and desperately in need of a cigarette. Do either of you have a light."

"Sorry," Ben said quickly, shifting the duffel bag to his opposite shoulder, "but neither of us smoke."

"Thanks anyway," said Fred Ruskin, slipping the unlit cigarette behind his ear. "You two must be here for the funeral, though you," he indicated Ben with a nod of his head, "aren't exactly dressed for it, unless you happen to have a suit and tie in that bag of yours."

"What funeral?" asked Katy, speaking for the first time since her father had approached. She was starting to get a bad feeling about this.

Ruskin gave her a sideways look. "Tanner McGee's funeral, of course. He drowned at the lake on Tuesday. I'm sure you read about it in the paper."

"He was my third-cousin, Sheriff," Ben said, "and this is my friend Katherine. We're from Chicago, and she's never met my family."

"Chicago, huh?" he said, a distant look in his eyes. "Beautiful city. I grew up in Chicago, though that seems like a lifetime ago now." He smiled, shifting his gaze to his daughter. "And Katherine—that was my mother's name. It suits you well."

"Thank you," Katy said, blushing, knowing full well that she'd been named after her grandmother.

"Nice meeting you kids. Now I really need to get going." Ruskin turned to go.

"Wait!" Katy said, instantly regretting it.

"What can I do for you?" he asked, maneuvering a hand into his box of doughnuts to pull out a chocolate éclair.

"Sheriff, those doughnuts," she said, recovering. "They smell delicious. Where'd you get them?"

Ruskin smiled, and then passed the box to Katy. She felt like crying as his rough, calloused fingers briefly touched her own. "Here, they're yours. Got 'em from 'The Donut Shop' on the square, but I need to cut down anyway." He patted his stomach and sighed. "The uniform doesn't fit as good as it used to."

"Thank you so much," Katy said. "We really appreciate it."

"Hey, it's no big deal," said her father, between mouthfuls of pastry. He turned to amble down the stone steps and away from the church, calling out over his shoulder, "Besides, they're only doughnuts."

* * *

"This is so weird," whispered Ben.

He and Katy stood at the back of the church, watching as the mourners, one by one, paid their last respects to Tanner McGee. The abbey was miserably hot and stuffy, and he mopped his brow with the sleeve of his shirt.

"Look, I think it's your parents," said Katy under her breath, gesturing to the pair talking at the far end of the church.

Ben turned to follow her eyes. There were his parents, both aged fifteen, exchanging words beside his uncle's casket. This was all so surreal. His whole family was here—both sets of grandparents, his cousins, everyone—but decades younger.

So far, no one had really paid them any attention, but Ben knew they couldn't risk getting noticed. The time travel spell hadn't worked properly—or he'd somehow bungled it—and they'd wound up in June of 1975, a full two years and four months before the first Halloween murder would take place. Ben felt dizzy just thinking about it. There wasn't much they could do here. If they entered the old house, they might alter things that were better left alone. And whatever they were looking for might not be there yet anyway.

He watched in wonder as his father flipped the Buffalo-head nickel into the coffin. This is how it all started, so many years ago. He instinctively felt in his pocket for his own nickel, marveling at the implications. His heart skipped a beat as he thought back to their arrival in the alley. Oh shit! He must have dropped the nickel when he passed out. Without the coin, they'd never get home, let alone to 1977.

"Katy," he whispered, touching her arm. "We need to get back to the alley. I think I lost the nickel."

"What?" she said, a little too loudly. Several heads turned their way but quickly lost interest as she fell silent. "How could you lose... oh my God, Ben, look," she lowered her voice, pointing past him, "It's Michael, and he just dropped the jar in Tanner's coffin. We're witnessing some serious history here."

"Making it, more likely," he whispered, watching in disbelief as the man in the trench coat walked past him and out of the church. He recognized the man, and he was certainly no angel. "That's not Michael. That's…me."

Chapter 17

Ben couldn't believe his eyes. He'd just come face-to-face with his double. Aside from the beginnings of a moustache and beard, the two looked identical. Running out of the church, he leapt the stone steps that led down to the sidewalk but his quarry had vanished.

"Hold up," yelped Katy, trying to navigate the stairs in heels. "I'm really beginning to hate these shoes."

"Did you see him?" Ben asked, his eyes darting all around the church for a sign of the man in the trench coat.

The building stood on the corner of Fayette Street and Interstate Highway 136, the main thoroughfare that ran through Carthage. He could have gone anywhere.

"There he is!" Katy pointed south, down Fayette. Ben turned just in time to see the man slip around the corner, heading across the highway.

He shot off down the road, leaving Katy cursing in his wake. Was it really him, another version of Ben Spencer, traveling from some future point in time to fix something they had screwed up? Whatever the reason, the other Ben's presence had to mean that he had found the nickel. Didn't it?

"Wait up," called Katy. He turned to see her sprinting down the sidewalk, shoes in hand, trying to avoid the cracks in the pavement.

He crossed the street just in time to see the other Ben dart into a copse of trees behind the third in a long row of houses. He nearly jumped out of his skin when Katy's hand touched his shoulder.

"Come on," he said, "I just saw him."

"And there he is again," said Katy, pointing at Ben's doppelgänger.

He was on the move, circling the houses, heading down Fayette. Ben felt a chill crawl up his spine. His double was heading for the cemetery to watch his uncle's interment. At least he thought he was. The truth, as it turned out, was a lot less morbid than it was confusing.

When they finally caught up to the other Ben, he was climbing a huge oak tree in the back yard of the third to the last house in the row, right before the turnoff on Kiwanis Road to the graveyard. Ben hoped whoever owned the house wasn't home.

He stood stock still, watching as the man in the trench coat scaled a row of wooden planks nailed into the side of the tree. He squinted against the sun, following his double's progress to a sprawling tree house at the top of the old oak. The other Ben turned and winked before going inside.

"What the hell?" Katy asked, craning her neck to stare up at the wooden dwelling. "If he expects us to go up there, he's out of his freaking mind."

"I was such a weenie back then," called down another voice that Ben would recognize anywhere. It was Katy.

He could just make out her face through the little window cut into the side of the tree house. And then future-Ben was there, too, and they were kissing. And not just an I'm-glad-you're-not-dead kiss, but a full on, one-hundred percent I-want-to-feel-your-tonsils-with-my-tongue-and-have-your-children kind of kiss. Ben felt himself go weak in the knees.

Katy saw it too. "Oh, come on," she said, "that will *not* happen. Never, not in a million years. There's just no way that's going to happen."

"Wanna bet?" asked a smirking Ben, unable to tear his eyes away from their doppelgängers.

"Hey, dumb ass," his other self called down to him as he reached through the window, "You didn't just lose the nickel, you know."

Ben watched as something small but heavy dropped from the other man's hand to plummet to the ground. Ben knelt over to pick it up. It was a twenty-dollar bill, dated 1972, wrapped around a small gray rock.

"Get Katy some real clothes," Future Ben said, as he withdrew his hand from the window and retreated into the darkened recesses of the tree house.

"And maybe a nice pair of boots as well," came Future Katy's voice from the tree house, chased by laughter.

A flash of light followed and the tree house, Ben knew, was empty. They'd used the spell and gone back to wherever they had come from.

"Oh shit," groaned Ben, cradling his head in his hands. "Shit, shit, shit!"

"What's wrong?" Katy asked, still staring up into the tree house.

"The spell," he said, turning to face Katy. "It's gone, too."

Chapter 18

Ben scanned the horizon: trash, trash, and more trash, as far as eye could see, and tomorrow they'd bury this week's crop of trash and start the cycle all over again. It made him a little queasy to think how much trash the tiny city of Carthage produced in just a week's time. The ironic thing was that in 25 years the landfill would be gone, replaced by an upper-class housing development. He wondered if any of the doctors and lawyers living there would realize they were spending their time walking around on mountains of garbage.

"Okay, so let me get this straight," Katy had said, hands on her hips, as they stood in the little alley behind the church, "you're the one who lost the damned thing, but you expect me to help you look for it *at the dump*? In this dress, no less. Are you insane?"

It had taken them less than five minutes of searching to track down the nickel, but the spell was nowhere to be found. Katy finally noticed that the trashcan, which had been full before, was now empty. And then she remembered that Friday had always been trash day in Carthage. Someone had probably found the paper and, assuming it was trash, tossed it into the can along with everything else, where it had been taken to the dump.

"Pretty much, yeah, unless you can think of a better way to get it back." He said. "But, umm, I'll buy you something pretty to make up for it?" He held the twenty out in front of his face, grinning like a fool. She was still frowning. "Didn't work, huh?"

"Well, maybe a little." She snatched the twenty from his hand and slipped it into her purse. "So let's go shopping. There's no way I'm going dumpster diving in these clothes."

"But the quicker we get there, the better chance we have of finding it."

"Good point, dude. So why don't I go shopping, and you can high tail it to the dump and use your good luck to track down the spell?"

And that was how Ben had found himself alone and out of breath, searching through three tons of stinking, disease-infested trash at the town landfill. They'd made plans to meet back at the church in two hours, and he hoped with all that was in him that he'd have the spell by then. Between the dump and the fact that he'd worn the same clothes for the last two days, he was desperately in need of a shower.

He couldn't understand it. He'd gone through sixteen bags of trash, and still nothing. With his luck, he should have found it inside the first bag he opened. So far, he'd found 21 quarters, 37 pennies, 18 dimes, 9 nickels, 11 one-dollar bills, 2 tens, a five-dollar silver certificate note from 1934, and a perfectly good Timex watch (and, if the watch was to be believed, he finally knew what time it was—12:25—and set his own watch accordingly). The spell, however, was nowhere to be found.

Covered in rancid spaghetti sauce, dirt, and God only knew what else, he decided to call it a day and head back to the alley. He wasn't sure how they were going to get to 1977, but one thing was clear— wherever the spell was, he was pretty sure it wasn't in this landfill. If it was, he would have found it by now. Stuffing his findings into the blue duffel bag, he swung the heavy load over his shoulder and began the long walk back to town.

* * *

Katy walked down the sidewalk, marveling at how little Carthage had really changed over the years. She'd grown up here and remembered walking around the town square years from now. Of the businesses dotting the square, only a few still remained in her time—Men's

Firestone, the public library, the Hotel Carthage, Royalty's—but the ones that had replaced it weren't all that different. It was a heady experience walking these streets, though she wished she could do it in more sensible shoes.

Katy passed Sherrick's Drugstore, Ben Franklin Five and Dime, the Sheriff's Department, and the Laundromat, before finally coming to Jo's Swap Shop, a used clothing and trinket store long gone even before she had left Carthage. She pushed at the glass door and enjoyed the tinkle of the little bell connected to the handle as it swung open.

She'd often heard her mother talk about the thrift shop and the little treasures she'd found there. The store had closed by the mid-eighties, and so she relished the chance to experience something her mother had enjoyed years before she was even born.

She took in the store: macramé hangers, wicker baskets, comic books, paintings, clothing, toys, pots and pans—the store was just as eclectic as her mother had remembered. It offered a little bit of everything, and the price seemed to be right. She'd yet to see anything marked above five dollars.

Other than the cashier, a brown-haired, hawk-nosed woman in her early thirties that she assumed must be Jo, the store was practically empty. She took her time and explored everything, glancing through old paperbacks and various knick-knacks. Moving to the clothing area, she first looked through a pile of winter coats. She'd do fine with the jacket she already had, but Ben would need something warm.

There were maybe a dozen different choices, and all had been marked down because they were out of season. But not for the lucky guy who'd soon be traveling to an October two years from now. She looked through at least half a dozen coats before finally settling on a practically-new pea-green ski jacket from Sears that was discounted to a dollar and a half. Not the most attractive coat imaginable, but it would do. She imagined he'd be pretty grubby after his visit to the dump, and so she picked out an old "Blue Boys" Carthage high school football sweatshirt and a pair of bell-bottomed Dungarees to replace the clothing he'd been wearing for the past two days.

Next she picked through a big spinning rack of blouses. By the time she was finished, she'd found a nice white peasant blouse, a faded pair of blue jeans, a thin leather belt, and a scuffed-but-sturdy pair of black leather boots hidden away behind a row of tennis shoes in the back room—total price, before tax, including Ben's clothes: seven dollars and fifty cents. Ben's expression when he found out how little she'd spent for a complete wardrobe for both of them: priceless.

And that brought her thoughts around to him again, and the kiss they'd seen their future selves share. Damn it all, anyway. She couldn't get involved with Ben. He was just a kid.

But she always had an excuse, didn't she? She'd had her share of dates in high school and more in college, but she'd never been in a relationship that lasted more than a few weeks. And it wasn't always the guy's fault. She'd definitely dated a few losers, but most had been nice, decent people who hadn't deserved the grief she'd put them through.

She'd always used her nightmares as justification for not getting close to a guy. If she couldn't keep her own shit together, she reasoned, what chance did she have of making a relationship work? But she knew there was more to it than that. She was always running in her dreams, always hiding. She guessed some of that had rubbed off on her waking hours as well. So maybe it was finally time to stop hiding and take a stand, in her dreams as well as in the real world.

Katy's reverie was interrupted by the sound of the front doorbell followed by a tug on her shoulder. Startled, she spun around to see Ben standing in front of her covered in garbage. She managed to suppress a giggle but felt the corners of her mouth edge up into a smile.

"Wow, Sherlock. You look great with a touch of tomato sauce and a few dabs of dirt! How could a girl ever resist?" she asked.

"Yeah, yeah," he said, rolling his eyes. "So, did you find anything?"

"I did indeed," she said, "But the real question is," she glanced at Jo behind the counter, and lowered her voice, "did you?"

"It wasn't there. I found a lot of treasures among the trash, but that wasn't one of them. It must still be at the alley."

Katy felt her heart sink. They'd scoured the alley from top to bottom. If it wasn't at the dump, where else could it be? "Are you sure?"

"Pretty sure, yeah. I looked everywhere, Katy."

"I guess your famous luck isn't so infallible, after all."

"Excuse me," said the woman from behind the counter, wrinkling her nose at Ben. "But what are you looking for?"

Katy guessed it wouldn't do any harm to explain. "Well, my friend dropped something in the alley behind the Catholic church. When we realized it was missing, we went to look for it and noticed the trash can had been emptied. And that's when I realized today was trash day. He went to the dump to look for it, but apparently he didn't look quite hard enough."

Jo gave her a quizzical look. "Honey, you must not be from around here. Trash day was last Wednesday, just like it's been for as long as I can remember. They probably just emptied the trash into the dumpster behind the shed. I helped out in a city-wide trash clean up last year and that's where we dumped a lot of the trash before the trucks came to haul it away—in the dumpster behind the big tin shed in back of the church."

But that couldn't be right, could it? Trash day had always been Friday. And then she realized that it must have changed. It had been Wednesday at some point, obviously, and had been changed to Friday sometime after she was born. Her face turned a deep shade of red. She'd been wrong, after all.

* * *

The spell finally in hand, Ben clambered out of the dumpster and dropped to the worn and cracked pavement below. He was in desperate need of a shower, not to mention a fresh change of clothes. The jeans and sweatshirt he had on needed a good washing or, preferably, to be burned. He thought he was even filthier now than he had been at the landfill, which he'd previously thought impossible.

"You know, we could stay the night..." Katy bit her bottom lip, letting the words trail off. "I mean, we've got all the time in the world, right? I have close to twelve pre-1975 bucks in my purse, which should be more than enough for a hotel in Carthage in this time period. And if we jump now or in the morning, assuming the spell actually works this time, we'll still get to 1977 exactly when we're supposed to. We're both exhausted, you definitely need a bath, and I'd love to get out of these clothes. If we're going to stop the Halloween murders, we need to be well-rested and ready. Don't you think?"

He studied the brown haired 24-year-old in her slinky black dress and diamond stud earrings, feeling a familiar stirring in his stomach. Spend the night together? That wasn't how she meant it, of course. But she was right; they'd have a much better chance of stopping the murderer if they could take time out to relax and catch their breath, study the information he'd downloaded from the Web, and plan their strategy to ferret out the killer.

"We'll be staying in separate rooms, of course," she added, as if reading his mind. "So whaddya say, dude?"

He sighed. Separate rooms it was, then. "Sure—like you said, what could happen?"

Chapter 19

"The rooms are $24 a night," said the gray-haired woman with parchment skin who sat behind the reception desk. Her nametag cheerfully announced that her name was Clara. "And checkout is by noon."

Ben's eyes grew wide. Apparently, rooms in 1975 weren't as cheap as they'd thought. Between them, not counting the silver certificate, they had a little more than fifty dollars. They could cover the rooms, but wouldn't have enough to eat. He looked at Katy, who met his glance with a shrug. They were both exhausted, and he didn't really want to go anywhere else.

They were in the lobby of the Hotel Carthage, the little hotel on the east side of the town square. The building was decorated in a style that would have been tacky for their time but felt strangely appropriate now. Crushed red velvet curtains surrounded all the windows, and a plush gray carpet cushioned visitor's steps. The restaurant opened off to the left of the lobby, while the rooms—all eight of them—occupied the entirety of the upstairs. The hotel section had vanished by Ben's time, but the restaurant still thrived.

"If you can't afford the rooms," the woman said, gazing pointedly at Ben's stained and dirty clothing, "I'm sure the Starlight Motel on 136 has vacancies. I'll be happy to give you directions."

"Excuse us for a minute," Katy said, pulling Ben aside. The woman glanced up at the clock, as if she had someplace better to be. Katy rolled her eyes. "We have, what, fifty dollars?"

"Pretty much, yeah," he said in a low voice. "We can do it, but no dinner."

Katy sighed. "Okay—if we share a room, can I trust you?"

"You know, I think you can," he snapped, handing her the silver certificate. "Here. I found this at the dump along with everything else. It's probably worth more than five dollars, but I'm sure it'll still work as cash."

Katy took the money from his hand, whispered, "I guess you're right," and then she turned back to the receptionist, clearing her throat to get the woman's attention. "Well, Clara," she said, "it looks like we'll only need one room after all. But, you know, it's your fault that we'll be spending the night in sin."

The old woman surprised Ben by smiling back. "Honey," she said, her watery blue eyes twinkling with laughter, "I've worked here for over twenty years. Carthage may seem a little pedestrian to folks from Chicago, and in some ways it probably is, but the things I've seen go on at this place…"

Ben couldn't help but grin at Clara's revelation. They were just two in a long line of many to grace her desk, and she'd probably seen it all countless times before. He passed the money for the room over the desk to the woman's outstretched palm and accepted room key number eight in exchange.

He didn't wait even five minutes after opening the door before going into the bathroom, stripping off his clothes, and stepping into a hot shower. He felt disgusting, but the steaming water slowly worked to eliminate the stink from the dump and the general wear and tear he'd put his body through for the last two days.

He thought about Katy as he worked shampoo from the tiny hotel bottle into his long blond hair. He was alone in a hotel room with the woman of his dreams. Never in a million years had he thought that would happen, and certainly not before he was even born.

This whole time travel stuff was mind-boggling, though not nearly as mind-boggling as Katy herself.

He heard a knock at the door, followed by Katy's voice. "How long are you going to be?" she asked, "I desperately have to pee."

"The door's unlocked," he said, grinning to himself as the water washed over his body. He was almost finished, but he couldn't help himself.

"Hey, you promised you'd be good."

Did he? Yeah, he guessed he kind of did. "Sorry," he yelled through the steam, as he worked to wash the soap from his body. "I'm almost done. Just give me a few more minutes, okay?"

"Hurry," sounded Katy's muted reply through the door.

Ben turned the water off, quickly toweling his hair dry before wrapping a second towel around his waist. He clambered out of the shower, brushed his teeth with the freebie toothpaste and one of the little travel toothbrushes the hotel had provided, snatched up his new clothes, and swung open the bathroom door.

"Hey!" yelped Katy, standing up from the bed. "You could have gotten dressed, you know. It wasn't that big of an emergency."

"Just trying to be good," he said, moving out of her way as she padded toward the bathroom. "Don't worry, I'll be dressed by the time you're done."

"Better be," Katy said, as she closed the door behind her.

Ben chuckled to himself as he pulled his new sweater over his head. A perfect fit. The Dungarees were a little loose, but they weren't going to fall off. The bell-bottoms made him feel like a member of the Brady Bunch. When in Rome do as the Romans do, he guessed. Things could always be worse.

He studied the room. It looked almost like an extension of the lobby, red velvet curtains and all. Two brown leather easy chairs sat on either side of a small round table, opposite a dresser and an ironing board complete with iron. A 15-inch RCA television stood atop an oaken stand beneath the window that looked out over the town square, and a king-sized bed filled the middle of the room. Everything looked clean and smelled fresh.

He thought about the bed. There hadn't been a room with two standard beds available, so they'd been forced to settle for the king. Ben, of course, offered to sleep in the easy chair.

"You look…very 1970's," said Katy. He turned around to see that she had changed into the clothes they had purchased at the thrift store.

"I miss the dress," said Ben, flashing his best smile.

"Yeah, I bet," she said, rolling her eyes at him, but he could swear the corners of her mouth fought a grin. "So why don't you get some sleep? For now, you can take the bed."

"I am pretty zoned," he said, looking at his watch. "It's four-thirty, but it feels more like the middle of the night to me. I guess this is what jet lag feels like."

"No doubt, maybe even worse."

"So what are you going to do?"

"What a girl does best, of course," she said. "Go shopping. I figured I'd try to sell the watch and the silver certificate at the swap shop and use whatever I can get to buy some snacks at the grocery store. I'm starving."

"Just be careful," he said, lying back in the bed. He could already feel himself drifting off. "See if you can pick me up some socks and shoes, will you? Mine are in pretty bad shape. You can take the rest of our cash."

"Already done, dude," she said, heading for the door.

Katy glanced at her watch; it was nearly half-past five, and she wasn't sure what time Super Value closed. She quickened her pace, passing Ben Franklin's Five and Dime as she rounded the corner to leave the town square. She'd spent almost thirty minutes haggling with Jo over the price of the watch and the old five-dollar bill, but finally came away with ten dollars in addition to a pair of Adidas sneakers and two pairs of socks for Ben. She could buy a lot of 1975-era snacks with ten bucks, and was seriously looking forward to diving into some sweet chocolate goodness and a big bag of Sterzing's potato chips.

She definitely had the munchies. She'd felt like this once in high school, when she'd let her best friend Lisa talk her into smoking pot after a dance. Did that mean that time travel had some of the same effects as marijuana? She giggled to herself, remembering how woozy she'd felt after her singular experience with the drug.

And there was Super Value. The grocery store had disappeared when she was a little girl, leaving Bill's as the sole provider of groceries to the town of Carthage. Ironically, it was Ben Franklin's Five and Dime, which she'd just passed, that had replaced the grocery store, moving from the small store front on the square to take advantage of the bigger floor space the empty building had provided.

She walked up to the double glass doors and stepped on the black floor mat in front of them, watching as they slid open to let her pass. She walked past an alcove that hosted a peg board where patrons could advertise garage sales and lost pets, knowing that in just a few short years the space would be filled with video games such as Space Invaders, Asteroids, and Pac-Man.

An old-time comic rack incongruously stood just inside the entrance, and she could see brand-new issues of Batman, Spider-Man, Casper, Shazam, Superman, The Hulk, Archie, Richie Rich, and others that she'd only vaguely heard of littering the slots. Some of these comics had to be worth a small fortune in her time, but she resisted the urge to buy even one.

What if, for instance, she purchased the last copy of a rare issue of Spider-Man? And what if some kid wasn't able to buy the comic he wanted and therefore couldn't sell it for a $1,000 twenty or thirty years later and use the proceeds to start a drug research company that would go on to save countless lives? Sure, it was a long shot, and quite a bit of "what ifs," but her even being here had probably already started to change things, and she didn't want to risk changing the time they had come from any more than necessary. That thought didn't, however, deter her from flipping through several issues anyway. She could read them, she decided, as long as she left them there when she was done.

She commandeered a shopping cart and then moved on to her true destination—the candy aisle. All around her, sweets were calling her name. Hershey, Mars, M&M's, Snickers, Space Sticks... space sticks? She'd read about those and always wanted to try them, but they'd been pulled from the marketplace by the time she was a kid. She greedily snatched up two boxes—one chocolate, and one peanut butter—and dropped them into her cart, along with two Hershey's Special Dark bars, a couple of Marathon bars, and two packages of Winston candy cigarettes.

She found it hard to believe that tobacco companies had been able to get away with marketing candy cigarettes to kids in an effort to "train" them to smoke the real things later, but apparently they had. Ben would get a kick out of this.

Content with her candy purchases, Katy rolled the cart further down the aisle and picked out a huge bag of Sterzing's potato chips. As far as she knew, Sterzing's were only made and sold in Missouri, Iowa, and parts of Illinois. She'd never been able to find them in Chicago and missed them desperately. The 1975 version was probably even greasier and therefore more delicious than the chips that came from her time. She was looking forward to this, waistline be damned.

"But, mom, all the other kids have them," came a little girl's voice from the very next aisle. Katy froze. Something about that voice...

"I'm sorry, Samantha, we just can't afford it." It was her mother, which meant that 'Samantha' was her sister Sam.

Oh my God! She was halfway down the other end of the aisle before she remembered—they wouldn't know her from Eve. Her parents weren't even together yet, and the world hadn't come to a screeching halt when she'd encountered her father, so why would she have any effect on her mother and half-sister?

"I never get to have anything!" Samantha whined, stomping around the corner of the aisle and into Katy's view.

Katy pretended to look away, but she knew the girl had realized she'd been seen, because her face turned red. She knew Sam had just celebrated her twelfth birthday. She studied the girl's face, recognizing the kind brown eyes and ponytails she'd seen in pictures. She'd never been very close to Sam, but right now it was all she could do not to run up to her sister and throw her arms around her.

"Hey, kid," she whispered instead, keeping her feelings in check. She pushed her cart back toward the potato chips. "Don't worry about it. What were you after anyway?"

Samantha glanced over her shoulder to make sure her mother hadn't yet rounded the corner. "Freakies cereal," she whispered back, her eyes darting back and forth between Katy and the other side of the store. "All the kids at school are eating them, but Mom says they're too expensive. All I ever get is the crappy generic stuff."

Katy suppressed a grin, remembering her sister's infamous ability to cut to the core of a problem. "Don't worry so much about what all the other kids are doing. They'll wind up with rotten teeth, and you won't."

Samantha giggled. "That's what my mom always says."

"So listen to her already. She has a lot on her plate as it is. Cut her a little slack. You'll make out better in the long run."

Samantha shot her a suspicious glance. "Do you know my Mom?"

Uh-oh. "Sure don't," she said, shrugging her shoulders. "But isn't every Mom overworked and underpaid?"

"Yeah, I guess so."

"Samantha?" Her mother's voice was closer now. "Where are you? I'm ready to go."

"Well, bye," said the girl, flashing a shy smile at Katy. She started to walk away.

"Wait," Katy whispered, slipping two dollars into the girl's palm. "We girls gotta stick together. Just tell your Mom you found it on the floor or something."

"Gee, thanks!" Eyes wide, Samantha stared at the money in her hand. "Are you sure, though? I mean, I can't pay you back. I don't even know your name."

"I'm Katy," she said, choking up, "and you don't have to pay me back. Just do me two favors, okay?"

"Sure, if I can."

"First, be nice to your sister."

Samantha scrunched up her face. "But I don't have a sister."

"You will," Katy promised her, trying not to think about what this might be doing to the future. "Just hug her a lot and make sure she knows you love her, okay? Even if you're older than her, the two of you can still be close."

"Well, okay. If I ever have a sister, I'll be nice to her. What's favor number two?"

Katy reached into her purse, making a decision. She pulled out a piece of stationary and a ballpoint pen and quickly scribbled something. She folded the paper in half and stuffed it into the envelope for her cell phone bill. She sealed the envelope and then wrote "Fred" across the top.

She knelt in front of the girl and held out the envelope. "Someday soon, your Mom's going to meet someone, fall in love, and get married. Don't tell anyone I told you this, and for God's sake don't tell anybody about the envelope. Just give it to the man your mother marries on the day your little sister is born."

"Huh? I don't think Mom's even had a date in forever. She's not gonna get married again."

"Just trust me, okay?" Katy said, smiling. "Just do this one little thing for me and I promise your life will be all the better for it. A lot better. Can you give me your word that you'll do it?"

"Samantha?" repeated her mother's voice, rounding the corner.

"Okay," Samantha agreed quickly, taking the envelope and folding it into the back pocket of her jeans. "Total weirdness, but I promise."

Katy grinned. So that's where she'd gotten that phrase. "No, it's not mine, but thanks for asking," she said, as their mother moved closer. "Maybe it's a gift from a guardian angel?" She said, earning herself a shy smile from Samantha.

"What's going on?" asked Candy Martin, a frazzled blonde in her early thirties. "Ma'am, is my daughter bothering you?" She pushed her cart to rest beside Katy's. Where Katy's cart contained frivolous snacks, her mother's contained mostly day-to-day staples like hamburger meat, bread, and cans of vegetables. Katy felt strangely guilty.

"She's not bothering me at all. In fact, your daughter found two dollars in the aisle and asked if it belonged to me," she replied, glancing at the girl, "but it doesn't."

"Mom," Samantha said, putting her hand on her mother's shoulder, "can I get the Freakies now? Please?"

"Well, we'll ask if anyone reported losing the money when we check out. If they haven't then, sure, you can have the cereal." She smiled at Katy over her daughter's head, shrugging as if to say, *Kids. What can you do?*

"I have a bit of a sweet tooth myself," Katy said, gesturing down into her basket.

"My name's Candy, so I know what you mean," the woman said, laughing. "Candy Martin. Are you new here?"

"Just passing through from Chicago. I came with a friend for Tanner McGee's funeral," Katy said, deciding it was better to stick with the story they'd told her father. "My name's Katy Rush," she almost said 'Ruskin' but caught herself, "nice to meet you and your daughter. She's a very sweet girl."

"When she wants to be," Candy said, reaching out to tousle Samantha's hair. The girl rolled her eyes. "Well, we'd better get going. I have to be to work in just a few hours."

She remembered her mother had worked as a waitress at The Peacock, a low-rent bar on the outskirts of town. *Just hang on, Mom,* she wanted to say, *in just a few years, you'll own your own restaurant and be happily married.* Instead she said, simply, "have a nice night," and rolled her cart past her family and to the next aisle.

"Mom, are you pregnant?" she heard Samantha ask just as soon as she thought she was out of earshot. Katy chuckled, and then headed down the soda aisle to pick up a six-pack of Frosty root beer.

Chapter 20

Katy quietly let herself into the hotel room, shoving her foot in the door while she retrieved the big paper bag of groceries from the hall. Ben was still sound asleep. In fact, he was snoring. That was not a good sign of the night to come. She desperately wanted to wake him, not only to stop the noise but to share her stash of goodies. He'd only been sleeping a little over an hour, however, so she decided to let him keep sawing logs until seven. Room service closed at eight, so that'd give them plenty of time for dinner.

She sat down in one of the easy chairs and rummaged through her bag of groceries. She'd given into temptation and added a box of Freakies and a half-gallon of milk to her purchases. Given enough time and an empty stomach, she was sure she could send herself into a diabetic shock. She reached into the bag and snagged a Hershey's Special Dark bar and quickly shed the chocolate of its wrapper. She finished it in three bites, savoring the bitter taste of the candy on her tongue. It was wonderful. She washed it down with a Frosty. Despite the sugar rush, she felt her head begin to get heavy. Before she knew it, her eyelids were drooping shut of their own accord.

Shaking herself awake, she stood up and padded over to the bed. "Move over, doofus," she whispered, pushing Ben from the middle of the mattress.

He sleepily obliged, rolling onto his side. Katy lay down beside him and was out the moment her head hit the pillow.

* * *

Oh lord, not this again. Katy stood in the middle of an enormous dining room, her heart pounding against her ribs and her breath caught in her throat. She was surrounded by dust and cobwebs as far as the eye could see. It was pitch-black, but, like every other time she'd visited the house, a glowing ball of light hovered above her, just out of reach, providing illumination wherever she went.

A great cherry-wood table surrounded by twelve chairs stood in the center of the room, and a delicate crystal chandelier hung from the ceiling. It, too, was completely encased in the trappings of time—dead bugs littered the spider webs that filled the space between the burned-out lights. She wrinkled her nose as the sour smell of mildew hit her in the face.

The hard wood floor beneath her bare feet squeaked whenever she took a step. As always, she was wearing her pajamas, the pink fluffy ones she'd had as a kid. Her teeth chattered. It was freezing in the old house, and the light that hovered above her offered no discernible warmth.

She knew she was dreaming and, like all of the other times, was powerless to do anything about it. She couldn't wake up and she couldn't control the nightmare. It was all she could do to simply hang on and wait for it to be over.

Because she'd had the dream hundreds of times before, she knew the drill by heart. Soon she'd hear a noise from some remote corner of the house, perhaps the howl of the creature that always pursued her or maybe the thump of furniture being moved. And then she'd begin to run, skittering around doors and running through hallways, always staying mere steps ahead of whatever pursued her. She'd had the dreams since she was twelve, yet never actually seen her pursuer. Thank God, she always woke up just before he cornered her.

A loud thump followed by a low scrape sounded somewhere to the south, in the direction of the living room. It was starting. Katy sprinted through the hallway toward the staircase at the back of the house. She took the stairs two at a time, at the same time trying to stave off the adrenaline that flooded her body. She fought to keep moving, to pump her legs faster, and it was all she could do not to scream.

She was on the second floor, between the studio and one of the bedrooms, and could hear doors opening and closing beneath her. She ran down the hallway, past the library, and into the master bedroom. The room hadn't changed since her last visit. Hands on her knees, she struggled to suck oxygen into her aching lungs. She stood beside a sturdy oak nightstand just to the right of a huge, rotting bed. She remembered hiding under the bed once, when she was thirteen or fourteen, and seeing the shadows of her pursuer's feet as he circled the room. She'd woken up just as a hand snaked out to wrap itself around one of her ankles.

That was the first and last time she'd tried to hide. After that, she'd just kept moving, running, rounding the corner just as whatever chased her bounded into the room. Sometimes, though, she could swear she felt her pursuer's hot breath on her neck, tickling the hairs on her skin.

The slam of a door vibrated ominously through the house, followed by the heavy scrape of flesh against wood. It was getting closer. Katy ran to the far end of the room and through the open door into the master bathroom. From here, there was only one way out—the balcony. She'd never managed to escape the house and didn't want her first time to be a nosedive through the air to land on the hard winter ground two stories below.

She quietly closed the door that separated the bedroom from the bathroom, willing it not to creak. It creaked anyway. Holding her breath, she took in the room. An old, crusty tube of toothpaste and a rotting red toothbrush sat upon the marble counter, while a threadbare towel lay draped over the side of the claw-footed bathtub. She'd moved the toothbrush once, flung it off the balcony, just to see if she could. It had been there again when next she visited the nightmare, as if it had never been moved in the first place. After that, she pretty much avoided touching any of the objects in the house.

Another thump echoed through the mansion, this time just outside the bathroom door. She stared in horror as the knob slowly began to turn. She tried to move but stood frozen in her steps. She should be waking up about now—at least she always had before. Slowly, agonizingly, the door began to creak, opening wider inch by torturous inch, mirroring her staggered breaths and the staccato beat of her heart.

And then she could move again. She threw herself through the door leading to the balcony, hitting the railing with her hip and nearly tumbling over. She shifted her weight, falling to the floor just as the door swung wide open.

Oh God, it was different this time. He was going to catch her. She scrambled to her feet and pulled the balcony door shut just as a hand snaked around the corner. Katy screamed, hanging onto the handle with all her strength, but it wasn't enough. Her pursuer slammed into the door from the other side, forcing the hinges to move in a way they weren't meant to go. The door came apart with a splintering crack, knocking her backwards as she struggled to keep her balance. The small of her back hit the railing, flipping her over, sending her spiraling though the air.

She caught the railing with one trembling hand, just barely hanging on. But her fingers were so cold, she could barely feel them. And then he was upon her, leaning over the railing, his hot, fetid breath turning to steam before her eyes, clouding her vision. She saw a hint of wiry black fur, and a snout where a nose should have been. A white hot pain shot through her arm as something sharp and dangerous raked deep across the back of her hand. She was falling again, her fingers having lost their grip on the cement balcony, and all she could see was a haze of blood as the ground rushed up to meet her.

Chapter 21

Ben awoke to the sweet smell of roses. He stretched, rolled over, and snuggled closer to the woman sharing his bed. Katy? He sat up in bed, perfectly awake. Katy snuggled closer to the pillow, moaning something unintelligible in her sleep. When had she decided to share the bed with him?

He swung his legs off of the bed and stood up. It was nearly nine o'clock. Shit, they'd missed room service. Katy must have gotten tired, curled up on the bed beside him, and dozed off. If it was a choice between her and food, he'd take Katy every time. Smiling to himself, still enjoying the smell of her perfume on his clothing, he walked over to the television and turned it on.

The TV buzzed loudly as it came to life. No cable, of course, but at least it was in color. Channel 10 swam into view just in time to show the end credits for *The Rockford Files*. He'd caught the show a few times on TV Land, but it was interesting to see first run episodes—or second run, he supposed, since this was summer and therefore the show was probably in reruns.

He watched in fascination as a commercial for Close-up Toothpaste played out across the screen. It was amazing how far advertising had come in only a few decades. The commercial, while having a certain kitschy charm, looked amateurish and was almost painful to watch. A young girl couldn't get her boyfriend to skate with her, but all it took to turn his head was the use of toothpaste. He didn't think that would work with Katy, though he was willing to give it a shot.

He settled into the leather chair across from the TV and began to root through the bag of groceries Katy had brought back to the hotel. Candy bars, Space Sticks, root beer, cereal… maybe not as filling as the steak and shrimp dinner he'd planned to order from room service, but it would do.

She'd also purchased a carton of milk, which now rested atop a small plastic bucket filled with ice that she'd probably gotten from the lobby. Good thing, too. What was cereal without milk?

He popped open the box of peanut butter Space Sticks, peeled back the wrapper of one of the individually-wrapped "nutrition bars," and bit into it. It was chewy like peanut butter, but didn't seem to stick to the roof of his mouth. Not bad. Not bad at all, but better when washed down with a glass of milk.

He stood up to get one of the little plastic hotel cups from the sink when he heard Katy scream. He dropped the half-eaten Space Stick and ran to the bed, watching in horror as an angry, jagged gash appeared out of nowhere across the back of her right hand. Her face was ashen white, her mouth fixed in a look of desperation and terror.

"Katy, wake up!" He yelled as he knelt beside the bed, shaking her shoulders. "Katy!"

"Help me!" she screamed. Her eyes snapped open, darting frantically around the room, as if looking for some unseen tormentor. "Oh God, oh God, oh God," she cried, tears streaming down her cheeks. She sat up in bed and flung her arms around him, sobbing hysterically into his shoulder. "I thought I was going to die." Her sobs slowly turned into soft hiccups.

"It's okay," he said, stroking her hair. What in the hell had just happened? She'd obviously had a bad dream, but nightmares don't normally manifest themselves in the real world—Freddy Krueger films notwithstanding. "It's okay now, you're safe," he whispered, holding her close.

"Ben?" she asked, pulling away from him, "what happened?"

"You called out in your sleep. I thought you were just having a bad dream, but..." he trailed off, taking her hand in his. She didn't pull away. "But this," he said, indicating her cut. "Dreams don't normally make you bleed, do they?"

She looked as though she might pass out. "This has never happened before. I've been having the nightmares since I was little, but never one like this."

"Nightmares?" he asked, letting go of her hand. "Why didn't you ever tell me?"

"I've never told anyone, Ben," She looked embarrassed. "Well, my Mom knew I had them as a kid, and my father knew, but beyond that... Not anyone. Not Mel, not even Sam."

"Let me go get something for that," he said, nodding toward her hand. "And then we're gonna talk, okay?"

"Okay," she whispered, brushing her fingers against his cheek. "Be careful what you wish for, Ben. You're about to find out more about me than anyone ever has before. I just hope you don't think I'm crazy."

"You say that like it's a bad thing," he said. "I'm the supposed schizophrenic, remember? And misery certainly does love company, especially yours."

* * *

Katy felt like she was going to cry again. Ben had left to find a first aid kit, and she was terrified to be in the strange hotel room all alone. She carefully washed out her wound with soap and water, but it still looked awful and felt worse. She could barely comprehend the fact that she had almost been killed tonight. She always assumed the dreams were a product of some disturbed part of her mind, her imagination running rampant, but all of that had changed. Thank God Ben had been there to wake her.

But then, when hadn't he been there? It was her who kept pushing him away. Even as a kid, before his adoration of her had turned into a full-blown crush, she'd kept him at arm's length. Hell, she kept every-one at arm's length, even her own sister.

The door opened and Ben entered the room. "No first aid kit," he said, rolling his eyes. "But Clara was able to scrape together some gauze and a roll of medical tape. Now let me see that hand."

She let him tend to her, watching as he carefully wrapped her hand in gauze and taped it all together. It felt good to give up control for once, to be in someone else's care. She'd always resisted that, never wanted to be weak, but perhaps real strength lay in the liberation of opening up to another and taking the chance, however slight, that they wouldn't let you down. She'd have to think about that.

"Okay," she said, forcing a smile. She wanted to tell him about her dreams, but the words wouldn't come easy. "Let's sit down, and I'll tell you everything."

And she did. She told him about the house that haunted her dreams, about her frantic sprints through its halls, and the monster that was always half a step behind her. She even told him about her dream sanctuary, the only place she'd ever truly felt safe. She'd never told an-yone about the little cabin she'd built in her mind, not even her father.

"Wow," he said, simply, after she was finished. Silence filled the room.

"That's it? I spill my guts and all you can say is 'wow'? So, what, do you think I'm nuts after all?"

"Not even," he said. "I think you're incredibly brave, especially for volunteering to come with me to 1977 knowing full well that we'll probably have to go inside the real house. It's just that that's the most you've shared with me in, well, practically forever. I never knew about the dreams. I wish you'd trusted me enough to tell me, that's all."

Her face turned red. "Ben, I'm telling you now." She reached out to take his face in her hands, looking deep into his eyes. "Doesn't that count for something?"

He looked at her for a moment, hesitated, and then pulled away.

"What's the matter?"

"I promised to be good, remember?" he said, flashing a lopsided smile. "You're just so beautiful."

"So you keep saying," she said. "But why, Ben? Why me? I've been nothing but horrible to you. I've pushed you away at every turn. Why do you care so much about me?"

"God, isn't it obvious? You're smart, you're beautiful, you're funny. I know it's a cliché, but you take my breath away. You always have."

She felt tears well up in her eyes and slowly cut salty tracks down her cheeks. "Ben, I'm a lot of things, but I'm not beautiful."

"What are you talking about? The dream version of you, yeah, I'd agree with you there. Blonde, big hair, blue eyes. Now *that's* cliché."

She blushed again. She had hoped that he hadn't noticed the appearance she took on when she dream walked, but of course he had.

"But the real you," he said, finding her eyes, "the inside as well as the outside, is what real beauty is all about. You're special. I love you, Katy. I can't deny it, and I don't want to. But if I don't get off this bed right now and eat a big bowl of Freakies, I'm probably going to do something that'll get me into a world of trouble."

He started to stand, but she reached out with her left hand to touch his cheek. "Don't go," she said softly, caressing his face.

"Katy, I promised I'd be good…"

"Yeah, well," she said, leaning in to brush her lips against his, "I didn't."

* * *

Ben woke up to the sight of the morning sun streaming in through the window to frame Katy's delicate, pale features. She looked so peaceful, so beautiful, lying there asleep in his arms. Though they hadn't made love last night—had stopped just short of it—he wouldn't trade their time together for anything. He could still smell her perfume on his chest, taste her kisses on his lips.

He had put the brakes to full-blown lovemaking. After all these years of her pushing him away, he told her, he wanted her to be sure. A part of him regretted that decision, though she promised him that there'd be other days and nights to come.

Ben glanced at the clock radio on his side of the bed—just a little after six in the morning. He yawned, fighting the urge to stay under the covers. He could think of nothing he'd rather do than spend all morning and afternoon in bed just watching Katy sleep, but there was still work to do. He slipped his arm from under her head, replacing it with his pillow, and rolled off the bed to pad over to the bathroom.

A quick shower later, he retrieved the milk from the bucket of ice Katy had gotten from the machine last night and prepared a bowl of Freakies. Total sugar shock, he admitted to himself, as he stood beside the sink spooning the fruity goodness into his mouth. In his time, everything was supposed to be good for you. Though he couldn't see himself eating like this often, he could understand why people like his father yearned for the "good old days."

He dug deep into the box and pulled out a little plastic "Boss Moss" figure. Boss Moss, proclaimed the story on the back of the package, was the self-appointed leader of the Freakies. He grinned at the little green lump of plastic and shoved it into his pocket.

Cereal finished, he found his duffel bag and removed the laptop and its charger. As he knelt to plug it in, however, he realized that the plugs were all two-pronged without a ground connection and his power cord was three-pronged. Shit. He hadn't even thought of that. He only had about an hour's worth of charge left on the battery, so he'd have to work fast.

According to his website extractor program, he'd only been able to download about a third of the information relating to Carthage between the years 1977 and 1981 that was available on the Web before he'd had to pull the plug. He hoped to find something to work with, because he didn't have a clue how to stop the murders before they'd even started. He and Katy could probably keep his grandfather safe, but that didn't necessarily stop the killings. The killer might simply go on to another victim or strike at a different time.

He pulled up the data and mentally cringed as he noticed there were over 2,500 entries, and that was just what the program had time to download. He'd set the Boolean search to ferret out anything with the term "Carthage, Illinois" along with the individual years. He redefined the search and told it to show him only information from 1977—461 articles, definitely better than 2,000.

The majority of the hits were obituaries and class reunion notices, but he did find other mentions of the murders here and there. Nothing, however, seemed to tell him anything more than he'd already learned from the article in the *Journal-Pilot*.

He broadened the search again, listing information that related to any mention of the house between '76 and '78. There wasn't much to go on. The Journal had run a piece on his grandfather after he'd officially been granted the deed to the house, another when they'd turned it into an apartment building, and a third when it'd been renamed "Huffman Heights." That was it, and nowhere in any of the stories did the newspaper mention even a clue as to anything unusual happening that involved the house.

He wished he had another set of files with which to compare the files he'd downloaded. If he did, he could track down the changes and quickly figure out the focal point. Otherwise, he had no way of knowing what was part of the original timeline and what had changed, unless it was blatantly obvious—the Halloween Murders, for example.

He read through the *Journal-Pilot* articles from October of 1977. Not much there. In fact, the only thing that was notable—other than the murder on the 31st—was the lack of news.

Frustrated, he was just about to give up and power down the laptop when he felt Katy's hands caress his shoulders. He leaned back into her, enjoying the feel of her hands, and then reached up to stroke her cheek.

"Hi sleepyhead," said Ben, powering down the laptop.

"Hi yourself," she said, nuzzling his neck. "I didn't know you brought that with you. Talk about destroying the space-time continuum."

"Yeah, well," he said, turning his head to stare into her deep brown eyes, "it only has about thirty minutes worth of juice left anyway, and after that it's just a very expensive paperweight."

"So did you find anything?"

"Not really, just more of the same," he said. "I guess there's no point in putting this off. Just let me know when you're ready and I'll read the spell."

"We have, what, four more hours before Clara kicks us out?"

Ben glanced at his watch. "Just about."

"So, come back to bed," she said, patting the covers.

They held each other tight, sharing kisses before falling asleep again, waking only when the radio alarm clock they'd set earlier began to play Earth, Wind, and Fire's *Shining Star*, a signal that they had only fifteen minutes left before checkout. Fourteen and a half minutes and one long kiss later, they were on their way downstairs to turn in their hotel keys and begin the next leg of their journey.

Chapter 22

March, 1977

The Reverend hadn't had a vision in months, and was beginning to think that the Lord had no more use for him, but he hadn't lost His favor after all. He was in Euless, Texas, in the middle of a sermon on vanity, when the vision came. It knocked the breath from his lungs, rocking him to his knees.

The crowd gasped as the giant collapsed to the floor. His leather Bible tumbled from his hands, and many feared that the Lord had called him home. With the help of Joyce and Anthony, two loyal members of the flock, he'd slowly risen on shaky legs to the cheers and hallelujahs of the crowd. But he couldn't continue his sermon. He didn't have time, not if he wanted to make it to Dallas to slay the demon before it escaped.

The vision was puzzling. A middle-aged Asian man knelt beside a bed, tending to an elderly Asian woman. Two other women, twins, stood helplessly on the other side of the room, their eyes closed as if in prayer. The man was dressed in a suit and tie and looked like every other businessman the Reverend had ever run across in the big city. He withdrew something from a small metal box that sat upon a nearby nightstand. He clutched the object tight in his fist and closed his eyes, passing his free hand over the woman's chest. A smile crept across her face, and she sat up and embraced her healer.

The man returned the hug, and then stood up. The two women, tears in their eyes, ran to the bed to throw their arms around the elderly woman. The healer stepped away, snatching up the box from the nightstand. He opened the box and put the object, which Dowd could now see was a necklace of some sort, inside. There was something else within the box as well, but his vision didn't allow him the vantage point to tell what it was. Now the two women were hugging the healer, congratulating the man on his miraculous work.

And then the vision ended, but not before Dowd caught a glimpse of a room service menu clutched in one of the two younger women's hands—it was the Fairmont Hotel, and the words emblazoned across the menu said it was located in historic downtown Dallas, an area he'd visited many times before.

But why would the Lord bless him with this vision? The man was doing God's work, was a healer…unless the old woman wasn't supposed to be healed. Yes, he understood everything now. She, along with her younger sisters, was another of Satan's minions. The businessman was possessed by a demon, called forth to make whole one of Lucifer's whores so she could continue her mission to bring about the apocalypse. And Dowd, the right hand of God, would not let it happen.

It took him 45 minutes to drive there in his old rusted-out red Dodge pickup, and then another thirty to actually find the building. He hoped he wasn't too late. But even as he thought it, he realized that he couldn't be, for it was all part of God's divine plan. Just as he'd eventually track down the Anti-Christ and his whore, today he would destroy the nest full of demons awaiting him at the Fairmont.

Dowd parked the truck in front of the hotel as he surveyed the lay of the land. They were still in there; that much he could tell. And, as he got closer, he'd be able to tell more. Like a ship to a beacon, he would be drawn to the enemy, would seek them out and put them to rest. He would smite them, just as the Almighty intended.

He reached beneath the tattered and torn seat and pulled out a leather sheath. It was his Samurai sword, his weapon of choice, next to the Bible, of course. He'd found the blade at a flea market in Iowa and it had sung to him, wanting to be part of his crusade. Two-hundred dollars was a small price to pay for such a weapon, and he was sure that the Lord had intervened on his behalf when the vendor had agreed to let him have it for a hundred and fifty.

He removed an oiling cloth from the tackle box on the floorboard, wet it with a bottle of Choji clove oil, and slowly pulled the sword from its casing. Tenderly, lovingly, he cleaned the weapon until it shined as beautiful and as bright as the sun. And then he was ready.

Dowd let himself out of the red '67 pickup, not even bothering to kill the engine. He knew that God would protect his chariot, just as He would bless his sword and make his aim true. He didn't plan to be gone long anyway. He strapped the sword to his back, slipped on an old tan trench coat to conceal its shape, and dropped his Bible into one of its many pockets.

"Sir," said a voice to his right, as he strode toward the hotel, "if you want valet parking, just pull around to the front entrance and…"

The boy's words fell silent as the Reverend turned to meet his gaze. The kid had red hair and freckles and was dressed in blue slacks and a red jacket and carried a ring full of keys, and couldn't have been a day over twenty.

"I'll be just a moment, son," he said softly. "Don't worry about the truck."

"I…yes, sir," he said, backing away. "Sorry to have bothered you, sir." The boy scurried back to his post by the entrance, studiously looking away as the Reverend walked past him and into the hotel.

The Fairmont was beautiful, bordering on ostentatious. A huge crystal chandelier hung from a vaulted ceiling several stories above the lobby, while balconies surrounded the open space as far up as he could see.

He closed his eyes, concentrating. His quarry was on the seventh floor. He walked purposefully toward the elevator, pushing past a bell-hop loading a luggage cart. He entered the elevator, pressed the button to close the door, and then tapped seven. The doors slid closed, gravity pulling at his body as the elevator car rose.

He glanced at himself in the mirror, taking in his full height. His hair was starting to get long. He'd have to ask Mary Alice to give him a shave and a haircut when he got back to the tents. Only a few of his followers knew about his missions: Jim Felt, who'd been with him almost from the beginning, and a handful of others. The rest, bless them, never questioned his excursions or asked him where he went when he heard the Lord's call. They knew he was on God's clock, and that was good enough for them. At least for most of them.

One day a few years back, a young sheep by the name of Lyle Brown had followed him on one of his missions. Afterward, the man had confided in Felt what he'd seen, threatening to call the police. Felt had come to Dowd, of course, and it was then that Dowd realized that Lyle Brown was a pawn of Satan, sent to bring him down. Dowd had been forced to dispatch the man, and had since been careful never to expose the majority of his flock to the violence that he was called upon to perform in the name of the Lord Jesus Christ. They couldn't see, they wouldn't always understand, and solitude was a small price to pay to be able to continue to do God's good work.

The elevator opened and he stepped out into the hallway. He closed his eyes again and could see the Japanese man stepping off the elevator, walking down this very same hallway, finally stopping to knock on door 713. And there he had it. Hand on his sword, he opened his eyes and followed the man's phantom footsteps.

Tap, tap, tap, he knocked quickly three times in succession, calling out, "Room service." He heard voices beyond the heavy wooden door, and then the slide of a chain. The door opened a crack, and one of the two Oriental women peered out.

"We no order room service," she said in broken English, pushing the door closed again.

He took a deep breath and let the Lord's light fill his body. Stepping back, he slammed his size 17 foot hard into the center of the door. The wood gave way instantly, splintering and cracking as it flew open. The woman behind the door went sprawling backwards, a thick shard of polished wood protruding from her neck. Blood sprayed in an arc from an artery, and she was dead before she even hit the floor.

The Reverend reached over his shoulder to free the Samurai blade from its sheath. Stepping over the dead woman's body, he took stock of the room. The old woman stood up from the bed, her mouth open in shock. The twin screamed, cowering in the corner, while the healer fumbled with his luggage.

"Nani o shiteru?" screamed the man, his eyes a mixture of anger and fear. *"Wakatte nai na."* The suitcase fell open, spilling clothing and toiletries to the floor.

And there was the box, hidden between a pair of slacks and a golf shirt. The man was fast, but Dowd was faster. Already moving, he reached the healer just as he knelt to retrieve whatever lay hidden within the box. His sword flashed out, severing the man's arm from his elbow. Blood splattered the floor as the man screamed in shock and stumbled back, his good hand covering the stump.

"Dame dayo!" screamed the old woman, darting from the bed to snatch the fallen container.

She was deceptively fast, but still no match for Dowd. He plunged the sword into her stomach, running her through. She uttered a sharp cry of surprise as he pulled the sword back out again. She stared down at the blood seeping from the wound, looked up at him, and fell backwards onto the bed. The box tumbled from her hand, spilling its contents onto the green hotel carpet.

It was filled with pennies—several hundred, from the looks of it, both American and Canadian. The pennies scattered all over the floor, some rolling under the bed. And there among the pile of copper, half-buried, was a silver chain. He knelt to retrieve the chain. A small tooth dangled from it, perhaps from a lion or some other wild cat. And suddenly he could see as he'd never seen before. All around the country, Satan's minions did their master's bidding. An incense shop in New Mexico: a group of hooded moon worshipers in Missouri: a self-proclaimed psychic in Rhode Island—all agents of the devil, all working to bring about the downfall of the Lord. And Dowd could see them all, knew exactly where they were and what they were doing.

Dowd was caught by surprise as a kick to the ribs knocked him to his knees. It was the healer, determined to reclaim the necklace. Still cradling his bleeding stump, the man sent a roundhouse kick into the Reverend's face, knocking him flat on his back. He could taste his own blood dripping down the back of his throat and was sure he'd lost a tooth. The Lord was not happy, and neither was Dowd.

Still clutching the necklace, he kicked out with one of his massive feet and just missed the healer's kneecap. The man jumped back, maneuvering around the room, always careful to keep his body between Dowd and the woman. And that's when the Reverend knew he had him.

He moved closer, swinging his blade toward the healer, maneuvering slowly across the room. He feinted to the left then swung quickly to the right, catching the other man off balance. The female was left unguarded. Dowd, sensing his opportunity, flung the blade straight for the woman's heart. The healer threw himself in front of the woman, as Dowd had known he would, realizing his folly only when it was too late.

The sword buried itself deep into the man's chest, knocking him back into his companion. Dowd was on them in an instant, snapping the woman's neck in a single twist of his hands.

"Do shite?" asked the man, as his eyes slowly lost their glimmer. He was dying and he knew it. *"Abunaiyo. Contororu no shikata ga wakatte naina.* Why?"

Dowd placed a foot on the dying man's chest, withdrawing his blade. Blood sluiced from the hole in his chest, flooding his lungs, and he never got to hear the Reverend's reply.

"For the Lord," he said, walking across the floor to clean his blade on the hotel curtains, "and his sweet son Jesus."

He sheathed his Samurai sword and walked through the splintered door and into the hallway. His truck was still where he'd left it by the time he retraced his path down the elevator, through the lobby, and out into the humid Dallas evening.

Chapter 23

Friday, October 28, 1977

Shawn Spencer pulled his little yellow Pacer—the car he'd bought from Fred Ruskin this past August—into the Carthage High School student parking lot. He still had his parking sticker from last year, and no one ever seemed to notice anyway. He looked at his watch: it was just before noon, and Jenny's 45 minute lunch period would start in a few minutes.

He walked to the front doors of the school, peering through the huge glass panes. Students scurried to and fro, late for class or just finishing, but no Jenny. Her science class must have run late. Because he didn't have to go into Newsland until one, he'd made plans to take her to lunch. It was just going to be hot dogs or hamburgers at Tastee Freeze, but at least that would give them a chance to spend some time together.

Thank God it was Friday. He missed Jenny during the school week. He drove her to school most days, and always picked her up afterward, but it wasn't the same as when they'd both gone together and certainly couldn't hold a candle to the summers.

He leaned against the wall, nodding or waving as kids he recognized shuffled by or called out to him. He almost wished they wouldn't, because being at the school made him feel more than a little conspicuous. He no longer belonged there.

Because he was tall and lean, Shawn's billowing winter coat combined with his sandy blond hair gave him the appearance of a scarecrow. The crows that had taken up residence on the roof didn't help matters. He pulled the coat tighter around his chest, glancing up at the moving clouds, enjoying the silence after spending the morning listening to his father and Mr. McGee bark orders.

"Hey, handsome," said a voice from behind him, but it wasn't Jenny's. Steeling himself for what he knew was about to come next, he turned around to greet Kristen Hawks.

She'd moved to Carthage from Missouri at the start of the school year and for whatever reason had immediately glommed onto Jenny. He knew it had to be rough changing schools right before your senior year, but he wished she'd make an effort to find some other friends and give him the occasional moment of peace.

"Hey, Kristen." He forced a smile, doing his best to act friendly.

Kristen usually overdressed for school, and Fridays were no exception. Today she wore a low-cut red satin blouse and a plaid pleated skirt that ended just above her knees, something most of the other girls in her senior class probably wouldn't have the nerve to pull off.

He didn't know what it was about the girl, but she just rubbed him the wrong way. Kristen was beautiful, though often pretended that she wasn't. She had long, jet-black hair that contrasted perfectly with her porcelain complexion. That contrast, along with her high cheek bones and deep hazel eyes, combined to create an exotic beauty that was at once alluring and intimidating.

She was, for the most part, friendly, and definitely bright, but he didn't like the way she treated Jenny whenever she thought Jenny wasn't paying attention. And he especially didn't like the way that she always managed to insinuate herself into every aspect of their lives.

"Fancy meeting you here," she said, sidling up to give him a hug, "I guess this is my lucky day." She was a shameless flirt, but only when Jenny was out of earshot.

"Just here to pick my girlfriend up for lunch." He forced a smile, hoping she wouldn't invite herself along.

"And here's the girlfriend," said Jenny, running up to throw her arms around his neck.

Her long red hair fell past her shoulders, accentuating her freckles, and Shawn was reminded once again just how beautiful she was. He winced as Kristen shot her a look of pure jealousy that only he could see.

Jenny turned to Kristen. "Want to come with?"

"Well, if it's okay with your boyfriend," she said, raising her eyebrows at Shawn. A slow smile crept across her cherry-red lips.

What could he say? He was damned if he did and damned if he didn't. "Sure, if you want. We're just going to Tastee Freeze."

"My favorite," she said, twirling in a circle, the movement causing her skirt to creep perilously up her thighs. She smoothed down the material, smiling demurely. "So are we taking the mustard mobile?"

"Like always," Shawn replied, putting his arm around Jenny's shoulder.

For the first time in a long time, he almost couldn't wait for his shift at Newsland to start. This was going to be the longest lunch of his life.

* * *

Shawn had just picked Jenny up from school and was enjoying the thought of spending some alone time with her, but instead they ended up arguing about Kristen. Kristen had been a point of contention between them almost since she'd entered Jenny's life. He'd spent most of lunch listening to the girl complain about her food and jabber on and on about something or other—Shawn couldn't say for sure—and hadn't even had the chance to get a word in edgewise, much less talk to Jenny about anything meaningful.

And then, to top everything off, he'd been forced to run Kristen home after dropping Jenny back off at the campus, all because she hadn't had the foresight to remember to bring her science homework to school with her. Kristen, of course, had study hall the period after lunch, so she had the perfect excuse not to go back to school and torment Shawn for just a little while longer. She'd ended up making him late for work, of course. Elaine, his manager, had been none too happy about that, and he'd had to agree to work an extra shift next week to smooth things over.

"Why does Kristen always have to invite herself along?" asked Shawn, regretting the words almost the instant they left his mouth.

Jenny took a deep breath. "Look, Shawn, I don't know why you're always so down on her. She's our friend. She's a good person."

"*Your* friend, you mean."

"Okay, *my* friend. And she's new here and doesn't have that many friends yet. Why can't you understand that?"

"I *do* understand that. Believe me, I do. But maybe if she wasn't always hanging out with us she'd actually have the time to make a few new friends."

Gravel crunched beneath the Pacer's tires as he pulled the car into Jenny's driveway. Her parents weren't home yet, but she didn't seem in the mood to invite him in.

"Well, thanks for the ride," Jenny said, her hand on the door handle the moment the wheels stopped turning. She swung the door open and started to get out.

"Wait, wait," he said, exasperated. "Look, I'm sorry, okay? She just bugs me, that's all. I'll get over it. Say, do you want to go out tonight and get a pizza?"

She turned to look at him with those deep green eyes that could always melt his heart, but she wasn't smiling. "I have to study," she said, shrugging by way of apology. "And Kristen's coming over later so

I can help her get ready for an English test. I know you couldn't bear having to deal with her again."

He ignored the barb. "Okay, so how about tomorrow?" he asked, leaning across the seat for their usual goodbye kiss.

She gave him a quick peck on the lips before leaning into the back seat to snatch something from the floorboard. "What's this?" She held up a silver tube.

Shawn leaned in to take a closer look. "Lipstick?" he guessed, noticing the name *Revlon* emblazoned in gold lettering across the side.

"Yeah, silly, but who's? I don't use this brand." She looked at him curiously.

"I have no clue," he said. "Kristen's, maybe? She's been the only person back there other than, well, you know, us."

That brought a smile to her lips. "Yeah, probably." She tossed the cylinder into the air, catching it in her palm. "I'll give it back to her tonight."

"*Jen*," he said, playfully using the nickname Kristen had given her, "you know I love you, right? I'm sorry about what I said earlier, about Kristen. You're right—she's your friend. I'll get used to her. I guess I just miss spending time with you."

"You'll get your chance," she said, this time leaning in for a long, lingering kiss that left him wanting more. "I promise. Tomorrow."

Shawn sighed. "Tomorrow it is, then. Around six?"

"Wouldn't miss it for the world," she said, leaving the car to walk the length of the driveway before turning around to blow him another kiss goodbye.

* * *

Jenny dropped the tube of lipstick into the white china bowl that sat on top of her dresser before crossing the room to flop down into bed. She stared up at the ceiling. She couldn't understand why Shawn didn't like Kristen. Being one of "the smart girls," Jenny didn't have a lot of friends, so when the girl had moved to Carthage and they'd seemed to have a lot in common, Jenny had taken an instant liking to her. They both enjoyed science fiction novels, Beatles music, and the entire CBS Friday night line-up of *Wonder Woman, Logan's Run,* and *Switch.* What more could you ask for?

If push ever came to shove, of course, she'd choose Shawn over Kristen, but she didn't think it was fair of him to force her to make that choice. She loved Shawn with all her heart and wanted to spend the rest of her life with him, but she needed to be able to spend time with other friends as well.

Her thoughts drifted back to the summer of 1975, after her brother had twice been murdered and they'd killed the man responsible for his death. She'd fallen in love with Shawn that summer, when she was only fifteen, and they'd been inseparable ever since.

She had always promised herself that she wouldn't have sex until after she was married, but lately had been second guessing that decision. What were they waiting for? They were desperately in love and had been moving things toward that eventuality for two years. What hadn't seemed a big deal at fifteen—the decision to wait—suddenly seemed much bigger at eighteen. Her idea of God and religion had been flipped on its ear the moment she met a real, live angel, so she didn't much care what the church thought about pre-marital sex. She just wanted her first time to be special, and doing it in the back of Uncle Fred's old Pacer wasn't. Still, she wasn't sure how long either of them could wait.

She looked around the room, taking stock of her surroundings. A lot of things had changed in her life, but her room wasn't one of them. The walls were still pink, even if she had managed to get rid of pretty much everything else of that color. Her mother still didn't get it, but you had to grow up sometime.

Jenny kicked off her shoes and peeled the white gym socks from her feet. P.E. was her last period and she still felt grubby from the game of dodge ball she'd been forced to play. It'd be at least an hour before Kristen showed up, and she definitely needed a bath.

She forced herself up from the soft comfort of the bed, pulling her blouse over her head in one quick motion. She stepped out of her skirt, tossed it and her blouse in the general direction of the hamper she kept at the end of her bed, and then slid out of her bra and panties before wrapping the oversized terry cloth robe her parents had given her last Christmas around her body. She stepped over her discarded under-clothes and made her way toward the bathroom, intent on a long over-due soak in hot water and bubbles.

And outside her window, someone watched.

"Hey, did you drop this in Shawn's car?" Jenny asked, holding up the lipstick.

Kristen had been at her house for nearly an hour before she thought to say anything. She'd been on her way out the door to fix a bowl of Jiffy Pop when the tube of Revlon Cherry Red caught her eye.

Jenny walked back across the room to her bed, where the pair had been studying. "I said, did you drop this?" She held the tube in the palm of her hand. "I found it in Shawn's car."

Kristen's face was ash white, and a twin pair of tears trickled down her cheeks. She stared at the lipstick. "Um, yeah, I guess I did," she whispered, reaching out to take the silver tube from Jenny's out-stretched hand. "Thanks."

"Hey, what's wrong?" Jenny asked, dropping to her knees to sit be-side her friend. "Are you okay?"

Kristen wiped her eyes with the back of her hand, and then flung herself into Jenny's arms. "Oh, God, I can't lie to you. Jen, I'm sorry. I'm so sorry."

"It's okay, whatever it is, it's okay," she whispered, stroking the girl's hair. But she had a sick feeling in the pit of her stomach that she wasn't sure she wanted to hear what was coming.

"It's my fault, Jen. I'm so sorry. I should have said no," she said, her voice trembling as she sobbed into Jenny's shoulder. "He... this afternoon, during my study hall, when I asked him to take me to get my papers... He said you wouldn't have sex with him. That you were making him wait, and he was tired of waiting. I should have said no, I tried, I really did. I just didn't know what to do."

Jenny reeled back, pushing her friend hard against the bed. "What did you do?" she demanded, her fingers squeezing Kristen's shoulders. "What?"

"You're hurting me!" the girl yelped, struggling to break free.

"I said, what did you do? Answer me!"

"We had sex, okay? In the back of his car, behind my house. I'm sorry! He just said that if I didn't he'd make it so you and I weren't friends anymore, and I couldn't stand the thought. I love you, Jen!"

"You had sex with my boyfriend, and you love me?" Jenny finally released the girl's shoulders. Her heart was beating so fast that she felt for sure it would burst. She felt like crying, but wouldn't give either of them the satisfaction. "Jesus, Kristen, if you love me, you sure have a funny way of showing it."

"I didn't want to lose you!"

"I just can't believe Shawn would...I mean, are you sure?"

"What do you mean, am I sure?" she sobbed, burying her face in her hands. "Your boyfriend had sex with me, and then he hit me when I tried to tell him to stop, of course I'm sure. I wish it had never happened, but I won't lie to you. I'm so sorry."

"He hit you? Shawn would never hit a girl. He'd never do any of this!"

"Then what's this?" Kristen demanded, pulling her blouse up around her breasts.

The ribs on the right side of her stomach were bruised, and were starting to turn purple. Kristen winced sharply when Jenny reached out a tentative hand to touch the bruise. Jenny pulled her hand back, letting it fall to her lap.

Her thoughts flashed back to two summers ago, when Shawn's blood had mixed with the blood of the monstrous fetch. The connection had helped the fetch regain its humanity, but had also influenced Shawn's emotions, making him angry, even violent. But that had all ended when the fetch turned back into Collin Wainwright, hadn't it?

"He couldn't..." she began, but the words sounded hollow even to her.

"He did," Kristen said, dropping her shirt.

"What exactly did he say?"

"I don't know. I've been trying to forget it all day."

"Tell me!"

"All right, I guess you deserve to know. He said, 'Jen won't put out, and I can't wait any longer.' He said he loved you, but he wanted me. He kept...he kept calling me 'Jen' the entire time, over and over. 'I love you, Jen,' he kept saying."

Jenny felt like she was going to throw up. She had to be lying, but why would she? "Was this the first time?"

"The first time he hit me? Yeah, it was."

Jenny's hands were trembling. "No, that's not what I meant. Was is the first time you had... had..."

The girl looked down at her hands, mumbling, "Had sex? It's the first time I gave in, yeah. But he's hinted before, flirted with me, when he thought you weren't around."

"When?"

"That time we went to see 'Close Encounters' in Keokuk. It was crowded and I ended up sitting on the other side of him, remember?"

"I remember. What happened?"

"He just kept... touching me. At first, I thought it was an accident, but it kept happening, and then when you went to the bathroom, he...he kissed me, and pushed his hand up between my thighs."

"You're lying."

"I'm not lying, Jen. I swear to God. I just didn't know what to do. I know how much you love him, and I just kept hoping he'd stop. I thought if I told you, you wouldn't believe me. I begged him to stop, but he wouldn't listen. He kept pressuring me. I didn't know what else to do, and I was scared, so I finally gave in."

Jenny thought again to the fetch. Even under the horrid creature's influence, after Shawn attacked Mike Jackson and Rusty Boyer at the Tastee Freez, he'd never been anything but gentle and kind with her. And he'd never even tried to pressure her into sex. Kristen had to be lying, she just had to be.

"Get out," Jenny finally said, almost whispering the words.

"What?" she said, blinking away tears. "I can't leave now. I can't lose you, Jen. I can't. You're my only friend."

"Get out," she repeated, her voice louder this time.

"Jenny, we can't let him come between us."

"Get the *fuck* out of my room!" Jenny screamed, slapping Kristen hard across the face. "Get out! Get out! Get out!"

Kristen recoiled from the blow, falling back onto the bed. She raised a tentative hand to the angry red welt already forming across her cheek.

"Jenny?" said her mother's voice from the hallway. The door creaked open a crack. "Are you okay? What's going on in here?"

"Get this bitch out of my room!" Jenny jumped to her feet, screaming at the top of her lungs. "Get out!"

Kristen bolted from the bed in tears, her hand pressed tight against her swelling cheek. Sobbing, she ran past Jenny's mother and out of the room.

Abby watched the retreating figure of her daughter's best friend before turning back to Jenny. "Are you okay?" she whispered, walking across the room to lay an uncertain hand on her daughter's shoulder.

Jenny folded herself into her mother's arms and began to cry. "Mom, I don't think I'm ever going to be okay," she said between huge, wracking sobs, "never, ever again."

Chapter 24

Brody Huffman walked the perimeter of the property on Randolph Street, counting each step, wondering just where to start. They didn't normally work Saturdays but they were already behind schedule and so he'd volunteered to put in a half a day's work this morning. By the time they were finished renovating the old mansion there would be enough space for ten families, and it was one of his jobs to make sure they all had places to park.

He'd staked out a rectangular lot in the backyard that would connect to the driveway around the side of the house, and he'd managed to do it while avoiding having to cut down any of the huge oaks that decorated the yard.

Though he was more a man of action than contemplation, he liked to, upon occasion, reflect back on his life and how he had gotten to where he was today. That's why he enjoyed his work so much; he could do everything and still had time to think. He allowed his mind to wander back to over a year ago, when he'd first made his way through this little Illinois town, back before he'd decided to make it his home.

Back then he'd been tramping, a man without a home working his way across America one boxcar at a time. He'd gotten into Carthage hungry and tired but willing to work; Fred Ruskin had accepted those terms readily, hiring him on to help renovate the old Morgan Oil restaurant into Ruskin's Pizzeria.

He'd done construction and renovation work before and so was pretty good at it, but something had always happened to give him that itch, to send him riding the rail one more time. But it hadn't happened this time. He'd known he was going to stay when Ruskin had invited him to help celebrate Thanksgiving last year with him and his new family. It'd been years since he'd had a proper holiday, and the man had taken him into his home and fed him turkey with dressing and all the trimmings. How could he leave after that?

Other construction jobs had come after that, just a few hours a week at first, until finally he was working full time. He'd eventually moved out of the Starlight Motel and rented a trailer at the edge of town, and that's when he knew for sure that he wanted to stay.

He'd gotten to know Henry Spencer, Paul McGee, and their respective families through Ruskin, and later on his own merit, finally culminating with being hired to help McGee with the construction on Spencer Heights, Carthage's newest apartment building. He'd become fast friends with Shawn and Jenny, regaling them with tales of life as a grunt in Korea.

He'd lost his wife right after nearly getting his leg blown off in the battle of Porkchop Hill, just a month before receiving his medical discharge from the Marines. He'd arrived home in the little town of Beech Bottom, West Virginia on temporary leave, released early from the hospital, just in time to catch his brother screwing his wife on top of the kitchen table—the very same table they'd scrimped and saved for just two years earlier.

Something had broken in him then. He'd walked out without saying a word, without even announcing his presence, and hitchhiked his way back to the base in Colorado. He stopped replying to his wife's letters, and had never seen her or any of his family ever again. For all he knew, they probably thought he was dead. He had been, he supposed, at least until this past year. After years of traveling, he finally felt like he had a home.

He slipped his tape measure into his pocket and then glanced at the used Timex he'd picked up over the weekend, deciding he was due for a break. He couldn't seem to keep his mind on work anyway. He'd only been on the job two weeks and couldn't ask for a better pair of bosses than Henry Spencer and Paul McGee, but would be glad when it was over, and definitely wasn't looking forward to working inside.

There was some strange shit inside that house. He thought he'd seen someone in the library the other day, a man in a trench coat, but turned around to find he was completely alone in the room. Tools he'd been using had disappeared from where he'd left them, only to be replaced by things that weren't anywhere in the house during his initial walkthrough, and he'd heard frantic footsteps running through the hallways when he knew that nobody else was there.

He was sipping lukewarm coffee from an old Stuckey's thermos, counting every gulp, sucking down the beverage in swallows of three, when it happened. He thought he'd seen it all, but this took the cake. Between serving his time as a machine gunner for the 7th Marine Regiment in the Korean War and his twenty some odd years of civilian life since, not to mention the fourteen days he'd worked on this project, he'd been witness to a lot of strange shit, but never shit quite as strange as this.

Where moments before the bright morning sun flickered through the branches of the huge oak trees surrounding the property, everything in a ten yard radius immediately went pitch dark. The air, already a chilly 50 degrees, dropped past freezing in an instant, and the pressure changed to the point where he thought his eardrums might burst.

And then, as quickly as it had begun, it was over. The sun once again warmed the leaf-covered fall ground, its rays warming the space around him, and birds—whose silence he had failed to even notice—continued to sing to their winged brethren. He hugged himself beneath the old army jacket he wore and shivered, blinking his eyes exactly three times. The thermos fell from his fingers to splash to the ground beneath his boots.

Lying in the grass beneath one of the huge oak trees were two young kids, maybe in their early twenties, a boy and a girl. One moment they weren't there, and then the next they were.

"Hey, are you all right?" he asked, kneeling beside them, trying to avoid staining his jeans on the spilled coffee even now soaking into the earth. If that happened, he'd have to wash them three times and he'd be up all night.

The kids weren't moving, but at least they were breathing. He reached out a trembling hand to touch the brown-haired woman on the shoulder, jumping back to land flat on his ass as her eyes suddenly fluttered open.

"What happened?" she murmured, her eyes huge as saucers. She rolled to her side to rouse her companion. Her hand was taped in gauze, as if she'd been hurt. "Ben, are you okay?"

Brody continued to stare at the pair in amazement. Who were they, and where had they come from? He slowly clambered to his feet, his bum leg making even that movement difficult. He stood an even six feet tall, weighed two hundred and change, and sported a bullet-shaped head that wasn't helped by the fact that he was completely bald save for a cluster of salt-and-pepper hair that started behind both temples and covered the lower half of the back of his head.

He stared down at the pair with steel gray eyes, sticking out his lantern-square jaw, doing his best to hide his fear. He tapped his fingers silently against his leg. Three times, then six, then nine. If push came to shove he could brawl with the best of them, but he had to admit that right now he was scared shitless.

"Ben?" she pleaded, slapping the boy sharply across the face. "Wake up!"

"Huh?" her friend mumbled, finally opening his eyes. "Where are we?"

"Carthage," Brody answered, watching as both their heads whipped around to stare at him. "Where did you kids come from?"

"I mean what year?" the boy asked, instantly looking as though he regretted it.

What year? What kind of question was that? "It's 1977, at least for another two months. Hey, are you two okay?" Everything in him wanted to run, to lock himself in his trailer and count whatever remained of the beer stashed in his refrigerator, but he forced his feet to remain still.

"Never better," said the woman, rolling her eyes. "Somebody, um, knocked us out and robbed us, how do you think we are?"

Then why didn't they take your duffel bag, he wanted to ask? It had to be a lie, because he knew what he saw. One moment he was alone in the backyard, and the next he wasn't. There hadn't been any robbery.

"Hey, dude, can you help my friend up?" the girl said, climbing to her feet.

Dude? What kind of girl talked like that? "Yeah, sure," he said, willing to help despite his misgivings.

He limped over to the boy, knelt to the ground, and draped the kid's arm around his neck. In one quick motion he yanked him to his feet, backing away again as the kid clutched his stomach and hurled its contents all over the girl's shoes.

"Seriously, Ben?" she chastised him, but didn't actually seem angry. "Just how much of my clothing do you intend to ruin?" She drug her black leather boots through the dead winter grass, doing her best to clean them.

"You kids aren't on drugs, are you?" he asked. He smoked a little pot from time to time—it helped with the pain—but he stayed away from the rest of that shit.

"No," the boy said, wiping his mouth on his sleeve. "No drugs. I'll be okay."

"So where did you come from?"

The girl shot her companion a glance that Brody couldn't quite decipher. "Chicago," she said, slowly. "We were traveling through when we got jumped."

"Look," he said, putting his hands on his hips, "There wasn't any robbery. Everything went dark and then there you were. Now what really happened?"

The girl looked stricken but quickly recovered. "If it was dark, how do you know we weren't here?" she countered.

"Well, I mean…" He had to admit, that was a good question. "Okay, so how did the sun go out?"

"Eclipse?" the boy offered, squinting up at the sky. "What time is it?"

"Umm," Brody replied, looking at his Timex, "Fifteen minutes until nine, why?" Six. The number came unbidden into his mind. Fifteen plus nine equaled twenty-four, and two and four equaled six.

"Well, that explains it," the girl chimed in, "there was supposed to be an eclipse around 8:45 this morning. In fact, that's why we were out here—to watch the eclipse. But then those guys jumped us, and that's all I remember."

Brody sighed and scratched his stubbly chin. An eclipse? He guessed that could have happened, but he was positive they hadn't been there when he walked out here. The war may have left him a walking cripple, but, for the most part, it had left his mind intact. Still, the kids hadn't really done anything wrong, and with all the weird shit going on around the house as of late he was happy to dismiss this as something totally unrelated.

"Okay, you win," he said, "it was an eclipse, and I managed to survey the entire yard without noticing either one of you. It all makes perfect sense now."

"Works for me," said the girl, poking out her lower lip and shrugging her shoulders in an unvoiced apology. She looked at the boy, who shrugged in return.

Shrugs all around it was, then. Mystery solved, at least until the next time his tool belt went missing. "By the way, my name's Brody. Brody Huffman. You know, I don't think I caught your names," he asked, knowing full well they'd never been given.

"Katy Rush," Katy replied, "Sorry we had to meet under such weird circumstances."

"And I'm Ben... Matthews," he said, hesitating between the names. "We're pleased to meet you, Mr. Huffman, but I think we better get out of your way and let you get back to work."

"You know, if you were really robbed, I'd better get the sheriff down here."

"No!" they yelled in unison, trading furtive glances. "They didn't get anything important, and I'm sure the police have enough to worry about without having to drive over here on Halloween."

Halloween? Brody looked at her curiously. "Today's Saturday. Halloween isn't for another two days. Are you sure you're all right?"

She looked like the wind had been knocked out of her. "You know, on second thought," she said, slowly shaking her head, "I'm not all right at all." She leaned against Ben with her head in her hands. "Not by a long shot. But I'll get there."

"Okay, just get out of here and that'll be the end of it. But if you show up again, I'll have to tell Mr. McGee."

"McGee?" the girl asked.

Her mouth open as she looked past him, she seemed to notice the house for the first time. Her face turned white and she grabbed the boy by the hand and hurriedly walked away.

* * *

The Reverend awoke with a start, his body in a tent just outside of Hannibal, Missouri, his mind someplace else entirely. He was having another vision, one for which he'd hoped and prayed for much of the last two years. His heart hammered in his chest as he watched the scene unfold before him.

He looked on in fascination as a man and a woman—one of the pairs he had seen two years ago—literally appeared out of thin air and crumpled to the ground. Another man approached them and the woman quickly climbed to her feet, using a tree for support, and together they helped her companion rise as well. And then the man clutching his stomach, doubling over in pain, finally vomiting a rush of multi-colored chunks into the grass.

He ignored the demons in his vision, instead concentrating on their surroundings. Ever since he'd liberated the tooth from the demon healer in Dallas, his visions had been more frequent and far easier to understand. God had rewarded him for his dedication and persever-ance by opening his eyes just a little bit wider.

The vision quickly passed, as they always did, but he knew where they were now: Carthage, a small Illinois town that straddled the bor-ders between that state, Iowa, and Missouri. More importantly, he sensed the man and woman's connection to the Anti-Christ.

"*Padre?*" called a Spanish-accented voice from outside his dwelling. "Are you okay? I heard you yelling in your sleep."

It was Oscar, a brown-skinned slip of a boy from California who had been with the church for nearly seven years. He'd spent the first ten years of his life in Mexico City, in the heart of Mexico, until his parents had moved to the States for work. The boy had never taken to the change in culture, drastic even in California, and had become in-volved in drugs and gangs. He'd been fourteen when he first ap-proached their encampment and had joined them shortly thereafter. Oscar had proven to be one of Dowd's most loyal disciples and insist-ed on calling him *Padre*, though he wasn't a priest.

"Everything is fine," Dowd called out, rising from his cot to pull back the flap of the tent, "but come in. I need to talk to you." He retrieved his bible from the little table beside his cot, absently flipping through its dog-eared pages until he found the verse he wanted.

The black-haired boy, no taller than five feet four inches, slipped in through the opening and smiled shyly up at the Reverend. Oscar was dressed in khaki trousers and a plain green sweater, the usual fare for the flock. Dowd had impressed the urgency of dressing no better than the townspeople that came to hear testimony, to prove the point that they were all cut from the same cloth, and Oscar had followed his example to the letter.

"'When a prophet speaketh in the name of the Lord, if the thing follow not, nor come to pass, that is the thing which the Lord hath not spoken," he quoted from Deuteronomy 18:22, "'but the prophet hath spoken it presumptuously: thou shalt not be afraid of him.'"

"Beautiful, *Padre*. Are you ready for the sermon?"

"That's what I need to talk to you about," he explained, laying a huge hand on the boy's shoulder. "I've had a vision. There are people just south of here that are in desperate need of the Lord's word, and so we're going to have to cancel this morning's sermon."

Oscar had been through this many times before and, to his credit, the boy didn't even flinch. "*Sí, Padre*. I'll tell Felt and the others, and we'll spread the word. Would you like me to pack your tent when I'm finished?"

"That'll be fine, Oscar," he said, gently touching the boy's cheek. "The Lord surely did me a favor when he brought you into my flock."

The boy beamed, quickly scurrying out of the tent to make preparations for the day's unexpected travel.

If they packed fast they could be in Carthage by this afternoon, and have signs posted for a Monday morning revival by the end of Sunday. They'd trump Satan on his very own day of celebration, Halloween.

And when the Anti-Christ and his demons came—for they could never resist gazing enviously upon his brightness—he'd know who they were. And before the clock struck midnight on All Hallows Eve, he'd see every last one of them dead.

Chapter 25

Shawn had promised to help his father with some of the renovations on the house before starting his shift at Newsland but was already running behind schedule. He pulled his little yellow Pacer into the driveway behind Mr. McGee's red Dodge pickup. Ketchup and mustard, Jenny liked to say, whenever she saw the cars parked next to each other. That's when Kristen had started calling his car the "mustard mobile."

He never liked coming to this house and was glad his father had decided to turn it into an apartment building. The house had once been guarded by magical wards that kept anyone from even noticing much less entering the house. After the wards were destroyed and people started seeing it again, his father and grandfather had decided to file a claim of legal ownership over the property. The county had eventually approved the claim and they had been given joint ownership earlier this year. Neither of them knew anything about what had happened during the summer of 1975, and the three—Shawn, Jenny, and Fred Ruskin—had sworn to keep it that way.

He thought back to that summer nearly two and a half years ago. He'd lost his best friend, only to have him briefly come back in the form of his Galahad action figure to help Shawn and Jenny do battle against an ancient wizard and his other-worldly familiar intent on recovering a charm that Shawn's ancestor Colin Wainwright had stolen from them. With the help of the Archangel Michael they had eventually prevailed and Shawn still had the magic charm, a buffalo-head nickel, hidden in a jar full of pennies beneath a loose floorboard under his bed. He and Jenny had been chased, trapped, and nearly killed, but not everything that happened that summer had been bad.

He'd known Jenny practically all his life but had always thought of her as just Tanner's little sister. How wrong he'd been. They'd fallen in love that summer, and he knew they'd be together for the rest of their lives. Shawn had graduated high school last year but had decided to take a year off to work before going to college, so he and Jenny (who wouldn't graduate until next May) could attend Western Illinois University in Macomb together. So, no, not everything that had happened in June of '75 was bad, not by a long shot, though his heart would always ache with the loss of his best friend.

Shawn slid out of the Pacer, bumping the door shut with his hip. He scanned the sky, looking for the promised first snow of the season. "Quincy's favorite meteorologist" Melissa Rhoads had sworn it was going to snow, but it looked like the weather girl had bungled it again. The sky was clear for as far as the eye could see.

He took a deep breath, enjoying the smell of nature all around him. The oaks, the white lilac bushes, all of it—he hoped his father didn't intend to bring down any of the trees. Shawn hugged himself as a shiver ran down his spine. He felt a strange sense of foreboding cloud his spirit as he turned to stare at the house.

This place always had that effect on him, which is why he tried to visit as little as possible. He'd never even bothered to retrieve the yo-yo he'd lost in the library those two long summers ago, though he supposed if one of the construction workers found it he wouldn't mind having it back.

A lifetime of memories had been created during that awful, wonderful week in 1975, and thank God he had someone to share them with. He thought he might go crazy if he didn't. Since that summer, Jenny had always been there for him, and he tried to always be there for her, but he was starting to worry about their relationship. They'd been arguing a lot lately, mostly about Kristen, and she hadn't called him last night. She always called before she went to bed. And when he'd tried calling her, Mrs. McGee had acted strangely cold when she told him that Jenny was already in bed. He had a feeling something was wrong, but didn't know what.

Enough stalling, he told himself. He'd figure out what was wrong with Jenny later. Hands in his pockets, he started up the driveway just as Brody Huffman rounded the corner of the house.

"Brody," he said, "is my dad back there?"

"Hey Shawn, didn't know you were coming by today. No, he's in the kitchen trying to figure out what it will take to repair that big hole in the floor."

Oh, that. He and Jenny had crashed a dumbwaiter through the floor in the kitchen in an attempt to escape the fetch. He wondered if his dad had discovered the secret cavern beneath the house yet. The house held a lot of secrets, some that he probably didn't even know himself.

Shawn caught movement out of the corner of his eye. He turned to see a man and a woman walking through the yard, past the remains of the fence that had once surrounded the property, and toward the square.

"Who's that?" he asked, indicating the pair with a turn of his head.

"Just a couple of kids, no big deal. Found 'em messing around in the backyard, told 'em to get lost. Said they'd been robbed, but I think they must've been high or something. Girl talked funny."

Shawn stared after their backs, watching them retreat down the street. Something looked almost familiar about the man, from what little he could see of him, but he couldn't quite place what it was. It didn't set well with him that they'd been snooping around the house, but he guessed no harm had been done.

"Say, do you know what Microsoft is?"

"No clue. Why?"

"The boy had it written across the duffel bag he was carrying."

Chapter 26

Brody Huffman cursed his lame leg for the 33rd time that day. It was a struggle to climb the narrow wooden stairs in the old mansion, but he needed to take measurements for the two planned apartments on the third floor. He gritted his teeth against the pain, clenching his jaw in time to the beat of his heart.

He paused on the second story landing to catch his breath, letting the heavy floodlight he'd been carrying settle to the ground. Despite the deep smell of mildew at every turn, the house had held up remarkably well. They had a lot of work ahead of them, to be sure, but unlike many other sites he'd worked on, at least the stability of the infrastructure wouldn't be an issue. He'd checked out the foundation and all the supports and hadn't found a thing wrong with any of them.

If it were up to him, he decided, the first thing he'd do would be to install railings on both sets of stairs. He looked up the staircase and sighed. A dozen steps behind him and a dozen more to go, 24 in all. For the most part, he got around fine, but stairs were always a hindrance to him and had been since Korea, and lugging all this equipment didn't help.

He bent to retrieve his tool belt, but a noise at the top of the stairs—metal against metal, he thought—caught his ear. More ghosts? He rolled his eyes at the thought. He didn't believe in ghosts, but he'd seen enough strange occurrences at the site in the last two weeks to at least make him consider changing his mind.

He snatched up the floodlight and, hand against the wall for support, slowly began to climb the stairs. The steps ended in a landing that opened up into a huge, empty room. Shawn had told him that it used to be a ballroom, but he couldn't fathom climbing two flights of stairs just to spend an hour or two waltzing. After that, who could ever find the energy to follow the stairs back down again?

Brody sat down the battery-powered floodlight in the corner of the room and switched it on, flooding the room with an eerie orange glow. They'd turned the electricity on over a week ago, and though most everything else had worked, the third floor remained dark. None of the light fixtures would turn on, despite him completely rewiring every one of them.

All of the windows were open, but even that light seemed absorbed by the darkness that spread from the center of the room. He intended to use the floodlight so he could more easily mark off the room, but first he wanted to satisfy his curiosity and track down the noise he'd heard a few minutes ago. Afraid the harsh glare might scare whatever was up here away, he decided to stick to the flashlight for the time being.

He crept along the floor, wincing as every third or fourth floorboard seemed to creak beneath his weight. What if those kids had managed to sneak up here? If they had, he wanted to get the drop on them. He swept the light across the floor, catching sight of something metallic. He moved closer, kneeling down to get a better look. It was a necklace, a bright silver chain with a round star attached to its length. Little colored stones adorned each point of the star. It reminded him of the huge marble monstrosity in the center of the room, inlaid into the otherwise-beautiful rich cherry wood floor, because it also sported a star, albeit a much larger version.

Scooping up the necklace, he marveled at the way the light made it twinkle against his rough palm. He noticed a red fleck of paint on the chain, but other than that the piece looked brand new. It wasn't tarnished at all, so someone must have dropped it recently. He'd have to ask around. He knew Shawn and Jenny had been through the house once or twice, so maybe one of them would know.

He shoved the jewelry into one of the pockets of his gray work pants before crossing the room to set up the floodlight. There, that was much better. Light flooded the room, banishing whatever ghosts of the past might remain into only the darkest corners of the floor. Finally, he could get some work done. He clicked off his flashlight, looping it through his tool belt, and pulled out a measuring tape and a piece of white chalk.

The room was smaller than he'd thought, just 40x42 feet with a bathroom off the south side and the stairs going down from the north. The marble monstrosity wasted four square feet of that space, in the exact center of the floor. He wondered what it was going to take to rip it out. He dreaded damaging the floor but knew that eventually Mr. Spencer would want it yanked up and hauled out.

He pulled a hammer from his tool belt and headed for the star, intent on testing how embedded into the floor it really was. He knelt beside the marble, his bad leg creaking with the effort. The floodlight went dark the moment his hammer touched the ground.

"Shit!" he cursed, dropping the hammer and measuring tape and fumbling with his flashlight. And then the room was light again.

"Probably a short," he mumbled, chuckling softly when he realized he was talking to himself. He was starting to turn into his old man, who had conversed deeply with himself on a wide range of topics until the day he died.

He shook his head, reaching for the hammer he had dropped. His fingers found only air. The hammer had disappeared. The measuring tape was right where he'd dropped it, on the edge of the circle, but the hammer was gone. Brody fell back on his ass, quickly backing away from the center of the room. Talking to himself be damned, he had more important things to worry about. Three, six, nine, twelve, fifteen, eighteen, he counted inside his head, trying to still the bad feeling that settled in the pit of his stomach.

He clambered slowly to his feet, scanning the area for the missing hammer. It was nowhere to be found. Tools couldn't just disappear. It had to be somewhere. He shook his head, feeling a long, slow shiver begin to work its way up his spine. Cursing silently to himself, he limped to the staircase and began the long descent back down the stairs and to his car for another hammer.

Chapter 27

By the time they got to the Hotel Carthage, Ben had found nearly twelve dollars in change and a brand new, crisp ten dollar bill. He would have preferred twenties to the quarters and dimes, but he'd take what he could get. Between that and the two-dollar bills he'd lifted from his dad's safe, the money they had left over from 1975, and a 1977 ten-spot Ben had found in his wallet, they had a little over 80 dollars.

They could have stayed in the Starlight for half the money, but they both felt it would be better to be as close as possible to the house, and Randolph Street was just three blocks away. Ben was certain he could count on his luck to get them through, just like he always had. He knew he had a twenty dollar bill in his future, and was sure there were more where that came from. And they'd managed to get the same room they'd had in 1975, which Ben took as a sign that maybe things were starting to go their way.

"So how are we going to get into the house?" Katy asked him, lying back on the bed with her feet in his lap.

He massaged the soles of her feet, eliciting little moans of pleasure in response. "There are three potential ways in. The first is through the caved-in hole in the ground that used to be the garage, though there's a chance it's unusable because of the wreckage. And then there's the cellar, the way my dad and Tanner got into the house in the first place. And if none of those options end up working, well, we can always just break in."

"Great, that's what we need, to go to jail for B&E in 1977. I'm sure they'd think our crazy futuristic driver's licenses were just lovely."

"'Breaking and entering?" Ben asked.

"Yeah, breaking and entering. Sorry, I learned a lot of useless cop lingo from my dad. And from cop shows on TV too, I guess." She shot him a self-deprecating smile.

"Ah, you finally remember your dad being alive?"

"You bet. My other memories about not having a sister and my father dying when I was a little girl... I still remember them, but it's like they've faded to the back of my mind, like something I read a long time ago that didn't stick with me." Her face suddenly lost color and she sat up in bed.

"What's wrong?"

"Ben, if we succeed, then it'll be like none of this ever happened. If we stop the past from being changed, then we'll never have had the need to go back in time and fix it. What if I forget you? What if I forget us?"

"Then I'll just have to make you remember," he said, crawling across the bed to kiss her. "I don't think it'll happen, though."

"Why not? What's to stop me from forgetting all about you?" She smiled coquettishly, wrapping her arms around his waist.

"Do you want the real answer," he said between kisses, "or the smart-ass one?"

"Surprise me," she murmured, delicately trailing her fingernails down his bare back.

"I think it's like we're outside of time. I think whatever happens, for us, happens. There's the past, the present, and we're in the space between. You know, whatever happens in Las Vegas stays in Las Vegas. Otherwise, there'd be a paradox. If we stop the murders from happening then there's no need for us to go back in time, and so they happen until we fix them, in which case we don't need to fix them, et-cetera, etcetera, ad nauseum. Do you see what I'm getting at?"

"Yeah, I guess so," she said, biting at his lower lip, teasing it with her tongue. "So, what's your smart-ass answer?"

"I won't let you," he said. "I'm pretty persistent, remember?"

"How could I ever forget? So come on, doofus. It's been, like, what, two years since we last made out? What's a girl gotta do to get your attention?"

"You know," he said, kissing her fully on the lips, "I think you just did."

Chapter 28

Reverend David Allan Dowd's ragtag caravan of trucks, vans, and motorcycles pulled into Carthage just before six that night, parking in an open field beside the Carl Sandburg College and across the street from Ruskin's Pizzeria. They'd managed to break down their tents and stages in record time, and everyone was exhausted. The Reverend, however, was ecstatic and full of energy. He'd waited over two years to smite the Anti-Christ and his whore, and he was this close to doing it. All he had to do was find them.

As tired as everyone was from loading and unloading the vans, there was a certain buzz in the air, as if they all knew that something important was about to happen. Soon, he wanted to tell them. Soon, my flock, the Lord's enemies will be vanquished and the path will be clear for Jesus to once again walk the Earth, and then the rapture will begin. Stick with me, he wanted to tell them, and you'll spend eternity at the knee of the Almighty.

Satan's night would soon be upon them. October 31st, All Hallows Eve, the day when the dead would once again walk the Earth. And that was the day on which he'd strike, the day that the Anti-Christ and his minions would least expect. That was the day he would send them all back to hell.

"Dad," said the southern genteel voice of Jim Felt, a weathered 65-year-old veteran of the second World War. "Can I have a word with you for a minute?"

His face was tight as leather, made dry and papery from years working under the sun in Florida. He'd joined the ministry almost eight years ago and had quickly proven to be one of his most trusted disciples.

"What can I do for you, Jim?" he asked, laying a huge hand across the man's shoulders.

Jim had been an alcoholic when he'd first come to the ministry, but with the Lord's help Dowd had been able to get him off the bottle. He'd been clean and sober ever since.

"Well," he said, looking over his shoulder at a handful of the faithful, "everybody missed breakfast, and some of the boys are getting a mite antsy. You know, moving this way and that way at a moment's notice. A couple of folks had kin in Iowa and were looking forward to seeing them before plans changed. No disrespect intended, Reverend."

"Of course not, of course not," Dowd said, nodding thoughtfully, though a part of him yearned to tell Felt everything.

They were so close! But, as always, patience was a virtue, and virtue was its own reward. Still, he felt giddy, and couldn't help smiling.

"Reverend," Felt whispered, "are you all right? The flock will survive, but it's you I'm worried about. You haven't really been yourself since this morning. Can you tell me, what are we looking for here? Will more folks be joining us?"

"I can tell you this," he said, in a conspiratorial tone, "by the time we're finished with our good work in Carthage, a lot more people will see what we're really all about. And they'll open up their hearts to the Lord, just like you did, Jim, and let Him inside and His light will fill them to bursting. All that will happen, I promise you, Jim, and soon, very soon, the rapture will be upon us."

"Praise the Lord," Felt drawled, his eyes wide in wonder. "And God bless you, Reverend. It's just what I was telling 'em. Stick with Dad, and he'll never let you down."

"No, Jim," he said, "I'm just a vessel. Stick with the Lord, and He shall provide. But there is something that I can do."

He reached into his pocket and pulled out an old leather wallet. Donations had been down, but they'd been flush since he'd liberated the Oriental wizard of his money clip all those months ago. All told, they had over three thousand dollars in the coffer. He peeled two fifties from his wallet and folded them into the man's tanned hands.

"We need to celebrate, Jim. Today is a day for rejoicing, for our quest is coming near to an end. Take a few of the boys with you and pick up a dozen or so pizzas and a few cases of Coke, as much as that money will buy you. That should help to raise everybody's spirits. A man can hear the Lord's message a little easier on a full stomach." He winked with his one good eye and clapped Felt on the shoulder.

"Consider it done," Felt said, slipping the fifties into the pocket of his worn blue jeans. "I'll round up Oscar and one of the Tyler twins and we'll feed these good folks in style. God bless you, Reverend."

"He already did, my friend," said Dowd as he watched Felt weave through the crowd in search of helpers, "and I'm about to repay the favor."

* * *

"A large with everything, chief," yelled Marianne Sandling, shoving a ticket through the order window, "and two small salads, one Ranch and one Western."

"Got it," said Fred Ruskin.

Ruskin tossed a glob of pizza dough high into the air, caught it on the way down, spun it on his hand, and flung it back into the air only to repeat the process all over again.

He'd learned the art of pizza tossing from his uncle Salvador many years ago but had only recently returned to the practice. He and Candy had opened Ruskin's Pizzeria a year ago, using the money from Molly's insurance policy. He'd refused to touch the cash for sixteen years, and by the time he got around to calling the investment banker he'd left it with it had grown from a respectable $200,000 into a whopping three-hundred-and-fifty grand.

It was his wife's final gift to him. He'd used the lion's share of the money to start the Molly Ruskin and Tanner McGee Memorial Victim's Fund, a charity that helped the families of victims of violent crimes, and used most of what was left to buy the old Morgan Oil building and start his new business. He'd also invested twenty-five grand in various stocks and bonds in case the business went under, but right now business was booming. In fact, he was enjoying the restaurant so much that he never even thought about his former career in law enforcement. Well, almost never.

But making pizzas had been better to him than police work had ever been. He'd lost his first wife and eleven-year-old daughter to a serial killer in Chicago, and had spent the next fifteen years in a drunken haze. It was only through the grace of God that he'd met Candy Martin and managed to get his act together enough to help his niece and her boyfriend save the world from total annihilation.

Okay, maybe that was a bit melodramatic, but he shuddered to think what the old man would have done if they hadn't found a way to stop him. The whole thing still gave him nightmares, but he wouldn't change his involvement for all the marinara sauce in Italy. It had saved his life, in more ways than one, and had given him a family again.

He had met two angels that summer, one named Candy and the other named Michael, and in their own unique way each had given him wings. He knew now that God existed, and that buoyed his spirit and gave him purpose if not religion. Other than his nephew's funeral and the day he got married, he hadn't stepped foot inside a church since Molly had died and he saw no need to break the pattern.

Jenny had, upon occasion, asked him why he didn't go to church. "I once shook the hand of an angel," he always replied, "how much closer can you get to God than that?" Church was for people who needed to be convinced, and he no longer needed convincing. For him, it was as simple as that.

He slammed the pizza down onto the huge wooden counter that made up the bulk of the kitchen. The crust was ready for the sauce and the toppings, and within fifteen minutes another table of happy patrons would be served a piping hot pizza with everything. Feeding the hungry was a noble profession, he decided, even if it didn't put criminals behind bars. And it was definitely better than serving bench warrants and writing out parking tickets.

He poured sauce over the dough, spreading it evenly over the pizza with a wooden ladle. Next he covered it in a generous layer of cheese before adding the beef, pepperoni, mushrooms, onions, and a half a dozen other ingredients into the mix. Finally another layer of cheese and it was ready to be fired. He scooped up the pie with his long hardwood peel and carefully slid it into the hot brick oven.

He glanced at the clock over the counter. It was a quarter to three, which meant Mike Horner would be coming in soon to spell him for the evening shift. Horner was still an amateur when it came to tossing pies, but he was learning. The kid was a good worker and seemed eager to learn the fine art of pizza making, and he knew he could count on him, rain or shine, to always show up for his shifts.

"Hey chief," said Mike, stepping through the swinging French doors that separated the kitchen from the rest of the restaurant.

He was early, as usual, and already wearing his apron and hairnet. Ruskin started to call out a greeting until he noticed a look of consternation on the kid's normally jovial face.

"What's the matter?" he asked.

"More business than we can handle." he said. "I came in through the front today and overheard Clancy taking an order for a dozen larges. Don't they usually call big orders like that into us in advance?" He handed the order ticket to Ruskin.

"Usually," Ruskin said, looking at the other tickets that hung above the order window. Because it wasn't yet time for the dinner rush the orders were pretty light, but he knew Mike couldn't handle a dozen pies all by himself. "Tell you what. I'll stay as long as we need to get the job done."

"Are you sure?" asked Mike, relief evident in his voice.

"Yeah, I'm sure," he said, dropping the ticket on the counter. He could handle another hour of work, though Candy wasn't going to be happy. They'd promised to take Sam across the river to the Keokuk mall. "But I am going to take a break to head up front and find out who ordered all these pies."

* * *

"So, do you have a permit?" asked Ruskin.

He stood by the front counter with the man who'd just ordered a dozen large pizzas. The pies, he said, were for the churchgoers even now gathering in the huge empty lot across the street. According to the man, who gave his name as Jim Felt, there were nearly thirty members of the traveling ministry, and their reverend was a man named David Dowd. Two other members of their flock, a Hispanic boy named Oscar Reyes and a young red-headed kid named Teddy Tyler, had come along to help carry the food.

"Does the Lord need permission to step foot on the ground He created?" Felt answered with a twang. "Did Jesus ask permission to speak in Rome? The Reverend answers to a higher authority."

"So, I'll take that as a 'no'," Ruskin said. He wasn't the Sheriff anymore, so it wasn't his problem. Let Jesse Floyd sort it out.

"You should come to the revival on Sunday, Mr. Ruskin. Let the Lord into your heart. We can all be saved, if we only let the Spirit inside."

He sounded like an automaton to Ruskin, preprogrammed to take in and spit out whatever this Dowd character fed him. Already he didn't like the reverend and he hadn't even met him yet.

"I'll be sure to check it out," he said, lying. "But right now, I'd better get back to the kitchen so we can get started on your order. Just have a seat, and we'll get them out to you as soon as we can. Mary Anne," he said, motioning to one of the waitresses, "will get you some sodas, on the house."

He didn't feel like getting into a philosophical debate right now, especially when it might involve losing business. He'd learned that lesson the hard way when he'd debated a group of Mormons right out of his restaurant, leaving two half-eaten pizzas and a $30 tab behind them.

"Much obliged, Mr. Ruskin," Felt drawled, the papery skin around his mouth crinkling into a smile. "Much obliged. We surely do appreciate your hospitality, and look forward to sampling your wares."

Chapter 29

Shawn stared at the clock. It was nearly five, and he hadn't heard from Jenny all day. He tried calling her twice, and both times her mother had said she was busy and then more or less hung up on him. He didn't understand what was going on. Between Jenny's odd behavior and the kids hanging around the old house, he was starting to worry that someone was after the nickel again.

He pried open the loose floorboard beneath his bed and pulled out a big Mason jar full of pennies. He shifted the container from hand to hand, enjoying its weight. Slowly turning the lid, he let all 555 wheat pennies fall to the blue comforter stretched across his bed. And there, at the center, gleamed a 1931 Buffalo head nickel.

He plucked the coin from the pile, feeling electricity spark through his system. It had been like that ever since the summer of '75, when he'd used the combined power of the nickel and the other four talismans to heal himself and his friends. It was almost like the nickel recognized him and wanted him to use it. It was a scary feeling, and one he had a hard time ignoring.

He knew the coin wasn't malicious—it was just a tool and could be used for both good and evil—but a part of him had longed to take the power that the demon Azazel had offered him, to use it to bring his dead friend back to life, even knowing that it would corrupt him and forever separate him from everyone around him. It was a paradox; use the magic to help the people you loved, only to lose the capacity to love those very same people.

When he'd held the magic of the five objects combined, he'd felt more than human; he felt like a God. And in that instant, he'd almost lost everything he cared about. Only Jenny's love had saved him, but not before he'd used the power to heal all of them of their wounds, to cure Jenny's eyesight, and to bring Fred Ruskin back from the brink of death.

He wondered about that sometimes. Once you'd held such power in your grasp, had the world for your taking, could you ever truly go back? But he had gone back. In fact, he'd hardly even touched the coin since he hid it in the jar beneath his floor that same summer. Michael had entrusted him with the nickel, had faith in him to keep it safe, to do the right thing. That, combined with Jenny's love, had kept him sane. But he'd wondered these last two years how he'd feel if he ever again held that much power in his hands.

Just holding the nickel was enough to bring it all back again. He concentrated, centering himself, and the magnetic pull of the power lessened and finally disappeared. He didn't need it, because he had enough already. He'd use the nickel if he had to, to protect Jenny, his family, and even the coin itself, but that was enough. After all, he was its guardian, and that was his job. And now that he'd verified that the nickel was safe, he would put it away again.

He had scooped half of the pennies back into the jar when the phone rang. His parents were playing bridge with the Merediths, so he slipped the nickel into his pocket and went to answer the phone.

"Shawn?" It was Jenny, and he could tell she'd been crying.

"What's wrong?" he asked immediately. "I've been trying to reach you since yesterday, but your Mom wouldn't let me talk to you."

"We need to talk, in person."

"Okay, so let's talk. Are we still on for tonight?" The phone went silent. "Jenny?"

"I'm here, I'm just thinking. It's cold, but can we go to the park? We really need to talk."

"Sure. I can come pick you up right now. I'll be there in five minutes." His heart raced. What did she want to talk about that they couldn't do over pizza and Pepsis at Ruskin's?

"No, I'll meet you there." Her voice sounded cold, resigned.

"Jenny, it's freezing outside. I don't know what's wrong, but just let me come over and pick you up and we'll talk it through."

"Shawn, do you love me?"

What a strange question. "Of course I love you. With all of my heart."

"If that's true, then meet me at the park." She hung up without another word.

His heart sank. How could she ever doubt that? Something was definitely wrong, and for the life of him he had no idea what. With only Jenny on his mind, he grabbed his winter jacket and his car keys and walked out the door, forgetting entirely about the pennies spread over his bed and the nickel in his pocket.

* * *

He waited at the park for thirty minutes before she showed up, her teeth chattering against the cold as she rode her bicycle into the park.

"Jesus, Jenny," he yelled, leaping up from the picnic bench to run to her side. "Why didn't you just let me pick you up?"

He could see she'd been crying. Delicate crystal tears were frozen to her cheeks, and her eyes were red from the wind. She wore a flimsy pullover jacket and no gloves or hat. He was amazed she hadn't turned into an icicle on the ride over from her house.

"Here, put this on." He tried to drape his jacket around her shoulders, but she shrugged it away. "Okay, can we at least sit in my car and turn on the heat?"

"I j-j-just need to know," she said, teeth chattering, "did you have s-s-sex with Kristen?"

His mind reeled. Why on Earth would she ask him something like that? "Never in a million years," he said, putting his hands on her shoulders, "even if she didn't annoy the living hell out of me. I'm in love with you, Jenny. You. Why are you asking me this?"

"She told me, Shawn," Jenny said, backing away from him, "she told me that you had sex with her yesterday when you drove her home to get her homework. She said you told her I wouldn't 'put out' and that you wanted her." Fresh tears welled up in her eyes, and Shawn's heart ached.

"God, Jenny. If she said that, then she's lying. I've never had sex with anyone, and, other than you, someday, I don't intend to. I have the most beautiful, smartest, sweetest girl in the world. Why would I ever want anyone else?"

"That's what I've been telling myself," she said tentatively, but still wouldn't let him touch her. "But why would she lie? She confessed when I showed her the lipstick. She said you guys did it in the back of your car, and..."

"She what?" Shawn said, angry now. "She's lying. I swear to God, Jenny. I took her straight home to get her homework, drove her right back to school, and then I went to Newsland. I was late, you can ask Elaine."

"Yeah, well, wouldn't you have been late if you'd had sex with Kristen? That doesn't prove a thing."

"How can I prove a negative? How can I prove I didn't do something? You just have to believe me, have faith in me. Have I ever lied to you before?" He blinked, saw she was about to speak, and added, "Other than about the fetch? And I didn't half believe that myself."

"Shawn, about the fetch...Kristen said you beat her up when she threatened to tell me about the sex. And she has bruises all over her ribs. When the fetch bit you, it caused you to be so angry..."

"And all that stopped the moment the fetch turned back into Colin Wainwright. Before that, even. And as much as I dislike Kristen—okay, now I absolutely hate her—I'd never hit her. I'd never hit anyone, unless I was forced to."

"You hit Mike Jackson. You broke his nose, if I recall."

Shawn sighed. Why wasn't she listening to him? "We both know he deserved it, and besides I was under the influence of the fetch's blood at the time. I'm not now, and I haven't been for over two years."

"I know. I just…just tell me again, Shawn. Tell me you didn't have sex with her, tell me you didn't hit her, and I'll believe you. God knows I want to believe you. She just sounded so…convincing. And those bruises. She said that you'd been flirting with her and that you made a pass at her that time we went to the movies together in Keokuk."

He hesitated. Everything Jenny said about the Keokuk trip was true, but from his point of view, not Kristen's. Kristen had flirted with him, had slid her hand up his thigh at the movies. He ignored her and hadn't told Jenny, but he realized now that he should have.

She misread his hesitation. "It's true, isn't it?" she whispered, her eyes clouding over with confusion. "God, I am so stupid!" She started to back away again, her eyes darting left and right as if she wanted to run, to be any place that he wasn't.

"No," he said, reaching out to grab her wrists. She struggled against his grip, but he wouldn't let go.

"Just listen! All of those things are true, but I didn't do them. *She* flirted with *me*. *She* came on to *me* at the movies. She hugged me yesterday before you came out for lunch. I just… I should have told you, but I didn't want you to get angry, and I thought if I just ignored her long enough she'd get the message."

"Oh, come on," she said, finally wrenching free from his grasp, "do you really expect me to believe that? That she was the one who came on to you?"

"Yes," he said, "I do. Because, deep in your heart, you know how much I love you, and that I'd never intentionally do anything to hurt you. She's lying, Jenny. I don't know why, maybe because I didn't respond to her advances, but she's lying. I can't prove it, but..." he trailed off, suddenly remembering the nickel. He reached into his pocket and pulled it out, showing it to Jenny. "I can't prove it, but maybe this can?"

"Huh? Why are you carrying that around?"

"It doesn't matter, I'll tell you later. Here, just take it," he said, folding it into her hand. "Use it to compel me to tell the truth. Like Wonder Woman's lasso, or something."

She sighed, looking down at the nickel. "No, Shawn. You take it." She handed it back to him. "I don't need it, and magic can't do everything."

He stared at her. "So, that's it, then? You're going to break up with me?"

"Not in a million years," Jenny said, stepping into his arms. She started to cry again. "If I were to use the nickel to force you to tell me the truth, would I be any better than Aupuch?"

"Jenny...none of that matters now," he whispered, "I just want you to believe me. I'll do whatever you want. I don't want to lose you."

She stiffened under his embrace. "That's exactly what she said, except," she sniffled, pulling away from him to look into his eyes, "she called me 'Jen.' She said when you two were... were having sex, you kept calling out my name, kept saying 'Jen' over and over, saying that you loved me."

"I swear to God, Jenny, we never..."

"Hush. I know. The point is she called me 'Jen'."

"So? She always calls you that."

"Yeah, but you don't."

"So you believe me?"

"I do," she said, "but not because of that. Well, maybe that helps. I've just...Shawn, you should have told me about her hitting on you, but this is also my fault. I should have come to you the moment she made those accusations. It was the bruises that made me doubt, made me think of Mike Jackson and the fetch and all of that. Why would she do that to herself?"

"Why would she do any of this? I have no clue, but I'm sure as hell going to find out."

* * *

God fucking damn it! Up until now, things had been going so well. Deception and misdirection always worked like a charm on television. How was she to know that they'd actually get together and talk? They'd never have talked on *Three's Company*. Jack Tripper was always too dimwitted for that, but apparently Jenny and Shawn weren't.

Kristen Hawks hid behind a huge oak tree, eavesdropping. She couldn't hear everything, but she'd heard enough to know that she'd failed. She'd been watching Jenny all day and had followed her to the park for her meeting with Shawn. She'd been so shaken up that she hadn't even noticed Kristen following her in her father's Cadillac.

She immediately knew that she'd screwed up when she told Jenny what Shawn had said in the back of his car. Her one hope was that she hadn't been paying attention, but of course that would have been too good to be true. She'd just been caught off guard and said the first thing that popped into her head. Unfortunately, it had been the wrong thing. She'd said Jen instead of Jenny, and that little slip of the tongue had cost her everything.

But there was still hope. She'd been knocked down, for sure, but by no means was she out. Her plan was still salvageable, even if she had to shake things up a bit. One way or the other, Shawn and Jenny would no longer be a couple come Halloween. She was in love, and love couldn't be denied. Once that moron was out of the picture, they could be together forever.

Her ribs hurt when she breathed. She'd given herself a pounding, slamming a sack of potatoes into her side over and over again until she nearly passed out from the pain, but it was all for nothing. Even with physical proof, Jen didn't believe her. Her slip of the tongue was just icing on the cake. They were too close, and she'd played her hand too early.

She pulled her black suede coat tight around her face, protecting her delicate skin and full red lips from the wind. She was beautiful, and she knew it. She had long, sensuous hair, and a body to die for. Yes, she was beautiful, bruised ribs notwithstanding, but if beauty wasn't going to get her what she wanted, she was more than willing to kill for it. She'd heard that killing someone was easier the second time around, and she was about to find out.

Chapter 30

It was just past midnight when Ben and Katy arrived at the old house, dressed in black and ready for action. Their clothes were courtesy of the swap shop and blended perfectly into the night. The air was cool and crisp and filled their nostrils with the promise of rain. The evening news had predicted snow for tomorrow and if the low nighttime temperature was any indication, this was one weather prediction that might actually come true.

It was amazing to think that this was where it had all started. His father and his dead uncle Tanner had broken into the house two years and a lifetime ago, and now he was following in their footsteps.

Katy stood guard by the cellar door as Ben tried to clear his mind. He usually didn't even have to make an effort to use his abilities; things just happened. The lottery machine just happened to produce the right numbers; he just happened to come across a wallet filled with cash and no ID. Things just happened for him.

If he tried, that's when things fell apart.

"What's taking so long?" Katy whispered, dropping to a crouch beside him.

"I don't know," he said. "Let me keep trying." He finally found the combination on the fifth try. "Katy, this is seriously fucked. This just doesn't happen to me."

"Definite weirdness," she agreed. "But still, it's open now. Let's get inside before I lose my nerve."

"You don't have to go," he whispered. "Maybe you should stay out here and keep watch."

"Are you kidding me? It's just as creepy out here. Don't worry, I'll be all right."

"I promise, I won't let anything happen to you."

"My hero," she said. "Come on, let's get this over with."

Ben pulled at the old door, wincing as it slowly creaked open. He switched on one of the flashlights they'd bought at the Ben Franklin before walking down the concrete steps.

"Looks like someone cleaned down here," Katy whispered, sweeping her flashlight across the empty cement floor. Her beam rested on an old wood furnace, the only occupant of the otherwise empty cellar.

He was already moving up the interior stairs to the door that separated them from the house beyond. This one wasn't locked. He pushed open the door, stepping past the threshold into the house.

This room, a kitchen, was also empty, and smelled strongly of age and mildew. The space around them was huge and echoed with their every footstep. The floor was covered with a cracked and grimy tile, while the walls, once white, were colored a sickly brown. All of the cabinets and appliances had been removed, leaving only empty spaces and slightly less-grimy floor or wall spaces in their wake.

"I guess your grandfather ripped everything out," Katy said, shining her flashlight through the room and into the dining area beyond. "I'm not sure what we're going to find here anyway." She hugged herself. "Damn, it's cold."

"Michael said the evil originated in the house."

"Great," she said. "If the evil won't come to us, we'll go to the evil. Great plan, doofus."

"Hey, I do what I can," he said, walking across the tile and into the dining room.

Chalk lines separated various parts of the house into quadrants, and Ben assumed the work an early attempt to divide the floor into smaller living areas. He had been to the apartments a few times in the future and knew that the first two floors were divided into four individual apartments, so it was strange to see everything still connected.

As they started to climb the front stairs to the second floor, he noticed Katy hesitate. He knew she had dreamed about the house only the night before and wished again that she hadn't come. The dreams were dangerous—the cut across her hand proved that—and he could only imagine that whatever was really inside the house was doubly so.

He reached out to take her hand and they entwined their fingers together. "Are you sure you want to go up there?" he asked, turning to look into her eyes. Her face was as white as a sheet.

"I'm okay," she said, "let's just get this over with so we can go home."

He thought about the nickel in his pocket and the pentacle that hung from his throat. He had his magical bases covered, and the handgun hidden in the waistband of his jeans would hopefully serve to protect them against more mundane threats.

"Okay, then," he finally said, stepping onto the staircase.

The stairs creaked beneath their weight, but otherwise felt sturdy if tenuous. They quickly ascended the staircase, avoiding spiders and other assorted creepy crawlies that had sought shelter from the cold. The second floor more closely resembled the stories his father had told him than did the first, which probably meant that they hadn't done much work up here yet.

"It's...beautiful," Katy said the moment they walked into the studio.

She stood transfixed, staring at an oil painting of a man in Renaissance clothing caught in a silent scream. Like a marionette controlled by an unseen puppeteer, strings stretched from the man's hands and feet to somewhere off the edge of the canvas.

"Damn scary, more like it," Ben said. "That thing's in my attic, and I used to have nightmares about it when I was a little kid." The painting was chilling and emitted an uncontrollable sense of rage and frustration.

"Yeah," she admitted, "but the brushstrokes, the composition. It's amazing. Colin Wainwright did this?"

Ben shrugged, reaching down to snatch a wooden toy monkey from the floor. The thing's eyes seemed to follow him no matter which way he held it. "As far as I know, he made all this stuff. The guy must've had some serious issues." He sat the monkey back down again.

They searched the room from top to bottom but found nothing that seemed the least bit threatening. They had just stepped into the hallway when Ben heard a deep growl from further down the hall.

"Did you hear that?" Katy whispered, grabbing his arm.

He'd heard it, and there it was again. Ben maneuvered her behind him and slowly crept further down the hallway. "Stay back," he whispered, putting a hand on the gun inside his waistband.

They heard the growl again, like the angry snort of some wild animal. They stood outside of a huge bedroom, with the door open just a crack. The growls were coming from inside.

"This is just like in my dreams," Katy said.

Another snort, this one raspy and wet, echoed through the hallway. Whatever it was, it was just on the other side of the door. "Stand back," he warned her, letting go of her hand as he pulled the gun from his jeans.

He'd seen them do this hundreds of times on television. He turned his back to the wall beside the door and held the gun out in front of him.

"You have a gun?" she said. "Where did you get a gun?"

Ignoring her, he reached around the door frame and pushed the door open, quickly spinning on his heels to point the gun into the room. It was empty save for an old wooden dresser, a big oak nightstand, and a rotting four-poster bed. His heart thrummed wildly in his chest as he stepped across the threshold and into the bedroom.

There was nobody there. He could feel the tension release in his shoulders. Maybe it had just been the wind. He started back through the door just as a huge snorting growl echoed through the room.

"Shit!" he yelled, stumbling back into the wall. He struck the back of his head with a loud thump, his vision swimming as he tried to focus on the room.

Something was in the bed. A thin, wraith-like creature sat up from the tattered mattress, its long white matted hair falling down around its eyes. It grimaced at him with a mouth full of yellowed teeth and said something unintelligible, then shook a bony fist in his direction.

The gun went off in his hand, fire blazing out the barrel. The recoil threw his aim off, and the bullet struck the wall just a foot above the creature's head. The wraith ducked down, hands over his head, cowering among the tattered covers.

"Jesus, man," screamed a voice from the bed, "are you trying to kill me?"

Ben shook his head, holding the gun at his side. Had the creature just spoken? He took a tentative step toward the bed, first one foot and then the other, blinking against the shadows that fought the beam from his flashlight.

"Ben, are you all right?" Katy's voice carried around the corner, but he ignored it.

He'd just come a hair's width from taking a human life. He pointed the beam closer toward the cowering form under the covers.

"Who are you?"

"Jeremiah Watson. Please don't hurt me. I didn't steal nothing, I just didn't have nowhere else to go." He held out a bony hand, waving it in a sign of peace.

"Ben, what's going on?" Katy peered around the corner.

Jeremiah Watson. Why did that name sound familiar? "It's okay," he said to the man, slipping the gun into his waistband. "Come on out, I'm not going to hurt you."

"Ben?" Katy said, coming up behind him. "You're shaking. What's going on?" Her body went stiff as her eyes fell on the old man's head poking through the blankets. "Is that the killer?"

"Jeremiah Watson," Ben whispered. "Just some harmless old man, and I almost shot him."

"Do you work for McGee?" the old man asked, his watery blue eyes moving back and forth between Ben and Katy.

The man's face was a wealth of wrinkles, and thin wisps of white hair trailed down his head and covered his eyes. He looked as though he hadn't bathed in weeks.

Watson was the name of the drifter who'd been mentioned in the *Journal-Pilot* article from 1987, the one initially suspected of murdering his grandfather. The man looked old and frail, but looks could be deceiving. His hand instinctively went to his waist, feeling the hard metal of the gun underneath.

"Because if you do," the old man said, "I didn't mean no disrespect to him, and I'm sorry I raised cane. I just needed the work, man. Times are hard, and I needed the work."

"What're you doing in here?"

"I snuck in when they was working. Figgered if they couldn't offer me a job, the least they could do was put me up for a little while." Arms still in the air, Watson wearily rose from the bed.

The old man wore a pair of threadbare jeans and a stained sweatshirt that hung from his skeletal frame. His feet were bare. No wonder his grandfather hadn't hired him; he looked like he might snap in half if forced to carry anything heavier than the clothes on his back. He didn't look like a threat, and the police had exonerated him for the crime that had yet to even be committed. Ben motioned for him to lower his hands. There was no way this man could kill his grandfather.

"So what've you been eating?" Ben asked him.

"Stole some food from that guy with the limp. Been having a fun time with him, moving his shit around," The old man said, air lisping through his missing teeth. "Don't tell him, though."

"Wouldn't dream of it," Ben said, remembering their encounter with Brody Huffman. Between the old man's tricks and he and Katy's appearance this morning, the poor guy probably thought he was going nuts.

"Now you wouldn't happen to have a drink, would you?" Watson reached deep into the blankets and pulled out a dented flask. "Ran out today and I'm getting a little shaky."

"You can't stay here," said Katy, suddenly finding her voice. "And the alcohol isn't helping your job search one bit, you know."

The old man looked down at his feet. "Yeah, I know. Look, can I stay here until morning?"

Ben considered this. Tomorrow was Sunday, and he didn't think anyone would be coming in to work. "Sure," he nodded, finally moving his hand away from his waistband. "But you need to be gone before the sun rises. Understood?"

"Yeah, boss, I got it," said Watson, shrugging his bony shoulders. "Just don't shoot at me again, okay?"

* * *

He couldn't believe it. He ran everything through his mind again, and he couldn't believe it. He'd nearly killed an innocent man tonight, just some poor soul trying to stay out of the cold. His hands shook and he felt nauseated.

"It's okay," Katy said, kneeling beside him on the big hotel bed. "You didn't hurt him."

"But I almost did. I don't know what the hell I'm doing. I'm in way over my head here. I finally see—finally see!—why you didn't want to have anything to do with me. I don't know what got into you to change your mind."

"You did," she said, reaching out to touch his knee, "you got into my heart." That earned her a brief smile.

"I'm just… I rely on my luck too much, just because that's easier. If there's a choice between hard work and chance, nine times out of ten I'll just roll the dice and see where it takes me."

"And I'm a bit of a flibbertigibbet. I buy expensive clothes and shoes, and I spend way too much on both. So? Does that make me a bad person, too?"

"Of course not. But, Katy, I've never worked a day in my life for anything. I didn't ask to be given this magic, this gift, but boy have I taken advantage of it. And then I go off on this amazing adventure half-cocked, not sure what I'm doing. I could have killed him. Hell, I could have killed myself, or even you."

"But you didn't," she said, holding his head in her hands, touching her forehead to his. "You didn't, and we're on this 'amazing adventure' together, to get our lives back. What else could we have done?

"And the reason I didn't want to have anything to do with you, although that's not exactly how I'd put it, had everything to do with me and very little to do with you. I was scared. I still am. I've been alone all my life, at least inside my head. It's hard to let somebody in, especially somebody I care about as much as you."

He looked at her, not understanding. "Why?"

"Because I don't want to lose you, doofus, and because I'm scared of you getting to know the real me and not liking what you see."

"I've already told you that could never happen."

"Yeah, and I'm finally starting to believe it," she said, squeezing his hand. "I'm sorry I was such a shit to you about the whole age thing.

I'm still nervous about that, to be honest, but I can't deny there's chemistry between us. I can't say I'm in love with you because, well, I'm just not ready for that yet. But I think I could be, and I hope that means something to you. I definitely want to see where this goes, once we're back in our own time."

"It does mean something," he whispered, pulling her into an embrace. "So let's quit feeling sorry for ourselves and do what we came here to do so we can start working on that. Deal?"

"It's a deal," she murmured into his shoulder, holding him tight. "It's definitely a deal."

Chapter 31

The killer slept fitfully, tossing and turning, dreaming of the life that would be lost on Halloween night. He stood just outside the home of Paul McGee, a long butcher's blade in one hand and a length of rope in the other. The ground was covered in a fine new snow, and snowflakes danced and circled in the air all around him. The killer stuck out his tongue, feeling almost giddy as a tiny crystalline flake floated down to dissolve immediately in the warmth of his saliva.

He wouldn't enjoy taking the life, nor would it make him sad; it was just something that needed to be done, that he felt compelled to do, like taking a piss or breathing. He needed to take the life, needed to watch the light fade from McGee's eyes as he slowly drew the blade across his throat, needed to feel the man's weight in his arms as he hoisted the lifeless body onto his shoulders and strung him up from the top of the garage.

He knew he was dreaming, just as he knew that he would make the fantasy real in only three days' time. He wasn't ashamed of these feelings. They were just a part of him, as natural as eating or sleeping. He glanced down at the blade again, brought the tip to his mouth, and pricked the end of his tongue. Sharp. Blood ran down the length of the metal, dripping to the snow at his feet. He was ready.

This was the second night in a row he'd had the dream, but he knew the details by heart and felt as though he'd been living them forever. The dreams felt more like visions, maybe even predictions of the future. McGee would answer the door, surprised but cordial. He'd invite him inside, curious at this strange nighttime visitor. Before the man could utter another word he'd be upon him, sliding the knife deep into his throat, blood spraying the walls in a Rorschach pattern. And then he'd drag him through the living room, past the kitchen, and into the garage.

"Why?" the man would rasp before taking his final, dying breath, remaining still forever after.

The question bothered him. He had no answer, and this made him strangely sad. A man's dying request should always be fulfilled, but he couldn't answer something he didn't know. He'd shrug, the sadness fading as though it had never been. He'd kneel to carefully tie the rope around the man's bare feet before finally hoisting McGee onto his broad shoulders, balancing him there as he tied the rope to the mechanism that opened the garage door.

And then he'd leave. Just like that, as if it had never happened. That was the strangest part. Once the killing was over with, he wouldn't have to think about it ever again. Yes, the killer knew the dream by rote, and soon he'd follow it through into the real world. But tonight, right now, he still needed to practice.

He reached out, his finger poised over the doorbell, but never pressed the button. Something off to the left caught his eye. Curious, he abandoned the house and clumped through the snow to investigate.

It was a door made of frosted glass, illuminated by a shallow light somewhere within. But it wasn't attached to anything. It just floated there, about a foot off the ground, inviting him to enter. It was strangely appealing, this chance to explore a new world. The dreams were tiring, and he was sure he had the pattern down already. Ring the doorbell, go inside, kill, drag, then hang the body. Murder in five easy steps.

He moved closer to the door, feeling the frosted pane. As cold as it was outside, the door felt strangely warm and inviting. He pushed, but it wouldn't budge, and there was no handle or knob that he could see. He smashed the butt of his knife against the door, but nothing happened. This was frustrating. Why had the door appeared if it couldn't be opened?

Mother-fucking cock-sucking door! Didn't it know who he was? This was his dream, and all doors were supposed to be open to him. He slammed a beefy hand into the glass, but it bounced harmlessly back, not even making a crack. His hand hurt, and he was sure he had broken his knuckles. Goddamn fucking door.

He'd deal with it later. He shot the door one last baleful look before turning his back and stalking back up the McGee's sidewalk. He held the knife at his side and rang the doorbell.

* * *

Kristen awoke in a panic, the same as nearly every other morning for the past two weeks. She could feel his hands all over her, searching, his touch filled with desire. And then he was on top of her, doing what he'd always done. She shivered, pushed the memory of the dream out of her mind, and stood up from the king-sized bed.

She slept in the nude, something she'd taken to because she'd grown tired of having to replace the ripped and tattered pajamas. She no longer had to do that, of course, but that would take some getting used to. She looked down, enjoying the sight of her naked body. She ran her hands over her breasts, cupped them, and thumbed her nipples until they were standing erect. She sighed and wrapped a silky bathrobe around herself.

Right now, she wanted nothing more than to lie back on the bed and touch herself; to lose herself in the folds of her body; to think of her soon-to-be lover and what they would do once they were finally together; and to banish the remnants of last night's dream into the darkest recesses of her mind. But she didn't have time. She needed to get showered and ready. She had a full day ahead of her and didn't intend to waste a moment of it.

Chapter 32

It was six-thirty in the morning and Katy couldn't sleep, which was how she found herself walking down the square and through the snow toward The Donut Shop. They still had Space Sticks and Freakies from her sojourn into Super Value two years ago, but she couldn't get the thought of a chocolate éclair out of her head.

The store was open and already doing brisk business. She waited in line for a good ten minutes before finally getting her order—two éclairs, a bear claw, a cinnamon bun, and two white milks. Avoiding the chocolate milk that she so desperately wanted was her one concession to the sheer amount of sugar she'd been taking in since this whole odyssey had begun. After all, a girl had to stay fit.

The snow was coming down harder by the time she left the shop, and she wished for the umpteenth time this morning that she'd thought to buy gloves. She was going to freeze to death before this whole thing was over, if the Halloween Murderer didn't kill her first.

She smiled to herself at the thought of Ben sleeping in their hotel bed, the covers a mass of cotton and polyester wrapped around him like a big blue cocoon. Thinking of him made her heart skip a beat and her stomach turn little flip-flops, and that's when she finally admitted to herself that she was falling in love. She just wasn't quite ready to admit it to him yet.

She was in love with a nineteen-year-old boy. In ten years, their age difference would hardly matter, but now, with her almost ready to get her graduate degree and him not even having started college yet... *Stop it, Katy*, she told herself. *Live in the moment. Carpe diem*, and all that. She was in love, so she might as well enjoy the ride for as long as it lasted. And maybe, just maybe, she'd jump his bones once she got back to their room.

That thought put a spring in her step as she neared the hotel. Her eyes strayed to the dark clouds circling overhead and she nearly ran into a small Hispanic boy tacking a sheet of paper onto a wooden telephone pole.

"Apesadumbrado," the boy said, turning to look at her. "Pardon me, *senorita*. I'm sorry that I wasn't watching what I was doing." Now that she saw his face—he had dark skin and kind brown eyes—she realized he wasn't a boy after all, just a very young man, probably only a year or two younger than she was.

"No problem at all, I had my head in the clouds."

"You want to come?" he asked, giving her one of the mimeographed sheets of paper he held in his hand. It was an advertisement for, of all things, a church revival, to be held the day after tomorrow in the open field across from her father's restaurant.

"Thank you," she said, folding the paper and quickly stuffing it into her purse, quickly dismissing the idea of the revival. She'd been raised without a lot of religious influence in her life, and had grown to prefer it that way. "I hope the weather is nice for your event. It looks like it's going to snow quite a bit."

"Sí, senorita. Gracias. Me too. But the Lord provides. It will be as He intends it to be." He turned to get back to his work, then added, "God bless you, *senorita*."

"Thanks, and good luck with everything," she said as she walked away, chocolate the only religion on her mind.

* * *

Ben was awake by the time she walked into the room. He was sitting up in bed, naked, covered only by a sheet. "I was worried about you. I thought maybe you decided to leave without me."

"And go where?" she asked, tossing the bag of donuts onto the bed. She handed him a carton of milk. "Sorry, I didn't think you'd wake up before I got back."

"Missed you terribly," he said, beckoning for her to come back to bed. She was more than willing to oblige.

She crawled under the covers, and then dug into the white bag of donuts to drag out an éclair. She sank her teeth into the incredibly delicious chocolate pastry, savoring every last luscious bite. "Heaven," she moaned, toasting him with her milk. "Better than sex, even. Well, almost."

"Just almost?" he murmured.

"Just almost," she agreed, shoving a little of the éclair into his mouth. "Yummy?"

"Definitely," he said, licking his lips, "Though not nearly so much as you."

She smiled. "Sex and donuts, it's better than religion any day."

"Huh?"

"Ah, I ran into a guy outside posting an advertisement about a church revival. In the field across from my Dad's restaurant, if you can believe it, and on Halloween, no less, in the middle of a snow. Bet all of ten people show up."

He went rigid. "Are you sure? Tomorrow?"

"Yep," she said, digging into her purse to pull out the mimeograph. "That's what the paper says, five in the afternoon on Halloween. It's all about, and I quote, 'Exposing Satan's lies.' Weirdness, huh?"

Ben leapt out of bed, knocking his half-eaten bear claw to the green shag carpet. "Serious weirdness. Katy, this might just be what we've been looking for." He ran across the room in just his boxer shorts to pull the laptop from his duffel bag.

"What are you talking about? How could this be at all connected to the murders?"

"I don't know," he said, as he powered up the PC, "but I scoured all the *Journal-Pilots* from 1977 and I don't remember reading anything about a church revival. This is new, Katy."

"Yeah, but… c'mon, it's not exactly news, is it? Maybe it just didn't make the paper."

"You've lived here most of your life," he said, "so tell me—when has anything at all that happened in Carthage not shown up in the newspaper?"

"Good point," she said, suddenly interested. If the revival had brought the murderer to town, or somehow inspired someone to commit murder, then it had to be the focal point for the whole mess. But then she thought of something.

"The files on your PC just cover the new timeline, right?"

"Damn it," he yelled, slamming his fist down onto the table. She heard a monotone beeping sound coming from the computer.

"What's wrong? The paper had something about it after all?"

"How would I know?" he asked, shutting the cover of the laptop. "I'm out of power and none of the sockets in this time period seem to be grounded. If I can't plug in, I can't recharge the battery, and so I can't look anything up. We're sunk."

Katy rolled her eyes. "Boy, you are 19, aren't you?"

"What's that supposed to mean?"

"Well, doofus, just because hotel rooms didn't have grounded wall sockets in 1977 doesn't mean that they didn't exist. They do. Large appliances such as washers and dryers were using them years before '77. I think appliance stores sell adaptors, and places like, oh, I don't know…my Dad's restaurant, have the wall sockets."

"Seriously? How do you know?"

"An electrical engineering course I took before I decided to change my major. Learned a lot of interesting history about stuff like that." That earned her a strange look. "Hey, a girl's gotta be handy."

"So how about pizza for lunch?"

"Why, Ben Spencer, are you asking me out on a date?"

"You know, I think I am."

"Our first official date," she said, performing a mock swoon. "I thought you'd never ask."

* * *

Brody Huffman awoke screaming, bathed in a cold sweat. His eyes were wild, and he reached for a machine gun that wasn't there. The Gooks were after him again, lying in wait, ready to pounce at a moment's notice.

They had hunted him through the hills and valleys of Korea and out the other side, where they had finally tracked him down and taken him to ground in the old house he was working to remodel.

But thank God, it was just a dream, and it wasn't even a Gook after all. It had all seemed so real. Instead of a Korean soldier, the thing stalking him had been a huge, black-haired monster with a long snout and blood-red eyes. It had come after him with a murderous rage, pursuing him down a flight of stairs in the old Spencer house, and had finally cornered him in the dining room. It leapt for his throat seconds before he woke up.

"Three, six, nine, twelve, fifteen, eighteen, fifteen, twelve, nine, six, three," he said, reciting the numbers over and over. He multiplied by three until he felt his heart return to normal. He hated the counting, but he hated the dreams even more.

He'd suffered nightmares since the war, but last night's little romp through his subconscious was some seriously scary shit. He rolled over in bed and reached for the bottle of Pabst Blue Ribbon he had left on his nightstand the night before. It was half-full, but he drained it in three long gulps that left him wanting more.

Huffman glanced out the curtained window of his old double-wide trailer; it was barely light out. Snowflakes sparkled through the gleam of the street lights, and he wondered if it was as cold outside as it felt inside. He definitely needed to fix that heater. It only half-worked, but he knew himself well enough to know that he wouldn't get around to fixing the damned thing until it completely crapped out on him.

Sunday was usually his day to sleep late, but there was no way he was going back to bed after that nightmare. Instead he swung his bum leg over the edge of the bed frame, pulled himself up into a sitting position, and hoisted his body out of bed.

Huffman limped to the kitchen, filled a bowl with Kellogg's Sugar Frosted Flakes, and pulled a carton of milk from the refrigerator. He took a long drink and quickly spit it into the sink, nearly gagging at the taste. The shit was expired and smelled like rotten eggs, and tasted even worse. He dumped the milk into the sink, watching in dismay as it came out in clumps. How long had it been sitting in the fridge anyway?

He left the bowl of cereal uneaten on the Formica counter. He never could stand to eat cereal without milk. He rummaged through the refrigerator and cabinets but came up empty. He seriously needed to restock his trailer before it got any colder. His leg was even worse during the winter months, and he didn't relish carrying a bag full of groceries up the steps in -20 degree weather.

With no food in the house and an empty stomach, he guessed he was going out today after all. First to Prairie Winds for coffee and a Danish, and then to Bill's to stock up on groceries.

He took a quick shower, cursing again the heater that had failed him, and then got dressed and was almost out the door when, with a flash of guilt, he remembered the necklace. He doubted it was worth anything, but he wouldn't feel right keeping it if it did indeed belong to somebody else.

He snatched the necklace and the car keys from the hook beside the front door, tapped the door knob three times, and pushed his way out into the snow.

* * *

Shawn thought back to yesterday, wondering what those kids had been up to at the house. If he'd gotten there just a minute sooner, he might have had the chance to ask them. Michael had warned him that others might seek the nickel, so maybe he was a little paranoid when it came to strangers. Still, the thought of anyone sneaking around the house left him unsettled.

He shivered against the frigid morning wind. It had started snowing again late last night, the morning news weathergirl had said, and was expected to continue well past Halloween. There was maybe half an inch of snow on the ground right now, but he could see it floating down all around him. Unless it warmed up, they'd probably have two or three inches by nightfall. He pulled his hooded jacket close around his body before starting up the driveway.

Today was Sunday and so there wasn't much traffic around town. If someone wanted to break into the old house, now would be the perfect time. It wasn't even completely light out yet. He walked the perimeter of the property, looking for signs of a break-in. He stopped when he came to the cellar. He was certain there'd been a lock on the door the last time he'd been here. He felt around in the snow and came up with the combination lock. It wasn't broken, which gave him pause. The combination was 13-82-77, just a random combination of numbers. No one could have guessed it, so perhaps Brody or one of the others had simply forgot to put it back on before going home.

He was about to loop the lock through the metal clasp that separated the door from the frame when he heard a noise coming from inside. He tensed, sliding his finger through the loop of the lock to use as a weapon.

Shawn moved away from the door, pressing himself against the wall to the side of the cellar. He watched as the door creaked open and a white shock of hair poked out through the gap. He was on the intruder in an instant, grabbing him by the back of his shirt and driving him down roughly into the snow.

"Urk," the man shouted, his hands a flurry of movement as he tried to push himself up from the ground. "Please, don't hurt me. I'm leaving just like you said."

Shawn slid atop the man, straddling his back, pushing his face down into the snow. "Who are you?" He demanded, roughly yanking the man's head back when he didn't respond.

"Jeremiah Watson!" he said, wet snow dripping from his face. He was just a wrinkled and frail old man, but Shawn wasn't taking any chances.

"What were you doing in the house?"

"Sleeping, what do you think I was doing? You said I could stay!"

"What are you talking about?" he turned the man over on his back, carefully pinning his arms to his side.

"Oh, you're not you," he said, his eyes a sea of confusion. "Jesus, he must've been your brother, you look so much alike."

"What are you talking about?"

He repeated the story he'd told the previous night, adding the part about the young man and woman who'd nearly shot him to death.

Shawn rolled off the old man and held out a hand to haul Jeremiah Watson to his feet. "Sorry about that," he said, forcing a smile. "But you shouldn't have been in the house."

"I know that, but your brother…"

"I don't have a brother," he said. "What did these two look like?"

The closest he'd ever come to having a brother had been Tanner, and he was long dead. He'd had a sister once, a long time ago, but she'd died, too.

"Like you, I keep telling you that. At least the boy did. Longer hair than yours, I think, but the same color. Six feet, maybe, medium build. He was wearing a sports shirt."

"What kind of sports shirt?"

"Carthage blue balls, I think, or cow bells, or something like that."

"Blue Boys?"

Shawn's heart was racing. There was something going on here, after all. It was the same pair Brody had spotted. What could they be after?

"Yeah, that's it. Carthage Blue Boys. They seemed scared of me at first, almost as much as I was scared of them."

"And the girl?"

"Pretty thing. Brown eyes, I think, and short brown hair."

"Did they say anything else?"

"The girl asked if I was 'the killer,' whatever that meant. I've never killed anyone, I swear to God."

"I believe you," he said, digging into his pocket to pull out a worn leather wallet. He flipped it open and removed half the contents—two crisp, new twenty-dollar bills—and handed both to the old man. "Here, you go find yourself a decent place to stay. In fact, I'll drive you to the Starlight Motel myself. You can probably get three or four nights out of that, plus a little food. Beyond that, you're on your own."

"Thanks, son," he old man said, spit trailing down his chin from the gap between his teeth. "This town hasn't been kind to me, but you sure have."

"Least I could do after practically assaulting you," Shawn said, looking down at the lock in his hand. He closed the cellar door, kneeling to put the lock back into place. "How'd you get inside the house in the first place? Did you overhear someone giving out the combination?"

Watson looked puzzled. "No, I just snuck in while that guy with the limp was eating his lunch a few days ago. Cellar door was wide open. Tried to leave that night and it was locked, so I figgered I'd stay for a while."

How had their mystery visitors managed to get the lock open without breaking it? That didn't make sense, but he had other things to worry about for now.

"Come on," he said, gesturing down the driveway at his old Pacer, "let's get you to that motel, and then I've going to track down those kids and have a talk with them."

Chapter 33

It had been a strange two days but, thankfully, at least he didn't have to go into work today. As a kid hungry for comic books, Shawn had often cursed the fact that Newsland wasn't open on Sunday. Now that he was working there, however, it was a blessing. He intended to use the day to track down the kids Brody had seen at the house, more than likely the very same ones who had confronted Jeremiah Watson, but first he was going to take Jenny to lunch. Their relationship had been damaged by Kristen's lies, and even though he knew that Jenny believed him, things still seemed strained.

The whole Kristen thing was just weird. Could she really be so hot for him that she was willing to destroy her friendship with Jenny just to break them up? He shook his head ruefully at the thought. The sad thing was it had almost worked. He wondered if Jenny had talked to her yet, and what sort of explanation she had come up with to explain her lies. He resisted the urge to stop by Kristin's house for a visit, knowing it would only lead to trouble.

He stood in the library of the old house, thinking about yesterday. Two days ago, life had seemed perfect. He and Jenny were together, and their fathers were working (whether they knew it or not) to banish the horror of what had happened in the house by turning it into something hospitable. But things had definitely changed the moment he found out that someone had gotten inside the house.

True to his word, he'd dropped the old man off at the Starlight, and then drove back to the house to look for clues. He'd spent an hour searching through the mansion but hadn't found any indication that the intruders had taken anything. Then again, if they were after something he didn't know about, how could he tell?

Everything in here was exactly how he'd left it two years ago, books, broken furniture, and all. He could still see his green yo-yo, now covered in a thick caking of dust, resting just past the edge of the top shelf of one of the bookshelves. Maybe it was finally time to reclaim what was his.

He slipped off his brown leather belt and whipped it at the yo-yo. With a snap, the green chunk of plastic spun, slowed, and then teetered on the edge, finally falling into his outstretched palm. He dusted it off and attached it to his middle finger, spinning it at the ground and back up again. It still worked, though his formerly-sharp yo-yo skills were more than a little rusty.

Retrieving the toy brought back memories, and his thoughts soon shifted to the glowing door of light he'd found in the room that had hidden the final set of wards that protected the house. He'd only been there once and had never dared set foot through the door, but the room still gave him nightmares.

He'd stayed away from the house for the better part of two years, but maybe it was finally time to step through the shimmering curtain and find out what was hidden beyond. But not today. It was almost eleven, and he had a lunch date. With Jenny on his mind, he left the library and headed for the stairs.

* * *

Ben and Katy stood outside Ruskin's Pizzeria, across the street from the field full of trucks, vans, and tents. Ben was positive that her father wouldn't remember them from their brief encounter two and a half years earlier, but Katy wasn't so sure.

Shivering, she pulled her jacket close around her and thought again about the inviting warmth inside. "Maybe this wasn't such a good idea after all."

"We're wearing different clothes and, what? We talked to him for ten minutes, tops? Let's just get in and do this. He might not even be here."

"My Mom might."

"So?"

"Well," she said, drawing out the word, "there's something I might have forgotten to tell you."

His eyes grew wide. "I have a feeling this is going to be good."

"That night I walked to Super Value. My mother and sister were shopping, and, well, I might have talked to them for a few minutes."

"Might?"

"Okay, did. Definitely did."

"And…?"

"Well, not much came of it," she said, instantly feeling guilty. She knew she should tell him about the note, but there was nothing much that could be done about it now.

"Well, then it's probably not a problem. And we definitely need to go through the information that's on my laptop," he said, pausing to eye the growing gathering across the street, "so let's just take our chances. What have we got to lose?"

"Famous last words," she said, leaning in to give him a kiss. "But you're probably right. We'll order a pizza, eat, and about halfway through, you get up to use the bathroom. The plug's beside the sink. I remember plugging in the vacuum many times over the years when I would help out during the summers."

"Got it, chief," he said, shifting the duffle bag onto his shoulder. "Are you ready?"

She took a deep breath, held it, and let it out, trying to force herself to relax. "As ready as I'm going to be. Let's go."

They walked into the restaurant. It was just as she remembered it, more or less. The booths, replaced in the late 90s by fake mahogany monstrosities, were back to their original red vinyl, and an old-fashioned jukebox stood in the corner. The carpeting would be replaced several times between now and their time, but the layout, the structure, and even the atmosphere remained mostly unchanged. It was like coming home.

"Can I help you?" asked a young Asian woman that Katy didn't recognize. Like most restaurants, Ruskin's Pizzeria employed a handful of constantly-changing wait staff, and she supposed 1977 had been no exception.

"Table for two, please?" she said, glancing at Ben. She took his hand and together they followed the waitress to a large booth beside one of the windows that overlooked the parking lot.

The waitress laid a red-and-white checkered menu in front of each of them before offering to take their drink orders. They both settled on Pepsis, but let the girl persuade them to share a pitcher which, she explained, would net them four times as much soda for only twice the price.

"Whatever happened to free refills?" Ben asked as soon as the waitress was out of earshot.

Katy shot him a dirty look, kicking him hard under the table.

"Hey," he said. "What was that for?"

"You don't want anyone to overhear us, do you?"

"This from the girl who's made small talk with both her parents a good six years before she was even born?"

"Yeah, yeah…Good point, though. We've got to be more careful."

"More careful about what?" asked a voice from behind them. They turned to see her father, dressed in a long white apron and carrying a pitcher of Pepsi and a tray with two glasses, smiling down at them. "Say, you two look familiar. Have you been in here before? I try to remember all my customer's faces, though I have to admit I'm not nearly as good with names."

She was at a loss for words. She returned his smile, fighting down the urge to bolt from the restaurant. He had changed drastically since the last time they'd seen him. He no longer reeked of tobacco and cheap liquor, had lost a hundred pounds or more, and was clean shaven. More than that, though, he looked happy. Gone was the sadness he'd carried with him that morning at the church. He looked genuinely content, just like the man she'd known all her life.

"We've stopped by once or twice," Ben said, covering for her. "Love your pizza. Can't get enough of it."

That seemed to satisfy the former sheriff. He placed a clear red glass in front of both of them, filling each to the brim with ice-cold Pepsi. He deposited the pitcher at the far end of the table before saying, "That must be it, then." He was about to leave when his eyes strayed to the Microsoft duffel bag at Ben's feet.

"No, I remember now. Two years ago, at Tanner McGee's funeral. I tried to bum a light from you," he said, "but you were fresh out. Don't worry, though. I've long since given up the habit. You know, I've wondered for two years…what's Microsoft?"

Katy blanched. That damned duffel bag was going to be their downfall. Why couldn't he have brought something else instead? This time, it was her turn to cover for him. "It's for a failed line of clothing made with micro-fibers. It was supposed to keep the material soft even after several washings, but I think the company went out of business."

It was a stupid story, but it was the best she could come up with on the spur of the moment. Her father shrugged, and then asked to take their order.

"How about a large pizza with Canadian bacon, mushrooms, and extra cheese?" Ben asked Katy, who nodded her acquiescence.

"I have to warn you," Ruskin said, "it'll be about 45 minutes or an hour. That crowd over there," he motioned through the window, toward the tents across the street, "just put in an order for a dozen piz-zas, same as yesterday. The business is good, but it slows everything down."

"No problem," said Katy, anxious for her father to leave their table.

"And I'll have Lisa bring you some complimentary bread sticks and marinara sauce while you're waiting," Ruskin said, and then added, "Say, didn't you say you were related to the McGee's?" He looked at Ben.

"Umm, not related, just a friend of the family," Ben quickly responded. "Why?"

"Because," he said, gesturing behind them, "Jenny McGee is my niece, and she and her boyfriend just walked in. I thought you might want to say hello."

* * *

Neither Shawn nor Jenny felt the need to wait for a booth at Ruskin's Pizzeria. The man had saved their lives two years ago, and they in turn his, so whatever formality there might have existed between them turned into an easy friendship. Fred was Jenny's uncle by marriage, but had also turned out to be a good friend to both of them.

They always sat at the booth across from the register, simply because that's where they were seated the night of the grand opening. It quickly became "their table," and it always seemed to be available whenever they came in. Shawn had a feeling that Ruskin had instructed his staff to always seat that booth last, though he couldn't say for sure.

"Pizza?" asked Jenny, sitting across from him.

He'd always found Jenny attractive, but today she looked beautiful. Her emerald green eyes sparkled with laughter, and her freckled cheeks were flushed from the weather. She had on the amethyst earrings Shawn had given her for her eighteenth birthday, and smelled of patchouli and lavender. She looked like a knockout in a tight blue skirt and a matching top.

"Earth to Shawn, come in Shawn," she said, brushing back an errant strand of hair from her eyes. She wrinkled her nose at him. "Nickel for your thoughts?"

He smiled. Substituting a nickel for the proverbial penny was their private joke, a reference to the magical coin even now tucked into Shawn's pocket.

"Just thinking about you," he said, "and how pretty you look this afternoon."

She blushed. "I bet you say that to all the girls."

"Just the ones I'm in love with," he whispered, reaching across the table to take her hand. "Jenny, I don't know what I'd ever do if I lost you."

"It'll never happen."

"It almost did last night."

"Yeah, well, that was a mistake on my part. I'm sorry I didn't believe you. I was just scared," she admitted. "You have my heart, Shawn. Sometimes it's scary to love someone that much."

"I know the feeling," he said, squeezing her fingers. "But I swear to you, you'll always be the only woman for me."

"Woman?" she asked, tracing a finger along the back of his hand. "Well, not yet, but maybe soon…"

"So, you love birds want to stop cooing long enough to order?" said a bubbly voice.

Shawn looked up to see Lisa Wang smiling at them. She carried a tray filled with glasses of water and placed two of them at their table.

"Hey, Lisa," said Jenny, her face turning red again. "Sorry about that."

"Are you kidding?" the waitress said, laughing. "I don't have a love life, so I'll just live vicariously through you two." She noticed the look on Jenny's face, and then added, "I'm just kidding."

"Oh, I know," Jenny said, reaching out to touch the woman's shoulder.

Lisa was almost nineteen and was a student at the Carl Sandburg School of Nursing across the street. She'd been in Shawn's class, and she and Jenny had been friends despite their age difference.

She was also Maya Wang's little sister, and, because Maya had helped Jenny out of a jam two years ago, before Maya had left Carthage to take a nursing job in Texas, they had used their influence with Fred Ruskin to get Lisa a job at the restaurant.

"So…what do you guys want today?"

"How about a large pizza with Canadian bacon, mushrooms and extra cheese?" Jenny said, and Shawn nodded. It was their favorite, something they had often shared at the restaurant, and today seemed like a good day for comfort food.

"You got it," Lisa said, with a wink. "You know, I just overheard Mr. Ruskin taking the very same order. I guess you're rubbing off on people. Anyway, it'll take a little longer than usual because," she lowered her voice, gesturing with a turn of her head toward an older, white-haired gentleman sitting at the bar with a Hispanic boy and a big red-haired teenager, "this way creepy guy from the religious thing across the street just ordered a dozen pies. I think I can probably slip yours in, though. After all, you have friends in high places."

"No rush, Lisa" Jenny said. "Just bring us a couple of Dr. Peppers and we'll be happy."

"It's a deal," she said, rushing off to get their drinks.

"So," said Shawn, "have you talked to Kristen yet?"

"Tried to, but apparently she's not taking my calls." She felt a pang of guilt as soon as the words left her mouth, because she'd done the exact same thing to Shawn all of yesterday and part of the night before. "Speaking of which…"

"Don't worry about it. I forgive you," he said, seemingly reading her mind.

"Still," said Jenny, feeling awful that she'd ever doubted him, "I'm sorry."

"I'm gonna run to the bathroom before our drinks come," Shawn said. He rounded the table, leaned down, and gave her a quick kiss. "I love you, Jenny."

She smiled after him, watching as he crossed the room into the back. Some people waited a lifetime to find a love like they had, and she vowed never to let anyone come between them ever again.

Despite her bravado, Kristen's lies and manipulations still hurt because she had thought that they really were friends. Apparently, though, Kristen had only used her to get to Shawn, and had somehow thought that if she broke them up that she could move in and pick up the pieces. She wondered how many of the things that they seemed to have in common were real. She definitely owed Kristen a visit, and though she wasn't normally big on confrontations, she was really looking forward to this one.

Chapter 34

The pizzeria was busy with customers, but not so busy that they wouldn't be noticed. In fact, Fred Ruskin had already noticed them, and if his parents were here, that meant there was one more variable in an ever-increasing list that could interfere with their plans. But he had to get to that plug if he wanted to power up his laptop.

"They've never seen us," Katy said, "so at least that's something."

Ben knew it was true, but he didn't want to take any chances. He leaned out of the booth, surreptitiously surveying the restaurant. There they were, sitting in a booth near the cash register. There was no way to get out of the restaurant without walking past them, let alone into the bathroom.

He took a giant gulp of Pepsi and nearly did a spit take as he saw his mother rise from her booth and begin to walk toward them. He immediately swallowed the drink and leaned across the table to pull Katy into a long, lingering kiss.

"Mmph," she whispered, pulling away, her mouth open in surprise. "What are you...?"

"It always works in the movies," he said, turning his head to look out the window as Jenny walked past them and into the back of the restaurant.

"Doofus. And you think that made us any less noticeable?"

He glanced toward his parent's table and realized his father was absent as well. Now was his chance. Without another word, he snatched the duffel bag from beneath the table and walked quickly toward the restroom.

Ben reached for the door handle, twisted, pulled, but the door was locked. Great. He felt exposed, almost naked, standing outside the bathroom door, hoping his parents wouldn't wander back here and spot him.

"Just a second," said an all-too-familiar familiar voice from inside. The door swung open to reveal a skinny teenager with sandy blond hair wearing a pair of jeans and a blue sweater.

"Dad!"

"Dad?"

"I mean dadgummit," he said, dredging up an old word he'd heard on an ancient television show, "I just really have to go."

"No problem," Shawn said, his gaze shifting first to Ben's 'Blue Boys' sweatshirt and then to the duffel bag in his hand. "Well, then again…"

He grabbed Ben by the collar, spun him around, and shoved him into the tiny one-stall bathroom. Ben stumbled backwards, thumping the back of his head against the wall.

"Ouch! Hey, what the—"

Shawn stepped into the bathroom, locking the door behind him. "I know it was you snooping around the old house on Randolph, but what I don't know is why. What were you doing there?"

"Whoa, whoa," Ben stammered. He was about to get beaten up by his dad, and he didn't know whether to fight back or confess. "I didn't —"

"Yeah, actually, you did. Brody Huffman saw you outside, Jeremiah Watson saw you inside. So what the hell's going on?"

"Okay, you got me. My girlfriend and I, we were just trying to find someplace private, ya know? And the house seemed romantic, in a creepy, haunted sort of way. We didn't know anyone actually owned the old place."

Shawn rolled his eyes. "A broken down, rotting heap of a mansion is romantic? I don't buy it."

"You don't have to buy it," Ben said, feigning a sense of bravado, "but that's the way it is. Now unless you want me to go all Fight Club on your ass, you'd better back off."

"'Fight club'?" Shawn laughed. "What on Earth are you talking about?"

This was going from bad to worse. "Just let me pass, okay?"

"Fine, whatever," he stepped aside, motioning for Ben to move past him. But in one quick motion, he pushed him back against the wall and tore the duffel bag from his hand.

"Stop! You do not want to do that!" Ben warned his father. This was crazy.

"Too late," he said, unzipping the duffel and dumping the contents to the floor.

Ben dove for the laptop, managing to catch it before it landed on the white and yellow tile. He'd thankfully secured the gun in a zippered compartment inside the bag, but he'd brought along the printout, which Shawn now held in his hands.

"What the hell?" the sandy-blond teenager said, his facing growing pale. "1987? And all these people...my mother, Jenny's dad, Samantha... dead?"

"I told you that you didn't want to do that," said Ben, snatching the paper from his father's hand. He let out a frustrated sigh, took a deep breath, and shoved the laptop and the printout back into the bag. "Come on, let's go eat some pizza. I guess we've got a lot to talk about."

* * *

"So let me get this straight," Shawn asked, his face a mixture of wonder and disbelief, "you two are from the future, and none of that stuff was ever supposed to happen?"

He sat at the table with Ben Matthews and Katy Rush, self-proclaimed travelers from the future. He could barely wrap his mind around it, but they seemed pretty convincing. They knew all about Aupuch and the nickel, and Shawn knew for a fact neither Jenny nor Fred had ever breathed a word of their adventure to anyone.

Shawn wasn't sure what to believe. When he'd come back to the table he shared with Jenny he'd found her missing, presumably in the back somewhere talking with Fred. He really needed her here for this, but didn't want to chance leaving Ben and Katy alone while he went to find her.

"Pretty much, yeah," Ben said, shrugging his shoulders. "You weren't supposed to know. Nobody was. Michael…"

"Wait a minute," he said, lowering his voice, "the Archangel Michael?"

"He came to us," Katy said, glaring at Ben, "and sent us to 1977 to stop all of this."

"He gave me a spell," said Ben, "and, powered with the nickel, we're here to stop the murderer. Now all we have to do is find him."

"Okay, slow down," Shawn said, feeling his pocket. The nickel was still there. "Are you sure it's a 'him'? And you need the nickel? How do you even know about it?"

"I don't need it, I already have it," Ben reached into his own pocket and pulled out a very familiar-looking Buffalo-head nickel.

"Let me…"

"Sorry," Katy said, wrapping her hand around Ben's, "but that's probably not a good idea."

Shawn dropped his hand to the table. "But if you have it, then, wherever you come from…am I dead?"

"Hardly," Ben said. "You're very much alive."

"So, I *gave* it to you?"

"He really doesn't need to know any of this," Katy said to Ben. "Seriously, dude, we're getting in way deep here."

"Hey, I'm right here. Don't talk about me like I'm not here."

"Sorry...Shawn, but she's right," Ben agreed, putting the nickel away. "I've probably said way too much already."

"About what," asked Jenny, walking up to the table to put her hand on Shawn's shoulder, "and why'd you change tables?"

"Jenny," he said, kissing her hand, "meet Ben Matthews and Katy Rush. Ben and Katy, this is my girlfriend, Jenny McGee."

"What's going on?" Jenny asked him, concern evident in her tone.

Before he could answer, Fred Ruskin was at their table. Lisa Wang was behind him, and they both carried a piping hot pizza. "I see you two decided to join your friends," he said to Jenny, who looked at him in confusion. Nevertheless, she slid into the booth beside Shawn.

"Yeah," Shawn said, going along for the moment with whatever Ben and Katy had told Ruskin, "I hope you don't mind."

"Not a problem," the former sheriff said.

"I'll be back in a jiff with plates and silverware," the waitress said before scurrying off into the back.

"We ordered the same pizzas?" Shawn mused, eyeing the couple across from him. "What're the chances of that?"

"So, Shawn," Ruskin said, leaning against the table, "what's going on here? I met these two a couple of years ago at Tanner's funeral," he looked apologetically at Jenny, "and they said they were family. Today, they said they were *friends* of the family, but it's obvious by the look on Jenny's face that she's never met them before in her life."

Shawn stared at Ruskin, his mouth hanging open.

"Son, you can take the badge away, but I'm always going to be a cop. So…what's up?"

"That's what I'd like to know," said Jenny, crossing her arms.

"Why don't we just call a town meeting?" Katy said, rolling her eyes. "Let's wait for the waitress to get back so we can fill her in, too."

Shawn grinned. "Well, Fred," he whispered, "seems they're from the future, and they've come to 1977 to stop a series of murders from taking place."

Ruskin started to laugh, then grew silent as he took note of the seriousness in Shawn's face. "Oh, come on…"

"At least that's what they've told me."

Lisa Wang deftly maneuvered past Ruskin's broad shoulders to deposit a plastic cafeteria plate holding a fork and a knife wrapped in a napkin before each of them. She also carried their drinks, which Shawn now realized they'd abandoned at their table. She sat them on the table. "If you need anything else, just let me know," she said, glancing at Ruskin. When he made no move to follow, she just smiled, shrugged, and left to check on another table.

"So," Ruskin asked, leaning over Ben's shoulder, "if all this is true, where's your proof?"

"Show him the story," Shawn prompted. "After all, it concerns him too."

"Ben…" said Katy, but he was already reaching into the duffel bag.

"What choice do we have? Maybe they can help."

"Okay, fine…Mr. Ruskin," she said to Fred, "do you have a pen?"

"Always," he answered, taking a black ballpoint from the pocket in his apron. "Why, though?"

"Because," she said, snatching the sheaf of papers away from Ben, "the only way you're going to see this is in edited form."

* * *

Katy carefully blacked out any mention of her name in the article, or even the fact that her mother had ever been pregnant. She also deleted all mentions of Brody Huffman and "Huffman Heights." If his friends knew he was going to die in just a few short years, they might do something to change history. Kind of like she'd done with the note she'd asked Sam to give her father, she realized guiltily. But what was done was done, and she wasn't about to compound that mistake with another.

Finally finished, she handed the papers to her father. Ruskin took them, pulled up a chair, and spread them out between himself, Shawn, and Jenny.

"This is wrong," Jenny said, when they were finished, "it has to be. My dad…what do you want? Why are you doing this?"

"We're trying to save them!" said Ben.

"But what does this actually prove?" Ruskin said, focusing his attention on Katy. "Anyone could put something like this together with a decent electric typewriter, though I have to admit the typeface looks really smooth and professional."

"You don't need to see proof," Katy said, picking at a piece of pizza. It tasted wonderful, but she'd lost all appetite and her stomach felt like a pit of ice. "In fact, just forget you ever saw us. We'll deal with all of this on our own." She pushed at Ben, who started to slide out of the booth.

"Not yet," said Shawn, reaching out to touch his forearm.

A fiery-blue spark jumped between the two men, moving from the point of contact to spread quickly over the rest of their bodies. For an instant, probably less than a second, both men were enveloped in an unearthly azure glow. And then, as quickly as Shawn could yank his hand away, it was gone.

"Okay, what the hell was that?" asked Ben, rubbing his arm.

"Wow, are you okay?" Katy asked, touching his shoulder.

He felt warm to the touch, like he'd just spent the day working under the hot summer sun. The heat quickly faded, however, and in an instant his temperature returned to normal.

She looked around the restaurant, but thank God, no one else seemed to have noticed. "Serious weirdness," she mumbled, her hand going to her mouth. What had happened?

Ruskin gave her a funny look but said nothing.

"Do you...Shawn, do you have your...nickel?"

"I do," he said, his eyes wide. "And it exists in two places at once, and apparently that isn't a good idea."

"What an understatement," Ben said, putting his version of the coin on the table. "Here, let's try this again."

Katy watched as he reached out a tentative hand to touch his father's arm, but this time there were no sparks, no opaque blue lights, nothing. "Definitely the nickel," she agreed, sliding it back to Ben. She breathed a sigh of relief as he tucked it safely back into his pocket.

"Proof enough for you?" she asked Ruskin. "How can two objects exist in the same place at the same time if we're not telling the truth?"

She was tempted to show him the necklace with the melted wedding rings she wore beneath her blouse. She wondered if that would produce the same result as the nickels but didn't want to risk exposing her identity to find out.

"I believe you, Katherine," he said, squinting at her. "It's...total weirdness, and I didn't believe you before, but I certainly do now."

Chapter 35

He'd just had a vision. There they were, his enemies, plotting his demise. The Anti-Christ, his whore, the two demons he'd seen in the alley, and the Roman soldier, all sitting around a table eating pizza and laughing at him. And, this time, he knew where they were. They were across the street, eating the very same pizza that Oscar had brought to his tent not fifteen minutes earlier.

The Reverend looked down at the empty box from Ruskin's Pizzeria and felt an incredible anger surge through his veins. He felt like vomiting. He had eaten food made by the hands of one of Christ's betrayers. He had sinned. Not knowingly, perhaps, and certainly not intentionally, but he had sinned nevertheless. By accepting food from the enemy and, worse, inflicting that same food on the good members of his flock, he had betrayed the Lord Jesus Christ. He had tasted the foodstuff of Satan, swallowed it, felt sated by it, and his body was now impure and unclean.

He felt faint but forced himself to his feet. Stumbling to the opening of the tent, he latched it closed before returning to the cot. The Reverend withdrew a wooden-handled hunting knife from his pocket, removing it from its sheath with a practiced flick of his wrist. He stood up again to unfasten his jeans, letting them drop to the ground around his ankles.

He prayed God would forgive him. He had sinned and must do penance for his crime. He looked between his legs, at the roadmap of scars that marked both thighs. He lowered himself to the cot and, taking a deep breath, slowly drew the sharp blade across one of the welts, laying bare a layer of flesh a quarter of an inch deep.

He watched blood quickly fill the cut, flowing out of the wound to run down his leg, staining his jeans. He dabbed at the incision with a towel before making another cut, followed by another, and still another. fifteen cuts in all, three times five, the Holy Trinity multiplied by the number of his enemies. By the time he was finished, the white towel had turned completely red and his legs were a mass of open wounds. But he was clean again, his sins washed away by the tears of Jesus and his own lifeblood. He could once again carry on the Lord's work, smiting those who opposed Him with a clear mind and unfettered conscience.

They would show up tomorrow afternoon, on Halloween, secure in the knowledge that they were protected by all that was Evil on Satan's very own day of celebration. They would let down their guard, blissfully unaware of his impending attack. And attack he would, hard, fast, and deadly. He'd send them straight to hell or die trying, and Reverend David Allan Dowd knew that the Lord wasn't ready to call him home just yet. Not by a long shot.

He longed to put on his jeans, pick up his sword, and walk across the street to confront the Anti-Christ and his minions, to initiate the battle that would signal the beginning of Armageddon. But he knew that, if he waited, they would come to him. If his plan worked, they would have to. They would be drawn to him, and it would be all the easier to put them down. Of course, a little insurance never hurt…

Chapter 36

Ben crouched alone in the bathroom, waiting for the laptop to boot up. Katy still sat at their table, though her father had been forced back into the kitchen by the after-church lunch crowd. He still couldn't believe that he had eaten lunch with eighteen-year-old versions of his parents. No, he had to stop thinking of them that way. He didn't want to risk another slip up. There had been too many already.

Finally, the laptop initialized and was ready. He called up the search program and keyed in a variety of words, including "revival," "religion," and "traveling," but nothing. "Religion" got several hits, of course, but the *Journal-Pilot* had absolutely no mention of the revival. There had to be a connection.

The thing was, because all the searches came from the altered timeline, even if the revival was somehow connected it should have been mentioned. Assuming the newspaper wasn't just being sloppy, that could only mean that something they had done had brought the traveling ministry to town. His head hurt just thinking about it.

He keyed in another search; the name "Kristen Hawks." Shawn had mentioned her as a possible suspect. Apparently, the girl had a crush on Shawn and had tried to come between him and Jenny. He'd never heard the girl's name before, but that didn't mean anything.

He watched as the search engine churned out two articles. Apparently, she had won an award for perfect attendance her senior year of high school and then, two years later, saved a woman's life while working at The Good Apple printing press. So she was punctual and knew

CPR. That didn't really prove one thing or the other. Bad people, he knew, sometimes did good things, and vice versa.

Their best bet was still the revival. Someone there knew something, was maybe even planning something. And if they could find out who it was, they could stop them before it was too late.

* * *

Katy sat at the table with Shawn and Jenny, watching numbly as they finished off the rest of their pizza.

She'd just spent thirty minutes talking with her father, the very same man she'd buried three years ago, or, in another timeline, who'd died when she was a little girl. He had changed a lot since their chance encounter in 1975 and more closely resembled the man she had known and loved. She desperately wanted to tell him who she was, but she knew that she didn't dare. Giving him that note was bad enough; telling him that he would soon have another daughter was something else entirely.

"So, Katherine," Jenny started, using the name her father had called her, "what year are you from? Do you know us in the future?"

"I can't answer that," she said, slowly shaking her head. "Look, I know you're full of questions—I would be, too—but no good can come from knowing the answers. We're just…friends, brought into the past by Michael to help you, to prevent these murders."

"But why didn't Michael come himself?"

"He said he couldn't, that he was irrevocably tied to the present, and that only Ben, for reasons that I can't get into, could make the trip."

"So how did you get here?" Shawn asked.

"Ben read the spell, and I just sort of… tagged along. Though I had the focus…" She stopped in mid-sentence, realizing she had said too much.

"Focus?" Shawn asked. "Do you mean, like another talisman?"

"Something like that," said Ben, sliding into the booth beside Katy. "It doesn't really matter, does it?"

"I guess not," Shawn said.

"So, did you find anything?" Katy asked, trying to change the subject.

"Wow, that thing's really a computer," Shawn said, "and it can access other computers all over the world? Amazing."

"And Michael let you bring it into the past?" Jenny wondered aloud. "It seems…dangerous, in the wrong hands."

"Well, I guess we didn't give him much of a choice," Ben said. "And, no, I didn't find anything on the show across the street, which is confusing."

"How so?" asked Jenny, finishing off the last of her drink.

"Well, unless something we did in 1975 changed things—and I can't imagine that it did—someone at the *Journal-Pilot* should have taken note of the revival, even if it wasn't part of the original timeline. Everything I downloaded was from the altered timeline, so whatever altered it, if it was newsworthy, would have been included.

"All of which means… hell, I have no earthly idea. It's like us coming here has somehow started a third timeline, which may or may not mean that the revival has anything at all to do with the murders."

"I do think someone would have mentioned it," Katy said, "especially with the first murder taking place on the same day as the revival. The Sheriff would have at least interviewed all these strangers in town, wouldn't he?"

"Jesse Floyd isn't the best Sheriff in the world," Jenny said. "He was responsible for Fred losing his job, so who knows? He's more about politics than anything else."

"Michael said whatever starts all this originated in the house," Ben interrupted. "We were trying to search it last night when we came across Jeremiah Watson. Regardless of whether or not the traveling ministry or Kristen Hawks are involved, I think our best bet is to get back inside the house and give it another search."

"I'm all for that," Shawn said, "but I can't imagine that, aside from the door in the secret room, there's an inch left that hasn't already been covered."

"But we've still got to try," Ben insisted, "and that door sounds like a good place to start."

"No time like the present," said Katy, wanting to just get it over with. "Unless you two have any pressing engagements, we should get in there and be done with it."

"Well, I don't have the key with me," Shawn said, then smiled as Ben tugged at a necklace beneath his sweatshirt. "But you do, huh?"

"If we're going to go traipsing around in that bug pit," said Jenny, "I need to run home and change into something slightly more comfortable—"

* * *

Everything suddenly went dark, and Ben didn't know where he was or what had happened. He tried to move, first wiggling his fingers, and then his arms. He groaned and sat up, but fell flat on his back again as a burst of pain exploded in the side of his head. He blinked his eyes, and this time could see the barest hint of light filtering in from somewhere above.

The last thing he remembered was sitting at the restaurant with Katy and his parents, making plans to search the old house. He remembered Jenny saying she wanted to go home to change clothes before searching the house, and then...

He remembered now. They'd agreed to meet at the house in an hour, and he and Katy had almost been there when a red pick-up pulled off the side of the road and asked them for directions. The next thing he knew, the driver—an old man with wrinkled skin—was pointing a gun at them. A Latino boy and two red-headed twins quickly jumped out from the back and grabbed Katy.

He sat up, ignoring the screaming pain that spread from his head through his eyes. Shivering from the cold, huddling against himself, he suddenly remembered Katy.

He'd tried to fight, but they had overwhelmed him. His luck didn't add up to much when the odds were four against one. Still, the twins had almost managed to knock each other out through a series of missed punches before the old man swung a tire iron at him. And that was the last thing he remembered.

He tentatively touched the side of his head, slowly running fingers through his hair, wincing as they came back slick with blood. He stumbled to his feet, swayed, but managed to steady himself against a crumbling cement wall. Where was he?

His eyes finally adjusted to the weak light, and he made out the shape of a door and steps leading up to it. He was in a basement of some sort. His head still felt full of cobwebs, and he shook it in an effort to ward off the fog. The motion sent a vibration of pain through his skull, driving him to his knees.

His vision fuzzy, he strained to hold onto consciousness. He heard voices and tried to concentrate on deciphering what they meant. Straining, he could just barely make out the words.

"…would they change…" said a man's voice.

"…you sure…" said a soft voice, perhaps a woman's.

"…take a look…snapped…two…" the man responded.

"…don't like…if…" the woman said, a note of urgency in her tone.

He thought he recognized the voices, but before he could place them his vision grew dark and he slumped against the stairs and could hear no more.

* * *

"This is weird," said Shawn, standing outside the old Spencer house. "Why would they change the lock?"

He stared at the entrance to the cellar. The combination lock had been replaced with a rusty padlock, and they could see no sign of Ben or Katy.

"Are you sure it's different?" Jenny asked, pulling her parka tight around her in a futile attempt to keep out the cold.

"Positive," he said, kneeling to study the padlock.

The gleam of metal half-buried in the snow caught his eye. He carefully dug through the white wetness, ignoring the cold shiver that went through his hands, and pulled out the broken hasp of the combination lock. "Take a look at this," he said, holding the broken lock up to Jenny. "Someone snapped it clean in two, probably with a crowbar or something."

"I don't like this, Shawn. What if someone else broke in?"

Shawn started to say something when he heard a low groan coming from the cellar. "Shit, someone's in there!"

He tugged hard at the lock, but it wouldn't budge. Glancing around for a rock or piece of metal to break the lock, he couldn't find anything. He didn't want to use the nickel but didn't feel like he had any choice.

"Go ahead," Jenny said, sensing his intentions. "It's all right."

They'd both agreed never to use the nickel unless absolutely necessary, but if someone was trapped in the cellar, that definitely counted as necessary. He withdrew the coin from his pocket, held it tight in his fist, and concentrated on the old padlock.

A bright white light briefly surrounded the lock, and then it was done. The hasp sprang open and Shawn removed it, yanking the cellar door in one quick jerk.

Ben Matthews lay unmoving on the cellar steps, his long blond hair matted with blood. But he was still breathing, even if those breaths were shallow and labored.

Jenny felt for a pulse. "He's alive," she whispered, "but he's lost a lot of blood. We need to get him to the hospital."

"I think I can do it," Shawn whispered, feeling the weight of the talisman in his hand. By the time they got to a phone and called an ambulance, Ben could already be dead. This was their only choice.

"Do what?" she answered distractedly, trying to stop the bleeding with her scarf.

"Heal him."

That got her attention. "Are you sure? Remember what happened last time."

"Do we have a choice? Look at him. Besides, that was with all five talismans. I only have the nickel now."

"You're right," she finally said, backing away from Ben's prone body. "Save him, Shawn. I get a good feeling from him."

"I know what you mean," he said, dropping to his knees in the snow. He reached out to touch Ben...

"Wait!" Jenny said. She reached around the man and snaked her hand into his pocket, pulling out the future version of the nickel. "We just don't want a repeat of what happened in the restaurant."

In the rush of the moment, he'd forgotten about Ben's coin. Trying to put everything out of his mind, he clutched his own nickel tightly in one hand and reached out with the other to touch the back of the man's head. He concentrated on healing the wound, seeing in his mind's eye the skin stitching itself together, magically mending. But nothing happened.

"I guess I was wrong," he whispered. "Little things like the lock are easy, but this..."

"Just try again," said Jenny.

He closed his eyes, ignoring the sound of the wind in his ears and the smell of the pine trees all around him. He concentrated on nothing save for Ben, imagining his wound reversing itself, the cut rapidly healing under his touch.

He opened his eyes. The wound looked a little better, but was still bleeding profusely, and Ben's skin had turned an ashen white. He was dying, and there wasn't a damned thing Shawn could do to save him. And then it hit him.

"Jenny, give me his nickel."

"Shawn, if what happened in the restaurant…"

Ben's shuddered once, jerked, and then was still. His breathing grew ragged, more labored. His body was shutting down; he was dying.

"Now!" he said.

But she didn't give him the nickel. Instead, she moved closer to Ben and reached out to lay a trembling hand on his blood-soaked skull. "If we're going to do this," she whispered, "we're going to do it together."

Shawn nodded, understanding. He reached out to lay his hand atop hers, willing the nickel to heal Ben.

"*Resarcio,*" Jenny whispered, repeating it two more times. "*Resarcio, resarcio.*"

He suddenly felt spiritually and mentally connected to both of them and could feel the fire in Ben's chest flickering like a half-burned candle in a windstorm.

He concentrated on snatching that flame in his fingers, on nurturing it, helping it to burn bright again, and he could feel Jenny doing the same. Together they tended to his life force, slowly bringing him back from the brink of oblivion. And then they turned their attentions toward mending his body. Skin stitched itself together, pulling tight over the wound, growing and healing…and then it was done, and Shawn felt the connection break.

He opened his eyes, blinked, and stared at Jenny. Tears ran down her face like little streams running to meet a river, but the tears, he knew, weren't tears of sadness. They were tears of joy, much like the ones running down his own face. They had healed Ben but, more than that, they had briefly been one with each other, had touched the depth of each other's souls.

And they had touched Ben's, and he theirs. There was a truth there, unspeakable but undeniable, and Shawn knew that the three of them would be forever entwined. After all, they knew him now. Inexplicably, they knew he was their son; blood of their blood, heart of their hearts, brought into the world through their love for each other. How they knew this they couldn't be sure, but know it they did, and what stronger bond could there be than that?

"Stop looking at each other all lovey-dovey like," mumbled Ben, his eyes glassy but open, "and help me up, will you? I've got a seriously killer headache."

* * *

Kristen Hawks crouched behind the remains of the collapsed garage, shivering against the frigid winter wind.

She had been following Shawn all day, waiting for her opportunity. She knew in her heart that if she just explained things to him, told him how she felt, that they could come to an understanding and everyone would be all the better for it. She didn't want to have to eliminate the competition—the thought made her queasy—but love cannot be denied, and she would do whatever was necessary to ensure her destiny. After all, she deserved to be happy, too.

She was almost positive she could make Shawn understand, if only she had the chance to talk to him alone. Jen was really upset with her. She didn't blame her, but she knew the girl would eventually get over it. It was Shawn that concerned her most right now.

She watched intently as he withdrew something from his pocket and bent over the door to the cellar. Something happened—she could see a brief flash of light—and then the door was open, and Jenny was walking down the steps into the cellar.

Kristen watched in confusion as an eerie blue light shone from within the cellar, growing ever brighter. She blinked, confused, but by the time she opened her eyes again, the light was gone. What on Earth was going on? She slowly backed away from her hiding place, but something caught her ankle and she stumbled backwards into the snow.

"Did you hear something?" Shawn's voice drifted over from the other side of the wrecked garage.

Her heart pounding heavy in her chest, she frantically edged away—only she wasn't moving. Her foot was caught in a tangle of canvas straps from an old bag half-hidden in the snow. She tugged at it, realizing too late that the zipper on her boot was tangled up with one of the straps.

She yanked hard on the bag but only succeeded in wrapping the strap tighter around her foot. It wouldn't come off! In desperation, she wiggled her foot free from the boot. She tried one last time to yank it from its canvas prison, and it finally came loose, taking the zipper with it. The bag fell open, revealing a large black box and a stack of papers.

Kristen kicked the bag away from her, but her foot struck something solid. She hurriedly dropped to a crouch, reaching into the bag, unzipping an inside compartment. A small, black gun poked out, almost daring her to take it.

Kristen stared dumbfounded at the gun. She needed to eliminate a problem, and it was as if the powers that be had just provided her with a means to that end. She watched herself reach out to wrap her fingers around the cold metal, lifting it from the snow. She shoved the weapon into her jacket, stood up, and quickly ran down the sidewalk.

* * *

"It was Kristen," Shawn said, walking towards them carrying Ben's duffel bag, "but she ran off before I could get to her. She ducked behind a house, but by the time I got there she was gone."

"We need to find Katy," Ben said, snatching the bag from his father's outstretched hands. "Please, you've got to help me." If the men that had taken her had hurt her… but he couldn't think about that yet.

"We will," Jenny whispered, tentatively reaching out a hand to touch his face. "Ben, I'm so sorry. If I'd known… if we'd known…"

"Known what?" he said sharply, his heart racing.

"Known you were going to get jumped by Kristen Hawks," Shawn said quickly. "I don't think she took anything, but you'd better check. And I also found this," he held out Katy's black purse, "buried in the snow by the bag."

"But it wasn't… shit!" Ben cursed, searching frantically through the bag. It was missing. The gun was gone. "Shit, shit, shit!"

"What's wrong?"

"There was a gun in the bag, but it's gone," Ben said. If someone had taken the gun, he'd just put all their lives in danger.

"I don't understand," said Jenny, her hand on his shoulder. "If you had a gun, how did Kristen…?"

"It wasn't her," he said. "I've never even met Kristen Hawks. It might not even have been her who took the gun.

"There were four of them, an old man, a pair of twins, and an Hispanic kid, in a brown Chevy van. They stopped just as we were walking up the driveway to ask us for directions. They jumped us, and the old man clocked me with a tire iron. As far as I can remember, Kristen wasn't even there. But…" he said, pausing, trying to capture a fleeting thought. There had been something familiar about their attackers.

"I've seen them before, at least the twins. They had bright red hair and looked like some sort of weird Irish farm boys; they're not exactly easy to forget."

"Where did you see them?" Shawn asked. "The description sounds familiar to me, too."

"At Ruskin's Pizzeria, that's where," he said, finally remembering. "They were sitting at the counter waiting for an order. A dozen pizzas, I heard one of them say. I think the Hispanic kid was with them, too."

"That order was for the ministry," said Jenny. "Fred kept complaining about the order when I went back to visit with him in the kitchen. I guess they're involved in this after all."

"And…shit," Ben exclaimed, "Katy saw a Hispanic kid putting up fliers about the revival. That's how we found out about it. It has to be the same person."

"And they left you for dead," Shawn said. "Nice people. But how do they even know about you?"

"That's a very good question, but I'm all out of answers. And if they haven't already killed Katy…"

He couldn't bear to even consider that possibility. He shook off the feeling of despair that threatened to engulf him. There just wasn't time for it.

"We'll get her back," Jenny said, moving to embrace him. "I promise. Together, we're stronger than they think. After all, we're family."

Ben straightened in her arms, started to pull away, but then gave into the embrace. "How did you find out?" he asked, his eyes turning salty. He let himself break down for a moment, crying with love for his parents and for the woman he feared he would never see again.

"Does it matter?" Shawn asked, putting a hand on his shoulder. "Boy, I never thought I'd be a teenage father, especially since we haven't even had sex yet."

Ben choked out a laugh and shifted in his mother's arms to awkwardly pull his father into the embrace. "I'm sorry I didn't tell you," he said, finally managing to stifle his tears, "but…hey, where's my nickel?"

He backed away from Shawn and Jenny. Reaching into his pocket, he came up empty. "What the...?" Ben asked, his hands shaking. "Oh, God, did they take that too?"

"No, I have it," Jenny said, "It's safe. It's right here." She pressed the coin into his palm. "That's how we healed you, and how we learned who you were."

He was about to reply when a blue Dodge Charger pulled into the driveway behind the Pacer, blocking the exit. He instinctively reached for the gun in his duffel, remembered it wasn't there, and then switched his attention to the nickel. If the people who had taken Katy were back for more, this time he wasn't going down without a fight.

Chapter 37

Oscar Reyes had a very bad feeling about this. They had done what the *Padre* asked, had kidnapped the girl, but he just couldn't understand why. The *Padre* had said she was a servant of Satan, but Oscar had never really believed in any of that stuff. He did, however, believe in the *Padre*, and so had gone along with it.

But someone had gotten hurt, or worse, and that definitely wasn't supposed to happen. They'd dumped the man in the cellar of that old, abandoned house, and Jim Felt had changed the lock despite his protests. Even if the man worshipped Satan, he could change. He could embrace God and move into His light. The *Padre* preached forgiveness for sin, so why didn't that apply to the man they had wounded and the girl they currently had tied up in the back of the van?

"Padre nuestro que estás en los cielos," he half-whispered to himself, in his native tongue, *"Santificado sea tu Nombre, Venga tu reino, Hágase tu voluntad, En la tierra como en el cielo, Danos hoy el pan de este día, y perdona nuestras deudas, como nosotros perdonamos nuestros, deudores y no nos dejes caer en al tentacion, sino que líbranos del malo. Amen."*

He had said the Lord's Prayer many times in his life, but never did the words sound as hollow as they did right now. He hoped God could forgive him not only for what he'd already done, but for what he was about to do.

"Reyes, you drive," said Jim Felt, coming up from behind him. He pressed a set of car keys into his hand. He was followed by Teddy and

Tommy, the redheaded Tyler twins, who carried a huge steamer trunk between them. Oscar knew what the trunk was for and he didn't like it.

"Do we really have to do this?" He asked Felt for the third time since the kidnapping. He already knew the answer, but he had to ask anyway.

"You don't have to, Oscar," Felt said, laying a rough hand on his shoulder, "but it'll get done whether you're involved or not. You don't want to disappoint the *Padre*, do you?"

No, he definitely didn't want to do that. He owed the man his life. He'd been running with the Spanish Dragons, a gang out of Los Angeles, when the *Padre* had first come into his life. He was so messed up on drugs that he'd just shot and nearly killed an old man at a *bodega*, all for 40 dollars in change, just so he could get his next hit.

The *Padre* had saved his life, both literally and spiritually. He'd managed to outrun the police in a fiery red Trans-Am he'd hotwired before the shooting, but he wrapped it around a telephone pole just outside of Alhambra, a few yards away from where the *Padre* was holding a revival.

Dad himself had pulled him from the wreckage, only seconds before the car exploded. Miraculously, he'd suffered only minor scratches and bruises. Jim Felt had been a medic during the Second World War and had easily tended to his injuries. They hid him from the police, took him in, and changed him. More than that, they'd brought him to God.

That was seven years ago, and he was just fourteen years old at the time. He was still an angry young punk then, but they hadn't given up on him. The congregation provided for him, fed him, and took him in as one of their own. Eventually, he'd accepted Jesus Christ into his heart. He'd been with them ever since.

So, no, he didn't want to disappoint the *Padre*, but neither did he want to be a killer. He hadn't actually swung the tire iron that killed the girl's *novio*—her boyfriend—but he'd been involved. Worse yet, he'd done nothing to stop it. The thought made his stomach go sour.

Without another word, he climbed into the old, rusted-out Chevy van and turned over the engine. He turned in his seat as he heard the heavy thump of the twins loading the steamer trunk into the back. He surreptitiously glanced in the rearview mirror at the girl. She was bound at the ankles and wrists with masking tape, and a red kerchief was tied around her mouth to prevent her from screaming. She was the same woman he'd seen on the town square, he knew, and that made him feel even worse. He'd even invited her to the revival. She certainly hadn't seemed Satanic at the time; in fact, she'd been nothing but pleasant and polite and had seemed anything but dangerous.

Oscar shook his head as he watched Teddy—or maybe it was Tommy, he was never quite sure—hoist the girl into the air and carefully lower her into the trunk. She was whimpering; pleading, he imagined, for a reprieve from her unknown fate. The twin slammed shut the trunk lid with a gleeful enthusiasm that made Oscar wince. He averted his eyes as the man locked the trunk, sealing the girl in darkness.

"Drive," said Felt, sliding into the passenger seat. The twins stayed in the back with the trunk, which was just fine with Oscar.

"Where to?" he asked, as he pulled out onto the highway. They'd only been in Carthage for a day, and he had no idea where anything was.

"Hang a right," Felt said, "We're taking her to the lake. Gonna bury her in that trunk."

"Mi Dios," Oscar said, his heart thrumming wildly in his chest. He'd always had an intense fear of being buried alive, and now he was going to participate in forcing that hell upon someone else. "Why?"

"Because the Reverend said to," the old southerner said. "Because she's a consort of Satan and because it's the right thing to do. That's why. Why do you ask so many questions? Has the Reverend ever led you astray?"

Oscar sighed. Felt was right. The *Padre* had been nothing but good to him, and who was he to doubt his judgment? After all, Reverend Dowd was the conduit through which God spoke. He would do his duty. He would help bury this woman, this creature of God. But he didn't have to like it.

* * *

She couldn't see anything, but she could tell they were driving. Every time the van hit a bump, her head managed to thump against part of the steamer trunk. If she lived to see a mirror again, she was sure her face would be covered in bruises.

Thump. Pain shot through her shoulder as the van drove over another speed bump. She thought she recognized the delay between the bumps that were spaced out over the winding road as belonging to the path that ran around the lake, but she couldn't be sure.

It felt like it had been at least an hour since the old man had hit Ben with the tire iron and he and his co-conspirators had abducted her from in front of the house. Her hands and feet were numb from being tied up, and her mouth was so dry from the gag that it was difficult to breathe, but she was mostly worried about Ben. He went down hard when the old man hit him, and there'd been so much blood that she couldn't bear to think about it. She prayed to a God that she only half-believed in that he was still alive.

She let out a silent yelp as the van hit another bump, this one sending waves of pain through her back and shoulders. She lay sideways in the trunk, her knees pushed up to her chest. Every inch of her body ached, and it was all she could do not to completely lose it. But if she wanted to stay alive—she had no doubt that they'd eventually kill her—she needed to keep her wits about her, and she needed to stay calm. And, more than that, she needed to sleep.

If she could sleep, she could use her powers to contact Ben, Shawn, Jenny, or even her father, assuming, of course, that one of them happened to be asleep and dreaming. She'd been trying to fall asleep ever since they put her in the trunk, but being bound and gagged in the back of a van wasn't exactly conducive to relaxation.

The van came to an abrupt stop, and Katy felt her heart go staccato in her chest. She heard the back doors open and the twins get out of the van. She started to hope that they'd simply abandoned the vehicle, but suddenly felt the trunk being hoisted into the air.

They were carrying her somewhere. She could hear muffled voices but couldn't make anything out. Katy felt a sudden and intense anger rise up in her. Unless she could somehow get away, which looked very unlikely at the moment, she would probably die and the Halloween Murders would go on as scheduled. Her mother would be attacked, her sister would die, her father would drink himself to death, and two of Ben's grandparents would be murdered, and Emily would never be born. And there was nothing she could do to stop any of it from happening.

The side of her head bumped sharply against the bottom of her prison as her captors stopped walking and let the trunk fall to the ground. Her teeth rattled and she saw stars. Her temple throbbed to the point where she thought her head was going to explode. She prayed to pass out so she could use her power, but stayed unmercifully awake.

* * *

"Puta madre," Oscar mumbled under his breath, glaring at one of the Tyler twins. He'd intentionally dropped the trunk as hard as he could, enjoying the poor woman's pain.

They were on the other side of the Carthage Lake, probably about a half a mile into the forest that surrounded it. The trees blocked most of the harsh wind coming in off the lake, but he guessed it was still close to freezing, if not colder.

"What'd you say, boy?" one of the twins challenged him, cocking back his fist. He shoved him hard against a tall spruce tree, ready to fight.

Oscar wasn't scared. He felt the comfortable weight of the switch-blade in his pocket, the very same knife he'd carried as part of the Dragons. He'd sworn never to use it again, but felt his fingers wrapping around the pearl handle just the same. Old habits die hard. But before he could do anything Jim Felt was between them, holding back the twin.

"Did you hear what he just said?" Teddy or Tommy said, his eyes locked with Oscar's. "He called me a mother fucker! That little wetback called me a mother fucker!"

"Let it go, Teddy," Felt said, "this is his first mission. The Rever-end thinks he's ready, and who better to judge than the Rev?"

"First of all, I'm Tommy," he said, still glaring at Oscar, "and sec-ond of all, I don't have to take that crap from nobody. We're doing the Lord's work here, and if he can't stomach it, then we need to cut him loose. You know that."

"Not your decision," Teddy said, laying a hand on his brother's shoulder, "even if the little spic deserves it."

Oscar felt his hands clench into fists. He took a step toward Teddy, waving the switchblade in front of him. "Just like this lady deserves to be buried alive?" he asked. "Just like those people deserved to be killed in Montana, and before that in Kansas?"

He watched Felt's eyes go wide and knew he'd said too much. He wasn't supposed to know about any of that, but he'd heard rumors, and by the look on all three men's faces he knew the rumors had to be true.

He dropped the knife to the ground, quickly back pedaling. *"Mi Di-os,"* he said, making the sign of the cross. "I am sorry, my friends. I see it all so clearly now. I confess that I have been very jealous. The *Padre* took all of you into his confidence before me. I see now, though, that he was right to do so, because I wasn't ready."

Felt let go of Tommy, walked over to Oscar, and pulled him into an embrace. He felt the man patting his shoulder and mirrored the dis-play of affection, patting the old man's back in return.

"Oscar, Oscar, Oscar," Felt said, his accent stretching out each syllable of the man's name, "my boy, whatever are we going to do with you? You're one of us, you always have been. We're all just doin' the Lord's work, whether it's preaching to the flock, collecting donations, or smiting demons. Your contribution is just as valuable as ours."

He saw one of the twins roll his eyes but tried not to react. "I know, Mr. Felt," he said, staring at the ground as though ashamed of his words, "but it's just been so hard, knowing I could do more..." He let his words trail off. "I see now that my misgivings were a sin of pride, of not understanding my place in the ministry. Do you think the Lord can forgive me, Mr. Felt?"

"Oscar, you know he can," the man whispered, "but can you forgive yourself? If you can do that, the Almighty will surely follow." He knelt to the ground, retrieved Oscar's knife, and slipped it into his pocket. "But until then, I think I'll keep this."

"All right, can we get this show on the road?" Tommy said, pulling a shovel out of the canvas sack they had hauled through the woods. "I'm over it now. No harm, no foul."

"Truer words were never spoken," Felt drawled, finally releasing Oscar from his embrace. "And we do need to get this 'show on the road,' as young Mr. Tyler here so eloquently put it. Boys?"

And with that, they started to dig. Oscar and the Tyler twins shoveled while Felt supervised. Because the ground was nearly frozen it took them almost an hour to dig the hole. By the time they were finished, soaked in sweat, teeth chattering, and tired to the bone, the hole extended down six feet and was a good three feet wide.

Oscar wiped his brow with the back of his hand, his arms and legs aching from the exertion. He tried to present a hard exterior, but inside he was shaking. He didn't want to do this, but if he didn't, he knew he might not make it out of the forest alive.

If only the *Padre* were here. He was certain that the *Padre* had not, in fact, ordered the woman's burial, and that Felt had instead taken it upon himself to do the deed without the Reverend's permission. The *Padre* would never condone their actions.

He would speak to him the moment they returned to the campsite. Dad would turn them over to the police. He was sure of it. But first, they'd race back to the forest and save the young woman's life.

"A little help?" asked one of the twins, dragging the end of the trunk. Felt and the other twin were leaning against a huge oak tree, drinking beer.

Why must he be the one to help bury the woman? He sighed, nodded, and lifted the other end of the steamer. Together they walked it to the hole, lifted it over the edge, and began to maneuver it down into the dirt.

"Fuck this," said Tommy or Teddy, letting go of his end.

The full weight of the trunk and the woman inside nearly wrenched Oscar's shoulders from their sockets. He tried to hold on but was finally forced to let go, and watched helplessly as the trunk turned end over end and finally settled upside down into the hole.

The redheaded twin laughed as he watched the trunk settle into the earth. Oscar wanted nothing more than to punch him in the mouth, to silence his laughter, but he held his fist as well as his tongue.

"She's gonna die anyway," said the man with a smirk, "either from freezing or running out of air, so what's it matter if she's right-side-up or upside down?"

Oscar's cheeks burned, but he shrugged and forced a smile to his lips. "Satan's whore," he said, "she probably deserves worse."

"Now you're getting it," said Tommy or Teddy, slapping him hard on the back. His shoulder cried out in pain, but he kept his silence.

"Okay," said Felt, walking over to them. "You two have earned a beer, and then we've got to put all that dirt back in that hole again."

He pressed an open bottle of Budweiser into Oscar's hand, which the boy gratefully accepted. Despite the cool October night, he was sweating and drained the bottle in three huge gulps.

And then they were shoveling again. It took markedly less time to fill the hole than it did to dig it, and they were done in no time at all.

Oscar couldn't help thinking about the girl and how much air she had left. The trunk was big, but not that big, and she filled up a good portion of it by herself. He'd be surprised if she lasted more than a few hours. The moment they got back to camp, he'd explain the situation to the *Padre* and then they'd race back here to dig her out.

"Oscar, you're staying here," said Felt, almost as if the man had read his mind. Felt walked toward the huge canvas sack from which he'd retrieved the beers.

"What are you talking about?" he asked, confused. He had to get back and talk to the *Padre* before the woman ran out of air.

"You need to stand guard," he said. He held a thin sleeping bag and a pup tent in one hand, and a green Coleman lantern in the other. "Here, take these," he said, pushing them at Oscar, "and try to keep warm."

"But...but..." Oscar said, something he sometimes did when he was upset, "but I can't..."

"You can, and you will," Felt said, "and you'll take this." He reached under his shirt and pulled out a small-caliber pistol, what looked like a .22, and handed it to Oscar. "In case there's trouble. Just pitch your tent over the trunk, crawl in the sleeping bag, and catch some shuteye. I'll be back around in a few hours to bring you some supper, and then again in the morning to take you back to camp."

"What about my knife?"

"The gun will serve you better," he said, turning to walk away.

He watched in astonishment as the Tyler twins each picked up a shovel and hoisted it onto their shoulders. "Hey Oscar, try not to shoot yourself in the foot," said Teddy or Tommy, as they left him to follow Felt through the forest to the clearing where they'd parked the truck.

Without the shovels, he'd never be able to free the woman in time. His heart filled with dread, he watched with a growing sense of despair as the three men entered a dense copse of trees and disappeared from view.

Chapter 38

It was nearly four in the afternoon when Brody decided to swing by the old house and check things out. He'd had an uneasy feeling ever since he'd caught those kids messing around outside, and because he hadn't been able to track Shawn down to ask him about the necklace, he decided to kill two birds with one stone and see if he and his old man were working today.

Shawn was there, as it turned out, but he wasn't working. Brody pulled his Charger in behind Shawn's Pacer and was about to get out of the car when someone—the boy from Saturday!—came running up to his car.

"Stop!" yelled Shawn, just behind the boy. "That's Brody Huffman. He's one of the good guys."

"Hey Shawn," Brody called out as he edged the door open. "Is everything okay?"

His hand tightened around the old baseball bat he kept in his car as he slid it out from under the passenger's seat. He drummed his fingers against the handle in three groups of three, counting off the numbers to calm his racing pulse.

"Sorry," the boy said, stopping just a few feet away, "but he has to get out of the way. We don't have time for this."

"I have a better idea," said Shawn, quickly walking over to the window. "Brody, are you up for a little adventure? We need your help. I don't have time to explain, but Ben's girlfriend has been kidnapped and we're going to need whatever manpower we can find to get her back."

"Kidnapped?" Brody said, confused. He didn't think Shawn even knew these kids. "Have you called the police?"

"We don't have time!" the boy shouted, pacing back and forth in front of the car.

Brody made a decision. He knew Shawn and Jenny well enough to know that he could trust them, and if there was anything he could do to help, he had to try.

"Okay," he said, sliding the baseball bat back into its resting place, "it's been a while since I had to kick anyone's ass, but I'm game. Get in, and tell me where we're going." He jingled the keys three times before starting the car.

* * *

Ben sat in the passenger seat of Brody Huffman's Charger, willing the man to drive faster. It had only been a few minutes since Huffman showed up at the house, but it felt like forever.

He went on and on about a necklace he'd found in the house, saying he didn't want to keep it if it belonged to someone else. Ben finally agreed to take the necklace, promising to give it to Shawn so he could find whoever had dropped it and return it.

Shawn and Jenny were behind them somewhere, no doubt caught in the traffic that they had managed to avoid. They'd decided to take both cars in case they needed to go to the police after all.

And then they were at the east end of highway 136, right across the street from Fred Ruskin's restaurant. The moment they pulled off the road, Ben was out the door and running. He immediately saw one of the twins who had attacked him standing beside the red pickup they'd been driving when they abducted Katy, chatting up a skinny blonde hippie chick like nothing had ever happened. The man's mouth gaped open in surprise as Ben hurtled toward him.

"Where is she, you piece of shit?" he screamed, tackling the man around the waist. He knocked him flat on his back, a sick thump resonating from the impact of his skull hitting the frozen earth. "Tell me where she is!" He punched the man hard in the nose, sending a splatter of blood spraying into the snow.

"Wait," Huffman yelled after him, but he was through waiting. He dug his knees into the man's ribs and bore down on him with his full weight, eliciting a shriek of pain.

"Hey, asshole," yelled his twin, running out of one of the many tents scattered across the field, "get the fuck off Tommy!"

Ben's luck was in full swing now. The redhead stepped on an empty Pepsi can, slipped, flipped head over feet like a vaudeville comedian doing a pratfall, and came down hard on his shoulder.

"Leave me the hell alone!" shouted his brother, but Ben met the plea with two more quick jabs to his face, bloodying his own knuckles.

"Tell me where she is," Ben screamed, clenching the man's shirt collar and shaking his head violently back and forth, "or I swear to God, I'm going to kill you!"

He felt a crowd gather around him, but he didn't care. Two more people tried to interfere; one only succeeded in twisting an ankle, while the other accidentally punched the grill of the pickup, the sound of broken bones echoing in the silence that followed.

"You heard the man," yelled Huffman, waving a Louisville Slugger baseball bat in front of him, swinging it like a spear. He limped over to Ben and kneeled down to check on the second twin.

"Out like a light," he whispered. "But there's more of them than there are of us, son. This could get real ugly real quick if any of them have half a mind to push it."

Ben ignored him, continuing to interrogate Tommy. "One more time: where is she?" Blood was everywhere, but he didn't care. These fuckers had taken Katy, and he'd do whatever he had to in order to get her back.

"You don't want to do that," drawled a man's voice behind him, so sweet it reminded him of syrup.

He craned his neck to see the old man who'd hit him with the tire iron leveling a rifle at his forehead.

"Now why don't you let that boy up all easy like and we'll talk this through. We're just a peaceful ministry traveling across God's great country preaching the word of the Lord. I don't know what beef you have with us, son, but it's only going to end badly if you don't get up right now."

"Fuck you," Ben said through gritted teeth. "Shoot me, if you think you can."

He concentrated on the rifle, willing it to explode in the man's hand the moment he pulled the trigger. He'd never know if his luck would have worked, however, because in that instant Shawn exploded from behind the Charger, hitting the old man with a body block that knocked the rifle from his hands and sent it spinning into the crowd of onlookers.

"You little shit," said the old man.

He threw a punch toward Shawn's head, but Shawn ducked and connected with a quick jab to the man's stomach that sent him to the ground wheezing for air.

"Enough!" bellowed a voice from behind the tents, vibrating through the field of canvas and cars.

All eyes turned to the voice, and Ben was astonished to see a giant of a man—he had to be close to seven feet tall—emerge from among the makeshift dwellings. He wore his hair shaved close to his scalp and a scar ran diagonally through the place where his left eye should have been.

Incongruously, he sported a pair of creased black slacks, a freshly-ironed white dress shirt, and a thin black tie. The contrast between the man's physical appearance and the clothes he wore struck Ben as absurd, and he would have laughed out loud had it not been for his sheer overwhelming presence. He walked through the crowd, moving closer. He carried an old, worn leather-bound Bible in his left hand.

"Let that man up," he demanded, his one eye riveted on Ben. "Thomas Tyler is a member in good standing of my congregation and has done nothing wrong."

"He kidnapped my girlfriend!" shouted Ben. "He and his brother, the old man, and a Hispanic kid left me for dead and took her God only knows where, and we're here to get her back."

"Thomas was with us all day," the man said, fully in control of the situation, "and everyone here can vouch for that."

"Amen, Reverend," chorused the fifteen or twenty men and women who surrounded them.

"He was here all day long," said one of them.

"We were playing cards just a little while ago," added another.

"Tommy wouldn't hurt a fly," said a third.

"Do you see?" the Reverend asked, leaning down to touch Ben's shoulder. "Tommy Tyler has a good heart, as do all the members of my flock. You're surely mistaken if you think he had anything to do with the disappearance of your girlfriend."

"Was he also mistaken about taking a tire iron to the back of his head from this asshole?" asked Shawn, pointing a finger at the old man.

Ben could see Jenny now, standing beside the car. Brody Huffman eased himself away from the crowd and toward her, evidently intent on placing himself between her and the Reverend's people. He still brandished the baseball bat, but it now hung innocuously at his side.

"And where is this wound?" asked the Reverend, circling Ben. "I see no mark upon him."

"He's a quick healer," said Shawn, moving toward the Reverend.

Ben suddenly knew they weren't going to win this fight, at least not here and not today. He quickly rolled off Tommy Tyler and ran his bloody hand through the snow before moving to stand beside his father.

"Just give us Katy," he said, his heart pounding in his chest. He felt weak and nauseated, all the energy he'd had earlier beginning to wane.

"If I had this young woman," said the Reverend, once again touching his shoulder, "I'd surely give her to you, if she wanted to go. But the truth is I've never seen her."

Ben leaned against Shawn, feeling weak in the knees and sick to his stomach. What was wrong with him? His vision grew dark and he struggled to stay awake. Shawn seemed to sense that something was happening, and slowly maneuvered him away from the giant.

"Now, if she were to show up tomorrow, on Satan's very own Halloween, and if she were to seek forgiveness for her sins, I'd certainly hear her out and give her whatever comfort I could, and I would surely guide her to the hand of God. And if you were to come back tomorrow for the revival, and she happened to be here…well, then, I'd have to do everything in my power to reunite you, wouldn't I? As a man of the cloth, it would be my duty to see that you, all of you, were together, exactly where you belong."

He was toying with them, playing with words. Ben wanted nothing more than to wipe the smug grin off his disfigured face, but his arms wouldn't move and his legs felt like anvils.

The next thing he knew, Shawn was on one side of him and Brody Huffman was on the other and they were half-carrying, half-dragging him to the car.

"One more thing," the Reverend called out to them, as Brody and his father maneuvered him into the backseat of the Charger, "and this is directed at you, my young blond friend, as the leader of this little band of ne'er-do-well thugs who go around beating innocent young men—next time, bring the Roman. I'll no longer eat his wares, but I'd surely like to meet the man himself before I reunite Ben with his lovely young Katy."

Chapter 39

"What happened?" Ben asked, coming fully awake. He was lying in a bed in a room he didn't know, surrounded by décor he didn't recognize, his teeth clattering as he spoke. "God, my head hurts like…" and then he remembered. "Katy!" He tried to stand from the bed but only succeeded in making himself dizzy. He slumped back down into the pile of sheets and blankets that surrounded him.

"That… priest," Shawn said, walking into view, "or whatever he was, he did something to you, made you weak. We barely got you into Brody's car before you passed out."

"How do you feel?" asked Jenny, standing beside Shawn. She wore a look of concerned frustration, as if she wanted to help but didn't know how.

"Like shit," he mumbled. "Where am I?"

"My trailer," said a gruff voice. Brody. "We didn't know where you were staying and Shawn didn't think it was wise to bring you back to his folk's house, so we brought you here. Sorry about the cold, though. I've been meaning to work on that heater."

"Don't worry about it," he said, shivering, trying once again to stand up. He finally succeeded in moving himself to a sitting position, but even that made him dizzy. "I have to get out of here, find Katy."

"Slow down," Shawn said, sitting beside him. "It's obvious they have her, or at least know where she is, just as it's obvious that he wants us to come back tomorrow, on Halloween. He thinks he's in control, and that gives us an advantage."

"How so?" asked Brody, moving closer to the bed. He tapped the bedpost three times, but then backed away guiltily as Jenny met his eyes.

"Because we won't wait for Halloween, of course," Jenny finished for Shawn, laying a hand on his shoulder, "though you don't have to be involved in this if you don't want to, Brody."

"I'm already involved," he growled, softening the rebuke with a smile, "and I've yet to run away from a good fight. I have a feeling I don't know half of what's really going on here, but you and Shawn have always been good to me, and if the two of you trust Ben here and are determined to help him, what kind of friend would I be if I didn't come along for the ride?"

Ben felt the man's sentiment oddly comforting. "Thanks, Brody," he said, the corners of his mouth briefly turning up before the movement made him feel like he was going to puke.

All he felt like doing was going to sleep. And then it hit him. "You don't mind if I take a quick nap, do you?" He leaned back onto the bed, watching as the room spun before his eyes. "In fact, if you happen to have any sleeping pills, I could sure use a couple about now."

"What are you talking about?" Shawn asked, clearly confused. "We have to be smart about this, but we can't give up."

"Never," Ben said, closing his eyes, "but the sooner I get to sleep the quicker we'll find Katy. Just trust me."

As it turned out, he didn't need the sleeping pills after all. The moment his head hit the pillow, he was out like a light and drifting deep into dreamland.

* * *

Katy's stomach grumbled, and her mouth was parched, but she knew she'd be dead from suffocation long before she had the chance to starve. That is, if she didn't freeze first. The trunk wasn't airtight and so she'd been in no danger of suffocating until they put her in the ground. Now, though, she could only guess how long her air might last.

She was buried alive, bound and gagged, and nobody knew where she was. She didn't even know where she was, not exactly, but she had a pretty good idea it was somewhere near the lake.

As her captors had carried her to wherever they'd interred the tiny, cramped coffin that had become her home, she was almost certain she'd been able to make out the sound of water pouring over the dam. That meant that she was probably somewhere on the other side of the lake, in the wooded area that stretched for miles in three directions. She'd be practically impossible to find, unless she was able to communicate that information to Ben or one of the others.

It felt like she'd been in the box forever, but she knew it had probably only been a few hours since the old man and his friends had attacked Ben and snatched her from in front of the house. She didn't know how long her air would hold out, but had a sinking feeling that it wouldn't last very long. If she had any chance of escape, she needed to go to sleep.

She took a deep breath of precious oxygen, already feeling a little light-headed from the carbon monoxide that was quickly filling up the trunk. She tried to will her body to relax, but it was no use. She was terrified, and every beat of her heart, every gasp of air, every shiver, took her one step closer to oblivion.

"Fuck it," she thought, and in desperation slammed her head as hard as she could into the side of the trunk. A multitude of colored lights danced and briefly flickered in her vision as she felt a wet rush of heat envelop her forehead. *Well, that was stupid*, she thought, just before she passed out.

* * *

Ben found himself in a graveyard. Was Katy dead? But he knew it was only a dream, his subconscious mind expressing his worst fears.

He didn't normally have lucid dreams, but this time he knew full well that everything he saw was all in his mind.

It was nighttime, of course, and the ground was covered in a soupy London mist, just like he'd seen in a hundred different horror movies. The moon was full tonight, and shone with a crystal bright intensity illuminating one spot in particular just over the hill.

He followed the moonbeam until he came to Katy Ruskin's grave. It was decorated by a huge piece of marble and granite, boasting an angel at the top of the stone. It lay in a row of similar headstones, all representing people he loved or at least cared about: Ellen Spencer, Paul McGee, Samantha Ruskin, Fred Ruskin, and Brody Huffman.

Five people dead, all because he wasn't smart enough or quick enough to stop their murders. He blinked and saw four more graves, open and without headstones, and instinctively knew they belonged to his parents, Emily, and himself.

He shook his head. This was bullshit. None of it had to be this way. If he could just find Katy, figure out where she was being held and rescue her, then everything else would fall into place.

He heard a noise, the snap of a branch or a footstep on the frozen earth that filled the graveyard. Turning away from the graves, he half-expected to see Katy but was greeted only with darkness. Another noise sounded, just past the headstones, and this time he knew it wasn't his imagination. It sounded like a half-strangled growl or a guttural curse spoken from across a chasm.

The hairs on his arm stood at attention, and he became acutely aware that he was not alone. He stared past the tombstones and into the trees beyond and could just make out a pair of glowing red eyes watching him from the foliage. Every fiber of his being urged him to run, to break from the tombstones and get as far away as possible, but still he held his ground.

Something had changed. The tombstones laid out in front of him were altered somehow. He stared at them in confusion, finally realizing that there was one less than there had been a moment ago. One of the graves had vanished. He squinted to read the names but could no longer make them out.

He heard footsteps echoing in the distance and realized that whatever had been watching him was gone. Another noise caught his attention, a low humming followed by a quick swoosh. It reminded him of the transporter in the original Star Trek series. He spun on his heels and was startled to see a frosted glass door just inches from his face. He stared at it in astonishment. Katy!

He recognized the door from her description; it was the portal she used to dreamwalk, but it was scarred and pitted, as if someone had been hammering to get inside. His heart once again in his throat, he slowly lifted his fist to knock.

* * *

Katy stood in the middle of her dream house, her head throbbing with pain. She touched her forehead and in an instant the pain disappeared, though she knew that she had one hell of a headache awaiting her in the real world.

Moving quickly to the couch, she grabbed up the remote control and turned on the widescreen television that dominated the living room. The screen sprang to life, showing her bound and bleeding form lying in the steamer trunk.

She felt the world around her began to waver and break up, but willed her subconscious to stay in the dream. Everything slowly swam back into view, and she quickly jammed her index finger against the button marked "Ben."

And there he was, wandering through a graveyard, looking for something or someone. She grimaced when he finally came to a headstone with her name on it, tears welling up in her eyes for both of them.

She loved him, she was sure of that now. She longed to be in his arms, to taste his lips against hers and to tell him—to finally just tell him—that she was in love, to finally take the terrifying risk of getting her heart broken.

A sharp pinprick of pain exploded in her temple, quickly spreading outward, almost rocking her out of the dream. She concentrated again on bringing the cabin back to view, but knew that she was dying. She was finally running out of air, had perhaps only minutes or even seconds before succumbing to her body's desperate need for oxygen.

Forcing herself from the couch, she stumbled toward the frosted glass door that separated her mind from the minds of those she monitored, rocking back on her heels as a knock vibrated against the glass.

"Katy," pleaded a familiar voice that she had to strain to make out, "let me in."

It was Ben! All thoughts of her physical body forgotten, she ran to the door, pulled it open, and threw herself into his arms.

"Oh God," she sobbed, ethereal tears running freely down her cheeks, "I thought I'd never see you again. How did you get in here?"

"No time," he gasped, looking past her and into the cabin. "Where are you?"

"I don't know," she said, "though I think they buried me at the lake, maybe past the dam by the spillway."

"Buried?" he asked, pulling from her to grip her shoulders. "You're not…dead, are you?"

She tried to suppress a frantic little giggle that sprang unbidden from her lips. "No, sweetie, I'm not dead, though I probably will be soon if you don't get your ass in gear and come find me."

"I'm on my way, just as soon as I can figure out how to wake up."

"I think I can help you there," she said, pressing her lips into his before pushing him through the door and back into his own dream.

"I love you," he said, and the anguish in his face tugged at her heart. He was terrified of losing her, just as frightened as she was of losing him.

"I love you, too, Ben," she said, feeling an incredible weight lift from her shoulders. "Now, wake up!"

* * *

Ben awoke with a start, elated in his knowledge that Katy was still alive. He scanned the room, squinting at the overhead light that flooded his eyes. Then he remembered; Brody Huffman's trailer. Other than his mother, he was alone in the room.

"You're awake," Jenny said, sitting beside him on the bed. "We were starting to get worried."

"I know where she is," he said, sitting up in bed.

He felt a lot better than he had when he'd first fallen asleep. Whatever the Reverend had done to him had apparently, thank God, only been temporary.

"Then let's go," she said, jumping from the bed to follow him out of the room.

"How long have I been out?" he asked, half-dreading the answer as he stepped from the trailer to the night beyond.

"Maybe thirty minutes," Jenny said, sliding into the back seat of the Pacer.

"Oh shit!" He said, bolting into the driver's seat, looking frantically for keys that he did not have. "I don't think we have much time."

"Where is she?" asked Shawn, following them from the trailer to the car. He carried a ballpoint pen and a pad of paper in one hand and a half-eaten sandwich in the other. "We called Fred. He and Brody are out looking for her right now. Tell me where we're going and I'll leave them a note."

"The lake," he said.

"I've been trying to work out a spell to help find her," Jenny said from the back seat.

She held up a pair of books; one was a dictionary that promised to help you 'quickly and effortlessly' translate English to Latin or Latin to

English, while the other was an old black book with a ragged, unlabeled cover that he didn't recognize.

Since when did his mother practice witchcraft?

"Here," said Shawn. He climbed into the passenger's seat and pressed a set of keys into Ben's hand, motioning for him to crank the engine. "Let's move."

The engine roared to life and Ben popped it into gear, squealing away from the trailer and out through the circular blacktop.

"Where at the lake is she?" Jenny asked, holding tight to the back seat as he pushed the car toward its limits.

The little yellow Pacer rattled and shook as he burst through the little gate that marked the entrance to Bower Trailer Park, hitting Locust Street at almost 70 miles an hour.

"I'm not sure," he said, swerving to avoid hitting a dog that darted out into the street, "but she thinks it's past the dam, and on the other side of the spillway. They buried her alive."

"*She* thinks?" Shawn asked.

"There're a few things I haven't exactly told you," he said, shooting down South Fayette to turn left on Highway 136. "We both have… abilities; we were born with them. I'm incredibly lucky, at least when crazy reverends aren't nixing my mojo, and Katy can dreamwalk."

"Dreamwalk?" Jenny asked, shouting to be heard over the roar of the engine.

"She can enter people's dreams, change them, and communicate with the dreamer. I fell asleep and we talked, and she told me where she thought they had taken her."

"Thought?" Shawn asked. "You don't know for certain?"

"No, not for certain," he said, driving past the Jaycee park and onto the lake road, "but she was pretty sure, because of," he said, pausing as the car hit a speed bump and flew into the air, coming down hard a second later, "the speed bumps."

Shawn winced.

"Sorry about the car, Dad."

"I'll make you a deal," he said, his hands gripping the side of his seat as the car squealed around a curve at breakneck speed, "don't call me that again until you actually exist, and you can do whatever you want to the car."

They shot down a steep hill, moving past the golf course and an old fishing shack, careening around another curve. Ben started to reply, but the words died in his throat as they finally reached the end of the road. And there, parked beside the spillway, stood the old red pick-up that the Reverend's goons had been driving when they abducted Katy, the very same truck they had seen in the field across from Ruskin's Pizzeria.

Ben slammed on the brakes and squealed to a stop. Then they were out the door, running fast across the dam toward the snow-covered woods where Katy had told Ben she lay buried.

* * *

Katy awoke to the all-consuming certainty that she was going to die. She tried to suck in air, her lungs gasping to bring in oxygen, but none would come. She strained hard against the duct tape that bound her wrists, but it wouldn't come loose. She finally managed to spit the handkerchief from her mouth, but it didn't help.

She pounded her fists against the top of the trunk, screaming, begging for somebody, anybody, to help her. She hit and scratched until her fingers were broken and bloody, then resorted to kicking, but to no avail. The trunk, she knew, was weighed down with hundreds of pounds of dirt and wasn't about to budge.

Closing her eyes, she prayed for God to help her. For the first time in a very, very long time, she prayed to a God that she had never really believed in. She prayed to stay alive long enough for Ben to rescue her, and to have the strength to hold on for just a little while longer.

She prayed to God, alternately cursing Him, blaming Him for everything from the nightmares to allowing her to be buried alive just after she'd found the man who she wanted to spend the rest of her life with; for taking her father from her not only once but twice; and for sending His angel to lure them into the past to stop a series of murders without even giving them a clue how to do it.

On the verge of dying, her lungs shutting down, it finally hit her: from everything her father had told her about his brief meeting with Michael, he wouldn't do the things she had just accused him of doing. When the angel had touched him, her father had told her, he had taken away his craving for alcohol and filled the darkness inside his soul with a blissful and undying bright light. He had literally saved her father's life. And a being that good, that pure, wouldn't—perhaps couldn't—send them to their deaths 28 years in the past without at least a chance to survive. Which had to mean…something, but she was no longer sure what.

The thought tingled in her brain, wanted to come out, but she was beyond words now. She drew her last breath of carbon monoxide, sighed, and blinked one last time before darkness enveloped her.

* * *

Oscar Reyes sat in his little tent, on top of the grave of the woman he had helped bury, praying to God for forgiveness. His teeth chattered as he completed the prayer, and he pulled the sleeping bag tighter around his shoulders in an attempt to keep out the bitter cold.

He poked his head out the tent door, shining the lantern through the towering pine trees and into the dark night sky. The snow was coming down harder now, and a good inch or two of the powdery white flakes surrounded his tent. His stomach grumbled, and he wished that he had something to eat. More than that, though, he wished he were back in Mexico or even California, and that he'd never gotten involved with the Dragons or joined the ministry.

That thought surprised him. He'd done nothing for the last seven years but eat, drink, and sleep the church, scouting new towns for them to visit, collecting money to support their mission, and trying to learn whatever he could from the *Padre*. But hadn't Reverend Dowd wondered where he was by now? He didn't believe, not for a second, that the man had condoned what had been done to that poor girl. But…what if he did? What if all the rumors were true and he'd been joining Felt and the Tyler twins on their secret missions all along?

It was funny but, if he was in the man's presence, he never would have even considered the thought, would have thought it almost blasphemous to even think it. But the further away he got from the *Padre*, the more he wondered about the ministry and what he'd been doing with his life these last seven years.

He was about to close his eyes and try to get some sleep when he heard a noise, the sound of someone crunching across the snow. His hand went instantly to his belt and he withdrew the .22 Felt had given him. He'd never even checked to see if it was loaded.

He slowly peered out the tent flap, his pulse beating like a drum. He tightened his grip on the gun and slowly edged his way out of the tent.

"Whoa, pardner," said Jim Felt, staring out at him from beneath several layers of clothing. His neck was wrapped in a huge white scarf and Oscar thought he looked like an abominable snowman. He carried a takeout bag from Tastee Freeze and a thermos, both of which he raised into the air in mock-surrender. "Don't shoot."

"You scared me," Oscar said, watching as his words condensed in the air. "Sorry about the gun." He slipped the pistol back into his waistband.

"Better safe than sorry. So how're you doing out here?" he asked, handing Oscar the food. "Brought you a couple of hot dogs, some fries, and a thermos full of coffee. Cold as a witch's tit out here, don't you think?"

"Si," Oscar replied, taking the food and quickly ripping open the bag. He was starving, though thinking of the girl buried beneath the dirt and snow tempered his appetite. "Thank you for the food."

"Least I could do," he drawled, rubbing his gloved hands together. "Sure didn't expect a blizzard when we set out, did we?"

"I'm not sure I'd call a couple of inches of snow a blizzard," said a voice behind them, "but then again, I also wouldn't kidnap and bury a defenseless woman."

Felt whirled around to confront the voice, while Oscar just stared into the darkness. He had heard the words plain as day, but nobody was there.

"Come out, come out, wherever you are," Felt half-sang into the night, his eyes wild with bridled fury. He reached into his waistband and withdrew another gun.

"Basta," warned Oscar, pushing Felt's gun toward the ground, "stop it. We don't even know what they want. If we let them have the girl, maybe they will let us live."

"Don't you get it yet?" Felt whispered. "We're not fighting men; we're fighting demons and devils."

"The only devil I see out here," said a different voice, this one closer, "is you."

"Deliver us from evil," spat Felt, firing blindly into the darkness. The gun jerked in his hand and he screamed in pain as the weapon misfired, exploding in a sea of sparks, metal, and blood.

"We surrender," Oscar called out, raising his hands in the air.

"Where's Katy, you piece of shit?" said the man they had assaulted in front of the old house as he stepped from the shadows to confront them.

"Fuck you, asshole," Felt growled, grabbing the gun from Oscar's waistband with his left hand. He pulled it free in one quick motion and aimed it at his attacker.

Time seemed to stand still as he cocked the hammer and shoved the muzzle hard into the man's chest. "Use your magic on this, motherfucker," he whispered, his finger tightening on the trigger.

"No!" shouted another man, one he'd never seen before, as he dashed toward them from the darkness. But there was no time.

Oscar didn't even think. He swung the lantern up in an arc over his head, bringing it down hard on Felt's gun. The weapon fired harmlessly into the ground, and then Oscar was upon him, wrestling the gun away from his hand and taking him down to the ground.

"Oscar, you little spic," Felt said, "what the hell do you think you're doing?"

"*Usted es Malvado*," he said, bringing his elbow down hard into the man's face. He felt a sickening crunch as Felt's arms went limp. "You are evil. You! Not them, not the girl, you!" He struck him again and again, until finally one of the other men pulled him off Felt's unmoving body.

"*Permita que mí sea,*" he yelled, filled with rage that he had let Felt and the others manipulate him. But then the rage dissipated, and he knew what he had to do. "Okay, okay. We have to save the girl."

Chapter 40

"Where is she?" screamed Ben, frantically searching for signs of a freshly dug grave.

Between the snow and the darkness, he couldn't make out anything. He felt a new dread settle over him. To come this far, only to be too late...

"There," the dark-skinned man said, pointing toward the tent. "God help me, but we buried her underneath. We must hurry." He scrambled to his feet.

"Why are you helping us?" Shawn asked, as he and Ben uprooted the canvas shelter and threw it aside.

Ben dropped to his knees, throwing clumps of earth over his shoulder as he dug into the earth with his bare hands. But it wasn't going fast enough. And then the Mexican was beside him, tearing up great clods of earth and handing them off to Shawn who threw them away from the hole.

"We did a terrible thing," the boy said helplessly.

"I found shovels," said an out-of-breath Jenny, joining them beside the makeshift grave. "They were in the back of the red pick-up." She handed one to Ben and the other to Shawn.

Ben stood up, burying the shovel deep into the earth, yanking it out again to throw more dirt away from the hole. Shawn joined him, and Jenny and Oscar worked to excavate the larger clumps from the hole. After what seemed like hours, their shovels finally clunked against something solid.

His heart raced as he leapt into the hole, frantically digging with his hands. A huge steamer trunk lay upside down in the dirt, wedged into the bottom of the pit.

"Oh my God," he whispered, seeing for the first time Katy's subterranean prison.

He grabbed the trunk, yanked, but couldn't get any purchase. He dug along one side, found a handle, but wasn't strong enough to pull it out of the hole. And then Shawn was beside him, pulling at the other side. Together they managed to lift it maybe three or four inches before it became wedged against a gnarled and ancient tree root.

And then Oscar was in the hole, chopping at the root with the end of one of the shovels. As soon as the root was gone, he managed to squeeze himself between the side of the hole and the trunk. He heaved at the trunk and, between the three of them, they managed to right the makeshift coffin and haul it out of the hole.

Ben clawed at the lid but it wouldn't open. "Katy," he screamed, pounding his fists against the trunk. "Katy, can you hear me? Katy!"

"Ben, it's locked," Jenny said, kneeling beside the steamer. She beat at the padlock with the butt of the gun Katy's abductor had dropped earlier, but it wouldn't budge. "Stand back," she said, aiming the muzzle of the gun at the lock's hasp.

"Wait," Ben said, concentrating, trying to calm his racing mind.

Praying his luck would hold true, he cocked back his middle finger with his thumb and lightly tapped the lock. It fell open, and he threw it aside and flung open the lid.

Katy's hands and hair were smeared with blood and her feet were bound with duct tape. She wasn't moving, and he didn't think she was breathing. Her lips were blue, and her skin was cold to the touch. He gently lifted her from the box and laid her atop the canvas tent. Jenny dropped to her knees beside the girl's still form, checking for a pulse. She shook her head and then, together, they began to administer CPR.

Jenny tilted the girl's head back, lifted her chin, and checked her breathing. She blew two quick breaths into her mouth, and then knelt back as Ben located her sternum. He placed his hands in the middle of her chest and began compressions, counting to fifteen before pausing to let Jenny blow oxygen into her lungs.

They went on like this for five minutes before Shawn finally motioned for them to stop. "I'm sorry," he said to Ben, tears in his eyes. "You did all you could. I'm sorry it wasn't enough."

He stared down at Katy's lifeless body, her skin a pale chalky white, her mouth caught in a silent scream. "The nickel," he said, suddenly remembering. The nickel could save her. He reached into his pocket.

"No," said Jenny, reaching out to still his hand. "It doesn't work that way. We were able to save you because you weren't dead, but even then just barely."

"If we'd gotten here a few minutes earlier," Shawn said, looking lost, "we might have been able to save her."

Something clicked deep inside of Ben, some secret knowledge he hadn't known he possessed, and he knew exactly what to do. He looked at his watch: it was twenty minutes after eight. Just a few minutes earlier… The world seemed to slow down all around him, and he saw an infinite number of delicate gossamer threads dancing before him. The strings fluttered this way and that way, like a thousand butterflies, all transparent, fragile, and intertwining.

He reached out to touch one, felt its weight, considered it, and then let it fall away, where it fluttered into the background. There were hundreds, perhaps thousands, of such threads forming patterns in the chaos laid out before him, and they all led to different probabilities. Some were near-identical and others were drastically different. Each one, he knew, branched off in an infinite number of different directions, and represented an alternate outcome for every choice he could possibly make. He watched in silence as seven threads disappeared and twelve others appeared to take their place. He touched another thread, then another, trying to find the reality where Katy was alive, but he couldn't sense her presence in any of them.

And then he found it, a string where he had awoken from his nap in Brody's trailer three minutes earlier. He touched the string, looked at his watch, and saw that it was exactly three minutes earlier than it had been a moment ago. But it was enough. It had to be. He could feel her life, her vitality, flowing away into the ether, almost gone. But there was something. She wasn't alive, but she wasn't quite dead yet, either.

He grabbed the thread, tugged at it, concentrating on changing reality. He watched as, one by one, all of the other strings collapsed into themselves, not truly disappearing but somehow sliding just out of sight. First three, then five, then fifty, then two hundred, a thousand, three million, a billion...

And, finally, there was only one. He blinked his eyes and watched as the thread disappeared, and then he was back in real time.

"I'm sorry," Shawn said, repeating the words he had said earlier. It was like watching an instant replay on Tivo. "You did all you could. I'm sorry it wasn't enough."

"No, I didn't," Ben whispered, slamming his fist down hard into Katy's chest, "but I am now."

All eyes turned to Katy as she awoke with a start, gasping for air, her eyes open wide and her mouth twisting into a scream. She sucked in huge gulps of oxygen, her breath rattling and rasping in her throat, before rolling over on her side and vomiting out the contents of her stomach.

"*Mi Dios,*" Oscar exclaimed, his eyes wide in wonder. "It's a miracle. How?"

Ben pulled her into his arms, stroking her hair, no longer able to hold back the tears. Something inside him broke and he sobbed, water streaming down his face to crystallize in the harsh winter wind, and he held the woman he had loved for as long as he could remember in his arms.

"Buh-buh," she rasped, struggling to speak.

"Shh," he whispered, trying to warm her body with his own. "You don't have to talk." He nodded gratefully as Oscar pulled a sleeping bag from the snow, shook it off, and wrapped it around her shoulders.

"Buh-buh-Ben," she finally managed to get out, her eyes gazing at his with confusion, "is this re-re-real, or am I d-d-dreaming?"

"It's real," he whispered, drying his eyes with the back of his hand. "Thank you for coming back to me."

She smiled up at him, shivered, and then whispered back, "There's no other place I'd rather be."

Chapter 41

Oscar Reyes had betrayed him!

Dowd was sitting on the cot in his tent drinking hot tea when the vision had taken him. It was just a flash, lasting no longer than a second or two at most, but he could clearly see Oscar standing beside the Anti-Christ as the long haired boy, another of Satan's minions, pounded on the chest of his dead whore.

They had surprised him. When he'd made the decision to go after the girl, it was more of a whim than anything else, a way to get their attention. He didn't expect that they'd actually seek him out or try to rescue her, and certainly not before Halloween.

His lark had cost him dearly. Both the Tyler twins were hurt, Oscar had left him, and Jim Felt—well, he didn't know what had happened to him, but he had a bad feeling about his absence. He had left to take dinner to Oscar quite a while ago, and he should have been back by now. He feared that the Anti-Christ had murdered him or, worse yet, turned the man against him, like he'd done with Oscar.

It was the sin of pride, he now realized, that had finally made him abandon his original plan and instead go after the girl. He had sinned and would have to be punished. He fingered the hunting knife in his pocket, knowing that all sin came with a price. God would forgive him his failings, he knew, but the only way to grow as a minister was to learn from his mistakes, to take himself to task for his transgressions.

But that would have to wait. First, he must deal with the devil. He rose from the cot, found his sword, and strapped it to his back, secur-

ing it behind his long trench coat. The devil wouldn't wait until tomorrow, he knew that now. They'd be here soon. And he'd be ready for
them.

Chapter 42

It was almost nine o'clock by the time they got back to Brody's trailer. The first Halloween murder wasn't supposed to take place until sometime tomorrow evening, but Ben didn't want to take any chances. As soon as they could get Katy settled and make sure she was all right, they had to find out what Jim Felt knew.

They had bound the man with the tape they had taken from Katy's arms and legs and gagged him with the handkerchief she had been gagged with. What goes around comes around. Shawn and Oscar loaded him into the back of his own pick-up and drove him to the old house, while Ben drove Jenny and Katy to the trailer.

The plan was to track down Fred Ruskin and Brody Huffman and get Katy set up in a safe house and then go back to interrogate Felt, but Ben was happy to see both Brody and Fred's cars (at least he hoped the brown Ford Bronco belonged to Fred Ruskin) parked in front of the trailer.

The snow seemed to be letting up a little, but it was still cold. Ben wrapped his coat tight around Katy as they climbed out of the car, but her teeth were still chattering and her skin felt like ice. He wanted nothing more than to get her into a hot bath and some dry clothes, but didn't feel comfortable taking her back to the hotel with the preacher and his people still out there.

Katy had trouble walking, so Jenny took one side and Ben the other and together they helped her ascend the steps that led up to the trailer. The door opened from inside and Brody met them on the porch.

He helped them navigate Katy through the entrance, and soon she was under the very same covers Ben had covered himself in less than an hour ago. Jenny stayed with her, while he brought Fred and Brody up to speed.

"I'm so glad you found her," Ruskin said. "We looked everywhere, even managed to catch a few of the church kooks outside their camp, but we couldn't get them to tell us anything. Not sure if they actually *knew* anything, to be honest."

"After a while, we just came back here," Huffman added, "because we didn't know what else to do."

"They had her buried alive on the other side of the lake, just past the spillway," Ben said, glancing over his shoulder toward the bedroom. "They had two guys guarding her, but one of the men, a kid named Oscar Reyes, turned on the other and probably saved my life."

He was pretty confident that the gun never would have gone off, but no one else needed to know that, especially Oscar.

"My God…" Ruskin said, his face pale. "Is she okay?"

Ben thought back to what he had done. He'd altered reality just enough to find a reality where they had arrived at the grave a few minutes earlier, just in time to save Katy's life. He still didn't understand it, not exactly, but he was sure that he'd been doing it for half his life; he just hadn't seen the mechanics until now.

"I think so," he said, "She's weak, but I think she'll be fine."

"Where's Shawn and this Oscar Reyes?" asked Brody, tapping his fingers against his thigh. "And can we trust him? Reyes, I mean."

"They're at the house. I didn't think the preacher would think to look for them there. As for Reyes, I honestly don't know," said Ben. "But I do know Shawn can take care of himself. And we didn't have a lot of choices."

"I think we can," added Jenny. "The remorse in his eyes…it's like he got in over his head, and regretted ever being part of it."

"We need to get Katy settled in somewhere safe and then I'll meet up with Shawn and we'll find out what Felt knows," Ben said.

"I think you meant 'we', son," said Ruskin, a gleam in his eyes that made Ben nervous.

"Brody," Ruskin added, turning to the other man, "can you take Katy and Jenny to my house? I'll call Candy and let her know what's going on. Up until now, I've had no involvement in this, so they should be safe there. And you'll be their insurance."

"I can do that," the vet said, with a smile, "just let me grab a few things first."

"And give me a few minutes to check on Katy," Ben said, already walking out of the room. He paused, called over his shoulder, "and then maybe we can finally get some answers from Felt."

Even if they didn't yet know all the questions, he silently added. Like why, for instance, if the Reverend was the murderer, didn't his little revival show up in the papers? And what about Kristen Hawks? She'd stolen his gun. If she was the murderer, which he doubted, then had he changed things? In the original timeline, the murderer had bludgeoned Paul McGee to death before cutting his throat and hanging him upside down from the roof of his garage. Would he now be shot instead?

He forced the image of his grandfather's corpse from his head. He needed to be upbeat and positive for Katy's sake. A great and powerful rage burned deep in his heart when he thought about what Jim Felt and his merry band of sadists had done to her. And Oscar Reyes was part of that. Oscar had helped them in the end, but he still had issues with the man, ones that would have to be settled soon.

He smiled as he walked into the room. Katy was sitting up in bed, tentatively sipping water through a straw. His mother sat beside her, arm protectively strung around Katy's shoulder. Even now, at the tender age of eighteen, Jenny had the maternal instinct he would come to know so well.

Impulsively, he leaned down and kissed Jenny on the cheek.

"What was that for?" she asked.

"Just for being you," he said, "Mom."

"You *told* her?" Katy asked incredulously, "What, did you tell her about me too?"

"What about you?" Jenny asked, turning to stare at Katy.

"No, but I think you just did, at least in a roundabout sort of way," he said. "And, no, I didn't tell her about me. She and Shawn figured it out all on their own."

"How?" she asked, taking another sip of water.

"He was hurt pretty badly," Jenny said, reaching out to take Katy's hand, "and I think he probably would have died if we hadn't found him. Shawn and I, we…healed him, using both the nickels. And, in doing that, we all connected in a way I'd never experienced before. It was amazing. Afterward, we just knew."

"I'm jealous," she said, smiling. "You guys got to experience all sorts of new psychic weirdness and family bonding stuff and all I got was this lousy t-shirt." She gestured at the Led Zeppelin tee she was wearing, courtesy of Brody's dresser.

"If you don't like it, I'm sure we can find another one for you," said Jenny, looking perplexed.

Ben rolled his eyes, playing along. "It's an expression from…our time," he said, nearly blurting out the date they were from, "she was just expressing her usual weird sense of humor."

Jenny sighed, smiled, and said, "Yeah, that's it. Tease the backwater girl, why don't you? You know, it's not my fault I was born…umm, a few decades too early?"

She was uncomfortably close to the truth. "Okay," he said, eager to change the subject, "I'm out of here. Brody's going to take you over to Fred's house, and I'm going to meet Shawn at the old house."

"You're going to the house?" Katy asked, a look of dread passing over her face.

"I'll be okay," Ben assured her, squeezing her hand. "We have Jim Felt, one of the men that kidnapped you. One way or the other, we're going to find out what's going on." His stomach did flip-flops at the thought of torture, but they no longer had time for niceties.

"Normally I'd be writing Amnesty International, but in this case, I'm all for torture. Go all 'Abu Ghraib' on his ass for me, will you?"

"You got it," he said, forcing another smile to his lips.

He didn't know what was going to happen tonight, not even if he'd come back alive; but he knew they had to stop the murders, and—he glanced at his watch—they only had a few hours left to do it.

"I love you, Katy," he said, gently pressing his lips against hers.

"I love you, too," she whispered, and then added, "but I'm going to be mighty pissed off if you go off and get yourself killed. So be careful, okay?"

"You know I will," he said, hoping he would see her again.

The house looked even more sinister at night. The trees had all lost their leaves, and the light from the moon combined with the hundred-year-old oaks to throw an eerie array of shadows against the house. Ben wasn't sure he could think of a more desolate and lonely place to spend a Sunday night.

Fred Ruskin walked beside him, and he pondered telling the man the truth about Katy. He knew it would probably do more harm than good, but Ruskin was risking his life to help them, and he felt that they owed him the truth. He was spared from making the decision, however, at least for now, when Shawn and Oscar met them at the cellar entrance.

"How is she?" he asked, holding the door open.

Even though they could have gone through the front door, they decided to keep using the cellar so as not to attract unwanted attention from any neighbors who might be watching. They didn't want to involve any more people in this than was absolutely necessary.

"Better," Ben answered. "She's still pretty shaken up, though. Brody's taking her and Jenny to Fred's place."

"He's going to stay there and keep guard," said Ruskin, "just in case."

"So, where's Felt?"

"On the second floor," Shawn said. "He's in pretty bad shape, but he refuses to talk."

"He's real pissed off," added Oscar.

"How about you?" Ben said, whirling to face the man who had helped to bury Katy alive. "You finally did the right thing, sure, but not until you were forced. What are you even doing here? Why are you helping us?"

"You do not understand," Oscar stammered, looking down at his feet. "I never wanted to do these things. *Mi Dios.* I didn't even know what we were doing until just a few minutes before we approached you."

"And that makes everything okay?" Ben asked. Ruskin laid a hand on his shoulder, but he shrugged it off, shoving Oscar hard in the chest.

"Un no definitivo," Oscar said, backing away, "definitely not. I'm sorrier than I could ever say or explain. It's just...you don't know the Reverend. When you're with him, he makes everything seem like it's going to be okay. Even now, I have a *mucho* hard time believing that he ordered Mr. Felt to do these things. Yet the longer I am away from him, the more it seems possible."

Ben softened a little at Oscar's words. After what he'd experienced at the hand of the preacher, he had no problem believing Oscar's story. Dowd was some sort of psychic vampire, leeching just enough of his congregation's energies to make them pliable and open to suggestion.

He'd turned on all the juice with Ben, and it had come close to killing him.

"And as for why I'm here," Oscar said, "there are two reasons. First, I have some responsibility in all of this, and second," he said, a brief look of regret crossing his face, "I have nowhere else to go. I have been with the *Padre*—excuse me, Reverend Dowd—for seven years, a third of my life. I know nothing else, though I will most certainly have to learn."

Oscar probably wasn't the enemy, but that didn't mean Ben was ready to forgive him. He had accepted the man's help in the heat of the moment, when Katy's life was on the line, but he couldn't get past the thought that Reyes had helped bury the woman he loved.

Still, they might need his help again before the night was over. Reluctantly, Ben held out his hand. "This isn't forgiveness, but a truce. Do you think you can live with that, for now?"

He seemed taken aback by the gesture but slowly reached out to clasp Ben's hand. *"Sí. Gracias,"* he said, laying his other hand over Ben's. "For now, yes, I think I can. Thank you."

They walked into the kitchen, through the hallway to the stairs, and up into the second-floor library. Shawn explained that he and Oscar had decided that was the room best insulated for sound, and if things didn't go as planned Felt was probably going to be doing a lot of screaming.

The thought made Ben queasy, and he was sure none of them felt excited over the prospect of torture. But this was bigger than any of them, and they would do whatever they had to in order to get the information they needed.

Felt sat in the middle of the room, gag in place, his hands and feet tied securely to an intricately carved wingback chair. He stared defiantly at them. His nose had stopped bleeding but was probably broken, and his left eye was swollen to the point where Ben doubted he could even see out of it.

His right hand had suffered considerable damage from the explod-ing pistol, and he'd lost both his thumb and forefinger from the first knuckle up. Someone had wrapped the hand in a white towel, but the cotton was quickly turning red.

Ben almost felt sorry for the man, but reminded himself that this son of a bitch had nearly murdered Katy. He felt an incredible rage rise up within him and it was all he could do not to strangle the life out of the old bastard.

"Okay, it's time," said Ruskin, cracking his knuckles. "You three might want to step outside for a while. This could get ugly."

They had no intention of torturing the man if there was any other way, but of course Felt couldn't know that. They had briefly considered drugging him and having Katy dreamwalk into his mind, but there just wasn't enough time, and Katy was still so weak.

"I'm not going anywhere," Ben said flatly. "I think, after tonight, I've earned that."

"It's up to you, but don't say I didn't warn you."

"I'm staying, too," Shawn said, though he didn't look too sure.

Oscar echoed the sentiments, standing beside the door with his arms crossed. He didn't look like he could be convinced, so Ben decid-ed to focus all his efforts on his father.

"Shawn," Ben said, "you really don't need to be here for this, and, besides, I was hoping you could do me a favor. We have clothes and stuff at the hotel. Would you mind checking us out and taking our stuff to," he glanced at Felt, not wanting to say too much in front of the man, "the safe house? Besides, someone should check up on the girls."

"Yeah, I guess I can do that," he finally agreed, looking torn.

He'd played hardball, mentioning his mother and Katy, but he seri-ously did not want his eighteen-year-old father to have to help torture this man. He watched as Shawn left the room. "All right, let's get this over with."

Chapter 43

Katy sat in her bedroom—at least the room that would be hers several years from now—feeling very much alone. Jenny had tried to keep her company but eventually gave up and went to the kitchen to help Candy with dinner.

Maybe some of Ben's luck was rubbing off on her, because Sam was spending the night with a friend. Her mother didn't remember their conversation in Super Value two years ago, but she was almost certain Sam would. So at least that was something.

It's not that she didn't want to talk to Jenny; she just didn't know what to say. She was scared to death for Ben, Shawn, and her father, and at the same time kept picturing herself buried alive in that horrible steamer trunk.

She had come so close to dying. Actually, she corrected herself, she *had* died, but they'd managed to bring her back. The huge purple bruise across her chest attested to the fact. She'd thought her nightmares were terrifying, but they couldn't hold a candle to being buried alive. Perhaps next time she had the dream she'd remember that feeling and finally have the guts to face her attacker.

Her body ached in places she didn't even know could ache, and every time she moved or even stretched her muscles she immediately regretted it. She sighed and looked around the room. It wasn't anything like she remembered it; it was a guestroom in 1977 and as such had that antiseptic, unlived-in feeling that you came to expect from hotel rooms. Gone were her collection of Steiff stuffed animals, her awards from high school, and the paintings from the brief time in her life when she had decided to go from studying art to making it.

She knew that back in her time everything was exactly how she'd left it, but it still bothered her. It was as if her life has been erased instead of simply rewound. Of course, she reminded herself, if her father were to die tonight, she'd never be born in the first place. She wondered what would happen to her then. Would she simply disappear, or would she go back to a future where nobody knew who she was, a future where Katherine Grace Ruskin never existed? It was a sobering thought.

"Can I come in?" said Jenny, peeking around the door. "I come bearing hot tea and cookies."

"Yummy," said Katy.

No matter how warm she'd managed to get since being rescued from her makeshift grave, she still felt as if she had ice in the pit of her stomach. Something hot to drink might be exactly what the doctor ordered.

Jenny maneuvered a tray laden with cookies, two cups, and a steaming teapot through the room and placed it between them on the bed. "How are you feeling?" she asked, pouring each of them a cup of tea.

Katy carefully sipped the hot Earl Grey and bit into a cookie, savoring its texture and taste. She immediately recognized them as her mother's "special recipe" made-from-scratch peanut butter and pecan cookies that she'd so loved as a little girl. They were just as she remembered them.

"You can talk to Candy, you know," said Jenny. "She doesn't suspect a thing."

Katy stared at her for a long moment, then smiled and slowly shook her head. "You're good," she said, biting into another cookie. "What gave me away, my comment to Ben at the trailer?"

"I'm not *that* good," she admitted. "It's just that when I was getting you into your clothes, I couldn't help but notice this."

Katy watched as Jenny reached into her pocket and pulled out the melted wedding rings that she had worn around her neck since her father's death. So paralyzed by the entire kidnapping and being buried alive experience, she hadn't even realized it was missing.

"Don't tell anyone, okay?" Katy asked, taking the necklace and slipping it over her neck to let it fall beneath her t-shirt. "I'm not lucky like Ben. I want to make sure I get born."

"Your secret's safe with me, Katy Ruskin," Jenny promised, reaching across the bed to touch her cheek. "God…I'm going to miss you guys when you go back to your own time."

Katy found that her eyes were wet, and realized she was going to miss Jenny as well. "Well, you'll be seeing plenty of me sooner or later," she said, with a smile. "I am, after all, pretty smitten with your son."

"The one that's actually older than I am? Yeah, I kind of noticed that," she said, laughing, a beautiful alto that reminded Katy of the woman she knew and loved in the future.

"You know," she said impulsively, "we're actually friends in the future. You've never been anything but kind and generous with me, especially after my father…" her voice trailed off.

"Died? Don't worry, I kind of figured that out, too, after the way you looked at him in the restaurant, like you'd seen a ghost. I mean, I didn't know then that you were his daughter, but now that I've put the pieces together, it all makes sense."

"Yeah, well, I've lost him twice in two different timelines, one when I was a little girl and the other, the real timeline, just a few years ago. I don't want to go through that again."

"You won't. Things have a way of working out."

"So…you and Shawn," she said, changing the subject, "won't your parents wonder where you are?"

"Shawn's eighteen and out of school, so he can pretty much do what he wants, though he told his parents he's spending the night with a friend. Me, I'm babysitting all night for Fred and Candy because they had to go out of town on an emergency, something involving Candy's great-aunt. My parents weren't happy about it, because tomorrow's a school day, but Candy talked to Mom who'll smooth it over with Dad, so it'll all be okay."

"Clever," she said. "So, you and Shawn…I don't quite know how to ask this, but you already seem so close, and…"

"Not yet," Jenny said, blushing. "The plan was to wait until we're married, but…I dunno…" She turned away, embarrassed.

"Hey, I'm not trying to pry, and it's none of my business."

"No," she said, "it's okay. I just really want to, you know, and so does he, at least I think he does. When Kristen did… what she did, when she lied to me about her and Shawn, it really made me stop and think. I mean, what are we waiting for? I know I'm going to spend the rest of my life with Shawn, so what does it matter if we put the cart before the horse or I give the milk away for free, or any of those other goofy euphemisms that my mother's so desperately fond of using?"

Katy took her hand, touched by her innocence. "I keep forgetting how young you are," she whispered, impulsively pulling her into an embrace. "Just follow your heart, and do what feels right, in here," she touched a hand to Jenny's chest, "and here," and then touched her forehead, "and if you listen to them, really listen, they'll never lead you astray.

"But," she added, as an afterthought, "don't let anything you've learned about the future affect what you do now. I mean, I guess that's impossible, but all this weirdness…just live your life, Jenny, as best you can. Trust me. You're going to turn out great."

* * *

Brody Huffman stuck out his tongue to catch an errant snowflake, and then he did it twice more. He'd never quite gotten over the magic of the little crystal structures falling downward from the heavens to disappear with an imagined sizzle as they landed in the heat of his mouth.

Gazing up into the night sky, he watched as a gibbous moon poked out from behind a row of clouds that strongly resembled a pair of huge mating sheep. He turned the baseball bat in his hand, trying to ignore the deep ache that resonated through his bad leg. It bothered him all the time now, but it was always worse during the winter.

And, damn, winter had hit hard and fast this year. He wrapped his hands around the hot cup of coffee Mrs. Ruskin had just brought him, greedily gulping down three long swallows of the warm caffeine. He sighed with pleasure, enjoying the heat that filled his stomach.

He sat on a green and white nylon lawn chair outside Fred Ruskin's place, surrounded by a white picket fence, keeping watch for whatever might decide to intrude on Fred's little corner of the American dream. He didn't mind, really—after all, he didn't have anyone to go home to, and he owed all three families more than he could ever repay—but he wished someone would tell him what was really going on.

He had seen a lot of weird shit in his lifetime, but never quite as much of it as he'd seen these last few days. Relaxing in the chair, enjoying the crisp night air, he almost didn't hear the soft crunch of someone walking on snow in the distance. Lowering the half-drained cup of coffee to the ground, he tensed, ready to climb to his feet, but relaxed again as a woman dressed in a black suede coat appeared from around the corner, walking down the sidewalk.

The woman wore black stockings and pumps, and despite the jacket, just from the way she moved, he could tell she had a body that would put most women to shame. Her hips rolled as she walked, like a young Jayne Mansfield or Marilyn Monroe.

She turned to wave, apparently feeling the weight of his stare, and it struck him again how beautiful she was. Her long black hair contrasted perfectly with her pale, delicate features, and she moved like a cat on the prowl. Her face, however, looked young, probably no older than eighteen or 19 at best. Oh, to be twenty years old again.

Get your mind out of the gutter, Huffman, he chided himself. He smiled politely at the girl and offered a half-hearted wave before turning away. It'd been years since he'd gotten laid, but that was no excuse for drooling over someone young enough to be his daughter. Hell, she was probably no older than Jenny. He felt dirty. He averted his eyes as she passed in front of him, counting to three over and over in his head.

"Gotcha," a voice whispered, startling him. He looked up to see her standing in front of him, a handgun leveled right between his eyes. She circled around to his side, pressing the muzzle of her weapon deep into his ribs. "Now drop the baseball bat...slowly...and stand up."

He dropped the bat to the ground, watching helplessly as it buried itself in the snow. This is what he got for thinking with his dick. When he was in the Marines no one would have gotten the drop on him, gorgeous teenage girl or otherwise.

"Guys like you never learn," she said, gesturing impatiently for him to stand up. "You see a beautiful girl and all you can think about is getting in her pants."

"What do you want?" he asked, pain shooting through his left leg as he forced himself to his feet. Three, six, nine, twelve, nine, six, three.

"Not you, that's for sure," she said, scrunching up her nose as she pushed the gun deeper into his ribs. "You're not exactly my type, if you know what I mean."

He started to turn but stopped the moment he heard the gun cock. "No funny stuff, mister. I don't want to kill you, but I will if I have to."

"Are you from the ministry?" he asked, stalling for time. He clucked his tongue three times, then three more times, and three times after that, trying to calm his racing heart. It wasn't working.

"Yeah, that's it, honey. I'm a nun. Now, come on. I know they're in there."

"Nobody's home," He said automatically, knowing she was talking about Katy. He'd die before he let anything happen to her or anyone else in the house. "I'm just house-sitting for some friends."

"You're lying," she said, pushing him hard with her other hand. "Now move. We're going to go around to the back of the house, and I'm going to tie you up."

He walked slowly, trying to figure out how to get out of this. But his gait wasn't entirely an act; his leg hurt like hell.

"Move it, old man," she said, pushing him with the gun.

That's when he made his move. He whirled on her, snaked his hand out to grab the weapon, but hadn't fully taken into account his stance. His leg, already in pain, gave out on him and he crumpled to the ground. The last thing he saw was the gun as it slammed down into his forehead.

* * *

This wasn't going anything like she'd planned. She hadn't wanted to hurt the old man, didn't even want to talk to him, but had no other choice. She was a hunter, a sleek lioness, and her prey waited just inside. She'd do whatever she had to do to get what she needed.

Crouching down beside him, she took a coil of rope from her purse. With great effort, she rolled him over onto his stomach and looped the rope around his wrists again and again before tying it off with a reef knot. Finally, something useful out of all those hours wasted fishing with her father.

Hal Hawks. He was a housing developer first, a fisherman second, and somewhere much further down the list, her father. He had always wanted a boy but had instead been cursed with a girl, and he'd never let her forget it. He and her mother had tried to get pregnant again for the next seventeen years, but to no avail. They were stuck with her.

After her mother died in a car wreck, however, the same wreck Hal Hawks himself had almost perished in, he hadn't seemed quite so disappointed. She was barely a woman when her father started coming into her bedroom. He'd been drunk the first time and she could almost forgive him for that, but she hadn't smelled a drop of liquor on his breath the time after that or any of the countless times later.

She knew now that she should have gone to the police after the very first time, but she'd been so scared and hadn't known where to turn or who to ask for help. They had no relatives to speak of—just an aunt, her father's sister, in Minnesota, and she wasn't sure Aunt Enid would believe her anyway.

Last year, a junior in high school and still in Missouri, she'd finally told someone. She'd grown close to Mr. Jordan, her AP algebra teacher, and so one afternoon when they'd been working out a problem she confided in him. He'd been the only good man she'd ever known, and she still regretted what followed.

He immediately reported her father to child services and she briefly spent a month in foster care. Her father, however, a powerful man in the growing city of Joplin, had greased enough palms to get visitation rights. The moment he'd been alone with her, he'd threatened to draft her best friend Amelia, who'd always been fond of her father, to take her place.

All she had to do to prevent that from happening, he said, was to recant her story and tell the authorities that it was Mr. Jordan and not her father who had repeatedly raped and abused her. She'd done as she was told, and Mr. Jordan had eventually been sentenced to three years in the state prison for statutory rape. He hung himself his first week in, and Kristen still mourned his death.

After that, her father had forced them to move to Carthage, to get a "fresh start," but he'd quickly taken to bedding her again. No longer, however, was there any façade of lovemaking; he'd just enter her room, growl at her to get on her hands and knees, and take her from behind.

Three, sometimes four nights a week, more on the weekends, he'd enter her room, repeatedly raping her, leaving her battered and bruised in his wake. His appetites were insatiable, and she'd had three abortions to prove it. Soon there'd be another to add to the list, if her missing period was any indication.

The abuse had finally come to an end two days after she'd found out that she might be pregnant again. Her father came into her room that night, grabbed her by the hair, and forced her to go down on him. She did as he asked, letting herself get into it, almost enjoying it when, just before he climaxed, she suddenly stopped, let his dick fall out of her mouth, and stared him straight in the eyes.

"Finish!" he commanded, slapping her hard across the mouth.

Well, she'd given him a chance. That was more than he'd ever done for her. She carefully lowered her mouth to his crotch, took him deep into her mouth, and bit down as hard as she could, right at the base, straight through his penis.

It'd been harder that she thought it would be; it was like chewing through a gristly steak. But she hadn't stopped, not even when, screaming, he'd pounded his fists into the back of her head, nearly causing her to black out.

His member had finally come off in her mouth, spraying blood everywhere. It stained the walls, the ceiling, and even her brand new pink pajamas, the ones she'd bought after spending the night the week before with Jen. She rolled away, spat the *thing* out, and casually walked to the door, never once looking back.

Her betrayal had been planned down to the last meticulous detail. Earlier that year, she began sneaking out of her room; he responded by barring the windows, a fact that she hoped hadn't been lost on him as he lay there dying. Her phone had also been removed, and she'd changed the lock on her door herself, installing it so that it locked from the outside rather than from within. She needn't have bothered; from his screams, she'd estimated that he bled to death within the hour.

She buried him in the backyard. His greatest fear, the one that had always driven him to make money, was to be buried in a pauper's grave without a headstone, just like his grandfather. She'd been more than happy to make that nightmare a reality.

Eventually, she knew, someone would come looking for him. She'd already fielded dozens of phone calls, playing up her father's long-standing battle with lung cancer. He was sick, she said, too sick even to come to the phone. But that couldn't go on forever. Someone would send flowers, or come round to check on him. And then, it would all be over. But by that time she'd be gone, free to live the life she deserved, the life her mother had always wanted for her. She'd finally be free.

Her father had never been a huge believer in banks and had kept stockpiles of cash hidden in various places around the house. From everything she'd been able to find, she now had nearly ten thousand dollars with which to plan her new life. And she didn't intend to do it alone.

Once she'd dealt with the only person who stood between her and the love of her life, they'd escape to New York or Los Angeles or anywhere else equally as large and anonymous and start anew. She'd be happy again, the way she'd been before her mother had died. And, just like the night she had killed her father, she'd never look back.

But first, there was work to be done. She slowly crept back around the house, holding the gun she'd found in the duffel bag at her side. She was thankful for the pistol. She'd planned to use her father's hunting rifle, but this was much more convenient.

She'd been following Shawn and Jen all day and had tailed them to the old guy's trailer earlier tonight, intending to do the deed there, but hadn't brought enough rope. And so she'd had to pay another visit to Western Auto, and this time she'd purchased five sets of nylon cord at six feet each—more than enough to deal with all of them, save her true love, who she'd never allow to be bound by anything other than the adoration and desire that they shared. But by the time she'd arrived back at the trailer no one had been home.

She'd driven first to Shawn's house and then to Jen's, peeking in windows, looking around corners, but neither of them were home. She'd checked all their usual haunts and was about to give up for the night when the old guy whizzed past her in a beat-up Dodge Charger. She'd caught sight of Jen in the backseat and figured Shawn was probably with them. After that, it was simply a matter of driving around town looking for the car.

She'd been to Fred Ruskin's house once, a few months ago, when she and Jen babysat for his step-daughter Samantha. She liked the little girl and her mother, but something about Ruskin made her skin crawl. The way he moved, even the air he breathed, just didn't set well with her. He reminded her of Hal Hawks. She'd hated eating at his restaurant and had often wondered if he had the same relationship with Samantha that she'd had with her father. She hoped not, or she'd have to kill him, too.

She knocked at the door and was surprised when Candy Ruskin answered. She'd been expecting Candy's husband, and would have enjoyed putting a bullet in his jowly face.

"Kristen," the woman said, looking anything but happy to see her. "What are you doing here?"

"I'm sorry, Mrs. Ruskin," she whispered, bringing the gun up below her chin, "but if you say another word, I'll have to blow your fucking brains out. Now step outside, turn around, and do exactly what I tell you to do."

She led the woman outside and around to the back of the house, where she gagged and tied her up beside Huffman. She took great care to make sure the ropes were tight enough to keep her from escaping, but not too tight as to cut off her circulation.

"Don't worry, Mrs. Ruskin," she whispered, watching as the woman's tears turned to frozen crystals of salt halfway down her cheeks,

"I'm not going to hurt you. In fact, no one's ever going to hurt you or your daughter ever again."

Chapter 44

Despite his bravado, Fred Ruskin had never tortured anyone. Sure, he'd interrogated people—that's what cops did—and he'd even tuned up a few uncooperative suspects in his day, but he'd never resorted to out-and-out torture.

He'd been given a second chance with Candy Martin and her beautiful daughter Samantha, and it made him feel sick to think he was risking his soul on a piece of crap like Jim Felt. But one way or the other, they had to know what they were up against. If it came down to it, he was fully prepared to extract that information by whatever means necessary and worry about the consequences later.

"Okay, Mr. Felt," he said, removing the gag, "tell us about this preacher of yours."

"Go screw yourself," Felt said. "He'll come for you, you know. And when he does, even Satan himself won't be able to help you."

"Oh, cut the crap," Ruskin said, "This isn't about God or Satan, and you know it."

"Our Father which art in heaven, hallowed be thy name," started Felt, "Thy kingdom come. Thy will be done in earth…"

Ruskin slapped Felt hard across the face, opening up one of the cuts he'd received in the fight with Oscar. Blood trickled down his cheek to soak into the corner of his mouth.

"As it is in heaven," he said, continuing as if nothing had happened. "Give us this day our daily bread. And forgive us our trespasses…"

Ruskin punched him in the stomach, knocking the wind from his lungs and sending him into a coughing fit. "I said, cut the crap."

Oscar started forward, but Ben stopped him. "Don't," he whispered, "he knows what he's doing."

Thanks for the vote of confidence, thought Ruskin, *but you've never been more wrong in your life.*

He watched as Felt recovered and continued his litany. This wasn't working; it was time to bring out the big guns. He slipped the pistol he'd taken from Oscar out of his waist band, cocked back the hammer, and held it to Felt's head.

"No!" Oscar yelled. "You said you wouldn't kill him."

"Oh, I'm not," replied Ruskin, moving the gun to point at Reyes. "At least, not yet. But I have to convince your former friend that I'm serious."

He pulled the trigger and a crack echoed through the empty room. Oscar clutched his chest, looking at Ruskin in shock before falling to his knees, teetering, and landing face-first on the dusty floor.

"My God, Fred," Ben said, staring at Reyes' back. "He helped us. Why on Earth…"

"Tell me all about the reverend," Ruskin said to Felt, ignoring Ben, "or the next bullet is for you."

"Fuck you," Felt said. "You can't do this. Why did you kill him?"

"No," said Ruskin, once again cocking back the hammer of the old pistol. He shoved it hard against Felt's temple. "Fuck *you.*"

He watched as Felt dissolved into a quivering mass of sobs and screams, his eyes filling with tears. "Okay, okay. All right! Please don't kill me."

"I know a thousand ways to torture a man," Ruskin said, "and we're just getting started. By the time I'm finished, you'll be begging me to put this bullet in your brain. But I won't. I'll leave you here, in your own piss and shit, and you won't be able to do anything but whimper into the darkness." The threat sounded hollow as soon as it passed his lips, but he couldn't come up with anything better.

"All right, all right," Felt said, talking several deep breaths. "He sees visions, and they lead him to people like you. He saw you earlier this year. The Roman soldier, he called you, standing beside the Anti-Christ and his red-headed whore. He watched you take down a man of the cloth, and he's been gunning for you ever since."

"Wait a minute," said Ben, stepping forward. "What in the hell are you talking about?"

"You know exactly what I'm talking about, demon," he screamed.

"Should I maybe break a few of your fingers on your left hand," Ruskin asked politely, "or perhaps work my way across to your right, which has already sustained considerable damage…" He let his words trail off, hoping the implication would be worse than any actual threat he might come up with. "Or maybe shoot your balls off. Which would you prefer?"

"All right! The boy that was with you earlier, the one you called Shawn," Felt said, blood trailing down his chin, "He's the Anti-Christ, at least as far as the Reverend is concerned, and he intends to kill him."

"My God," Ruskin's face went white, "The priest…he's talking about Aupuch. That was no man of the cloth. That was a monster."

"And the Anti-Christ's whore," Ben started, working it out, "must be Jenny?" Ben lunged for Felt's throat, and it was all Ruskin could do to pull him off before he choked the life out of the man.

"What else?" Ruskin asked, putting his own body between the two men.

"There's not much else to tell!" he yelled, flinching as though Ben might attack him again. "He's…I don't know, he sees visions, and we take advantage of that. Me and the Tyler twins, I mean. It's all a game for us, but for him—for most of them—it's real."

"Go on," Ruskin said.

"He goes on these…missions, he calls them. Sometimes we go with him. For him, he's killing agents of Satan. For us, well, it's a chance to make a little money, knock a few heads, and sometimes even get a little pussy."

Ruskin backhanded him, sending a spray of blood across the room. "Manners," he warned, noting the look on Ben's face. If he hadn't hit the man, he had a feeling Ben would have done much worse.

"We didn't do anything to her, I swear," he said, the words falling out of his mouth in a rush. "The twins wanted to, but Oscar was with us and it was his first mission. We didn't want him to come, but the Reverend insisted. And we didn't want him reporting back that we'd consorted with…with the girl."

"So all this time, you've been playing him?"

"Yes and no," said Felt, apparently eager to spill his guts now that the cat was finally out of the bag, "when you're with him, you really *believe*. There's something about him, something he does to you. Even a half an hour ago, I wouldn't have been able to tell you any of this. When you're with him, it's like you're caught up in the rapture."

"So he controls minds as well as sees visions?" Ben asked, walking back toward Felt. "What else can he do?"

"I think he feeds off of us, a little. That's part of why we stay, in a strange sort of way. He feeds from us but gives us something else in return, something sweet and wondrous. Even at my most lucid—now, for instance—I've never been able to figure it out."

"He's a psychic vampire," Ben said, shaking his head. "Makes sense, with what he did to me at their camp."

"Doesn't matter what he is," Ruskin said, taking back control of the conversation. "So how many missions has he been on?"

"Dozens, hundreds, who knows? I've been with him ten years, and he's probably gone on 30 or 40 in that time. I've went on maybe half, and the twins probably only nine or ten."

"What happened to him?" Ben asked. "To his face, I mean."

"Farm accident when he was a teenager. Grain silo exploded. He was in a coma for a month. It's probably what gave him his visions. As soon as he came out of it, he said, he started receiving these messages from God."

"Is there any rhyme or reason to his visions?" asked Ruskin, feeling like he was going to be sick. He wanted this conversation to be over, but he knew they still had much to learn.

"They all involve magic, of some sort or another," Felt said. "Yeah, I know all about magic, psychic stuff, you name it. Sometimes it's big, sometimes it's small. Whatever it is, it seems to trigger his visions, and he's always assumed the visions are God's way of directing him to kill the minions of Satan. He would've given up on the lot of you, though, if he hadn't seen him," he nodded toward Ben, "and his girlfriend appearing out of thin air behind some building a couple of years ago. He was able to use that vision and another vision of them by that old house earlier this week to get a lock on you. And that's why we're here."

"Oscar," Ruskin said, "you can get up now."

"Thank you," Oscar said, pushing himself up from the floor. He dusted himself off, smiling at Felt, seemingly none the worse for wear.

"What?" Felt asked, staring at Oscar. "How? He shot you!"

"Blanks," said Ruskin, stuffing the pistol back into his waist band. "We're not like you, Felt. Beyond a few punches, I'm not about to torture someone. Even if they probably deserve it. But we had to make you think we were serious."

"We brought him?" Ben said, his face pale. "We're responsible? And if we hadn't…"

"Something else would have," Ruskin finished for him. "He's the murderer, Ben. It has to be him. It sure the hell isn't Kristen Hawks, and there's no one else left."

Was there? He desperately hoped not because, if there were, then they were up the proverbial creek and there wasn't a paddle in sight.

Chapter 45

It was nearly ten by the time Shawn had gathered up all of Ben and Katy's stuff and checked them out of their hotel room. A part of him felt guilty for not staying at the house, but an even bigger part felt relieved that he hadn't. After all he'd gone through two summers ago, he wasn't sure he had the stomach for interrogating someone. He hoped Ben was made of stronger stuff than he was.

Throwing everything in the back seat of his Pacer, he drove the seven blocks to Fred Ruskin's house. He'd grown up in Carthage, but he and Jenny would be leaving to go to college in Macomb next year—and while he was sure he'd enjoy getting to know Macomb better, he was going to miss the convenience of being able to make it across town in less than two minutes.

The moment he pulled in behind Brody's Charger, he knew something was wrong. Since the whole mess with Aupuch and the fetch he'd developed a sort of sixth sense for trouble, and right now it was going off like gangbusters.

He hopped out of the car and jogged through the little gate to Ruskin's house. An old green lawn chair sat next to the front door, and beside that, on the ground, a now-cold cup of coffee and, sticking out of the snow, Brody Huffman's baseball bat. Brody himself, however, was nowhere to be seen.

He started to knock but instead crab-walked to the window. The warmth of his breath immediately blurred the glass, but he made out the shape of a woman, probably Candy, walking toward the back of the house.

Breathing a sigh of relief, he realized he'd been wrong after all. He began to walk to the door when she briefly turned toward the window. Their eyes met, but she turned away again, the glare from the lights inside blinding her to the outside world.

He only saw her for an instant, but there was no doubt in his mind—the woman inside was Kristen Hawks. He watched in horror as she walked through the house, opening and closing doors at random, finally disappearing down the back hallway.

Moving quickly to the front door, he tried the doorknob but it was locked. Where in the hell was Brody? He slipped the nickel from his pocket and felt the world around him float away as he concentrated on opening the lock. The latch finally popped and then he was inside, creeping quietly through the house.

Following the hallway through the living room, he stopped just short of the door that led into the guestroom as he heard voices:

"Who did you kill?" asked Jenny, her voice fraught with disbelief.

"My father, of course," replied Kristen's voice, echoing into the hallway.

Still holding the nickel, he edged closer to the door

* * *

"Did you hear that?" asked Katy, between bites of spaghetti and meatballs. She was still weak, so Candy had brought in trays so they could eat together.

"Hmm?" Jenny asked, her mouth full. The food was delicious but the forkful of food grew cold in her mouth as she forced herself to swallow, her pulse quickening as she eyed the door.

They'd heard a knock from the front door just a few minutes earlier but hadn't thought anything of it, assuming it to be Brody needing another refill on coffee or wanting to check up on them. It had been silent after that, but after a while they had heard various doors opening and closing throughout the house and what sounded like footsteps outside the bedroom door.

Candy knew where she was going, and Brody wouldn't traipse through the entire house unless he had a very good reason.

"Be quiet," Jenny said, as she slowly set aside her tray and stood up from the edge of the bed. "It's probably nothing, but I don't want to take any chances."

"I'm feeling much better," Katy said, starting to push up from the bed.

Her movement shifted the purse Shawn had recovered from the snow earlier in the day, and it rolled off the bed and fell to the floor with a clunk. Jenny spun around just as the door to the bedroom swung open behind her.

"So there you are," said a voice from the doorway. She turned to see Kristen Hawks dressed in a black suede jacket, pointing a gun straight at her. "I wondered where you'd gotten off to. Hey, who's that?" She used the gun to gesture toward Katy.

"Kristen," said Jenny, her eyes wide with surprise. "What are you doing here?"

"I could ask you the same question. Does Shawn know you're seeing someone else? Someone female?"

"What're you…" she said, trailing off as she finally understood. "No, you've got it all wrong. I'm not gay. This is Katy Rush, an old friend of the family." She used the same story Katy told her father.

"Pity," the girl said, her eyes gone cold. "If you were, it would make things a hell of a lot easier."

"So, you must be Kristen?" Katy asked, bending as if to get up off the bed. At the same time, she picked her purse up from the floor and anchored it between her leg and the mattress, hiding it from the other woman's view.

"Sit down!" Kristen said, waving the gun. "I don't want to kill you, but I will if I have to. I've been through way too much to stop now, not when I'm so close to getting what I want."

"You know," Jenny said, "sometimes it's a lot easier to get what you want if you're not waving a gun in someone's face."

"Sorry, Jen, but it can't be helped. Besides, I've already killed once. What's one more in the overall scheme of things?"

Jenny's heart raced. "Who did you kill?"

The girl looked at her blankly. "My father, of course."

"Your father?"

She'd only met Mr. Hawks once, when she'd had dinner at Kristen's house. She always seemed reticent about inviting her over, despite Jenny's insistence that she wanted to meet her best friend's family. She'd only been in Kristen's house that one time, and the man had seemed warm and friendly.

"Yeah, honey, my father," she said, a faraway look in her eyes. "He's been fucking me twice a week since my mother killed herself. I finally got tired of it, right around the time I met you. He's dead now, buried in the backyard. And if I did it once…"

"My God," Jenny heard herself say, "I didn't know. I'm so sorry."

"…I can do it again," she finished, tightening her grip on the gun.

"I'm sorry too," said another voice. All three women turned their eyes to Shawn as he walked through the doorway. "And if all of that's true, then I'm glad your father is dead. But there's no way in hell that I'm going to let you hurt Jenny."

* * *

She almost doubled over with laughter. "Hurt Jen?" she asked, training the gun on Shawn. "Why on Earth would I do that?"

"So you could be with me," he said, lifting his shoulders. "I'm sorry, Kristen, but I'm in love with her. Killing her certainly won't change that. So why don't you put the gun down and we'll talk?"

She did laugh then, long and hard, until tears came to her eyes. "You really thought," she said, after the laughter had subsided, "that it was you? That I wanted you? *You?* God, men are such self-centered, arrogant pricks."

"If not him," Jenny asked, her eyes clouding in confusion. "Then who?"

"You, honey," she said, smiling. "It's always been you, Jen, from the day we first met in the school cafeteria. I'm in love with you, and if you give it half a chance, I think you can fall for me, too. We can have a life together, far, far away from this miserable little town and people like my father!"

"I love Shawn," she said, her eyes drifting between Kristen, Katy, and her boyfriend, "and nothing you can do will change that."

"Oh really?" she said, pulling back the hammer of the gun. "How about if I blow his brains out? Then will you love me?"

"You can't *make* someone love you," said Shawn, holding his hands out in front of him. "Sure, you can kill me, but what will that do? Then you'll have to kill Katy, and then Candy Ruskin and Brody Huffman, if you haven't already. How many people are you willing to kill?"

"As many as I have to," she said, shoving the gun into his face. "They're both still alive, by the way, but they won't be for long, not if I don't get what I want."

"You're no better than your father," Shawn said flatly, dropping his hands to his side.

"I'm a hell of a lot better than my father!" she yelled, this close to putting a bullet in his brain.

"He's right," said Jenny. "It was horrible, what your father did to you; awful and unforgivable. He took you without your consent, turned you into something you never wanted to be. He made you his slave in more ways than one. But don't you see? If you took me from Shawn, killed the man I love, you'd be doing the exact same thing to me."

"But it's *not* the same thing!" she screamed, tears welling up in her eyes. "Don't you understand? Jen, I know you love me. And I'm giving you a choice. My father never gave me a choice."

"We all have choices," Shawn said, moving a step closer, "whether anyone gives them to us or not. You made your choice when you killed him, and it sounds to me like it was a long time coming. Kristen, your father was a piece of shit. You deserved better than that. He stole your innocence, and he almost turned you into a monster."

"Almost?" she asked, lowering the gun just a little.

"Almost," he repeated softly. "You're not there yet, but you're getting closer. You need to stop before it's too late."

"Someone tried to help me once," she said, thinking back to Mr. Jordan, "a teacher in Missouri. But my father forced me to accuse him of rape, and that was the end of that. He killed himself in prison."

"Your father's doing, not yours," he said, his eyes showing a kindness that she'd never noticed before.

"Kristen," Jen said, moving closer, "I'm angry with you, but I do love you—just not in the way that you think you want me to. But if you take Shawn away from me, if you force me to go with you, then you'll be stealing *my* choices, just like your father did to you. And if that happens, I won't love you anymore, and nothing on Earth or in heaven will ever force me to love you again."

"Well, then," she said, tears cutting streaks down her face, "I guess this little conversation is over."

They were right, both of them. Kristen's father had stolen her life from her, and she couldn't do the same thing to Jenny. It wasn't right. She'd just been deluding herself. She knew what she had to do.

"Just hand me the gun," Shawn said, "and we'll talk. I know you can't see it right now, but everything is going to be okay. We'll help you get the help that you need."

"Nobody can help me now," she said, turning the gun toward her temple. "But I must admit, Shawn, I underestimated you, and I'm sorry about that. You were dead-on with almost everything you said, but there was one thing you were wrong about. I *am* a monster."

She felt her finger tighten around the trigger, heard the crack of the gun as the bullet discharged from its muzzle, but after that, mercifully, she knew no more.

* * *

Shawn watched in horror as the gun sparked and thundered, delivering its payload into Kristen Hawk's skull. She had closed her eyes before pulling the trigger, but at the moment of impact they had sprung open again, wide in surprise, and for a moment she looked like the girl he imagined she had been before her father had done those awful things to her.

And then the moment passed and she was falling to the floor, hitting halfway between the thick shag rug and the hardwood floor that surrounded it, hitting with a sickening thud, dead. Blood leaked from a tiny hole in the side of her head, and he pondered briefly just how such a small wound could cause so much damage.

"No!" Jenny screamed, running to her side. She fell to her knees, cradling the girl's face in her hands. "Shawn, do something! She can't be dead. Do something!"

"What can we do?" he asked, kneeling to pry the gun from Kristen's fingers. He stood up again, put the weapon on top of the dresser opposite the bed, and bent down to touch Jenny's back. "The nickel isn't strong enough by itself, and Ben isn't here. We can't help her. I'm sorry."

"Jesus..." Katy said, walking over to where they crouched beside the girl's lifeless body. She held a small purple metallic device in her hand, but quickly slipped it into her pocket.

"What is that?" Shawn asked, taking Jenny into his arms.

Her wracking sobs shook his body, but he pulled her tighter, stroked her long red hair, and wished with all his heart that none of this had ever happened.

"It's a portable phone. Everybody has one where I come from," Katy said, her eyes riveted to the corpse before them. Her face was white as bone china. "I was going to make it beep or something, try to distract her, but it doesn't matter now."

"Try to heal her," Jenny said, between sobs, "she might not be dead yet."

He felt the weight of the nickel in his palm and almost wanted to try, but he knew it wouldn't work.

"We can't help her," he said, his eyes filling with tears. Jenny's grief was palpable, and he cried for her as much as he did for Kristen. "I wish we could, but we can't. Nobody can. She's gone."

Chapter 46

It was nearly eleven when they finally left the house. Felt told them all he knew, Ben was convinced, and they left the man tied to the chair in the library simply because they weren't sure what else to do with him. Fred had given Felt some Dilaudid pain pills he'd been prescribed years ago after a dental procedure but never used, so at least the man wasn't feeling any pain, and they'd wrapped him in blankets to keep him warm. That would have to do.

If they were able to stop Dowd, they reassured him, they'd be back for him later; if not, well, he'd better get comfortable, because it was going to be a long wait.

Ben had a plan, though it was tenuous at best. If they could somehow distract Dowd, use his own power to blind him, he reasoned, they could get in, deal with the preacher, and get out again with his flock being none the wiser. They had little more than an hour to do this, and after that all bets were off. His grandfather wasn't scheduled to die until Halloween evening, but if they couldn't stop Dowd tonight he might decide to accelerate his timetable.

Nobody seemed to want to talk about what they were about to do, and they were driving toward Fred Ruskin's house in his new Ford Bronco when Oscar finally broke the silence.

"I want to come with you," Oscar said. "I know you said I don't have to, and I appreciate that, but I need to. I need to talk to the *Padre*; I need to see for myself that all of what Felt said about him is true."

"It's going to be dangerous," Ruskin replied, "and we might not come out of it alive. This isn't your fight."

"Maybe it wasn't before, but it is now. I'll never forgive myself for what I did to that poor girl. I have to make amends."

"You already did," Ben said. "When it really counted, you did the right thing. Katy's alive, and I couldn't ask for more than that."

"And if you hadn't gone along with them," Ruskin added, "they would've just buried you with her, or worse. So no, son, this isn't your fight."

"Then I'm volunteering," he said, smiling.

It was the first time Ben had seen the man smile, and somehow it touched him. This kid—*no,* he corrected himself, *Oscar's older than I am*—this man had been through a lot, and he was still standing. "All right," Ben finally said, "you're in."

And then they were at Fred Ruskin's house. Brody wasn't at his post, and they immediately knew something was wrong. The door was hanging wide open, and Ben felt the tension in the air increase as Ruskin shifted the truck into park and was out the door with a quickness that belied his size.

"It's okay," said Candy, stepping through the threshold of the house just as Ben and Oscar were leaving the truck. "Everyone's okay. Well, almost everyone."

"Where's Brody?" Ruskin demanded, taking his wife in his arms. "He was supposed to—"

"I know," she said, cutting him off, "but we had some trouble. Kristen Hawks. She knocked out Brody and tied both of us up in the back yard." She rubbed her wrist, the indentation of the rope still evident in her skin. "Everyone's fine now, but Kristen...well, she's dead."

"Dead?" Ben asked, his mouth dropping open in surprise. He was so sure the girl hadn't been involved.

"She killed herself," Katy said numbly, peering over her mother's shoulder. "It's a long story, but I'm pretty sure she wasn't the Halloween killer."

"And we're pretty sure that David Dowd is," said Ben, moving through the door to wrap his arms around Katy.

"Hey," he whispered, under his breath, "I'm glad you're okay. I missed you. But are you sure you should be out of bed?"

"I'm fine now," she said, squeezing his hand, "and I missed you too. Besides…" Katy's face grew white as for the first time she noticed the man standing beside her father.

"That's one of the men who kidnapped me!" she shrieked, pointing at Oscar. "What's he doing here?"

"*Senorita,*" Oscar said, his hands trembling, "*Mi Dios,* I am so sorry! I didn't know what…what they planned to do to you."

"It's okay," Ben said, laying a reassuring hand across her arm. "He helped us out at the lake. Without him, you might not even be alive."

"Without him," she countered, "I might not have had to go through that in the first place!"

"Katherine," Ruskin said, using her full name, "he's right. Oscar was caught up in some shit he didn't understand. Trust me; he wouldn't be here if he posed any threat to you whatsoever. That preacher, he has some serious mojo. To one degree or another, he has control over the whole flock. If you don't believe me, ask Ben what he can do."

"What's he talking about?" she asked, turning to him.

"He's psychic, he can control people. He nearly killed me."

"My God, are you okay? When was this?"

"It happened before we rescued you, and I'm fine. But Oscar… He's genuinely sorry for his part in what happened, and he wants to make amends."

"All right," she said begrudgingly, "but I don't have to like him."

They followed Katy into the house where they found Shawn and Jenny sitting on a gold brocade couch. Both of them had been crying.

"I'm sorry for what happened," Ben said, "but I'm glad you two are okay."

"Yeah, I'll bet," Shawn said with a smile. "Maybe your luck is retroactive?"

Ruskin and his wife looked confused by the exchange but let it pass. It was bad enough that Shawn and Jenny knew he was their son; they didn't need to complicate things any further by going into detail about Ben's powers.

"Everything's been taken care of," Brody said, walking into the living room from the back of the house. "Don't know what we're going to do with her, but she's ready for travel."

"Kristen's body," Candy explained to her husband. "It seemed…unwise to call the police."

"You're right," Ruskin said, nodding toward Brody. "Jesse Floyd would be all over this. And besides, time's running out. We need to go after the preacher before midnight."

He explained to everyone what they had learned from Felt, leaving out what they had done to get the information. Everyone listened with rapt attention, and Katy was the first one to speak.

"Maybe," she said, stretching the word out, "I could enter his dreams. I've never tried to do anything destructive when I dreamwalk, but with a little incentive I'm guessing I could cause some major damage or at least distract him long enough for the rest of you to get in and take him out."

"Too risky," Ben said. "With his abilities, there's no telling what he can do. Besides, your dream walking is a form of magic, and if he can detect when magic is used, he might wake up before you even had the chance to do anything."

"So what do we do?" asked Jenny. She kept sneaking glances toward the back of the house, as if she expected to see Kristen Hawks walk out of the guestroom.

"Hit him, and hit him hard," Ruskin said, slamming a fist into the palm of his hand to illustrate his point. "With Shawn and Ben's magic and my shotgun, he can't possibly take us all on at once."

"But what if he can?" Shawn asked, looking up from the couch. "If he can keep, what, 50 some odd people under his sway, there's no telling what else he can do. I say we go pick up Jenny's parents, my parents, and Sam, and bring them all back here and barricade the doors. He can't kill what he can't find."

"And then what?" Ben asked. "The more people we involve in this, the messier it's likely to get. Already, too many people know about Katy and me."

"So what would you suggest?" Shawn asked, clearly frustrated.

Ben smiled. "I thought you'd never ask."

Chapter 47

It was a few minutes before midnight by the time that Brody and the girls arrived at the old house. The air was frigid but still, and the night sky was clear for the first time in days.

Baseball bat in hand, Brody grunted in pain as a jagged stab of lightning shot up through his leg. *It's these damn stairs*, he thought, as he climbed through the cellar into the kitchen.

"Are you okay?" asked Katy.

"Just a reminder from the war," he said, using the bat as a make-shift cane.

He held the door open for the women, letting it swing shut as soon as they were through. He pressed his hand against the cold wood for a full three seconds before moving to follow them.

Fred and the boys had gone to the woods to do a little magic, and he'd been relegated to playing nursemaid for Katy and Jenny. Even Candy had gotten out of babysitter duty by begging off in favor of spending the night with her daughter at Tom and Irene Knouff's house. He'd held his own in the confrontation at the campground, and couldn't understand why he kept getting assigned the shit work.

"This is the first time I've been in here since...well, since everything happened," Jenny said, looking at Katy. "Bad memories."

"Tell me about it," the girl said. "I've been having dreams about this place all my life. Every time I'm actually here, it feels majorly weird."

He had no idea what they were talking about. Ordinarily it wouldn't bother him to be left out of the loop—hell, he'd been in the dark half his life—but, tonight, for whatever reason, it made him feel stupid. More than that, it made him angry.

"Move it, ladies," he yelled, pointing the baseball bat toward the stairs.

"Hey, it's midnight," said Katy, looking down at her watch. "The witching hour, and all of that. Happy Halloween."

"Trick or treat," Jenny said, rolling her eyes. "What a way to spend a holiday."

"Go on," he said, sick and tired of listening to the two little bitches prattle on and on about nothing. "I'll catch up in a minute."

He tapped the head of the bat three times fast against the edge of the door frame, trying to calm his racing heart. He needed to rest, just for a second, needed to calm his fraying nerves.

"Are you okay?" asked Jenny. "Is it your leg?"

"Just…go on," he said, between gritted teeth. "Third floor, you remember. Take these." He handed Jenny a bundle of blankets he'd been carrying and passed the baseball bat to Katy. "I'll be up in a second." He clacked his teeth together three times, biting down hard on his tongue.

"All right, but be careful," Jenny said, reluctant to leave his side. Katy just shrugged and followed her up the stairs.

He watched as the girls walked up the stairs, their tight little asses swaying as they moved. Three, six, nine. What he wouldn't give to…

Stop it! What was wrong with him anyway? Why was he thinking like that at a time like this? The staircase spun before him, and he squinted as a migraine began to take shape in his temple. He leaned against the wall to steady his shaking legs, trying to keep from throwing up. He owed his life to Fred Ruskin and had vowed to do everything in his power to protect him and the people he loved. Why, then, he wondered, with an increasing mixture of curiosity and fear, did he desperately want to see every last one of them dead?

Chapter 48

Ben, Ruskin, and Reyes stood in the parking lot of Ruskin's Pizzeria, just across the highway from Dowd's encampment. Shawn stayed with the Bronco, but would make his "appearance" approximately five minutes after they did. All of them would play a crucial role but, if this were to succeed, it would be on Ben and Shawn's shoulders to make it happen. He just hoped they could pull it off, because, if they couldn't, none of them were likely to see morning.

Ben's only weapon was luck and the nickel, but Ruskin carried an old .38 caliber service revolver in a shoulder strap under his police jacket while Oscar carried the .22 he'd been given by Felt. Their armament wouldn't stand much of a chance against Dowd's psychic powers and fifty-plus people willing to do his bidding, but, if he and Shawn went down, it was better than nothing.

They were about 50 yards from the encampment when Ben finally clutched the nickel, said, "Here goes nothing," and willed an ethereal glow to appear around all three of them. A hush fell over the camp as white light sprung up all around them, lighting the area for three hundred yards in every direction.

Tone it down, he told himself, adjusting the glow accordingly. He wanted to draw attention from the camp but not from the restaurant. But it wasn't all for show. He needed to keep up the glow to continue to engage the nickel and hopefully give Dowd a headache. If all went according to plan, that would be enough of a distraction to let them get close enough to take the Reverend down.

"Dowd!" he shouted, as they entered the camp.

People all around him were staring, weeping, and dropping to their knees. "It's the savior!" called one. "Praise Jesus!" yelled another. "The rapture!" bellowed a third, falling prostrate to the ground in front of Ben.

Incredible. They actually thought he was an angel or some sort of other unearthly being. Well, why not? Dowd had filled their heads with so many tales of the supernatural and had them wrapped so tightly around his little finger that they probably didn't know which way was up.

"Bring me Dowd!" he yelled again, scanning the crowd for the Reverend.

He moved further into the throng of worshipers, watching in amazement as, one by one, they dropped to their knees or fell to the ground to let him pass. To put it in Biblical terms, it was as if Moses were parting the red sea. He just hoped there wasn't a tidal wave awaiting him on the other side, or, worse yet, a shark.

"I am the Reverend David Dowd," said a booming voice from behind the crowd.

More people parted to let him through, and, squinting with his one good eye, the man stumbled, nearly dropping his Bible. Their plan was working! Dowd was seeing them in person but also in a vision triggered by the magic Ben was using to power the glow. It must be like floating above your body watching yourself while at the same time being in your body, seeing things from two different points of view at the same time.

"Dowd, we know who you are, and we're here to bring you in," Ruskin said, removing a pair of handcuffs he still had from his days as the sheriff of Hancock County.

Ben looked up just in time to see a long, silvery blade swinging in an arc toward Ruskin's neck. Without thinking, he raised his arm to block the blow. The sword cut through his wrist like butter, separating hand from arm, sending a fine spray of blood raining down over the snow.

He fell back in agony and the glow around him and his companions immediately disappeared. And then the members of Dowd's flock were upon Ruskin and Reyes, pinning their arms behind them before they even had a chance to go for their weapons. Ruskin's handcuffs fell to the ground, disappearing into the snow.

"You must think me a fool," Dowd said, walking toward Ben. "Did you really think that would work? Actually, it might have had the Lord not gifted me with this." He held up a small tooth on a necklace that hung from his neck. "The good Lord protected me from your tricks by granting me a talisman of my own."

Ben held the bloody stump of his wrist to his stomach, trying not to look at the protruding bits of bone. The pain was unbearable, and his eyes kept closing of their own accord; he knew he must be going into shock. His luck had prevented the blow from severing Katy's father's neck and instead sacrificed his own hand, but the end result would eventually be the same. They were all going to die.

He inched backwards across the frozen Earth, moving away from Dowd. He had to warn Shawn. He wondered if, using the nickels, they might somehow be able to communicate. And then it struck him—he'd been holding the coin in his right hand. The nickel was gone. He immediately scanned the ground for his severed hand, and saw it lying perhaps five feet away, at the Reverend's feet, half-buried in the snow.

"Looking for this?" asked Dowd, bending to pick up the lifeless hand. He studied it for a moment, as if contemplating its existence, before tossing it away as if it were nothing more than a common piece of trash. "Or perhaps you were looking for this?" He smiled, holding out the nickel. "Interesting. Is this your source of power? I can feel a great energy coursing through the metal, much like my necklace. It will serve me well."

"How… did you know?" asked Ben, slurring his words. His vision darkened and he knew he had very little time left.

"Simple, Benjamin Spencer. I could hear your thoughts the moment you activated that silly glow. And did you really think me so weak as to not be able to shut out the vision when it no longer served me? I cannot be blinded so easily, demon, for the Lord has granted me the ability to truly see."

"That was the plan," Ben said, crawling across the snow toward Dowd. "You're an evil piece of shit, and I have to take you down."

The preacher ignored him. "And that's not all I know. You were sent here from another time, another place, by a powerful demon, to aid the Anti-Christ in my destruction. In fact, your 'Anti-Christ' should be making himself known," he glanced at his watch, "anytime now."

"If you can hear my thoughts," he whispered across the deep canyon that seemed to separate them, "then you must know I'm no threat to you. I'm trying…" everything went black, and he struggled to regain his foothold in consciousness. "I'm trying to save lives. My grandfather…"

"Your grandfather is of no concern to me," Dowd replied. "He never was; neither is your grandmother, Fred Ruskin's step-daughter, or any of the others. But then, you knew that, didn't you?"

"What…what do you mean?" He felt strangely numb.

"It's all a lie, that's what I mean. These 'Halloween murders.' I've never killed an innocent, and I never will. I will admit there are still some things I don't understand, but there *are* one or two things I see more clearly now."

"Like what?" he asked, trying to ignore the sound of his pulse raging like a river in his ears. He felt so cold.

"I assumed all of you were simply constructs, beings created by Satan so that you might walk the Earth. But you have families, and so I was wrong about that. Instead, you possessed innocent people, ruined lives that are even now calling out for freedom. And, soon, they will have it.

"And I was also wrong about Shawn Spencer being the Anti-Christ. That distinction most clearly belongs to you. I'll force him to admit that before I take his life, and then, when all the rest are gone, you'll join them."

Ben slumped in the snow, his breathing ragged and strained. His companions, he noticed, no longer struggled. They both stared ahead, unblinking. Dowd had them under his control. He only hoped Shawn wasn't next. If that happened, they didn't have a chance.

* * *

They'd been waiting up on the second-floor landing for a full two minutes, and still Brody hadn't shown up; moreover, he wouldn't answer their calls. "Do you think he's okay?" Katy finally asked, glancing over her shoulder at her companion.

Jenny shined her flashlight down the stairwell. "Don't worry, here he comes."

Katy heard a noise and time seemed to come to a standstill; it was almost like she was having another nightmare, though she knew for certain that she was awake. She heard a loud thump followed by a low scrape, and then another thump, and it finally hit her where she'd heard the sound before.

"Oh… my… God…," she said under her breath, her eyes going wide as her face turned an ashen white. She couldn't move, couldn't speak another word.

"What's wrong?" Jenny asked. "Are you all right?"

Thump, scrape. Thump, scrape. It was getting closer, and still she couldn't speak, couldn't move. Sound echoed up the stairwell, and she realized it was Brody climbing the stairs, his good leg taking a step, his bad leg pulled along behind him.

It was the very same sound she had heard hundreds of times be-fore, the sound that had terrified her since she'd been a little girl. And, all along, somehow, it had been Brody Huffman. She finally found the will to speak. "Jenny, run!" She grabbed the girl's wrist and propelled both of them up the stairs, half-dragging Jenny behind her.

"Slow down! What are you doing?"

"It's him," she managed to eke out, her heart pounding against her ribcage as she tried to take in air. Half of her life had been leading up to this moment, and she felt a profound sense of déjà vu as she ran for her life from a monster that wanted nothing more and nothing less than to end her life. "Brody's the killer."

"What are you talking about?" said Jenny. "Brody's just...Brody. He wouldn't hurt a fly."

Thump, scrape. Thump, scrape. He was almost to the landing, just a few steps from where they stood.

"Please," she begged, the staircase swimming before her eyes, "we have to hurry. If we don't, he's going to—"

A strangled scream halted her words, and then came the laughter. Raw, maniacal laughter, as though a small, demented child had just fin-ished torturing his first kitten and realized how very much he liked it.

"Jenn-eeey," called the voice from below, Brody but somehow not Brody, like a creature trapped in between, changed to something else that in a perfect world could never have existed. "Jenn-eeey," the voice repeated, closer now, "Sweet, sweet meat. I'm baaaack..."

Katy felt gooseflesh cover her arms and legs and tasted bile in the back of her throat. She wanted to run, desperately needed to get the hell out of there, but her legs had stopped working again. She felt hot tears running down her cheeks, and knew she was about to die.

Jenny looked stunned, like she'd just been punched in the stomach. "The fetch?" she whispered, her hand finding Katy's in the darkness. "But...Colin Wainwright was the fetch, and he's dead."

And then they saw him. It was still Brody Huffman, but changed. Gone were the kind eyes that Katy had first encountered behind this very house, replaced instead by a hungry stare that terrified her. There was nothing left of the man but the form he wore, and even that seemed to be changing.

Where Brody once walked like a normal man, albeit one with a limp, this new version *loped* up the stairs, like an injured wolf in search of prey. And everyone knows an animal is at its most dangerous when hurt.

"And tasty, tasty Katy, three times fast," he called to her in a sing-song voice, lewdly licking his lips, "when I'm through with Jenny, I'll have your heart for dessert…"

He was almost upon them, just a few steps away, and still neither woman could move. It was finally Katy who broke the spell, as she swung the baseball bat straight at Brody's face.

He was quick, though, and caught it with his hand, twisting it away from her with a flick of his wrist. At the last second, desperate and frightened out of her mind, she pushed at the bat with all her weight and watched in surprise as he lost his balance. He teetered then fell backwards, tumbling down the steps, landing with a heavy thud at the bottom of the landing.

"Move!" she screamed, spinning around to take the stairs two at a time.

They had almost reached the third floor when they heard his loping gait again, thump, scrape, thump, scrape, as he methodically resumed climbing the staircase.

Jenny tripped coming off the top step, careening into Katy, and both women tumbled to the ground, skidding across the room in a frantic tangle of arms and legs. Katy watched helplessly as her flashlight fell from her hand to skitter across the floor, spinning to a stop against the wall on the other side of the room.

"There!" Jenny said, pointing her flashlight at a spot in the middle of the floor. "The pentagram, it's our only chance."

Thump, scrape. Thump, scrape. He was on his feet again, just a few feet from where they lay. "Sweet meat," Brody gurgled, "I'm really gonna enjoy this."

Chapter 49

Shawn stood hidden behind the Bronco, in the parking lot of Fred Ruskin's restaurant. He put down the pair of binoculars he'd found in Ruskin's truck. He could no longer see Ben and the others. He'd watched in disbelief as a huge crowd of people opened ranks before them, almost swallowing them up, but now they all stood in his way, making it impossible for him to see. He glanced at his watch. It was nearly time to make his entrance.

The plan was to essentially blind Dowd with two different visions at the same time, and then to attack him using their nickels. But if the Reverend was as powerful as he seemed...he shook off the thought and clutched the nickel tight in the palm, feeling the magic course through him. He stepped away from the truck and willed an aura of fiery red to spring to life around his body.

"Demon," said a familiar voice to his right, and he nearly dropped the aura as he spun to confront the intruder. "You need to come with us."

"Fred?" he blinked, confused, "What are you doing here?" Fred and Oscar stood beside the truck, weapons drawn and trained on him. They weren't smiling.

"Thank you for your gift," said Ruskin, his voice flat and his eyes unmoving.

"Without the nickel," said Oscar in the same monotone voice, not missing a beat, "I never could have done this. My abilities are growing."

"And," said Ruskin smoothly, "soon I'll have the power necessary to bring on the apocalypse. Give me your nickel, and…"

"…I'll let you live long enough to say goodbye to your son," finished Oscar, holding out the palm of his hand.

Sweet Jesus! He dropped the aura, backing away from his two friends. This had all gone horribly wrong, and now Dowd controlled Fred, Oscar, and maybe even Ben. He thought of Jenny and the child they'd eventually bring into the world, and the man he'd grow up to be, and a bitter resolve passed over him. He wasn't going to go down without a fight.

"And if you don't," Ruskin added, taking note of his hesitation, "you'll both die right now."

"The nickel," Oscar said, gesturing with the .22, "give it to me."

"Dowd," he said, circling away from his former friends, "if you want it, you're going to have to take it from me."

"And don't think I've forgotten about the whores," Ruskin said, "I know where they are. If you cooperate, their executions will be merciful."

"But you'll kill them all the same, right?" Shawn asked.

"Their bodies have been taken over by Satan, and they must be cleansed," Oscar said, "but I'm not an unreasonable man. The how and when of it, not to mention the where, are entirely in your hands."

Why was he so anxious to get him to surrender? And, come to think of it, why did he speak through both men, one after another? Felt hadn't mentioned anything about Dowd having the ability to possess minds, so perhaps this skill was new, and he was stretching himself too thin.

"All right," he said, feigning compliance, "I'll do it, but I'm not giving up the nickel until I see Ben."

"That is…" started Ruskin.

"…Unacceptable," finished Oscar.

"So kill me," he said, pouring his will into the nickel, "if you think you can." A glowing blue shield sprang up around him. "Either you let me surrender under my own terms or you risk a fight that you may not win. Are you so sure of yourself?"

"Very well," said Ruskin. "But the moment you…"

"…See your son," Oscar said, "you hand over the nickel."

"Agreed," said Shawn, noting that the interchange of sentences between the two men kept getting shorter.

Dowd was almost certainly having trouble keeping them both under control. The shield was probably also forcing a vision, straining his capacity even further.

He let the shield drop. He didn't want to give Dowd too much time to get used to the balancing act he had to be performing. It could be more advantageous to test his limits later rather than to show him all he could do now.

"Move it…" Ruskin said, waving the gun in his face…

"Or, as the kids say these days…" Oscar said.

"…Lose it," said Ruskin, stomping down the road toward the encampment.

Oscar waited for him to follow, and then joined in behind them. Their steps matched in stride and cadence all the way from the truck until they reached the field where David Dowd's ministry had set up camp.

The crowd once again parted ways, this time for him. For the second time in two days, he saw his future son lying at his feet, close to death. His hand had been severed, and he lay face down in the snow, covered in blood. And this time, Shawn couldn't heal him. This time, Dowd had won.

The Reverend stood triumphantly before him, a long Samurai sword in one hand and a Bible in the other. Around his neck hung an object he recognized. It was the tooth of the Jaguar, one of the five magical amulets that Aupuch had melded together so many years ago and which Shawn himself had briefly possessed. He'd punched a hole through Ben's nickel, which now hung on the leather string beside the tooth.

"Okay, you win," he whispered, staring into Dowd's disfigured face. "I give up. It's over."

* * *

One moment the room was pitch dark, the next it was flooded with light; Katy turned, blinked in confusion, and saw Brody standing beside the huge flood light that stood to the right of the stairwell, his hand lingering over the switch. She felt like a small animal trapped in the headlights, too terrified to move. Jenny lay on the cold wood floor beside her, slowly inching her way toward the pentagram.

The room seemed to turn upside down in her vision and for a moment she didn't know whether she was awake or dreaming. Brody thumped the baseball bat hard into his palm three times, sending a series of thwacks echoing through the huge open room. Her wolf analogy sprang to mind. He was like a hungry wolf, circling a pair of poor, defenseless rabbits who were about to become dinner.

She was tired of being a rabbit.

"Jenny," she whispered, "walk away from me, but do it very slowly." She rose to her feet, prepared to face the monster she'd been running from since she was a little girl.

"What?" Jenny asked, looking at her as if she were nuts.

"Trust me."

Only Jenny stood between her and Brody, and while she knew that she might have time to get to the pentagram and teleport to safety, Jenny would not.

"Poor little Katy, Katy, Katy," Brody said in a sing-song voice, moving closer, "whispering her little secrets, hiding away in her little house in the woods, watching all her little friends live their little lives but never living her own."

"What the hell do you know about it?" she yelled, trying to hide her trembling hands by pressing them hard against her hips.

"Katy Bear, Katy Bear, sweet little Katy Bear, gonna be so sweet, gonna be so good to eat."

Her father had called her "Katy Bear" when she was a little girl. How did Huffman know so much about her?

"It's not Brody," whispered Jenny, "it's the fetch."

"Very good!" said Brody, baring his teeth. "*Very* good. Your boyfriend took Colin from me, and now I'm going to take you from him. I'm gonna take everybody from him, three times over."

"But how?" Jenny asked, climbing to her feet. "You…died. Didn't you?"

"Could have killed you a thousand times," said Brody, ignoring her question, "a thousand, thousand times. But the old man had me on a tight leash. Called me up from hell, stuffed me inside of Wainwright and made me forget who I was, what I was, and when we got separated, I wound up here," he spread his hands to indicate the house. "Woulda stayed here forever, too, if not for good old Brody." He thumped himself hard three times in the chest.

"What *are* you?" Katy asked, positioning herself halfway between Brody and the pentagram. She dropped her purse to the floor, getting ready for what she knew would be coming.

"I'm your worst nightmare," He said, springing at her without warning.

But she was ready for him. In one smooth move she grabbed his shirt collar, pulling him toward her, at the same time planting her foot into his midsection. She fell back onto the pentagram, taking his weight with her, and disappeared…

...reappearing in utter darkness. She followed through with the roll, throwing him up and over her body before letting go. It was pitch black and she couldn't see a thing, but she heard him crash hard into the wall and slide to the floor like a sack of rotten potatoes.

"Little bitch," he said, sounding closer than she would have liked. "Gonna get you now, Katy Bear."

She rolled quickly to the side, away from the second pentagram that she knew must be beneath her, and then back again, making contact with her shoulder, and...

...her eyes were flooded with light. She blinked, trying to readjust her vision. She was back on the third floor of the house, lying atop the huge pentagram inlaid into the floor, and Brody Huffman was gone.

She rolled away from the pentagram, not wanting to risk accidentally touching it again and dropping herself into Brody's lap.

"Oh my God," said Jenny, her eyes huge. She fell to her knees beside Katy. "I thought he was going to kill you!"

"You know," she said, breathing hard, "that move is about the only thing I remember from the Tae Kwon Do course I took my freshman year of college, but, boy, I'm sure glad I didn't ditch class the day they taught us that." Her heart was pounding in her chest, and she'd never felt more alive than she did at this very moment.

"But how did you teleport? Do you have Ben's necklace?"

Katy smiled, reaching into her shirt to pull out the pentagram Ben had given her earlier before they split up. "Thank goodness for small favors, huh?"

"So what do we do now?"

"Get out of here so we can warn Ben and Shawn that Dowd isn't the killer."

"I don't understand any of this," said Jenny, casting furtive glances at the pentagram. "How could Brody be the fetch?"

"Michael said the evil came from within the house," Katy said, trying to loosen the tension from her shoulders, "and I think it did. Ben mentioned earlier that Brody had found a necklace in the house similar to this one, but I didn't put it together until now. I think that necklace enabled the spirit of the fetch to possess Brody's body."

"Then someone must have put it there," Jenny said, "since none of this happened in your timeline. We have to help him."

Katy was about to argue that saving Huffman couldn't be their first priority when a thunderous crash resonated through the house, coming from the wall above the staircase. Again and again it sounded, like a battering ram thrusting against the gates of a medieval castle, and then they saw the tail end of a claw hammer break through the wall.

"He's getting out!" Jenny screamed, pointing at the widening hole.

First the hammer was through, and then his arms, knocking aside loose bits of wood and plaster. He frantically scraped and scratched at the hole, making it bigger, like a termite burrowing through the wall or a snake after a mole.

"Sweet, sweet meat, daddy's coming for you," he sang tunelessly, his leg exploding through the wall in a cloud of chalky white plaster.

"No!" Katy screamed.

Jenny ran full-tilt for the stairs, ducking under him, but stopped short as his fingers caught in her long red hair. Her head snapped back and her feet left the ground as she clawed and fought against his grasp.

"Got you, *Jenn-eeey*," he said, his fingers tightening in her hair, "and I promise you, this is gonna hurt you a helluva lot more than it's gonna hurt me."

Katy took a step toward them but stopped short as she had an idea. The quickest way from point A to point B, in this case, wasn't necessarily a straight line, and might even provide her a weapon in the form of Brody's baseball bat.

She took a deep breath as she watched Jenny struggle against her nightmare monster, turned around, and placed one foot on the pentagram. "Here goes nothing," she whispered, and then was gone.

Chapter 50

Brody Huffman remembered everything now, for what good it did him. He remembered finding the necklace, touching the star, and appearing in that dark little room with the shimmering curtain of lights that promised to lead him to freedom.

Only, it didn't. Instead, it led him into a jungle filled with horrors darker and more twisted than anything he'd ever encountered in Korea. Tall, looming mountain ash trees surrounded him, and vines threatened to ensnare his feet. Bones and broken bodies lay scattered everywhere, testament to all who had come before him. Fresh corpses hung from the trees, hung up to bleed out by an unseen hunter, and blood gushed through the center of the swamp like a rivulet flowing out to some far-off sea.

He'd screamed, then, totally lost it, thinking the gooks had finally come for him after all these years. He turned on his heels, frantically looking for the exit, but it was no longer there. And then something was upon him, ripping into him, burrowing its way inside. He felt the skin around his spine tear open…

And the next thing he remembered was kneeling on the star, wondering what was wrong with the floodlights and just where in the hell his hammer had gone. He'd forgotten the jungle, the bodies, all of it.

But now, just three days later, he remembered everything. He still had his mind, even as he had lost control of his body, but was helpless to do anything as Leonard hunted down his friends.

Yes, Leonard. The goddamned monster inside of him was named Leonard. He would have laughed if he hadn't been so damned scared. Leonard sounded like the name of an accountant, not a monster that wanted to force you to kill everyone you cared about.

Leonard was a fallen angel, he inexplicably knew, a demon who had been trapped behind the curtain before he had inadvertently set him free. The necklace had been both the mode of transportation with which he had gotten into the room and the conduit through which the demon was able to enter his body and escape his confines to wreak havoc on the world once more.

In less than 24 hours, he'd forget everything he'd just remembered and would go back to being himself again. Back to his life of counting and washing, which, compared to this, was looking better and better all the time. Leonard had command of his body for the entirety of Halloween, but once the day had passed he'd remain dormant in Brody's body until exactly one year later, when it would happen all over again.

He didn't know how he knew all this, but suspected that whatever allowed the demon's mind to take over his body connected them in more ways than one. For what little good the information did him.

The demon's actions were confined to a series of loosely planned events, but either it didn't know who had placed these limitations on its actions or was hiding that information better than it'd hidden the rest. The amulet was the key. In addition to its other duties, the necklace had essentially "programmed" the demon on this particular course, much like a computer following instructions given to it on a punch card. But, unlike a computer, the demon had some leeway in how it accomplished its assigned tasks, and Brody knew it intended to do as much damage as possible within those parameters.

He ached to rail against the demon, break down the barriers that kept him from taking control of his body; but he knew he couldn't. All he could do was watch helplessly as the demon did its dead-level best to kill his friends.

That's right, old man, echoed a voice inside his head, *just sit back and shut up. Who knows, you might even enjoy yourself.*

Somehow, he doubted that.

Chapter 51

Katy materialized on a chalk pentagram at the end of a long, rectangular room. She'd been here before, of course, but hadn't really been able to see anything because of the darkness; this time, however, light from the flood lamp poured in through the hole Brody had punched in the wall, and she could see everything.

Brody was three feet away, half of him inside the hole and half hanging out, surrounded by bits of wood and plaster. One hand methodically swung a claw hammer against the wall, over and over, working to make the hole wider, while the other hand, she knew, dangled Jenny by her hair.

Four or five feet past Brody stood the curtain of shimmering light she had read about in Shawn's book. It wasn't as bright as she'd imagined—certainly not bright enough to light up the room—but still it took her breath away. All the colors of the spectrum rolled through the curtain, first blue, then red, violet, green, yellow, orange, and then blue again. But the moment she'd started to sense a pattern it changed, and green followed orange, then red, yellow, and blue. She shook her head, turning her gaze from the lights to the baseball bat that lay on the floor beside Brody's foot.

Steadying her trembling hands, she quickly snatched the bat from the floor. Backing up, she assumed her softball stance, screaming, "Hey, asshole, let go!" just before she swung the bat.

The wooden Louisville Slugger cracked hard into Brody's right shoulder, vibrating in her hands so hard that she almost dropped it.

The man screamed in pain and slumped against the floor, down but not out. She swung the bat again, this time into his bad leg, and winced as his whole body shook and he tried to pull himself through the hole. One arm hung limp at his side, the hammer dropped and forgotten, but the other, the one that had been holding Jenny but was now full of long, bloody strands of her red hair, pushed and prodded at the wall until a large chunk of plaster broke off and fell down into the stairwell.

He reared back but Katy pushed the bat hard into his neck, temporarily pinning him to the wall. She snaked her hand into his pocket, pulling out a set of keys she knew had to belong to the Charger.

"Jenny," she yelled, thrusting the keys out through the hole and over Brody's head, "get out of here, and bring help!" She dropped the keys, hoping Jenny would catch them.

"I won't leave you," Jenny said. She could just make out the top of Jenny's head through the hole; she was missing hunks of hair and looked as if she'd been scalped.

Katy ground the bat tighter into the back of Brody's neck. "Get out of here," she repeated, her arms aching from the strain of holding the bat, "I can't hold him for long."

"Get off me, you little cunt!" screamed Brody, maneuvering his arm back inside the hole, pushing hard off the wall.

She lost her footing, tripped over the hammer, and fell flat on her back. The baseball bat rolled through the curtain of light and was gone. She fought to regain her feet but he was on her in a second, pinning her to the ground as his arm wrapped around her throat.

"Katy, Katy, Katy, you nasty little bitch, you have no idea how much that hurt...but you're gonna," he said, frothing at the mouth like a rabid dog.

He finally let go of her throat just as she felt herself beginning to black out, rearing back to backhand her across the cheek. The room swam in her vision and she literally saw stars—at least she thought they were stars, but realized an instant later it was just the pulsating lights from the curtain.

"I'm gonna fuck you, Katy girl," he said, between gritted teeth.

His hand grabbed the hem of her t-shirt—the Zeppelin shirt she had borrowed from him—and he yanked it up and over her head, revealing not only her lacy black bra but her good luck charm she'd worn since her father had died.

"Sweet little tits," he said, licking his lips. And then his hand was all over her, cupping her breasts, pinching her nipples, groping her, working to unfasten her bra. "I'm gonna bite off your tits, Katy Bear, and then I'm gonna fuck you three times before I kill you. Brody ain't got no pussy in so long, I'm sure he's gonna enjoy it just as much as I am."

She struggled under his grasp, but he weighed twice as much as she did and there was no way she was going anywhere without his assistance. He pressed his knee into her stomach, knocking the wind from her diaphragm, and she instinctively fought back, trying to roll out from under him. Though she couldn't budge him, she did notice that every time he moved he worked to stay as far away from the curtain as possible.

She kicked up with her legs, leveraging them against the wall just below the hole, and pushed with all her strength, rocking his body toward the curtain. Immediately he moved his weight the other way, adjusting himself on top of her, fighting to stay away from the shimmering lights.

"Stop squirming!" he commanded, slapping her sharply across the face.

So hard was the blow that it rattled her teeth. She felt her mouth well up with blood and could feel a split opening on her lip, but she held on, rocking her hips beneath him, edging slowly toward the curtain.

"Figured it out, huh?" he said, reaching down to unbutton her jeans. "For what good it'll do you. I'm never going back in there. Never, never, never again."

He leaned back, loosening his grip on her for just a second, long enough to shove his right hand into her pocket. He pulled out the pentagram hanging from the broken chain.

"Mine!" he yelled, grabbing the waistband of her jeans and pulling them down to her knees.

Her arms were pinned to her sides, but she could still move her hands and feet. She pushed against the wall with one foot, rocking her hips in an effort to distract him, while she felt around the floor with the other. And there it was—the hammer! She caught the claw end with the heel of her boot, drew her foot back, and slowly edged it across the floor toward her right hand.

"Cat got your tongue?" he asked her, as he finally yanked the jeans from her body. He pulled the denim material out from under her and brought it to his face, inhaling deeply.

His eyes grew wide, and he threw back his head and laughed. "Sweet little tasty, tasty, tasty Katy. I wonder, does your boyfriend know just how ready—"

He never got to finish. She brought the head of the hammer down hard on his knee, hearing an audible crack as iron met bone and iron won. His scream filled the little room as he reared back in pain, his eyes on fire and his fist balled up in anger.

But she was already moving. She rolled back on her hips, throwing him off balance. As he fought to right himself, she pulled her legs out from beneath him and kicked him hard into his chest. He fell back against the wall, half in and half out of the hole, and then she was kicking again, screaming and kicking with all her strength, blow after blow after blow until he finally fell through the hole to land with a heavy crash on the stairs below.

She scrambled to her feet, steadying herself against the wall as she began to hyperventilate. Snatching up her jeans, she slipped them back on her legs, hands shaking as she finally managed to get them buttoned. Dizzy and nauseated, it was all she could do not to crumple to the floor in a fit of tears and hysterics.

"Bitch!" he screamed from the bottom of the staircase, the thump-scrape of his gait echoing up the stairs. "I'm gonna fuck you, then I'm going to kill you, and then I'll fuck you again!"

She felt hot bile rising in her throat, and then she was gagging, throwing up in spasmodic heaving tremors. Forgetting about her shirt, forgetting everything but getting away from him, she staggered away from the hole and fell backwards through the shimmering lights.

Chapter 52

It was over. Dowd not only had Ben's nickel and the jaguar tooth, but also his own more-than-capable psychic abilities. Ben was nearly dead, and Fred and Oscar were completely immobilized. Only a fool would even think of going up against the preacher alone.

Good thing he was willing to play the fool.

"Here," he said, holding out the nickel. He was only going to have one shot at this, and he had to play it for all it was worth. "Just take it and be done with it."

"I promise you, your death will be swift and merciful."

Katy had been dead after they'd dug her out of the ground. He remembered that, even if no one else did. He didn't know what Ben had done, but he'd done something; he'd somehow managed to change things around just enough to give them the few extra precious seconds they needed to revive her.

Whatever Ben had done, Shawn was about to gamble his life that, if sufficiently motivated, he could do it again.

"If it's all the same to you," he whispered, as his hand clasped around Dowd's, "I'd prefer drawn out and cruel."

They both began to glow an ethereal blue, just as he and Ben had at the restaurant. This time, however, he was prepared for the electric shock that coursed through his system, while the Reverend was not. Shawn reached out with his mind; using the power of both nickels combined with the jaguar's tooth, he directed the energy flowing through them toward Ben.

"Resarcio," he whispered, closing his eyes, repeating the Latin word he had heard Jenny say when they'd healed Ben at the house. *"Resarcio, resarcio."*

"What are you doing?" Dowd roared, yanking his hand away.

Both men watched as the nickel flew through the air, bounced off Fred Ruskin's chest, and rolled to a stop about an inch from Ben's outstretched hand.

"What the hell?" Ruskin said, shaking his head.

"Die!" screamed Dowd, his blade moving as he stepped toward Shawn.

* * *

Ben's eyes jerked open; he wasn't quite dead, after all. In fact, other than missing a hand, he felt great. He pushed himself up and out of the snow just in time to see Dowd's sword flash through the air toward his father's neck.

"No!" he screamed, reaching out, already knowing it was too late.

But then something unexpected happened: the world around him came to an abrupt and sudden halt. Even the air was still, and tiny snowflakes twinkled motionless in the night sky. Dowd's sword hovered in the air, its blade just touching Shawn's neck. A thin line of blood was visible where metal met skin, but the blood, like the snowflakes, stood frozen in time, unmoving.

Something caught his eyes—hovering in the air, stretching all around him, were the gossamer threads, the same threads he'd seen after they'd pulled Katy's body from her grave. There were hundreds, thousands, all floating this way and that, some as thick as shoelaces with others perhaps the width of a hair. Some, he could tell, were too fragile to be manipulated and dissolved before he could even look at them. Those, he imagined, were the realities that might have been if things were just slightly different. They only existed in the abstract, and collapsed into themselves as he even thought about them.

But there were others, and they were strong, albeit tenuous, and he knew if he were to grab hold and yank, he'd bring the reality they represented to the forefront, and all the other threads would fall away as if they'd never been. His hand brushed against one thread and he watched in horror as Dowd's blade decapitated Shawn, while another showed Shawn ducking at just the last second. A third thread had the sword breaking off from the hilt just before impact, while a fourth contained the miraculous transformation of the blade into a rubber chicken.

He shook his head at that last one.

An idea formed in his head. No one thread seemed to accomplish what he wanted, so he carefully gathered up three different threads, wove them together with a deft twist of his fingers, and pulled…

…and time seemed to resume again. Dowd's sword swished harmlessly through the air, just a few inches from Shawn's neck. The preacher spun from the momentum, tripped, and landed flat on his back in the snow.

Ben climbed to his feet, flexing his fingers, admiring his new hand. It was obsidian, made of a substance he didn't recognize, some sort of cybernetic replacement snatched from a future that may or may not someday even exist, but it was better than nothing. He hadn't been able to find a thread where he hadn't lost his hand. Perhaps some sacrifices just couldn't be undone.

"How…?" Dowd asked, staring at Ben.

"Praise Jee-sus, it's a miracle," he said, reaching out to yank the tooth from the leather strap that hung around Dowd's neck. Lucky for him, the knot that tied both ends of the leather together had frayed and the tooth easily slid off the strap.

"What are you—give that back!" Dowd commanded, abandoning the sword to move toward Ben. He stopped as he heard a collective gasp rise up from the crowd gathered around them.

"Look, he's healed the Reverend!" shouted one.

"Praise Jesus!" shouted another.

Dowd turned toward them, then back to Ben, eyes wide. Dowd had never been in the grain silo explosion as a teenager, had never been injured. In fact, the man who had been cursed with psychic powers after the accident that had now never happened no longer existed, wiped out with the simple twist of a knot and the pluck of a thread. The body had been healed, even if the mind were still as twisted as a rope. But he remembered what he'd been, what power he had held. He remembered everything. Ben had made sure of it.

"My God…" he cried, sinking to his knees. "I can't—I can no longer feel them, hear them think. What have you done to me? What have you done?"

"Something far more merciful than you were about to do to me."

"You will…do as I say!" he yelled, staring Ben straight in the eyes. "Change me back!"

"Bite me," Ben said, right before he punched Dowd in the jaw. The man fell backwards into the snow and lay still, sobbing silently.

He knelt beside the man, rolled him to his side, and removed the trench coat from his huge frame. "Sorry, buddy, but I'm going to need this more than you are."

"Jesus H. Christ, how did you do that?" asked one of the Tyler twins, stumbling out from behind a tent with his brother at his side. One walked with the aid of a wooden cane, while the other's face was covered in bruises and his nose appeared to be broken.

"Stay right where you are," said Ruskin, leveling his rifle in their direction.

"This man is a fraud!" Ben yelled, ignoring the twins and Ruskin to turn to the crowd. "Get out of here, go back to your families, your lives, and forget you were ever part of this…this…travesty!"

"But…dear Lord," said a woman with long gray hair, kneeling before him, "you healed him, we all saw it. You healed the reverend."

"And if I can do that," he said, baring his teeth, "imagine what I could do if someone really pissed me off. Now go! All of you: get out of here, before I change my mind! Go!"

The woman clambered to her feet at breakneck pace, running toward the cars and trucks parked at the other end of the field. The others immediately followed suit, abandoning tents and belongings in an attempt to get as far away as quickly as possible. In a matter of minutes, the field was clear of everyone save their group, Dowd, and the Tyler twins.

"You two," Ben said, staring down the twins. "I should kill you for what you did to my girlfriend, but I won't...as long as you do exactly what I tell you."

"Anything!" they said, speaking in unison.

"Take Dowd, hobble your asses down to the Sheriff's station, and turn yourselves in. Confess to every one of your crimes—every one!—and maybe even add a few in you didn't do for good measure. Make sure to implicate Dowd. As long as you're in prison, you'll be safe. But if I ever see either of you ever again, you're going to get what Dowd got, only in reverse. Got it?"

"Yes!" they promised together, avoiding his eyes.

"I'll know if you don't do it," he warned them, "and part of me is hoping that you won't." Both parts were a lie, but they didn't know that.

Ben watched as they hoisted the Reverend to his feet and began to drag him to the rusted-out brown van parked at the end of the field, the very same van they had used to kidnap Katy. *Poetic justice,* he thought, as he watched them walk away.

"Mi Dios," Oscar said, unable to take his eyes from Dowd's restructured face. "You...he...it's a miracle."

"A bit of one, yeah," Shawn said, as he walked up to join his friends. He slapped Oscar on the back, then walked over to Ben. "I never thought I'd hear myself say this, but I'm proud of you…son."

"Shawn…Dad…you healed me, just enough. I don't know how, but you did. We did this together."

"And yet, I don't think this night is over," said Fred Ruskin.

"You're a smart man, Mr. Ruskin," Ben said, stuffing the tooth and the nickel into his pocket as he turned to the former sheriff. "Dowd did a lot of really bad shit, but he's not the Halloween murderer."

"Then who is?" asked Shawn.

Ben had no clue but never had the chance to answer as Brody Huffman's Dodge Charger suddenly came barreling down the road, screeching to a halt beside the curb just a dozen yards from where they stood. But it was Jenny, not Brody, who jumped out of the driver's seat, running toward them at breakneck speed.

"It's Brody! Brody's the Halloween murderer," she said, nearly out of breath. "It's been Brody all along, he's been taken over by the fetch, and now he's got Katy and he's going to kill her."

Chapter 53

Katy was falling. She had no sense of balance and didn't know up from down, right from left, and her skin turned to ice within seconds of touching the curtain. She felt for sure that she was dying.

But then, inexplicably, she wasn't. She found herself standing in her little cabin in the woods, her sanctuary. The one that existed solely in her mind, only she wasn't dreaming.

What is this, Katy thought, *Being John Malkovich?*

She stood in the center of the make-believe living room, surrounded by exquisite artwork borrowed from some of the most prestigious museums around the world. The smooth Spanish tile echoed under her feet, and the comfy leather couch in the corner called to her like never before, promising to ease her aching bones and soothe her wounded spirit. Brody's baseball bat lay at her feet. Blood stained the light wood varnish, reminding her of how close she had come to dying.

None of it, save the bat, was real. It couldn't be, because she'd made it all up. She'd created this place, her *sanctum sanctorum*, to escape the terrifying landscape of her nightmares. It couldn't be real. Could it? And, certainly, it couldn't be on the third floor of the old house she'd been dreaming about half her life.

She walked along one of the walls, examining *Study of a Woman's Hands* by Leonardo da Vinci. The original, she knew, was part of the Royal Collection of Windsor exhibit currently touring London, but this was as perfect of a copy as she could conjure up in her mind. This was definitely her cabin.

How could any of this be real? She plopped down on the leather couch, located the remote and turned on the television, tuning in to Mel. She expected the screen to be blank because, of course, Mel had yet to be born. Instead, however, she found herself watching an Asian man walking hand-in-hand down a carnival boardwalk with a blonde-haired, blue-eyed woman that definitely wasn't Mel. What on Earth? She turned up the volume, listening in, but they spoke in a language that she couldn't understand.

Saving that puzzle for another day, she let the conversation fade as she switched the channel to Sam. And there she was, all of fourteen years old, dressed in her pajamas and dreaming of flight. She watched in awe as her big sister soared through the skies over Carthage, arms spread out at her side, long blonde hair trailing behind her.

Sam looked her way for a second, but of course she couldn't see her. She arced to her left, flew straight through a cloud, rolled, and shot out the top, a huge smile on her face. Her heart ached as she watched the little girl that she'd never known, the girl who had all but grown in-to a woman before Katy was even born. To glimpse her like this, so happy and carefree, almost made everything she'd gone through in the last few days worthwhile.

Almost.

She turned the TV off, leaving Sam to her dreams.

Limping to the bathroom, she gasped as she looked in the mirror. Her lip was cut and bleeding, one eye was nearly swollen shut, and bruises covered nearly half her face. With a wave of her hand, she transformed herself, healing her cuts and bruises, making herself whole. She stopped short of the whole blonde, busty warrior-princess thing. Ben loved her as she was, so maybe there was something worthwhile there after all.

She bit her lip, wondering what to do next. Brody was still out there, waiting for her. And even if Jenny had already returned with help, how would they know where she was? Another thought occurred to her, one that chilled her to the bone: what if Brody wasn't waiting, after all? What if he'd simply left the house to go after Ben's grandfather, figuring he'd come back for her later?

"Hey, I don't want any trouble," echoed a voice from outside the bathroom, "My name's Jim Felt, and you just need to come with me, okay?"

She whirled, coming face to face with one of the men who'd abducted her from the house. Without thinking, she punched him hard in the chest. She felt something within him break as he flew backwards into the television, knocking it from its stand to smash to the tile floor in a torrent of broken glass and metal.

"Shit," the man said, holding his chest. He lay atop the remains of the television, tears streaming down his craggy cheeks.

"What the hell are you doing here?" she asked, conjuring a green silk blouse over her bra as she stomped toward him.

"I...God, don't hit me again...he untied me and said he'd kill me if I didn't come in here and get you. Please, I don't want to die. Just come with me, and I'll leave you alone, I swear." His words came out in a rush, his lips trembling as he spoke.

"You lost your right to ask anything of me the moment you put me in a box," she yelled, hands on her hips. "Do you know how terrifying...how humiliating...do you have any idea what you did to me?"

"I'm sorry," he said, flinching from her words. "I swear to God, I just did what Dowd told me to do. I didn't have a choice."

"You always have a choice, Mr. Felt."

"You're gonna make me do this the hard way, aren't you?" he said, pulling his hand out from behind his back to reveal a pearl-handled switchblade.

He thrust the knife at her leg, but here, in her realm, she was much too quick for him. By the time the knife slashed through the space where her thigh had been, she was standing a full five feet away from him.

He stared at her, gaping. "I don't want to do this, but he's going to kill me if I don't. Don't you understand?"

"I understand," she said, walking toward him, "that you just tried to hurt me for the second time in less than twelve hours. And you don't get a third chance!"

She held out her hand and the switchblade wrenched free of his fingers to fly through the air, landing in the palm of her hand. She smiled as the knife dissolved in her grip, turning to mist.

"Now get out of here," she said, eyes locked on his, "or so help me, I'm going to throw you out. Deal with Brody, deal with me, at this point I really don't care. But if you fuck with me ever again or hurt any of my friends…" she let the threat hang there, afraid of the anger she felt but also wanting nothing more than to rip off his balls and shove them straight up his ass.

"I can't," he said, cowering against the remains of the television. "I told you, he'll kill me!"

"So will I," she whispered. "Choose your poison, Mr. Felt. Out there, at least you have a fighting chance; in here, you'll suffer a thousand deaths before I even get started. This is my *home*, my refuge, and you made one hell of a mistake coming in here."

It was really no choice at all. She watched as the man, defeated, rose from the splintered glass and plastic and walked slowly across the floor to the shimmering curtain of light. He hesitated, took a deep breath, and stepped through.

Katy stretched out on the leather couch, resting her aching muscles and trying not to think about Felt. She'd give it ten minutes and then take a quick peek through the curtain. If Brody was no longer there, she'd make a run for it. By now Jenny should have found Ben and the others, but if not she needed to get away and warn Paul McGee. If Brody managed to reach him, then the terrible future from which they came might happen all over again. And if that did happen, there wasn't much of a future for any of them.

Chapter 54

Ben reached the front door first and hit the wooden entrance running, knocking the door off its hinges as he slammed into it with his shoulder.

"Katy!" he screamed. "Katy, where are you?"

"For God's sake, son, be careful," whispered Ruskin, his gun drawn, as he pushed through the door. "They could be anywhere."

"Or they might not be here at all," said Jenny, coming up behind them. "What if Brody decided to go after my father earlier than planned?"

"We should split up," said Ben, knowing as he said it that it probably wasn't the smartest idea he'd ever come up with. Invariably, that's when Freddie or Jason got their next victims in *Nightmare on Elm Street* or *Friday the Thirteenth*. But, this time, it couldn't be helped. "Shawn, you and Jenny go to Grandpa Paul's house, Oscar, you keep watch out here in case he gets by us, and Fred and I will take point inside."

Oscar started to protest, but Ben waved him off. "We need someone out here. I trust you. Fair enough?"

"Fair enough," Oscar agreed, withdrawing the pistol from his waistband.

"Be careful," Jenny whispered to Ben, reaching out to touch his arm.

"I will be," Ben said, giving her a quick hug.

"Wait," Shawn said, holding out his hand to Ben. "I know you gave yours to Katy, and you might need this." He pressed something into Ben's hand before turning back to leave.

"Grandpa, eh?" asked Ruskin, after Shawn and Jenny had left.

He let the words sink in. Then he was moving into the house, with Ben just a step behind.

Jenny had said they were on the third floor and that Katy had teleported Brody into the hidden room before he'd broken out through the wall, so that seemed the most logical place to start. Still, they couldn't risk Brody hiding out somewhere else and escaping the house the moment their backs were turned. Oscar was more than capable of holding his own with someone like Felt, but he doubted the man was any match for a possessed Brody Huffman, gun notwithstanding.

"So, are you a cop?" Ruskin asked. "You seem to handle yourself pretty well." He clicked on the penlight, providing a barely visible line of illumination.

"Not even a cadet," he said, letting a brief smile crack his lips, "but I did spend an awful lot of time talking to one, so I might have picked up a thing or two."

"You'll have to tell me about it later," he whispered, as they reached the back stairwell. "Stay behind me and don't make any more noise than you have to. He probably already knows we're here. Brody's an ex-marine, and if this monster knows what he knows…"

He didn't finish; he didn't have to. From what his father had told him, the fetch had been a lethal fighting machine. Combined with the knowledge and combat training of an ex-marine, he could be near-unstoppable.

They reached the second-floor landing without incident and were halfway up to the third when Ruskin stopped Ben with a slash of his hand. Katy's father pressed his finger to his lips, clicked off the penlight, and motioned Ben forward.

Light poured down from above, and the steps were covered in jagged splinters of wood, crumbling plaster and, most disturbing of all, blood. And then he saw what Ruskin had really been pointing out; a ripped pair of jeans, which he instantly recognized as belonging to Katy. Ben felt lightheaded and his heart boomed almost audibly in his chest.

Ruskin pressed a hand to his wrist, looked him in the eye, and once again held his finger to his lips. Then he turned to continue up the stairs, taking one step at a time, instinctively avoiding the squeaky spots that Ben only managed to steer clear of by luck.

And then they saw it; a huge, gaping hole in the wall just above the final step, where his father had told him the hidden room was.

"We'll be going in there blind," whispered Ruskin, flat against the wall directly under the hole, "Bad idea, but unless you have any other suggestions it's our only option."

"Actually, I do," he said, remembering the pentagram that hung from around his neck. "Katy has my necklace, but Shawn gave me his. I also have a similar necklace that Brody gave me earlier, one he found in the old house. That can't be a coincidence. They're both teleportation devices to a secret alcove above the stairs, where that hole leads. I go in first with my necklace, you wait for me to yell, and then you come in after me." He reached into his pocket and withdrew the pentagram Brody had given him earlier in the day, passing it to Ruskin. "That way, no one has to be exposed going through the hole blind, and if you don't hear me yell… well, you'll know what that means, too."

"Not a bad idea," he said, nodding his head, "but I'll go first."

"But I have my luck on my side," Ben countered. "I'm more likely to survive, and…" He hesitated, afraid to let the words he wanted to say pass his lips.

"And, if I die, then Katy will never be born, so this whole mission will have been pointless," Ruskin finished for him. "I've known since the restaurant, I think. I just didn't put it all together until you referred to Paul McGee as 'Grandpa'."

Ruskin's eyes glistened in wonder and, Ben thought, maybe a little in sadness as well, for the daughter who had been taken from him so many years ago by the smiley-face killer in Chicago. While he couldn't do anything about that, Ben was determined not to let the man lose another daughter.

"Then you get my point," he said, dashing up the stairs before Ruskin could respond.

He crossed the room, noted the floodlight, and spied the huge pentagram inlaid into the wooden floor intersecting exactly halfway across the room's width and length and, beside it, Katy's purse.

In one quick motion, he picked up the purse and stepped on the symbol, disappearing and immediately reappearing on the other side. He found himself in a rectangular-shaped room filled with debris and—his heart skipped a beat—Jim Felt's corpse. Or what was left of it.

He stumbled wordlessly toward the body. Felt's face was frozen in a scream, and something had bitten huge chunks out of his arms and legs. A bloody, gaping hole lay in his chest where his heart should have been. He looked closer at the wounds: the teeth marks were human.

He sniffed at the air, recognizing a smell that mingled with the sweet decay of death. Roses? And then he remembered—Katy's perfume. He felt sick to his stomach. Katy had definitely been here. The smell of her scent was at once a visceral reminder of what they had shared while also bringing to focus the very real possibility that she might be dead.

"That wasn't very bright," said Ruskin. Ben whirled around to see the old sheriff clambering through the hole. "He isn't here, is he?"

"Doesn't seem to be," he said, unable to tear his eyes away from the body. "So the necklace didn't work?" He kept picturing Katy's body, and it was all he could do to keep from screaming.

"Didn't try it," the former sheriff said, crawling through the hole. "When in doubt, take the surest route. Besides, it seems too much like that transporter in *Star Trek*, and you know that…" He fell silent and his eyes grew wide as he spotted Jim Felt's corpse. "For the love of Jesus." He righted himself before walking across the room to prod at the body with the toe of his boot. "Brody did this?"

"I guess so," Ben said, his breathing rapid and shallow.

Where was Katy? And then he noticed the shirt Brody had loaned her lying in the corner, drenched in blood.

Ruskin's eyes followed his, and a look of grim determination passed over his face. "Yes, it's the shirt she was wearing, but *she's* not here. If he'd done the same thing to her that he did to Felt, there'd be evidence. Wherever he is, she's with him."

"Or maybe," said Ben, his voice shaky, "she was the main course and Felt was only the dessert."

"Guys, there *is* a third option," said Katy, stepping through the curtain of lights. "Like, maybe I kicked his ass and sent him packing?"

"Katy!" Ben yelled, running to embrace her. "My God, I thought you were dead."

She looked absolutely radiant in a beautiful green silk blouse and a gold wrap skirt, almost as if the last twelve hours had never happened. He felt hot tears streaming down his cheeks but blinked them away, embarrassed.

"Yeah, doofus, I heard," she said, kissing him tenderly on the lips before slowly wiping away his tears. "I'm okay, really I am. It was close there for a while, but—oh!" She pointed a trembling finger at Felt's body, backing away.

"Brody must have done it," said Ruskin, putting his body between them and Felt's corpse. "Let's get you out of here."

"No, no, you don't understand," she said, burying her face in Ben's shoulder. "I did it to him. It's my fault he's dead."

Ben looked at her, stunned. "What are you talking about? There's no way you could have done that to him. There's just no way."

"And you," she said, staring at Ben. "Your hand, it's black. What happened to your hand?"

"It's a long story, but I'll explain everything."

Katy took Ben's other hand and pulled him toward the shimmering curtain. "Come on, both of you. I have something to show you, and then we'll talk and you'll tell me how your hand turned black and I'll explain exactly how I'm responsible for Mr. Felt's death."

Chapter 55

It was nearly two in the morning by the time Jenny and Shawn reached her parents house. The snow had mostly stopped, though the wind kicked up enough flurries here and there to make driving slow. Jenny wondered if Brody had already broken in and murdered her father but pushed the thought away.

They'd decided at the start to keep their parents out of it, figuring they were safer if they didn't know what was going on, but she was starting to second-guess that decision.

Shawn killed the engine and let the car coast the remaining 50 yards to the house. The house, thank God, looked undisturbed. If Brody had already been there, there'd be signs—an open door, a broken window, something. At least she hoped so.

"We still have time," said Jenny, praying that it was true. Her hand inched toward the car door handle, but Shawn's fingers closed around her wrist, pulling her away. "What are you doing?"

"There!" he whispered, pointing across the lawn.

She squinted through the darkness. There, standing in the shadows by the side of the house, was a man holding a knife. He stood stock-still, surveying the house, perhaps trying to decide how best to gain entry.

"You stay here," he said, his hand tightening on the door handle. "I promise you, I won't let him hurt your parents."

"We do things together from now on," she corrected him, the tiniest of smiles flickering past her lips, "remember?" She stared across the yard. Why was Brody just standing there like that?

"But…"

"It's not him," she said, still staring out the window. "It's just a snowman holding a stick. Shawn, it's not—"

She threw herself back against the seat as the front window of the car suddenly exploded in a thousand spider-web cracks, showering them with shards of glass. "Was gonna get your dad," said Brody Huffman, reaching through the broken window to grab Shawn by the throat, "but you'll do. You'll definitely do."

He pulled Shawn through the windshield and out of the vehicle, swinging the hammer straight down at his head. Shawn rolled away just as the weapon clanged hard against the car, iron meeting metal in a burst of sound that rang loudly through the sleeping neighborhood.

"Hold still, Goddamn it!" Brody shouted, tightening his grip around Shawn's throat.

Before she could even think, Jenny was out the door and attacking Brody, hitting the back of his head, scratching at his face, anything to get him off of Shawn.

"Can't believe you didn't run away when you had the chance," he said, dropping the hammer to reach over his shoulder at her. "Stupid little cunt." His fingers caught in her hair and he dragged her around to face him, head-butting her full-on in the face.

Everything went black for a moment as his skull cracked hard against her forehead, knocking her flat on her back. The night sky swam before her eyes but she fought against the dark veil that threatened to engulf her, knowing if she let herself go under that they were both dead.

She saw Shawn's feet kick and twitch, heard him gasp, and then watched as his body went limp, slumping against the hood of the car.

And then she was on Brody again, wrapping her arms around his leg, pulling his leg, pulling him away from Shawn.

His scream echoed through the streets as he turned from Shawn to beat at her head and shoulders, trying to dislodge her from his ankle. "Get off!" he growled, kicking and punching, but still she held on.

And then she heard a heavy thump and Brody was falling, tumbling over her to land flat on his face in the snow. She looked up to see Shawn staring down at her, his eyes glassy, the hammer hanging loosely from his fingertips. He winced and the hammer slipped from his hand to slide down the hood, falling harmlessly into the snow.

She rolled onto her stomach, her vision growing dim once again, and threw up all over her attacker's feet.

"Jenny," Shawn said, lowering himself on shaky legs from the hood of the car. "Are you okay?"

"Better than ever," she said, sitting up, determined not to cry. "Is he dead?"

"I…don't know," he wheezed, dropping to his knees beside Brody. "He's breathing."

"There's some rope in the garage," she said, using Shawn's shoulder to climb to her feet.

The neighborhood spun before her as she stood up. She steadied herself against the car before putting one foot in front of the other and walking up the driveway.

"Don't wake your parents," Shawn called after her. "And see if you can find any duct tape."

She turned around to answer him, watching as he rolled Brody onto his back. Immediately the man's arm shot out, sweeping Shawn's legs out from under him, knocking him flat on his back. And then the ex-marine was back on his feet, climbing into the car. The engine turned over, shifted into reverse, drove around Shawn, and peeled out of sight.

"Shit!" yelled Jenny, the rope and her injuries forgotten as she ran to Shawn's side. "Are you all right?"

"I'm okay," he said, rubbing the back of his head. "But why didn't he kill me? He had the perfect chance."

He started to get up but slipped in the blood that had mixed with the snow to form a slushy puddle at his feet. His eyes looked glassy, and Jenny worried that he might have a concussion.

"Who knows? Come on, we've got to catch him." She pulled him to his feet, and together they sprinted for the garage. Thank God her dad kept a copy of his car keys hidden beneath his workbench.

She wasn't as brave as she liked to pretend, and she knew that Shawn probably knew that too. But once they got through this night— if they got through this night—there'd be plenty of time to be afraid.

Taking a deep breath, she unlocked the door and climbed into the truck, shifted it into neutral, and let it roll down the driveway before turning over the engine. Steeling her nerves, she readied herself to chase down Brody and finally, once and for all, put an end to this horror they knew all too well as the fetch. And, this time, they'd make sure he stayed dead.

Chapter 56

Ben was falling. His perspective seemed to shift, and it was like he was looking at himself through a telescope. He turned inside out, or at least it felt that way. It was a nauseating experience, one that made him feel dizzy and off balance.

He stared at his surroundings. It was Katy's cabin, the very same one he'd glimpsed earlier today in his dream. But how? He knew it wasn't real; it was just a construct formed from her imagination, a pit stop on her way to dreamwalking. Wasn't it?

"Whoa, what is this place?" Ruskin asked, stepping through the curtain behind Ben. His eyes strayed to the windows, seeing the falling snow outside. "How is this even possible?"

"Major weirdness, huh?" She said, spreading her arms to encompass the whole of the imaginary structure. "I have some theories, but first we'd better compare notes on what's going on with Brody and the reverend."

It didn't take them long to catch each other up to speed. When they were finished, Ruskin was the first to speak.

"You're not responsible for Felt, you know. He chose his path a long time ago. He knew what he was doing."

"Still, I condemned an innocent…" she said, then stopped herself. "Okay, maybe not an *innocent* man, but still—I could have let him hide out in here until you two showed up. Instead, I sentenced him to death."

"He got what he deserved," said Ben flatly, surprised at his own conviction.

But it was true, wasn't it? This man had tried to kill Katy and had probably hurt many others before her. If his death wasn't justice, then what was?

"So," he said, in an attempt to change the subject, "where'd you get the new clothes?"

"These old rags?" she asked. "They're not real. Beneath all this," she gestured at the designer top and skirt, "I'm a real mess."

"Katy, don't you realize—you left this room with those clothes on, and that's how we saw you. They're real."

Her jaw dropped. "I wonder…" She closed her eyes in concentration. "Okay, I 'healed' myself earlier. Just temporary, I thought, but I can't make it go away. I don't understand this at all."

"Healed?" Ruskin's face grew troubled, and he turned toward her. "What do you mean?"

"Brody," she said quietly. "He tried to rape me."

Ben picked up the baseball bat from where it was leaning against the couch, enjoying the feel of its weight and imagining how it would feel to use it against Brody Huffman. "I'll kill him."

"I said *tried*, Ben; he didn't do it, and it's not really Brody anyway. So put that bat down. It's a demon, the same demon that inhabited Colin Wainwright. I managed to fight him off, and I think I probably hurt him pretty badly. But I got really banged up in the process."

"But you're all better now?" asked Ruskin, the color draining from his face. "Thank God for that, but—"

"But how? Honestly, I have no clue. This place, this cabin, it's where I go when I dreamwalk. If Ben hasn't told you about that…well, I can enter people's dreams, alter them, even control them. That television over there, or what's left of it," she gestured at a pile of broken glass and plastic lying in the middle of the room, "is the way I look in on people, and that glass door in the corner is how I actually enter their dreams."

That reminded Ben of something. "The door," he said, squeezing her hand, "you've probably never seen it from the outside, but I have. It's pitted and scarred, like someone tried to get inside."

She shuddered. "Remember the nightmare? It seemed different, somehow, and my injuries in the dream manifested themselves in the physical world," she said, peeling off the bandage; that wound, too, had been healed. "I think it must have been because we were in such close proximity to the fetch. I'm linked to him, somehow, and all these years he's been chasing me through my dreams. But here, he's stronger, and now that he's inhabited a real, live body, he's almost unstoppable. As long as he's alive, he's going to keep coming after me."

"You're connected," said Ruskin, his face pale, "because of me, because of what I did to him two years ago. Because I tried to kill him."

"What are you talking about?" she said, her eyes moving to him and then to Ben. "How could you…"

"He knows," Ben said, in a low voice. "We've really botched this up, haven't we?"

"Don't blame him," Ruskin said, moving across the couch to take Katy's hand. "I was pretty sure before he confirmed it for me. The letter you left with Sam kind of clued me in as well."

"She wasn't supposed to give you that until…until…" she said, stuttering, her eyes wet.

"Until you were born," he said, taking her into his arms. "Which you still will be, I promise. Actually, she gave it to me the day your mother and I got married, and I promise you I won't go anywhere near Highway 136 on the date you mentioned. Now that I know you…I wouldn't risk not having you in my life for the world."

"You *told* him?" Ben said incredulously, "after all the lecturing about not changing the past, you told him?"

"I couldn't help it," she said. "I wasn't going to, but I changed my mind when I saw my mother and sister in the store. A woman's prerogative, after all. Forgive me?"

How could he not? Now that he knew where his luck came from, he realized he'd more or less made a career out of changing reality. "Always," he whispered, "no matter what."

"So how're we going to stop Brody without killing him," Katy asked, "if that's even possible at this point?"

"I love Brody like a brother," Ruskin said, "but if it comes down to it, I'll put a bullet in his brain before I let him harm anyone else. It's not his fault that he got caught up in all this, but I know he'd understand—there are casualties in war, and this is most definitely war."

Ben nodded, thinking of Jim Felt's body on the other side of the curtain and of all the people that Felt and David Dowd had murdered over the years. He thought also of Kristen Hawks, who'd taken her own life after being twisted and manipulated by her father.

This *was* war, and in war innocent people died. But they'd already changed too many things, and he didn't want one more death on his conscience if he could help it.

A high-pitched beep suddenly sounded from Katy's purse, ringing softly every two seconds. It sounded like a cell phone.

"It's coming from your bag," Ruskin said, looking perplexed.

"Here, I'll turn it off…wait a minute." The phone was in camera mode, and as soon as she moved the slider to open it a color picture of the archangel Michael flashed on the screen. "How weird, I must have accidentally taken a picture of him. Hope that's not against the rules of the angel union or something." She punched a few buttons but the phone wouldn't turn off. "Damn it, I hate these things. You want to try?" She tossed the phone to Ben.

"Hmm," he said, staring at the tiny photo. "From inside the garage, I think. Anyway…" he started to turn off the phone but stopped short as Ruskin touched his wrist.

"Wait a second," Ruskin said, looking over his shoulder. "Let me see that."

He took the phone and stared at it for a long time, ignoring the plaintive protests coming through the little stereo speaker in the side. Passing it back to Ben, he said, "I'm sorry, but that's not Michael."

The incessant beeping finally stopped as the phone, out of power, shut down of its own accord. Ben jabbed at the buttons, trying in vain to force it back on again. "Are you sure?" he asked, handing the phone back to Katy. "I mean, it has to be him."

"Just because he said so?" asked Ruskin. "Maybe his appearance changed, but the Michael I knew had longer hair, his features were more refined, his nose wasn't hooked at the end—and his eyes, I can still see them in my mind; a dazzling blue deeper than all of the world's oceans." His face grew red, embarrassed. "Well, you know what I mean. If you'd ever met him, you could never forget."

"But…" Ben felt his heart skip a beat. "If it wasn't him…"

"…Then who was it?" Katy finished the sentence, slipping the phone into her purse. "And what was his real reason for sending us into the past?"

Chapter 57

Oscar Reyes shivered beneath his thin flannel jacket, wondering if he'd ever feel warm again. He watched his breath turn to frost as he stood guard outside the old house, trying to figure out just what in the hell he'd gotten himself into. Sorcery was real, the Reverend was a fraud, and one of the men he'd met earlier tonight, Brody Huffman, was possessed by a demon.

He almost wished he was back in Los Angeles, still running with the Spanish Dragons, holding up *bodegas* while high on crystal meth. At least *that*, he understood. But no, he didn't really want that life back again. He'd turned himself around, done many good things in the last seven years, even if his spiritual mentor had turned out to be a monster.

Ruskin and the others had given him the opportunity to back out, but he couldn't take it. For whatever else he had been, Oscar Reyes was no coward. He had sinned against Katy Rush, and he would protect her with his life. It was a matter of honor. He knew his mama, God bless her soul, would understand. More than that, she would be proud.

Just as he was about to circle the property for the third time in ten minutes, the Charger roared into view, weaved, and coasted to a stop a few yards from the driveway. The entire windshield was missing, and little bits of glass clung to the dented and caved-in hood of the car like fleas on the back of a horse.

He was already moving when the driver's side door creaked open and Shawn tumbled to the road. "I'm hurt," he whispered, shuddered once, and then fell silent.

Mi Dios! "I'm coming, my friend," he called out, slipping the .22 into his coat pocket.

He ran around the car, dropping to his knees beside Shawn. Only it wasn't Shawn. The last thing he saw was Brody's steel gray eyes and the flash of a smile as the bloody hammer swung up toward his face.

* * *

Brody Huffman wanted nothing more than to close his eyes and pretend that none of this was real. But he couldn't. He couldn't do anything. He couldn't even count. All he could do was sit back and watch as the demon, controlling his body, shattered Oscar Reyes' skull with the hammer he had purchased just last year at Western Auto.

He watched in horror as the head of the hammer crushed bone, ripped flesh, and finally broke through to the gray matter beneath. And then the demon was pulling the hammer free from the dead man's skull, bringing it to his mouth, *licking* it, sucking the blood and bits of brain from the head of the iron tool, reveling in the taste, growing stronger.

He constantly felt the pressure of the demon's rage pushing down on him, battering at his mind, doing its best to squash him, and it was only by directing his own anger back at his tormentor was he even able to retain consciousness, much less think his own thoughts.

And he knew the demon had access to all of those thoughts, just as he seemed to have access to the demon's, or at least a portion of them. He knew that it was the pentagram necklace that had allowed the demon to inhabit his body, just as he knew that the demon was even now trying to figure out a way to use that necklace to stay on Earth forever.

If the demon used the necklace to switch bodies, he reasoned, the magic that directed him, that had set him on this course of destruction, would more than likely continue to control him. However, if he chose the right host, he might be able to overcome those limitations.

He knew that Brody had given the necklace to Ben, and that the boy possessed an incredible amount of magic. Magic enough to break free of the chains imposed upon him by the enchanted necklace? He wasn't sure, but he thought the plan had a good chance of working. And what did he have to lose?

And what can you do to stop me? The demon's thoughts echoed in his skull. *This has nothing to do with you. You're just the means to an end. Shut up and stop whining and I might even let you live after all of this is finished.*

"Damn you to hell!" he screamed inside his head. "You think I'd even want to live after you've slaughtered all my friends?"

As you wish, the demon laughed, walking toward the house with Oscar's body in his arms. *Just don't say I didn't warn you.*

Chapter 58

"We can't stay in here all night," Ben said.

The cabin was warm, peaceful, and could provide for any of their needs, but it wasn't real. Besides, his parents and grandparents needed him. Brody Huffman was still out there, doing God only knew what.

"I'll go first," said Ruskin, gun at the ready. "If it's all clear, I'll stick my hand through and signal. Katy, you stay here."

"Nothing doing," she said, standing with her hands on her hips. "I'm tired of running and—"

"Much as I hate to admit it," Ben said, interrupting her, "Katy's right. She has a right to be there, especially after what that...*thing* tried to do to her."

Katy looked at him in silence, a slow smile spreading across her face. "You know," she said, squeezing his hand, "maybe you're not such a doofus after all."

Ben was about to reply when Oscar suddenly stepped through the curtain—and was then forcibly yanked back, like a rubber ball at the end of a paddle. Ruskin was already moving, diving through the gate, with Ben and Katy sprinting after him.

Ben knew something was wrong the moment he stepped through. Oscar lay crossways across Felt, bleeding from a vicious blow to the forehead, eyes wide open in surprise, while Brody lay curled up in a fetal position at the end of the corridor. Ruskin, standing to the side of the curtain, held not only his own gun but Oscar's, both of which were trained on Ben's chest.

"No," he screamed, pushing Katy back the instant she stepped through the gate. And then Ruskin was upon him, throwing him against the wall, shoving one of the guns into his throat.

"Smarty pants," Ruskin said.

The former lawman casually turned and fired a bullet into Brody Huffman's prone body. Huffman jerked once, rolled over onto his side, and lay still.

"What're you—"

"It's taking all the self-control I have not to jack three bullets into your brain, asshole," he whispered, his breath hot on Ben's neck. "Drop the bat, listen to me, and do exactly as I say."

"I'm listening."

Ben let the baseball bat fall harmlessly to the floor. The demon was inside Ruskin, and he knew in an instant that he himself had provided the key in the form of the necklace Brody had given him and he had passed on to Ruskin.

"Tasty, tasty, tasty little Katy can live, and so can daddy dearest, but you, my friend, will have to make one very large sacrifice. Are you ready to do that?"

"Do I have a choice?" He stood stock still, but his eyes took in the room. Oscar was definitely dead, and the weapon that had more than likely killed him—the hammer—lay on the ground beside him.

"Smart boy," Ruskin said, an inch from his face. "Smarty pants, gave his father twenty whacks, and when he saw what he had done, he gave his mother twenty-one. Onion. Shit, I still got that guy in my head. Your boy Brody was one fucked up ex-marine, gooks and all. Trust me, he's better off dead."

"So what do you want me to do?" Ben concentrated on the nickel in his pocket, eyeing the bat at his feet, hoping to use one or both the moment he had the chance.

"Simple," Ruskin said, taking a deep breath. He cocked the gun he'd just used to shoot Brody and placed it against his own temple. Smoke still rolled from the barrel, stinging Ben's eyes. "You're gonna give me your body, or I'm going to kill both you and the old man and then your girly girl won't ever be born. My way, both she and her father get to live, and I leave the Spencers and the McGees alone."

"When you put it that way," said Ben, his teeth clenched, "how can I refuse?" The demon seemed to go back and forth between lucidity and madness, and he wasn't sure which was more dangerous.

* * *

What the hell was going on? Why had Ben pushed her like that? From what little she'd seen of the outside world, her father had everything well under control. She started to walk through the curtain again, but a single thought stopped her.

If Ben had pushed her, he must have had a damned good reason.

She had an idea. Quickly sprinting to the couch, she snatched up the remote, magically rebuilt the ruined television, and tuned it to Brody. He wasn't asleep, but if he was still being controlled by the demon perhaps she could make contact anyway. She'd never visited his dreams before and it usually took a few minutes to connect to someone, but the screen immediately flickered to life.

She saw a young man slowly walking through a lush field of corn, following a meandering path through stalks so high that they almost touched the sky. A gentle breeze rippled the husks and she watched, mesmerized, as they swayed back and forth to some unheard melody.

The sun shone a brilliant yellow in the east, lighting up a sky so blue that it could almost have been a river. Blue jays and cardinals sang songs to one another through the corn, soaring high above the path's lone traveler. The sun-drenched scenery called to her, inexplicably tugging at some part of her that wanted nothing more than to go home, and it was all that she could do to ignore the longing and concentrate on the task at hand.

She zoomed in on the young man and realized that it was Brody, but as he must have looked twenty or thirty years ago. He had a full head of wavy brown hair and a big smile on his face, and he walked without the limp he'd earned in the Korean War. He looked as though he didn't have a care in the world.

The path he followed wound this way and that, thinning out as he neared the edge of the field. Beyond that…a bright white light encompassed the whole of the field, spreading out as far as she could see. And that's when she realized Brody was dying.

Without another thought, she dashed through the frosted glass door and into his dream. She found herself behind him on the path, watching as he methodically covered the distance between where they stood and the end of the field.

The sweet smell of the corn was intoxicating. Huge green stalks bursting with full ears of beautiful yellow corn. The odor tugged at her, called to her, promising to envelop her in its silky soft husks and keep her safe forever. But beneath that smell, the odor that brought back images of picnics with her family and hot buttered ears of corn, was another less inviting: the cloying decay of death. It was that smell that she concentrated on, anchored herself to, lest she lose herself in the hypnotic allure of the field.

"Brody, wait up," she said, jogging to catch up with him.

The young man turned around, a puzzled look on his face. "Sorry, ma'am, but do I know you? Name's not Brody, its Bruce. Bruce Huffman."

She stared at him in confusion. He couldn't have been a day over eighteen, but she'd recognize those eyes and the jaw line anywhere; it was definitely Brody. Besides, it was his dream, so who else could it be? Brody must be a nickname he had earned later in life.

"You can't walk into the light," she whispered, taking his hand. "Ben, my father…Fred, Shawn and Jenny…they all need you. I need you. You have to fight the demon."

He laughed, a sound so full and rich that she wondered why she'd never heard it before. "Demon? Ma'am, what on Earth are you talking about? I don't see anyone else here."

"Brody, don't you know me? I'm Katy. Katy Ruskin. Fred's daughter."

"Now, look," he said, a twinkle in his eyes, "I don't know where you come from, but here in Beach Bottom…"

"Beach Bottom?" she interrupted. "What're you talking about?"

"Beach Bottom, West Virginia, ma'am. Born and raised. And here in Beach Bottom, we don't go around telling tall tales, at least not before lunch. Now if you'll excuse me, I have an appointment to keep."

"An appointment with who?"

He looked at her as if he were searching his memory for a name. "Well, that is funny. I can't seem to remember. But I know if I keep going, just over the horizon there," he pointed toward the white space that lay beyond the corn field, "I'll come to it. So if you don't mind…"

"The thing is, Brody, I *do* mind. I don't know you very well, but my father seems to care an awful lot about you, and I'm not going to let you go without a fight. You can't let him win."

She felt suddenly dizzy and reached out to steady herself against Brody. If she stayed here much longer, she knew, she'd be putting herself at risk of dying, too.

"I said, let who win?" He stared at her, blinking as comprehension slowly crept over his face. "Oh, you must mean Leonard."

Leonard? "No, Brody, there's a demon…"

"His name is Leonard," he said, shaking his head, "and he's a lower-level demon and sometimes-ally of Eblis, one of the major fallen-angels of hell, and right now he's working under his bidding. Now don't ask me how I knew that, because I have absolutely no idea."

"So you do remember?"

"I do, though I almost wish I didn't. Korea, the demon, the counting, all of it—gone, but now it's all back in my head."

"I'm so sorry for that," she said, holding his hand, "but you can't let him win. You have to fight."

"Why? What's to fight? I'm dying, Katy. He shot me."

"Shot you? What're you…" She let her sentence trail off as it finally dawned on her. The demon was no longer inside Brody; it had taken over her father.

He nodded, as if reading her mind. Hell, it was his dream; maybe he could.

"I'm sorry," he said, still smiling, "but there's nothing I can do. He wants Ben's body, because he thinks the boy's wild magic might be enough to free him from the spell he's under."

"What do you mean?" Katy asked.

She shook her head, doing her best to fight the pervasive scent of the corn. It was all she could do now not to lay down in the dirt, curl up, and fall asleep.

"The necklace, the one I gave to Ben, the same one Fred now has—it's how he jumps. Before that, he was trapped in a room behind a curtain of light. It's a spirit trap. Humans can enter and leave at will, can even use the room's magical properties to bend time and space, but a spirit, or a soul…is trapped in there forever. Or at least until someone who can be possessed enters the room, which is how I came to be involved in this whole mess.

"The necklace I found was the key. Using the necklace as a conduit, he was able to enter my body, where he remained mostly dormant until Halloween, and where he would have remained dormant after Halloween ends until next October 31st. But if he can use Ben's magic to break the properties of the spell…"

"Okay, I'm totally confused now. What properties? And how do you know all this?" She asked, yawning.

"The properties of the spell that was cast on the necklace. He's supposed to kill Fred, his wife, their daughter, Shawn's parents, and Jenny's parents, one at a time, each Halloween. And, after they're dead, he gets to keep the body and live out the rest of his host's natural lifespan. That's the deal."

"But that's not how..."

She was about to say *that's not how it happened*, but then she remembered the *Journal-Pilot* article. Brody was killed in a construction accident in September of 1981, and that's why the murders stopped.

"As to how I know these things, again, I have no clue. I seem to know what he knows, or at least most of it. Anyway, I'd better go," he said, eyeing the horizon at the end of the cornfield. "I don't want to be late for my appointment."

"But...but..." she stammered, refusing to let go of his hand. "Who's behind all this? Who left the necklace for you to find?"

"That, my dear," he said, the act crinkling the corners of his eyes, "is the $64,000 question. He didn't know, and so I don't know. But he suspected it was Eblis, the fallen-angel I mentioned earlier. Apparently, they'd 'worked together' before, and he'd never quite forgiven Eblis for turning him into a mindless killing machine he referred to as the fetch."

She knew there was a connection to the fetch—Jenny had said as much—but Eblis? Why did that name sound so familiar?

"Anyway, I hope everything works out," Brody said, gently removing her hand from his wrist, "but I really do need to be going."

She crossed her arms and frowned at him. "Do you really want to die?"

"Honey, it's just not a question of 'want'—it's gonna happen whether I want it to or not, and sometimes you've just gotta go with the flow. Besides, I'm really tired of all the pain, and the counting and the washing. I don't seem to feel the need to do that here, and my leg doesn't hurt one bit."

Counting? Washing? And then she remembered watching him tap his fingers, over and over, always in groups of three. He had OCD, obsessive-compulsive disorder. She told him as much, but he just stared at her.

"Katy, I don't know what this 'OCD' is, but I do know that I don't like it one damned bit. I could only ever calm down with the counting, but then it just seemed to bring back the fear all the stronger. It's a vicious cycle."

"But do you *want* to die?" she repeated, glaring at him. "And do you want me to die with you? I'm fading fast, Brody. If we don't get out of here soon, we're both goners."

He seemed to think about it. "If it was my choice, no, I don't expect I really do, even with the 'OCD,' and I certainly don't want you to die, I never did. But…"

"Then *live!*"

She reached out and touched his face, working to heal him through the power of her dreams. She'd never done anything like this before, but then again, she'd never entered someone else's dream while awake either. If she could conjure clothing that existed in the real world, could even heal herself, then why couldn't she heal someone else?

But she couldn't. Maybe because, here in his dream, there was nothing wrong with him, maybe because he didn't really want to be healed, but whatever the case, it wasn't working. The bright white horizon still loomed, and Brody Huffman was still dying.

"I'm sorry," he said, reaching out to brush away her tears, "but you did your best."

"But it's not fair," she said. "You didn't do anything wrong; you don't deserve to die, and neither does my father or Ben."

"It is what it is," he said simply, trailing off as he stared at something over her shoulder. "Say, what is that?"

She turned around but couldn't see a thing other than corn and the door back to her cabin. She froze. Could it be that simple? If he were in her realm, would she then be able to heal him? Ben had also seen the door, had come inside *her* dream, which she'd previously thought impossible. So why not this?

"Move!" she said, grabbing his arm and tugging him along behind her. "We don't have any time to waste." The white oblivion suddenly seemed much closer.

"Slow down," he insisted, dragging his heels. "Where are we going?"

"Back to the real world," she said. "Now go!"

They reached the frosted glass door just as the white space threatened to overtake them. Her legs felt like jelly, and the world began to move in slow-motion. She stumbled into the door, pushing for all she was worth, and then they were through.

"Yes!" she yelled, pumping her fist into the air, her malaise instantly gone. "We made it. Now all I need to do is…" Her face paled as she turned to look at Brody.

"What's wrong?" he asked, studying her eyes.

She passed a hand through his stomach, flinching as her fingers met no resistance. Moreover, she could see right through him. She hadn't saved him after all. Brody Huffman was dead, and his ghost was trapped in the spirit room.

Chapter 59

Ben stared at the demon wearing Fred Ruskin's skin, trying to decide what to do. He'd happily give up his own life to save Katy and her father, not to mention his parents and grandparents, but was it really that easy? He had no guarantee that the demon would keep his word, and he knew now that he possessed an incredible amount of power. Could he really unleash that power on the world by giving his body to the demon?

"So do we have a deal, or do I kill you?" asked Ruskin, one gun pointed at his own head and the other trained on Ben's chest. "You know, in this body, my thoughts are a helluva lot clearer. I don't really want to lose it, but I'll kill both you and Ruskin if I have to."

"We have a deal," he said.

"Good," said Ruskin, transferring the gun he'd been pointing at himself into his shoulder holster. He slipped one hand into his pocket and came out with Brody's necklace. "Now remove your necklace."

"Why?" Ben asked, feigning ignorance. He knew exactly why, but for every minute he kept the demon talking, he would gain another minute to figure a way out of this mess."

"Because I'm going to give you mine, and I don't want you to *accidentally* get them confused," he said, with a wink, "Throw it through the hole in the wall and remember, try anything with that *nickel* of yours and I put a bullet into the old man's brain faster than you can say 'cherry turnover.' And then I go into your little girly girl's hidey-hole and take over her body, and that's when things really start to get interest-ing."

Ben felt his stomach sink. It had to be a bluff—if he could take over Katy's body, or even enter the room, why hadn't he done it al-ready?—but he couldn't be sure, nor could he be sure that he could ef-fectively use the nickel or his abilities to do anything before the demon killed him. He slowly removed the necklace from around his throat and threw it out the gaping hole.

He'd used the threads twice; once to bring Katy back from the brink of death, and the other to change Dowd. But he couldn't see them now. Try as he might, he couldn't seem to activate whatever part of his brain controlled the power to step into that "inbetween space." Even the nickel wasn't helping.

The demon grinned. "I'll have to remember never to play poker when I'm wearing your skin. Your magic won't work here because it's not supposed to. Wainwright set it up that way. The spirit room, magic works like crazy; here, everything is dampened. This," he pulled the gun out of its holster, waving it at Ben, "is the most effective weapon you could have right now. Why do you think we're here?"

"If that's true," he countered, still trying to connect with the nickel, "how were you able to trade bodies with Fred?"

"Controlled magic," he said. "Wainwright worked it all out, and I had access to his mind for an awfully long time. Wild magic, like the kind you have, doesn't work so well here. Items enchanted for a specif-ic purpose, like the teleportation pentagrams and my necklace, work just fine.

"But enough stalling," he said, throwing the necklace through the air at Ben's head, "put the damn thing on and let's get this over with."

He reached for the necklace but watched helplessly as it flew past his outstretched fingers to bounce off the wall.

"Don't fuck with me, asshole," warned Ruskin, pulling out his gun. "Pick it up or I'll—"

"You'll what?" said Shawn, stepping from the pentagram at the far end of the room. He held his version of the nickel in his hand. Jenny stood by his side, and Ben could see that she now wore the tooth around her neck.

"Shawn!" Ruskin yelled, his eyes going wide. "You two stay back. The demon's taken over Ben's body, and..."

"We're not stupid," Jenny said, stepping from the pentagram. "There's a big hole in the wall, remember? We heard everything."

"Oh, that," he said, nonplussed. "Well, it was worth a try."

"There's no way in hell he's giving up his body," said Shawn, moving to stand beside Jenny.

"Oh yes he will," Ruskin countered, cocking back the hammer of the gun, "because my way, everyone gets to live. Even if," he gestured at Ben, "it's in a way some of us are not quite happy with."

"He's right," Ben said, slowly turning around to retrieve the fallen necklace from the floor. He dipped his neck to slip it over his head, angling his hip toward the wall so he could slide his free hand into his pocket. "If this is what I have to do to keep all of you safe, I'm willing to take the risk." He surreptitiously removed his hand.

"About fucking time," Ruskin said, turning to fire the gun into Shawn's shoulder. "That's for the hammer and that whole motorcycle incident."

Ben watched in horror as a small hole opened up in his father's jacket, the polyester stuffing mixing with blood from the wound beneath. Shawn stumbled back against the wall, holding his arm, eyes locked on his assailant as he slowly slid to the ground.

Jenny dropped to her knees beside him, putting her body between Shawn and Ruskin. Shawn's fingers twitched helplessly and the nickel fell from his grasp to roll across the blood stained floor, finally stopping as it encountered Brody's corpse.

"You said you wouldn't hurt them!" Ben screamed, going for the baseball bat.

"I lied," he said, turning the gun on Jenny. "But I could have shot to kill, and next time I will. Or, as Brody might say, 'I will, I will, I will.' Remember that, before you swing that bat," He pulled back the hammer of the gun again, "because if you do, mommy's dead and you'll never be born."

"And you'll have lost your host," said Ben. If this was going to work, he had to make it look good. But before he could do anything Jenny began to cast a spell.

"Animus intereo," she chanted, her eyes closed and her fingers wrapped around the tooth, *"animus intereo, animus intereo."*

"Oh!" said Ruskin, shaking with laughter. "Jenn-eeey knows Latin! Jenn-eeey knows Latin! Stupid slut. Tell her, meat."

"Magic doesn't work right here," Ben said, inching closer to Ruskin. "Something Wainwright did to the room. He wanted us here all along."

"It wouldn't have worked anyway, but, for future reference, you really don't have to repeat a spell three times," said Ruskin. "The 'rule of three' thing only applies to banishments and bindings. Same goes for Latin, or spells at all, for that matter. It's all just a focus. If you're strong enough, you don't need any of that shit."

"I'll remember that," she said, through gritted teeth, "when I banish your ass straight to hell."

"Blah, blah, blah," said Ruskin, turning to wave the gun at Ben. "She never shuts up, does she? Come on, let's get this over with."

"Leonard," said a voice from the curtain, "playtime's over. Get the hell out of my father."

All eyes turned to watch Katy as she leapt through the curtain of light, a glowing metallic orb clutched in her hand. She threw the orb at

Ruskin, but it zoomed over his head, missing by nearly a foot. It car-omed against the wall, bounced once, and landed on Brody's chest.

And that's when all hell broke loose.

"How did you know…" started Ruskin, staring at Katy. He shook his head, turned the gun, and fired point-blank into her chest, sending her stumbling back through the glowing gateway.

"No!" screamed Ben, swinging the bat into Ruskin's stomach.

The possessed former-sheriff shrugged off the blow as if it were nothing more than a nuisance. He grabbed the bat and snapped it over his knee like a twig. "This ends now."

"Not quite yet," said Brody Huffman, rising to his feet.

The lining of his stomach spilled out onto the floor from the gut shot wound he had suffered, but he didn't even seem to notice. He was on Ruskin in a second, wrestling the gun from his hands, flinging it away from him to career across the floor.

"I said, this ends now," Ruskin yelled, finding Ben's eyes in the chaos of the moment. "Bennie, come to papa!"

Ben released the object he'd been hiding in his hand, letting it fall to the floor. He blinked, stared at Ruskin, and, smiling, watched as the corpse of Brody Huffman locked his best friend in a bear hug.

"Get off of me, Brody," he yelled, pushing at the dead man. "It's me, it's Fred. I'm back. I promise, it's me. Now let me go! I have to get to my daughter."

Katy! Ben was almost to the door when he heard his mother's voice, and the all-too-familiar sound of the gun being cocked.

"Turn around slowly," she said, her voice trembling. "I'm not go-ing to let you take Ben."

"Mom," he said, wanting nothing more than to get to Katy, "it's still me. It didn't work. It's still me."

"Don't you lie to me, you bastard," she yelled, tears running down her freckled cheeks. "You've taken so much from me. You took Tanner, you took Katy, you almost took Shawn, and I'm not going to let you take Ben."

"Jenny," said Katy, stepping back through the curtain. "Put the gun down, it's all right. I'm okay, Ben's okay, and Shawn will be okay if you'll let me bring him into the room and heal him."

"Katy?" she stared blankly. "How are you still alive?"

"Same way I am," said Brody, who finally released his death grip on Ruskin, "though I won't be for much longer. It's the room, Jenny. It's…incredible."

"But…but…" she said, faltering, the gun still pointed at Ben. She risked a glance down at Shawn, but his eyes were closed. At least he was still breathing.

"Mom…Jenny…" Ben said, holding his hands in front of him. "It's okay. The demon's never going to hurt you ever again. He's never going to hurt anyone ever again. Can I show you something?"

"Slowly," she ordered, her finger tightening around the trigger.

"See?" He pulled the chain from his neck and held it out to her. The pentacle had been snapped off, and only a broken link remained where it had once hung. "No star. And no star means no demon."

"Then where?" asked Jenny, lowering the gun.

"Right here," said Brody, picking something up from the ground with his gray, lifeless hands. He carefully passed it over to Ben.

It was Boss Moss, the leader of the Freakies, and the pentagram from the necklace had been wedged around his outstretched arm. Ben held it out for everyone to see, avoiding touching the star, instead holding the conglomeration of metal and plastic by the figure's foot.

He shook the green plastic figure and the star fell to the floor. Ruskin knelt to the ground, removed a handkerchief, and gingerly retrieved the pentagram. He folded it inside the handkerchief before stuffing it into his pocket.

"The toy's from 1975, got it in a box of cereal. And as far as I can tell, the demon is trapped inside the figure. And as long as no one makes physical contact with the pentagram, he's there to stay."

"That's all well and good," came a weak voice from behind them, "but I'm bleeding pretty badly over here. Some help, please, before I pass out again?"

Chapter 60

She could never have imagined having visitors in her little imaginary cabin in the middle of a forest located somewhere that didn't exist. True, it wasn't her cabin, not really, and whoever had the strongest connection with the room could probably shape it to their own will, but that was Katy right now, and she wasn't complaining.

Ben and her father sat with her on the couch, while Jenny and Shawn occupied a plush red velvet love seat she'd conjured up—her little tribute to the décor of the Hotel Carthage. And poor Brody, well, Brody had dropped dead the moment he'd stepped through the curtain—or at least his body had. It had fallen backwards into the secret room, while his ghost had continued into her cabin.

She healed Shawn as easily as she'd mended herself after her father shot her. The wound had hurt like hell, but the moment she tended to it the pain and the gaping hole in her chest had immediately disappeared. Here in the cabin of her dreams, all it had taken was a thought, easier even than it had been to create the spyglass she'd pushed through the curtain in order to spy on the world outside.

"It's nothing, really," Brody said, walking through the widescreen television in the corner. "Being dead is kind of…liberating. And, hell, look," he ran through her father, did a handstand, and somersaulted back over the couch, "no limp."

"You saved all our lives, Brody," Ben said, squeezing Katy's hand. "Before you showed up, the demon's eyes hadn't once left me. If you hadn't distracted him, I never would have had the chance to wedge the pentagram onto the toy and ditch it before he tried to possess me."

"Least I could do," he said ruefully, "especially after what I tried to do to Katy and Jenny and what I did to Oscar. I've killed before, plenty of men in Korea, but never like that, and never with such...pleasure."

"But it wasn't you," Katy said, "and I knew that even when it was happening, and so did Oscar, I'll bet. He made his choices, and he died trying to right a wrong he'd committed. If he were here, I know he'd forgive you."

"But he isn't, so I guess we'll never know."

"Can't you help them, Ben?" asked Shawn. "I've seen what you can do. Can't you give Brody his body back, bring Oscar back to life?"

"I don't know how," he said. "I seem to have the ability to alter things that have just happened, or are about to happen, but the threads, the possibilities I see when I use my power...they disappear after a while. It's like once their time has come and the moment has passed, they're gone. And even if we changed the past, where would that leave us? If Brody hadn't killed Oscar and subsequently died himself, Katy would never have found out about the demon and they wouldn't have been able to help us, and Leonard would have killed us all. Still, I do have a few ideas..."

"So what're we going to do now?" asked Jenny, dread falling over her face as she broached the subject they were all doing their best to avoid. "We have three dead bodies outside and another one at Fred's house, not to mention Brody's ghost. And if this room is a spirit trap...how did he get outside anyway?"

"I'll deal with the bodies," said Ruskin, his tone making it clear that this part of the conversation, at least, was finished. "It's the least I can do."

"Brody got out through me," Katy explained, glancing at the ghost. "And not everything you saw was planned. The ball I threw at my dad, it contained Brody's spirit. I really was trying to hit him. I throw like a girl, what can I say?

"I'd been watching and knew Ben was up to something, though I didn't know what. So we came up with our own plan. Brody would enter my dad's body and duke it out with Leonard and at least hold him off until the rest of you could escape.

"But it didn't work out that way. I missed, but luckily," she looked at Ben, wondering if his luck had worked in the room after all, "the ball made contact with his body and he was able to reanimate it."

"Something I've been wondering about," said Brody, hovering a few inches off the ground, "is who sent Leonard. He mentioned another name..."

"...Eblis," Katy finished for him. "When you told me, I knew it sounded familiar. And...oh my God."

"What?" Ben asked.

"The spell," she said. "Do you have it?"

"I do." He pulled a wrinkled piece of paper out of his pocket.

"Let me see," said Jenny, crossing the room to take the paper. "I wish I had my Latin to English dictionary with me."

Katy snapped her fingers, and a huge Latin to English dictionary appeared in her lap. "Your wish is my command, o mistress."

"Hey, I could get used to this," Jenny said, picking up the book. "Could I also get a pencil and some paper?"

"Thy will be done," said Katy, and a sharpened number two pencil appeared sitting on top of a sheaf of notebook paper.

"Okay, let me see..." She scribbled a few lines, transposing words, working it out. And when she was finished, she read the translation;

"Father Time, Mother Earth, turn the sands of time,
The past be the present, the present be the past,

My thoughts the destination the between space,
My immortal soul bound to the angel Eblis,
Luck will be gone, grow weak"

"Oh, my God," said Katy, eyes wide. "Those last two lines. That's why your powers wouldn't work at first, and why we got sick. But who is Eblis?"

"'My immortal soul bound to the angel Eblis'?" Ben read aloud, over Jenny's shoulder. "What the hell?"

"That's a very loose translation," said Jenny, tilting her chin in thought, "but Eblis, if I remember my Biblical mythology right, is another name for," she looked at Shawn, who nodded, "Azazel, the fallen angel who started this whole ball rolling centuries ago. He was the demon who first tempted Aupuch and set in motion the events that led to pretty much everything bad that's happened in our lives during the last two years."

"Then Azazel," said Katy, putting all the pieces together, "must be our faux Michael."

"What are you talking about?" asked Shawn, rising from the love seat. "Michael was the one who banished Azazel."

"Katy took a photo of 'Michael' on her hi-tech camera-phone hybrid device—don't ask—and it definitely wasn't him," said Ruskin. "He had blond hair and wore a trench coat, but beyond that, it didn't look a thing like him."

"But enough similarities to someone who had never seen him before," Shawn added, his lip curling in anger. "Son of a bitch!"

"But whatever his plan was," said Ben, "it didn't work. We stopped the Halloween murders. They'll never happen."

"But think about what else we did," Katy said in a hushed tone. "Four people are dead. History has been changed, lives have been altered. Maybe this is what he had in mind all along."

"Or maybe he was after the nickel. But that couldn't be right, because I would have just given it to him if he'd asked."

"I think the intent is obvious," Jenny said, turning to Ben. "How many times have you said the spell?"

"Just twice," he said. "When we first left, and then again after we mistakenly arrived in 1975. Why?"

"The rule of three," she explained. "In order to be bound to him, you would've had to say it three times. And I bet landing two years further down the timeline than you intended was no accident. By forcing you to take the extra trip, he insured you'd read the spell three times."

"Four, but who's counting?" said Katy, remembering that they still had unfinished business in 1975. "So what do we do?"

"For starters, we remove the last two lines of the spell," she said, crossing out the words with her pencil. "The fifth line bound you to him, and the final line short-circuited your luck and left both of you weak, probably so that when you returned, you'd be powerless against him. The spell should still work without those two lines."

"I'm not even sure you need the spell in the first place," said Shawn. "While I was lying there bleeding to death, Leonard said that the whole 'power of three' thing wasn't necessary, and neither was the Latin, that it was all just used to focus the magic."

"But why does he want me?" Ben asked, seemingly perplexed.

"My God, Ben," said Shawn, laying a hand on his shoulder. "Why wouldn't he? What you did at the campground with Dowd…you altered the fabric of the universe, and you didn't even have to use the nickel to do it. You," he turned to Katy, "both of you, because of what I did, when I healed myself and Jenny and Fred…you can do things that Aupuch probably only dreamed about, that he might not have even be able to do when he had all five of the charms. And Azazel wanted him and, heck, he even wanted me. So why wouldn't he want you?

"And at Jenny's house," said Shawn, putting the pieces of the puzzle together, "the demon could have killed me, but he didn't. It all makes sense now. If he killed me, you never would have been born."

"He's making sense," Ruskin said, from the other side of the couch. "What you can do without the magic…imagine what you might be able to do if you had all five talismans. Imagine what power you could wield. And if that power was his to command…"

"Armageddon," whispered Katy, bile rising to the back of her throat. She felt sick to her stomach.

"Oh, come on," said Ben, staring open-mouthed at her, "you can't be serious."

"The only one way to find out," she said, determined to take back control of her life, "is to go back to the future and take him down."

"Or you could stay here," Jenny said meekly, "and avoid the problem altogether."

Katy loved the girl for offering, but knew they couldn't take her up on it. They just didn't belong here, no matter how tempting the thought might be. They both had lives to live and a future to create, no matter how fraught with peril that future might turn out to be.

"If there's one thing the two of you taught me, or will teach me, or whatever," Ben said, smiling, "is that you don't get anywhere in life by avoiding problems. Dealing with Azazel is something I have to do," he said, staring at Katy as she punched him hard on the arm, "I mean *we* have to do, together."

"I couldn't have said it better myself," she said, smiling ruefully, "though I think I speak for Ben as well when I say we'd be more than a little amenable to staying around at least another couple of days while we figure out what the hell to do about Azazel."

"But first," Ben said, rubbing his shoulder, "I think I might have an idea about how we can reduce our fatality count and save Fred from one hell of a carpet cleaning bill."

Chapter 61

April, 1972

Hal Hawks was angry, and he didn't like being angry. Lizzie had found the magazines last night, and she hadn't been amused. He'd tried convincing her that someone had planted the magazines and that he wasn't a pervert, but of course she hadn't believed him. Finally, after she'd accused him of wanting to hurt their daughter, he'd just shut down. It was all he could do not to strangle the life out of the holier-than-thou bitch, but instead he'd spent the night on the couch.

He'd been a good husband and father, better to his daughter than his own parents had been to him. Sure, he desperately wanted to sleep with his twelve-year-old daughter—who wouldn't? But he'd resisted, hadn't initiated her into the club into which he'd been drafted at the tender age of eight. Hell, he'd even been careful of how he touched her, even if he couldn't help himself from looking. But now if he didn't have the magazines, his only outlet, what choice did he have?

If Lizzie told anyone...but he knew she wouldn't. She had too much pride. No, instead she'd keep him in the doghouse for a month, and then try to get him to sleep with her, something he'd managed to avoid for nearly two years now. But, eventually, he was sure she would turn him in. The police would confiscate the porn and take him to jail, and he'd be the laughing stock of Missouri. His real estate development business would probably go under, and he'd be left with nothing. And he'd rather be dead than be left with nothing.

When Lizzie woke this morning, he feigned a complete turnaround. He had breakfast waiting for her—scrambled eggs with cheese, bacon, hash browns, and orange juice—and told her over and over again how sorry he was, and how he didn't want to lose her. She'd softened immediately, as he knew she would, but insisted that he get help, that they both get help, and get their marriage back on track.

He'd taken off work and, after they both walked their surprised and a little confused daughter to the bus stop for school, he'd pretended to call a therapist. Which is how he found himself in the passenger seat of his brand new red Ford Country Sedan, with Lizzie driving.

In reality he'd called Bruce Diamond, their family doctor and his sometimes golfing buddy, saying he needed to see him, making an appointment for the indigestion he'd been suffering from for the past couple of weeks. He'd cut back on fried food and was feeling a little better, but the real doctor appointment he'd made would be his alibi for their trip to see imaginary marriage counselor Dr. Oliver Nussbaum.

"I'm still feeling a little under the weather," he'd said after seeing Kristen to the bus, "do you mind driving?"

She was a little taken aback because he rarely allowed her to drive but quickly acquiesced, even seemed to enjoy it. They had the windows down, and Lizzie was smiling, seemingly enjoying the wind in her face. She reached her hand out for his and he almost didn't take it, but finally forced himself. He rubbed her palm with his thumb, looking out the windows as they sped down the highway, trying to force his racing heart to relax.

They were on Range Line Road and had just passed the new Ramada Inn that had opened just a few months ago. There was a group of offices just about a mile up the road, where the fictitious Dr. Nussbaum had his pretend practice, but Lizzie would never know that the good doctor existed solely in his mind.

He didn't really want to admit it, but he supposed he'd been plotting something like this for some time. By most men's standards, he knew, Lizzie would have been considered gorgeous. She was a petite five-foot-three, weighed a hundred and ten pounds, and had long, silky black hair which perfectly matched her pale, exotic features and her deep green eyes. Her breasts were round and full, her body firm and athletic from her part-time volunteer job as a swim coach at Kristen's school.

She disgusted him. The way she used her sexuality to get what she wanted, always making sure her groceries were double-bagged at Harp's, never failing to talk her way out of a traffic ticket...and why couldn't she shave? Her thick triangle of black hair made him sick, almost made him throw up whenever he accidentally saw it. When Kristen hit puberty, he'd make sure she shaved.

He released her hand, then moved his own hand to her shoulder, gently caressing her back, trailing his touch slowly down her side. She seemed startled at first, but quickly took to the affection he'd so long denied her. His hand slipped past her hip and slowly unlatched her seat belt.

And there it was, the telephone pole he'd remembered, the one some drunken teenager had smashed into just last month. He suddenly grabbed the steering wheel, yelled "Look out!" and jerked it hard to the right, sending the Ford off the road and straight at the already-damaged pole. Lizzie screamed, threw up her hands, and then he blacked out.

* * *

Ben Spencer sat in the passenger seat of a 1969 Chevy Impala he had "borrowed" from a local used car lot, with Fred Ruskin driving. They were just a few cars behind Hal Hawks' brand new Ford, following him and his wife on a course that would end at a telephone pole and result in Elizabeth Hawks losing her life. Using Ruskin's police contacts and the Joplin Public Library, they'd researched Elizabeth Hawks' death. They'd hit the pole going almost 50 miles an hour and

Elizabeth, not wearing a seat belt, had been thrown through the wind-shield, dying almost instantly.

Her husband had been wearing his belt and, aside from a broken arm, would have survived unscathed had he not had a heart attack a few minutes after the accident. Fortunately for him, a passing motorist had seen the accident and stopped at the Howard Johnson Inn to use their phone and call the police. It had taken paramedics less than ten minutes to arrive at the scene, and they had managed to resituate Hal Hawks and save his life.

Newspaper reports said that the man had been clinically dead for almost three minutes before he was successfully brought back, and therein lay Ben's plan. Hawks' hadn't actually abused his daughter yet and so they couldn't justify ending the man's life, (Ruskin hadn't agreed with him on that score, arguing that, yes, he would have gladly stran-gled a baby Hitler in his sleep) but Ben had another idea.

"Are you sure we're doing the right thing?" Ben said as they passed a brown Dodge, moving one car closer to Hal and Elizabeth Hawks.

"What's right?" said Ruskin, his eyes scanning the road. "Was it right that poor girl had to go through what she did, and was it right that Brody lost his life?"

Ben felt the heft of the glowing metal ball in his jacket pocket. In their timeline, Kristen wasn't supposed to die, and because they could think of nothing that she did or said that would affect the overall out-come of their fight with Dowd or the demon, Ben felt they owed it to her to at least try to save her life. And if they were going to fix that, they might as well go back a little further and fix the whole damned mess. It was the best solution they could come up with, this side of murdering Hal Hawks.

They watched an hour earlier as a very young Kristen boarded the school bus, her mother and father taking turns giving her long hugs goodbye at the bus stop. They looked like the perfect family, but perhaps whatever sick feelings Hawks had for his daughter hadn't yet manifested. After that, they'd gone back into the house, and about thirty minutes later had left again, climbing into Hawks' red station wagon. According to the statement Hawks would later give to the police, he'd stayed home sick that day and decided to see his doctor because of a bad case of indigestion, and his wife had insisted on driving him.

"We're almost there," said Ben, their car now directly behind Hawks.

And then it happened. Abruptly the car jerked to the right, running off the road, heading straight for the telephone pole. Tires screeched as brakes were applied, but the momentum was too much. The Ford Country slammed hard into the pole, wrapping itself around the wood, and Elizabeth Hawks' body was thrown through the window to land at the side of the road some 50 feet in front of the car.

"Did you see that?" shouted Ruskin, pulling over to the side of the road. "That was no accident. The son of a bitch grabbed the steering wheel! He *made* her swerve!"

Ben hadn't seen it, but he had no doubt it was true. Ruskin was a brilliant detective and had an eye for taking in the world around him that most people would envy. The accident was no accident, after all. Ben held out his hands, bracing against the dashboard as Ruskin slammed the brakes, pulling off to the shoulder of the road about 50 yards behind the wreckage.

They started in confusion as Hal Hawks' door flung open and he stumbled out of the car. All of the reports said he had been found still in his seat, unconscious. The future child molester stumbled against the smoking car, righted himself, and walked in a beeline toward his wife's body.

Ben and Ruskin were already out of the car when they saw Elizabeth Hawks flail one arm and then roll over on her back. She wasn't dead yet. Her husband dropped to his knees beside her, covering her mouth and nose with his good arm, suffocating her.

Despite his age and girth, Fred Ruskin reached them first, tacking Hawks, pulling him away from his unconscious but still breathing wife. "Get off of her, you son of a bitch!" he growled, punching the man in the stomach.

"I was…help me…" he whispered, gasping for air. "My wife, we had an accident…"

"That was no accident," Ruskin said, straddling the man. He reared back to punch him again.

"Fred, stop," said Ben, taking hold of the former cop's arm. "I know this isn't how we planned things, but we need to save her if we can."

Hal Hawks swung an arm up at Ruskin, hitting him on the side of his head. Ruskin tumbled off his quarry but was back on his feet in an instant, lunging for the man, Ben barely able to hold him back.

"Molly and Jessica," he said, straining against Ben, "my wife and daughter, were taken from me by someone like this piece of shit. I'm not going to let it happen again. I'm just not."

And then Ben understood. This all hit a little too close to home for Ruskin. "It's not going to happen again, Fred," he said, pulling Ruskin around to face him, "because we're not going to let it happen."

"Who are you…" Hawks asked, then clutched his chest. "Oh fuck, I think I'm having a heart attack." His eyes were wide, and he was sweating. "The indigestion…Oh, Jesus, help me!"

"I'd rather help your wife and daughter," said Ben, turning away from the man to walk over to Elizabeth Hawks.

She was still breathing, sucking in shallow, ragged breaths, but had taken a tremendous amount of damage. The left side of her face was a mass of cuts, and she was losing a lot of blood from a huge gash across her forearm. Ben was pretty sure he could see bone. More blood gurgled from her mouth, and he feared she'd suffered internal damage as well.

They'd come prepared to heal Hal Hawks heart attack, but Ben had no clue if he could repair this much damage. Still, he had to try. Despite what the history books said, he wasn't going to leave this woman to bleed out on the side of Range Line Road.

He held both the future version of Shawn's nickel and Dowd's jaguar tooth in his left hand, and hoped that the combined magic of the two talismans would be enough to repair some of the damage that Hal Hawks had done to his wife. He laid his right hand, the black, cybernetic one he'd given himself yesterday, on Elizabeth Hawks chest.

He closed his eyes, concentrating, allowing the energy to flow through him, imagining Elizabeth Hawks' cuts closing, her insides healing, and her face once more the face of the woman he'd glimpsed saying goodbye to her daughter at the bus stop less than an hour ago.

"Ben," Ruskin said, touching his shoulder. "Hawks has stopped breathing. We need to do what we came here to do."

Ben opened his eyes. Elizabeth Hawks was still covered in blood, her breathing still labored, but she looked much better than she had just seconds earlier. Gone were the deep cuts from her face, replaced by more shallow cuts, and she wasn't spitting up blood. She would live.

Sirens sounded in the distance. They didn't have a lot of time left. Ben stood up from where he'd been kneeling beside Elizabeth Hawks, walking over to her husband. Hal Hawks wasn't breathing, but he didn't need Ben's help. The ambulance would be here any minute, and the paramedics would resuscitate him.

Ben pulled the metallic ball that contained Brody's spirit from his pocket. The ball was still glowing a deep shade of blue, powered by whatever strange magic Katy has infused it with from the spirit trap room.

He held the ball in both hands, bringing it down hard on Hal Hawks' chest. The ball split in two, shimmered for a second, and then disappeared. Ben waited and, for a moment, nothing happened. And then, like a car that had just been jump-started, the body suddenly gasped, sucked in air, and began to breathe. The breaths were ragged at first, greedy and all-consuming, but they finally settled down.

"This is...interesting," said Brody Huffman, though the voice didn't sound anything like him. "This feels strange and wonderful all at the same time. I can't describe it. It's...amazing. And the counting, the obsessions...it's all gone."

He'd told them about his OCD before they'd made the trip. People still suffered from the disease in their time, of course, but it was a lot easier to get help through medicine and therapy than it had been 40 some odd years earlier. To suffer from Obsessive-Compulsive Disorder in the 70's must have literally been a living nightmare. Ben was glad that Brody was going to get a second chance, even if he wasn't entirely comfortable with the means they had performed to achieve that end.

"Are you alone in there?" Ruskin asked, kneeling beside the man he had wanted to kill just moments earlier.

"I think so, yeah," Brody said, trying to sit up.

Ben put his hands on the man's shoulders, stopping him. "Whoa, Brody. You just had a heart attack, or rather your new body did. And the paramedics will be here any second. Just play dumb and do what they tell you, okay?"

Brody nodded, settling back onto the concrete. "This is going to take a lot of getting used to. I'm...what? A good three or four inches shorter and probably 40 pounds lighter? And my leg feels fine. Not as much fun as being a ghost, maybe, but it'll do. It'll definitely do."

Chapter 62

From The Joplin Globe, Tuesday April 12, 1972

Local Housing Developer and Wife in Car Accident
By Madeline Francisco

Elizabeth, 33, and her husband Hal Hawks, 37, president of Joplin 4-Star Development, were involved in a car accident on Monday on South Range Line Road in Joplin.

The accident, which happened near the intersection of South Range Line and Highview Avenue, was brought on when Hawks' husband suffered from a minor heart attack as she was driving him to a doctor's appointment. Hawks lost control of the vehicle and slammed into a telephone pole. She was thrown from the car and suffered a broken wrist in addition to minor cuts and bruises but was otherwise unharmed.

In addition to the heart attack, Hal Hawks also suffered a broken arm and a concussion. Though suffering from temporary amnesia due to head trauma, doctors expect him to make a full recovery.

Chapter 63

November 1, 1977

The majority of Halloween, as it turned out, was fairly uneventful, and that was just fine with Ben. To everyone's relief, Kristen's body vanished from Fred Ruskin's guestroom, and Candy, the only person not involved in the decision to travel back to 1972, didn't remember a thing. And true to his word, Ruskin disposed of Jim Felt's and Oscar Reyes' bodies. He didn't say how or where, and no one had the nerve to ask.

After the trip to 1972, everyone had gone home; they met up later to celebrate Halloween and say their goodbyes. That had been yesterday, and today Jenny was back in school, Shawn was working at Newsland, Fred was probably making pizzas, and Ben and Katy were finally, blissfully alone.

It hadn't taken much persuasion on Katy's part to convince him to delay their return to the future another day so they could enjoy the night together before taking their final trip to 1975 and then home.

He'd borrowed the twenty he knew he'd have to give to himself from Ruskin, promising to someday pay him back with interest. And, if everything worked out the way they hoped, he'd be alive and well to accept the money.

Ben yawned and stared out the window, watching as the morning sun melted the icicles hanging from the eaves and overhangs outside. Katy's cabin was amazing, and the couch he currently lounged on was probably the most comfortable he'd ever experienced. Truly, if he didn't know it was all an illusion, he'd think he was somewhere in Vermont in the middle of a winter ice storm.

"Sleepy?" asked Katy, her hand on her hip and a crooked smile on her lips. "I just might have to do something about that?"

"Oh really?" he said, gazing up at her. "I'd like to hear what you have in mind."

"I think I'd much rather show you instead," she said, taking his hand in hers and pulling him to his feet.

She wrapped her arms around his neck, drawing him into a kiss. At first tender and tentative, the kiss quickly turned hungry with passion as her tongue slipped past his lips and into his mouth. She pulled him away from the couch, through the living room, toward her bedroom.

She slowly pulled his sweatshirt up and over his head, meeting bare flesh with trailing little kisses. A throaty moan escaped her lips as his kisses trailed slowly down her neck, and it was all he could do to pull away and stare into her deep brown eyes.

"Are you sure?" he asked, his hands sliding under the black lace bra she'd slept in last night. "I want you—God knows I've wanted you forever—but only if this is really something you want to do."

She stared up into his eyes and smiled. "If I didn't," she said, moving his hands along her bra and to her breasts, "would I do this? Or this?"

She reached behind her to loosen the hooks and let the brassiere fall away, leaving only his hands to cup her full, pale breasts. Her nipples were hard, and she arched her back as he caressed them with his fingers.

"I want you, Ben," she said, her hands sliding down under his waist band. "You and only you, now and forever. I want you to make love to me. I have only one concern…"

"Don't worry, I have protection," he said, holding a little plastic packet in his hand.

"Not that, silly," she said, leaning in to kiss him, "though we'll certainly need it. My concern is this—how can I possibly compare to the girl of your dreams?"

"I have a feeling," he said, between kisses, "that you'll blow the competition right out of the water, though we might have to run multiple tests just to be on the safe side."

They made love three times that night, first with a frenzied desperation, and then later with a lazy, slow abandon, taking their time, exploring and enjoying each other's bodies, moving together, becoming one.

* * *

Ben awoke to the sounds of birds chirping just outside the window and for a moment he didn't remember where he was. The weight of Katy next to him, still lying in his arms, brought everything back. He smiled to himself, idly wondering just how the birds outside of this illusionary bedroom could exist when the one who had created them was sound asleep beside him.

He inhaled deeply, enjoying the smell of her body and the rose perfume that still lingered on her skin. They lay together, arms akimbo, tangled in the sheets of the king-sized bed she had led him to last night. He almost wished they could stay here forever, in their own perfect dream, but they couldn't avoid the future forever. Besides, if everything went according to plan, they'd have the rest of their lives to spend together once they returned to their time.

"Hunh?" mumbled Katy, snuggling closer. Her eyes fluttered open, and she smiled. "This feels good. Boy, I'm such a sleepyhead."

"After the last few days, who could blame you?" he said, brushing his lips against hers. "Besides, we've got all the time in the world."

398 | Joe DeRouen

"And we can come back here whenever we want," she said, returning his kiss. "Dad said he'd pull the Pentagram up from the floor and have it waiting for us, and Shawn promised to wall up the hole in the wall and make sure it was left intact. Just think—our own little hideaway!"

"Wherever I am, if I'm with you, I'll be happy."

"I bet you say that to all the girls," she said, playfully sliding her hand beneath the covers to trail her fingers up his thigh.

"Only the girls that I'm madly, deeply, passionately in love with," he whispered, gently biting her earlobe. "I know we need to get going. 1975 waits for no man, and all that. But do you think we have time for—"

"Definitely," she whispered, swinging her hip over his to straddle him. She brushed the hair from her eyes, bending down to kiss him deeply. "Like you said, my love…we've got all the time in the world."

Chapter 64

Present Day

"Hey, Dad, this came for you earlier today," thirteen-year-old Emily Spencer announced as she strode into her father's office, her long red bangs in danger of tumbling over her deep green eyes, "maybe a present?"

Shawn took the package and examined the return address, setting the box on top of his laser printer. Emily would be fourteen in a few weeks and was hoping for a new cell phone, but this wasn't it.

"You're right about this being a present, but it's one I bought for myself," he said, thinking back to the summer of 1975.

It had been over 40 years, but he could still remember just about every detail of everything that had happened. After he had rejected Azazel and used the power he had been offered to split the talisman back into its original five parts, the police had finally shown up, fully prepared to believe that a drifter had abducted both he and Jenny and that Sheriff Ruskin had swooped in at the last second to save the day. Ruskin was declared a hero, much to his own chagrin, and had been offered his job back with a big raise to boot. He turned it down flat and instead traded in his badge for an apron and opened up a restaurant at the edge of town.

Shawn had finally taught Jenny how to swim, on the last day that the pool was open that summer, on his sixteenth birthday. He could think of no better way to celebrate the day of his birth than by keeping the promises he had made to his best friend and the girl he loved.

They'd had another adventure two years later, when their adult son Ben and Fred's daughter Katy had time-traveled to stop a series of murders from taking place. He still didn't know what time they'd been from, though he suspected it would be happening any day now. Whatever the case, he hoped they could deal with Azazel when the time came. He and Jenny had surreptitiously researched the matter, keeping the information from the kids, and he had a few surprises in store for the demon.

Ben meant the world to him, and he wouldn't lose him without a fight. The years had been good to him and Jenny, and they'd been blessed with three beautiful children; their fraternal twins Colin Frederick and Benjamin Tanner, and of course Emily Margaret.

They'd had much success in their chosen fields as well; Jenny was an English teacher at the University of Chicago, and Shawn had written a string of critically and commercially successful fantasy novels.

Shawn remained in possession of the nickel and because of that, at over 50, both he and Jenny were in perfect health and looked to be at most in their late twenties. Though neither had asked for the youth that the coin provided, they both accepted it as part of the contract Shawn had signed (by tacit acceptance, if nothing else) with the archangel Michael. It did, however, freak out their kids, and made Jenny the envy of all the other female professors at her college, not to mention the object of desire for most of her male co-workers and students.

"Dad?" said Emily again, trying to get her father's attention. "Earth to Dad, earth to Dad—come in, Dad!"

"Sorry, Em," Shawn said. "I was just daydreaming."

"Are you about ready to go to supper?"

It was supposed to be a surprise, but both Shawn and Jenny knew that Ben and Emily had arranged a party for them at one of their favorite restaurants. They'd been married 25 years today. 25 was a milestone, he knew, but perhaps not as much of one to a couple who could potentially live forever. He wasn't sure if he wanted that, couldn't stand to think of watching his children die before him, but he'd cross that bridge when and if he came to it. Perhaps someday he'd pass the coin on to Ben or one of their other children. For now, though, it sat in a jar of pennies in the safe hidden behind a painting in their bedroom.

"Just about," Shawn finally said as he took the package from the monitor. "Give me five minutes and we're gone."

"Cool, I'll go tell Mom," the girl said, as he ran out of her father's office.

A few years ago, Shawn had begun writing down the events of that summer in 1975. With a few details changed, he thought it might make a good book. Even he was surprised, however, when first it sold for a $250,000 advance and then hit number three on the *New York Times* bestseller list, where it stayed for an impressive seventeen weeks.

While doing research for the book, he'd chanced upon a website called The Mego Museum, where he'd discovered photos and information on Galahad, the action figure that had once housed his best friend's spirit. He was part of a line that Mego had dubbed the "Super Knights," one of five figures that also included King Arthur, Ivanhoe, Sir Launcelot, and the Black Knight.

Five years later, his memories had finally got the better of him and he'd managed to track down a mint-in-box Mego Sir Galahad on eBay. The final bid had ended at almost $450, but he'd won, and the figure had finally arrived. He knew he should get going lest he risk being late for his own surprise party, but he really wanted to see the knight.

Shawn ripped open the priority mail package to find another, smaller box, carefully packed inside its bigger cousin. Finally, after bypassing about a million Styrofoam peanuts and two layers of bubble wrap, he held the action figure in his hands.

Carefully opening the box, he released the knight from the prison that had been its home since it had left the line in Hong Kong many decades before.

The figure was beautiful. It looked just as he remembered, complete with a bright orange shield, a sheathed sword, and a yellow feather coming out of the top of his helmet. Smiling to himself, he set the knight's box aside and stood up from his chair to position the figure on top of the desk.

Chapter 65

Ben and Katy appeared in a burst of light in the middle of the garage, exactly where their journey had started. Azazel was waiting for them, in the guise of the angel Michael, but they were ready. Ben immediately began the spell that Jenny had prepared, and Katy leveled the gun at the demon's heart.

"*Redimio vox Eblis!*" he shouted, as she pulled the trigger in an explosion of noise and gunpowder.

Her aim was true; a small hole appeared in his chest, and he staggered back against the wall, his face turning white with shock. Inexplicably, however, he began to giggle, a wry chuckle that slowly turned into bellows and snorts of laughter.

"Oh, that was good!" he said, the laughter subsiding as an ear-to-ear grin split his face. "You're far smarter than I gave you credit for. Your father would be proud."

"*Redimio vox Eblis!*" he repeated, gripping the nickel tight in his fist. "*Redimio vox Eblis!*" Why wasn't this working?

"The rule of three only works," said Azazel, as the blood drained from his face, "if the wizard knows the subject's true name, which you do not. In any event, you cannot bind someone when you yourself have already been bound."

"But he's *not* bound," Katy said, her hands shaking under the weight of the gun. "We removed the last part of the incantation. He never said it a third time!"

"What do you want?" asked Ben, putting himself between her and the demon. "The nickel? Here, take it." He held the coin out to Azazel, who quickly backed away.

"Ben," Azazel said calmly, holding a palm out toward him, "keep the nickel, and please take my hand."

He felt his body moving despite himself. It was as if he were floating above the room, looking down, watching himself sleepwalk. His heart pounding wildly in his chest, he could do nothing as he watched himself reach out to clasp the demon's hand.

"Oh my God," he said, thinking back to the cabin. He had read aloud the words Jenny had translated even if he hadn't been casting the spell. He bound himself to Azazel without realizing it.

"That's right," the demon said, tightening his grip. "You said the words. You're mine now, Ben Spencer. I'm sure we're going to have a grand old time together."

And then Azazel was falling to the ground, his legs crumpling under his own weight. The trench coat flopped open to reveal a University of Chicago sweater. He took one final, shuddering breath, and then lay still. Katy stared at him as if she'd seen a ghost.

"Tom Logan," Katy said. "That's why I recognized him. He's aged, somehow, but it's the same person."

Tom Logan? And then Ben remembered; he had been Katy's date the night that all this started. If he hadn't stood her up, she never would have come over, wouldn't have traveled back in time with him. It couldn't be a coincidence.

He felt a sudden, incredible pain erupt through his body, first in his stomach, then his genitals, down to his toes, through his chest and into his head. It felt like every nerve in his body was firing at once, over and over, and it was all he could do to keep from screaming.

He was being possessed by the demon; Azazel was claiming his prize.

"Katy," he said, fighting against the pain, "kill me, before it's too late." And then he was gone.

* * *

She aimed the gun at Ben's chest, her insides twisted into knots. They had talked about this, what they'd do if, despite their preparations, the demon's plan worked. Ben said he'd rather die than become Azazel's pawn, but she couldn't make herself pull the trigger. And the demon knew it.

"You're thinking to yourself," the demon said through Ben, "that you might find a way to undo this, that you might not lose your lover. Sadly, this just isn't the case. Deep down, you know I'm speaking the truth. And yet you can't bring yourself to kill me, even though you know you'll probably never again have the chance."

"You're a monster," she said, cocking back the hammer. "Ben wouldn't want to live like this."

"And you're a human," he said, taking the gun from her trembling fingers, "and the same spark that enables you to create art and music, to love and to dream, also curses you with hope. There is no hope. You know that—you *know* that—but you persist in believing just the same. It's incredibly naïve, but you can't help it; as I said, you're human. It's both your gift and your curse."

"Why?" she sobbed, battering her hands against his chest. "Why Ben?"

"I think you know why," he said, folding the gun into his pocket. "The boy can do amazing things, more than his father, more even than Aupuch or any before him. He can perform miracles of Biblical proportions. He's *important.*"

"But why did you send us into the past? The Halloween murders—it was all your doing, wasn't it?"

"Call it a dress rehearsal. I needed him to realize the full extent of his abilities and to learn how to use them, so that, in turn, I could use him."

"All that pain…the deaths…all for your amusement?"

"You intrigue me, Katy Ruskin. I bear no ill will toward any of you. In fact, you fascinate me. I do what I must, nothing less and nothing more. Nothing more, and nothing less. Men were not meant to rule the Earth, and it was a grave mistake to allow it to happen for as long as it has. And now I'm taking steps to rectify the situation."

"Let my son go," said Shawn Spencer, stepping through the door that separated the house from the garage.

He clutched a wooden branch in one hand and something that she couldn't quite make out in the other. Jenny stood behind him, holding a small glass vial.

"The gangs all here," whispered Azazel, gesturing at Shawn. "Give me the nickel."

The nickel? What was he talking about? He already had the nickel. Unless… but no, it couldn't be.

"Let's trade," said Shawn, his jaw squared in determination. "My son for the talisman. You can take my body instead."

"And why would I want to bargain," he asked, with a sad shake of his head, "when I can just take what I need?"

"Over my dead body."

"Tempting," said the demon, as Shawn edged forward, "but hardly necessary."

Katy watched helplessly as Shawn's foot caught the edge of the door frame, making him stumble. He immediately caught himself, but it was too late—the nickel flew from his hand and fell to the ground, bouncing twice before rolling to a stop directly in front of Azazel. Staring in surprise, Shawn wordlessly let the branch slip from his fingers to fall to the cement floor.

The demon scooped the coin from the ground, and touched it to the other, identical coin he held in his other hand. "What luck!" he said, as the coins combined to cover his body in an ethereal blue glow. "Now I won't have to take it over your dead body. Pity, I know how much the men in your family enjoy being martyrs."

The glow quickly subsided, and Azazel held up his hands to show that, where once two coins had existed, only one remained. He twirled it around in his fingers like a stage magician, and Katy could see that the coin now had two heads.

"It was his ability to manipulate causality, wasn't it?" Katy asked, staring defiantly at the demon that wore her lost lover's body. "The nickels…they shouldn't both exist, and that's why you stopped Ben from giving it to you. If it had left his body, it would have disappeared, just like Emily's image in the photo or his middle name on the driver's license."

"It's amazing how you humans eventually grasp the obvious," said Azazel, tipping an imaginary hat in her direction, "even if it is too late to make any real difference. But, yes, if I'm to accomplish my goal, I need the paradox of the same object existing twice in the same place and at the same time. And now I have it, and soon I'll have everything else I need."

"Then you don't need Ben," Jenny said, stepping forward to join her husband. "Please, I'm begging you. Let him go."

"One son for another," he said cryptically, shrugging his shoulders. "Jenny, your son is as much a paradox as the coin I now hold in my hand, perhaps more so. I'm truly sorry, but I need them both."

"You're not sorry," said Jenny, "but you're going to be."

She threw the vial at him, but it stopped just inches from his face and fell harmlessly into the palm of his hand. He closed his fingers around the glass container, and when he opened them again it was gone.

"Holy water? Really? You've had all this time, and all you can come up with is a vial of holy water and a Rowan wand? I tire of these games and your feeble attempts to distract me," he said, reaching down to snatch up the branch. He snapped it in half, tossing the two halves at Shawn's feet.

"Michael will find you," Shawn promised, "And when he does, you're toast."

"Find me? You still don't get it, do you? He doesn't need to find me; he knows exactly where I am."

Azazel waved his hand, and a glimmering portal of light appeared before him. Without another word he stepped through the doorway and was gone.

Epilogue

Six Weeks Later

It had been nearly a month and a half since Azazel had taken Ben away, and Katy still couldn't sleep through the night. Her nightmares were gone, replaced by an aching emptiness that almost made her miss them.

She'd tried making contact with Ben through her dreams, during the few hours of sleep she'd managed to snatch every night, but he remained invisible to her. It was as if he were nothing more than a memory, a fleeting thought of the perfect idea that you could almost but not quite remember. In a way, she supposed he was. After all, she was in love with a man who'd been possessed by a demon, and he in turn possessed her heart. What could be more fleeting than that?

Of course, she'd looked for him. They all had. She, along with her father (who had wisely avoided driving on the day in question, thus saving his life) and Ben's parents, had literally traveled the world, seeking out experts on the occult and those known to speak to both angels and demons, but no one could help them. They'd tried every conceivable action to get the attention of the real Michael, but nothing had worked.

Though it was almost unfathomable, they were forced to consider the possibility that Azazel had actually been telling the truth and that he and the Archangel really were working together. That, or Michael just didn't give a damn. His parents and her father were still out there; it was only she who had given up, had returned to Chicago and her dreary little apartment empty-handed and with a broken heart.

In this new and improved timeline, her father's investments in Microsoft had helped him to fund a national chain of Ruskin's Pizzerias. Together with Hal "Brody" Hawks, who had sold 4-Star Development to invest in the Ruskin's Pizzeria chain, they built a financial empire worthy of Bill Gates himself. And as of last count, they were the number two pizza delivery chain with a bullet, just behind Papa John's and catching up fast.

Hal Hawks had never fully recovered from his "amnesia," giving Brody the perfect excuse for not remembering things he never actually knew in the first place. He and his family had moved to Carthage just before Kristen's senior year of high school, and Jenny and Kristen had met just as scheduled.

Brody had proven to be a wonderful husband and father, and had passed away in his sleep last year at the ripe old age of 85. Kristen and Jenny were still friends to this very day, and not even once had Kristen ever tried to shoot anyone.

The biggest change, of course, was that Ben had a twin brother. In this timeline they'd had a falling out over that Burgundy chick that Ben had dated once upon a time, Colin had moved out of the house, and no one had heard from him in months. According to Shawn, Colin—Ben's twin—had no powers, which had always caused tension between the two siblings. Burgundy was just an excuse for a storm that had been brewing all their lives.

Though she'd never met him, Colin scared the hell out of Katy. There had to be some reason for his existence, but without powers of his own she couldn't quite figure out what use he might be to Azazel. Katy had tried on more than one occasion to bring up Colin and the fact that he shouldn't even exist with Ben's parents, but neither of them even wanted to discuss it. She supposed she really couldn't blame them.

Because of her father's money, Katy no longer had to work or go to school, and lately felt little incentive to do either. Surprisingly, not much else had changed about her life. She and Mel were still roommates, but Mel had just been offered a job in Dallas on the staff of the Morning News and would be leaving her alone in the apartment within a month.

Well, not entirely alone. Emily Spencer, Ben's little sister, had become her de facto roommate as soon as Katy had given up on the search. Em, who had just celebrated her fourteenth birthday, had been staying with friends of Shawn and Jenny while they were off searching for her brother. Katy made the offer the moment she returned home and found out Mel would soon be leaving, and, to her surprise (and, she had to admit, relief) the girl accepted. It was good for Katy, and, she hoped, for Emily, too.

Christmas was less than two weeks away, but she wasn't looking forward to celebrating. The only present she wanted had been taken from her by a fallen angel, and she was certain that she wouldn't find Ben wrapped in a large red bow under her tree.

No, that wasn't going to happen. Whether or not anyone wanted to believe it, Ben was never coming back. It was over.

She sat in the bathroom, one of Emily's *Seventeen* magazines in her hand, staring at the clock. It had been nearly five minutes. She was almost sure the results would be false, but some small part of her clung to the idea that, if they were positive, at least she'd always have a part of him with her. She almost laughed at the thought. That was the last thing she needed at the ripe old age of 24.

And yet there it was. The little stick showed a plus sign, and it had turned pink; there was no doubt now. Katherine Grace Ruskin, unwed, unemployed, undereducated, depressed, and heartbroken, was pregnant. She didn't know whether she should laugh or cry, so she did a little of both.

"Katy, are you all right in there?" It was Emily's voice, just outside the bathroom door. "I'm sorry, but I heard you crying. Anything I can do?"

She dropped the magazine, threw the EPT strip in the trash can, and opened the door. Though they didn't look that much alike—Emily had red hair where Ben was blond, she was short where he was tall— she resembled him enough that nearly every time Katy saw her, she had to hold back tears.

"I miss him, too," Emily said, surprising Katy with a fierce hug. "God, I spent so much of my life hating him, resenting him, wanting to be better than him, but now I'd give anything in the world to have my obnoxious, overbearing, luckier-than-thou brother back. Sad, huh?"

"Well," said Katy, instantly deciding to share the news, "maybe I can help with that, at least a little."

"What do you mean?" she asked guardedly, arching an eyebrow.

"I'm pregnant, Em. Ben's a daddy, and you're going to be an aunt."

"Are you serious? Oh! You are!" A slow smile spread across her face, quickly disappearing in a whirlpool of doubt. "I mean, wow, you're going to keep it, right? Is this what you want?"

"I want Ben," she said flatly, her eyes burning with tears, "and now I'll always have him. So, yes, I want this baby, with all of my heart."

Emily grinned mischievously. "Maybe you can have both."

"What are you talking about?"

"What Ben can do, what you can do…think about it."

She thought about it, and Em was right. If Ben could do so many amazing things, if she could literally control a person's dreams, and if these powers were given to them by their parents, who had only briefly been touched with magic…what might her baby be able to do?

Maybe it wasn't over yet, after all.

Be sure to read **A Pattern of Shadows**, the final book in the Small Things trilogy, available now!

For news about Small Things and Joe's other books, visit www.JoeDeRouen.com.